HOLLOW WORLD

NICK POBURSKY

ISBN: 978-0-9854706-9-2

Published by Bamboo Forest Publishing
First Printing: November, 2013

Visit us Online at:
www.bambooforestpublishing.com

For Savanah.

1

"What the hell are you doing still lurking around the office, Walker?" asked Captain Pete Valdez in the most sarcastic of tones. "Aren't you supposed to be on vacation? It's kind of dark in here and you're starting to creep me out."

"I know, Cap. It's just that I really need to knock out the paperwork on the Navidson case before I get out of here. You know how I am—me and my OCD."

Detective Charlie Walker was, in fact, not diagnosed with obsessive-compulsive disorder, but his dedication to his work—his *art*, as he occasionally referred to it—often bordered on fanaticism.

At thirty-two years old, the man was an honest-to-God genius but he didn't lord it over the masses—as some of his ilk were prone to—nor did he make anyone feel ill at ease when working with him. When he'd first made detective, the old warhorses in the precinct wouldn't give him the time of day. They never took well to new blood moving in on their territory but it didn't take Walker long to command the respect he deserved.

Case after case, Walker had proven that you had to be one slick son of a bitch to put even the smallest detail past him. In his six-year tenure as a Detroit detective, Walker had shown that seeing and comprehending were two entirely separate affairs. Repeatedly would a senior officer find himself rifling through a crime scene and coming up with nothing only to have

Walker find the most obscure detail and turn it into a concrete lead.

It was this sharpness of mind that never allowed him to quit before his work was thoroughly complete with every avenue explored and every lead pursued. Even something as minute as paperwork held the utmost importance in his mind. Late nights at the office were a specialty of Charlie Walker's.

"Charlie," pleaded the Captain, forgoing his usual gruff sarcasm for a gentler, more fatherly tone. "It's almost ten o'clock. You have less than seven hours to sleep. How do I know this, you may ask? Meghan sent me an email with your flight itinerary."

Ignoring the bemused look on Walker's face, Pete lifted his reading glasses to his eyes and leaned in closer to his monitor.

"Along with the flight info, there was this dainty little note: 'Pete, get my damned husband home before he oversleeps and we have to run to make our flight again.' Get out of here, Charlie. Put the Navidson file over on Martin's desk and I'll have him take care of it in the morning. He may be a dummy, but the kid's a data entry savant; you've got nothing to worry about. You know that I love all the hard work that you do—honestly—but for the next ten days you belong to Meghan and the girls. Go home, sleep and enjoy your damn vacation, son."

Walker looked at his friend and superior in silence for a few moments. With a smirk, he then neatly placed the file folder he had been holding onto Martin's desk.

"Thanks, Pete. They've really been looking forward to this and—I'm not going to lie to you—so have I."

"I don't doubt it. You're a different kind of guy, you know that, Charlie? I look around at everyone's desks and I see Red Wings and Tigers gear. I see pictures of these guys on hunting trips. I see them getting drunk on their idiot cousins' boats over in Crystal Bay. When I look at your desk, I see a picture of Meghan and the girls in Disney World, I see an EPCOT Center postcard from God-knows-when and I see an air freshener shaped like a damn Mickey waffle."

"What can I say? To each his own."

"You hit the nail right on the head, my boy. You're here every day, dealing with dead bodies and the worst filth the Earth can throw at you—and you still manage to be a kid at heart, sifting through crime scenes with that Club

33 pin on your jacket."

Walker looked a bit taken aback at the mention of his lapel pin.

"You know what this is?" he asked, his hand subconsciously tracing the silver numbers.

During his first year as a detective, the small token had been given to him by an elderly man—also a Disney fanatic—as a reward for his service. Charlie had helped recover a stolen jewelry box: the only item taken when the poor man's house had been broken in to. Only upon returning the box to its owner did Charlie learn how precious the contents really were. Inside, among other various pieces, was the wedding ring of the man's deceased wife. And it was from this very box that he'd presented Charlie with the Club 33 pin that he'd worn on duty ever since.

With a small wink, Pete said, "I haven't spent my entire life behind this desk. Get the hell out of here, son."

And with that, Pete went back to work and Charlie Walker left for what was promising to be a very relaxing, well-deserved vacation.

2

The Walkers' house was a modest little number in the suburbs, thirty minutes or so south of Detroit. Charlie did well enough on his detective salary and Meghan was an English literature professor at the University of Michigan, so they lived relatively comfortably. The Walkers were a very happy family and they were thankful for all that they had, knowing that many people these days couldn't say as much.

Upon pulling into his driveway, Charlie was surprised to see his two young daughters—seven-year-old Violet dressed as Belle and her six-year-old sister, Katie, dressed as Cinderella—running circles around the front lawn waving fluorescent glowing wands back and forth and blowing bubbles. The beautiful but exhausted Meghan Walker watched them helplessly from where she sat on the porch steps.

Stepping out of his car, Charlie checked his watch. The high-quality Rotary timepiece dutifully informed him that it was ten-thirty-eight PM yet his girls were playing like it was the middle of the afternoon. He shot a bemused look at his wife and it seemed that all she had the energy left for was a shrug and a slight grin. Charlie grabbed his two little princesses and gave them each a kiss on the top of their head before releasing them to resume their royal duties.

"What are my two favorite princesses up to this fine evening?" he asked, playfully.

"We're just doing magic tricks, Daddy!" shouted Violet, running gracefully after a large cluster of bubbles that had somehow managed to escape her.

"I should have known! No better time for magic tricks on the front lawn than seven hours before a flight!" he joked, making his way toward his wife.

"I know!" Katie screamed, zooming past him with all that mysterious energy that young children seem to find at any hour of the day.

Letting the two maniacs continue their magic show, Charlie dropped himself down next to his wife and put his arm around her.

"Magic tricks, eh?" he asked with a smirk.

"I can't stop 'em, Charlie," she said with an exasperated laugh. "I was upstairs packing about an hour ago and the two little demons got a hold of a two-liter of Dr Pepper. The bottle was full when I saw it this morning— it's now empty. I've said it once and I'll say it again: we have created two scheming juggernauts of destruction."

Charlie kissed his wife on her forehead and laughed. This wasn't the first time his two angels had conspired against their mother while he was away. It seemed as if the girls concocted some new scheme once or twice a week. The girls were beyond their years in intelligence and, so far, they'd used this precious advantage for nothing but evil.

"I figured," Meghan said, still watching her daughters race back and forth across the yard, "that since they had so much energy, I'd put them in their princess dresses, set them loose on the lawn and let them wreak havoc on some bubbles for a while. They have to burn off all of that caffeine somehow."

"Of course," Charlie agreed. "Aren't you worried they'll ruin the dresses, though?"

"I'm *counting* on it. Remember? I've signed them up for the princess makeover in the castle tomorrow. They'll get new dresses."

"Good plan," he agreed. "Same dresses this year?"

"No doubt in my mind," replied Meghan. "Violet will get another Belle dress; Katie will go with Cinderella again."

"Could be worse," Charlie joked. "They could decide to switch and then we'd have to dye their hair."

"*That* would be a fun time," Meghan shot back, sarcastically.

Violet took after her Dad with straight, dark hair while Katie was the opposite, proudly sporting a full head of wavy golden blonde locks, just like her mother. A smile broke out on Charlie's face as he watched his daughters endlessly dash across the front yard, giggling and screaming, probably driving the neighbors mad. He let his shoulders ease back, the tension of the job melting away and the Navidson case all but forgotten.

"Took the day off work today, eh?" Charlie ventured, mischievously.

"I did. How did you know?" Meghan asked, surprised.

"That's an easy one," he replied. "Your car hasn't moved since yesterday. Tree buds are still sitting on the roof and rear windshield wiper. Give me something harder next time."

Meghan subconsciously shot a glance toward the automobile that had betrayed her. "I can never put one past you, but that was an easy one," she laughed. "I went to—"

"I'll take it from here, babe," he interjected, with his characteristic diabolical grin slowly making its way across his face. "You went down to Mexican Gardens for lunch. You weren't alone—your sister picked you and the girls up. She brought Greg with her—and their kids too. After that, all of you went to the mall. You didn't buy anything for yourself, though. There was traffic on '75. You promised you'd get Amy and the kids *Tron* Vinylmation figures—*if* you remembered."

"Sometimes I wonder if you're really a human being," Meghan joked, shaking her head and laughing. He'd just rattled off a flawless list of everything she'd done that day, in chronological order.

"Go ahead and ask," he prodded, watching the girls ricochet around the yard.

"Ask what?" Meghan replied playfully, pretending she had no idea what he was talking about.

"Ask me how I know."

"No way," Meghan shot back, sarcastically.

Charlie simply stared at her for a few moments, still grinning that dangerous grin of his. He'd always been able to do this to her; to know *exactly* what she'd done and everywhere she'd been just by observing the mundane details that were presented to him.

At the beginning of their relationship, it had made her nervous. Once, Meghan had even accused Charlie of following her around and spying on her. He'd told her that he didn't have to and that the keen observer can make monumental deductions from the smallest, most obscure details. It sounded like a weak excuse. She hadn't believed him, and had seemed genuinely offended at this alleged invasion of her privacy until Charlie had walked her through his mental processes. Afterward, Meghan had laughed about it; it had all sounded so simple after Charlie had explained it to her. It seemed as if these deductions should be as easy for everyone as they were for Charlie.

"Fine!" she laughed. "Fine...how'd you know?"

"Your first mistake was letting the girls play hooky from school today and come with you," he stated with a light chuckle, purposely having left this detail out of his earlier deductions to achieve a greater dramatic effect now.

"How in the hell—"

"Hold on," he interrupted again, raising his pointer finger. "I'm just getting started, woman. Katie sold you out—not on purpose though! She still has a little sour cream in her hair. She always somehow manages to get sour cream in her hair at Mexican Gardens. We don't keep any in the house, and we never go to any other restaurants where she can get a hold of it—*especially* not with Amy and Greg.

"Vi's wearing a new bracelet. Same kind she always talks you into buying when you go to the mall, just a new color. The mall is on the far side of the restaurant from the freeway. So: food first, mall second. You just recently finished packing and that tells me that you got home *much* later than expected. Friday at four or five o'clock—'75 is bound to be backed up."

Meghan tried not to look impressed. "You're on a roll, Sherlock. Carry on."

"Figuring out that you went with Amy was simple. Since your car hasn't moved, you *had* to have had someone else take you—that's a given. You like seeing your sister before we leave on our trips so it was a safe bet that it was her. Amy's kids didn't have school today because of that massive power outage that knocked out half of Woodhaven this morning, so she obviously brought them. Greg doesn't work on Fridays so, naturally, Amy wouldn't have left him behind."

"Amy's come out here on Friday afternoons plenty of times and Greg's stayed home; you couldn't know that she would have brought him this time," Meghan stated, thinking she'd finally caught him taking advantage of a lucky guess.

"Sure I could," he countered, not missing a beat. "*You* told me. Oh—not with your words," he pointed out. "With your hair."

"My *hair?* Come on, Charlie, this is too much."

"You asked," he reminded her, chuckling. "Picture this: Meghan Walker takes a day off work to relax and prepare for her trip. Hell, Meghan Walker takes a day off work to go out eat with her *sister,* alone. Pick whichever one you like best. In either scenario, you would have left your hair down, because you were taking a *you* day. Add to that the fact that the kids were with you, and my theory gets stronger. Oh! I see you're following me, now," he laughed again, enjoying himself. "Good, because here comes the *coup de grâce*. I know that Amy brought Greg because your hair is done up like you were going to one of those gala dinners at the university. You absolutely *hate* how Greg always comments on how the two of you look *so* much alike. It makes you uncomfortable, so you—knowing Amy would show up with her hair down, like she always does—made yourself up to be her polar opposite."

For a second, Charlie simply stared at his wife, waiting for her to tell him how wrong he was. Instead, she broke out in a wide smile and laughed that musical laugh that he could never get enough of.

"It never ceases to amaze me how you notice these things that *I* don't even realize I'm doing," she said.

"The human subconscious is a fickle bitch," Charlie joked. "I just happen to know how to take advantage of her."

"I'll give you that," she admitted. "But riddle me this, oh master of subtleties: how'd you know about the *Tron* Vinylmation?"

"Lucky guess," he joked and Meghan burst out into another loud, clumsy bout of laughter that caught the attention of the girls, who momentarily stopped their graceful wizardry to gaze at their mother.

"Seriously!" Meghan slapped him lightly on the arm.

"Honestly?" he began. "That was the easiest of them all. Before our last three trips, you've promised Amy and the kids those figures, and all three times you have forgotten to get them. At this point, it's standard operating procedure for you to make that promise."

Charlie smiled at his wife, satisfied that he'd made his point. Meghan sighed and nodded, conceding yet another victory to her unstoppable husband. Secretly, Meghan loved that aspect of Charlie's personality. The idea that he could tell you nearly anything you wanted to know about a person simply by looking at them never ceased to amaze her. Charlie had saved her from some pretty disagreeable situations by merely observing the people involved and advising her not to put her trust in those who didn't pass his inspection. Meghan knew that the infamous city of Detroit was an immeasurably safer place with a man like her husband protecting it, and she was increasingly proud of him every day. Her husband was a hero, but no matter how much he did—no matter how many lives he saved or how many criminals he put behind bars—he never considered himself as such: he simply said that he was "just doing my job, same as anyone else would."

"I love you, detective," she purred with a smirk.

"I love you too, professor," he replied with his usual carefree suavity.

For a while, Charlie sat side by side with the woman that he loved more than anyone else in the world, watching the two miracles they'd created race wildly around their front lawn. He breathed in deep, enjoying the mild spring air feeling that desirable jolt of excitement, knowing that in just a few short hours, he would be in his favorite place in the world with his favorite people in the world.

"Are you as ready as I am to get the hell out of here?" he asked, pulling Meghan closer to his side and leaning back against the top couple of porch steps.

"What do *you* think?" she asked, playfully. "I even sent Pete an email this time."

"I know," he laughed. "The old man practically threw me out of the office after that!"

"Good. Otherwise you'd have been there all night and then I'd be dragging two exhausted girls and a half-dead cop through the airport tomorrow morning. Just like last time…and the time before that."

She joked, but her fingers found the three-inch long scar at the base of his throat, just inside the collar of his shirt. A few short months after he had finally become detective, the fates had brought him face-to-face with the serial rapist, torturer and murderer that the department had been hunting for several months. In an abandoned apartment complex on the city's east side, her husband had been forced to fire his weapon for the first and only time in his career. The brilliant but savage criminal had been expecting him and was faster on the draw than the young detective—his single shot catching Charlie in the throat. Before falling, Charlie had squeezed off three rounds, the second finding a spot just above the murderer's eye, putting a permanent end to a brutal spree.

Meghan felt a phantom pain in her chest and remembered the tense and terrible days after the incident. Charlie had lain on an operating table for four hours while surgeons frantically tried to repair the ragged hole in the young detective's neck. The carotid artery had been nicked and the injury would have proved fatal had he been delayed at all in getting to the hospital. With no small bit of luck and perseverance, the surgeons successfully saved

Charlie's life. The next day, he was conscious and responsive. Within a couple of months he had made a full recovery but neither Charlie nor Meghan ever forgot how close to death he had been.

Charlie gently took hold of his wife's hand and brought it away from his throat.

"This is going to be the best one yet. I promise," he said, with his most disarming smile.

"You'd better be right," she said, and they both quietly laughed. The girls still buzzed around the yard before them; two blue and yellow blurs ricocheting across the yard with no signs of slowing any time soon.

The Walker clan had visited Walt Disney World a couple of times every year since Violet had been born, only missing a single trip while Charlie was recovering from his injury. Charlie and Meghan had even gone at least once a year since the beginning of their relationship, long before the birth of their children. They were all lifelong Disney fanatics, and the World held a special place in all of their hearts. The biyearly vacation was always booked on the last day of each trip. It tended to make the bittersweet last day a little easier on the girls—and secretly on Charlie and Meghan—giving them all something to look forward to during the flight home.

Charlie sat for a few more minutes with his arms around his wife, simply enjoying the mild March evening and the sight of his girls expending all of their caffeine-enhanced energy. He thought back to the last trip they'd taken to Walt Disney World the previous September.

The entire vacation had been a disaster from the get-go. Charlie had been following up on a case until two hours before their flight and had not slept in almost two days. The girls had lain awake all night with excitement. All of this sleeplessness led to Meghan being forced to tow her three near-zombified loved ones through the busy airport early in the morning. Exhausted as they all were, father and daughters were asleep the moment they'd fastened their seatbelts on the plane.

Shortly after their arrival at Orlando International Airport, they were boarding one of the packed automated trams when Violet dropped her favorite ball. Catching an unlucky bounce, it rolled back out onto the loading platform. Frantically, the seven-year-old chased after it, only to have the doors close behind her, sending the rest of her family off toward the Hub, leaving her behind. For a frantic fifteen minutes, Charlie shouldered, elbowed and pushed his way through the throng of vacationers, hurrying to board the tram heading in the other direction. He breathed a long sigh of relief when he returned to where Violet had fled, only to find her waiting patiently near the large glass window, tapping her foot and checking her little white Hello Kitty watch, knowing that her Dad would be back for her any minute.

The next few days of the trip went remarkably well until, on the fourth night, both the girls picked up a nasty strain of stomach flu and had the entire family quarantined to their room. Two nights later, the girls had recovered, only to have passed the curse on to Charlie and Meghan. Finally, after four days of being holed up in their room, the Walker clan emerged to enjoy the last couple of days of their trip.

Charlie was hesitant when booking the next trip, but he knew that this was a freak occurrence and that they'd gotten their inevitable bad vacation out of the way. He was determined to make this trip the best one yet to make up for the train wreck that was the previous year's fiasco.

Charlie had spared no expense on this trip. Using extra money from his holiday bonus, Charlie had secretly upgraded their standard room at the Caribbean Beach Resort to one of their newly remodeled pirate suites. His girls—while understandably infatuated with princesses—utterly *adored* everything pirate related. They owned all the *Pirates of the Caribbean* films on Blu-ray and it wasn't an uncommon occurrence to see Violet and Katie marauding through the house—decked out in full princess garb—with cutlasses strapped to their waists. He'd known that this little surprise would make his girls extremely happy ever since he'd seen Violet and Katie swooning over a picture of the newly remodeled room on Meghan's iPad. Charlie had also spent extra money on the Deluxe Dining Plan. He'd figured that since his family spent so much time expelling their food on the last vacation, they might as well have the freedom to overindulge this time around.

§

Pulling his iPhone from his jacket pocket, Charlie called up a weather app and checked the forecast for Walt Disney World. The weather couldn't have been more perfect: low- to mid-eighties all week and sunshine for the entire trip. Smiling at his good fortune, he pocketed his phone and stood.

"I reckon I'll head inside and get out of this monkey suit," he told Meghan. "Hopefully by the time I get all my last-minute nonsense packed up, Penn and Teller over there will have finally run out of gas." He leaned down and they kissed.

Meghan gave his hand a gentle squeeze and turned back once more to watch the girls as Charlie headed into the house. Passing through the kitchen, headed for the back stairs, Charlie saw the results of his daughters' glorious plan firsthand. He couldn't help but laugh aloud as he saw, on a chair near the table, two small, pink Hello Kitty teacups sitting on a matching tea tray. On the floor nearby lay the empty Dr Pepper bottle.

The Walkers' dog—a five-year-old German shepherd named Zeus— casually wandered into the room and sniffed the cups and bottle, recognizing the scent of his two favorite girls. German shepherds have extraordinarily expressive faces, so it wasn't difficult for the detective to spot the look of mischief written across his beloved friend's face.

"Oh, Zeus," said Charlie, shaking his head slowly in mock disappointment. "Valiant protector, loyal friend…and shrewd partner in crime. I'll bet you had something to do with this, didn't you? Yes? I'll bet a shiny buffalo nickel that our clever little Vi sent you upstairs to distract your Mom, didn't she?"

Zeus gave a slight whine and held up his paw to be shaken: his gold-standard canine apologetic gesture. The dog was smart—the move worked every time. Charlie obliged, then knelt down and scratched Zeus behind the ears with both hands. He spotted a small bit of soda remaining in one of the girls' cups and he placed it on the floor before the dog.

"Don't tell Mom," he said, as he stood and headed for the staircase. He could hear the dog eagerly lapping up the remnants from all the way up the stairs.

Finally making his way to the bedroom that he and Meghan shared, he dropped heavily down onto the bed and removed his jacket. Unclipping the service pistol and badge that had been digging into his hip, he opened the top drawer of his nightstand. Taking up the entire space within was a custom-made handgun lockbox, complete with a biometric lock. Pressing his finger to the scanner, the lid quickly opened and he was free to stow the weapon. From within the space, he removed his smaller off-duty weapon—a Walther PPS—in its corresponding holster.

Leaving the unloaded weapon on the nightstand, Charlie showered, changed and began packing all of his last-minute necessities into his carry-on bag. Into the black canvas military backpack went the usual suspects: phone chargers, various medicines, bandages for all of the scraped knees and elbows the girls were destined to suffer from, a few sets of headphones, Meghan's iPad and the most recent book that he had been reading—*Phantom* by Ted Bell. Noticeably absent was Charlie's own laptop, for he had long ago learned never to bring his work with him on vacation.

Charlie had just laid his backpack atop the stack of other luggage and dropped back onto the bed when Meghan glided into the room.

"Want to hear a funny story?" she asked.

"Always," Charlie shot back, grinning at his wife.

"It goes like this: I *finally* got the girls into bed and, next thing I know, there's a wide-eyed German shepherd whining at me with a Frisbee in his mouth. It's almost eleven-thirty; Zeus should be knocked out cold by now. How *strange* that he should be ready to play this late at night."

"That is pretty strange," Charlie agreed, laughing lightly.

Lying down on the bed next to him, Meghan said, "I saw the cup on the floor, genius."

Charlie laughed again before pulling her over and kissing her.

"I had nothing to do with it…I swear."

"You may be good at catching liars, Charlie Walker, but you're very bad at *being* one. You know that?"

"I have my moments," he said, earning him a light punch on the shoulder for his trouble.

Within fifteen minutes, the entire Walker household was asleep—save for a newly nocturnal, Dr Pepper-fueled German shepherd patrolling the house, endlessly searching for intruders or someone to throw his Frisbee for him.

For once, the family's vacation was off to a decent start. Maybe Charlie would actually make good on his promise this time.

3

harlie awoke to find three sets of eyes patiently gazing at him from only a few inches away. When he was able to shake off the cobwebs of a deep sleep, his visitors came into focus. Violet, Katie and Zeus all sat—statue still—on the floor directly next to the bed, clearly anticipating the moment of his awakening.

Zeus recognized that his master was conscious and leaned forward, licking Charlie directly across the forehead.

"Thanks, Zeus. Love you too, buddy," Charlie said as he sat up, wiping the slobber from his forehead. Zeus's characteristic paw shot up for another handshake, and Charlie obliged.

"To what do I owe this glorious wake-up call—um—an hour before the alarm was supposed to go off?" asked Charlie, noticing the time as he slipped his watch onto his wrist and fastened the clasp. He also noticed that Meghan's side of the bed was empty.

Still sitting cross legged on the floor, between Zeus and Katie, Violet volunteered to answer.

"Mommy said we had to get up extra early today because we have to take Zeus to the dog-hotel and you have to talk to the airport people about your gun. She said that it took longer than we thought last time and she didn't want to have to run to the gate again."

"Makes sense. How was your sleep last night?" he asked. Zeus' ears pricked up as he heard some rustling downstairs in the kitchen. He quickly took off toward the sound, hoping to catch Meghan in time to scam a treat out of her.

"Really good!" Katie exclaimed.

"Yeah," agreed Violet. "It was like, as soon as we got done doing magic tricks, we just got super-tired. Magic isn't easy, Daddy."

"Hardest thing in the whole wide world," Charlie agreed as he stood, lifting his girls to their feet. "That's why I'm glad you guys are so good at it— you can do it for me and I can retire early. Why don't you head on downstairs and see if Mom's got any breakfast happening, I'll meet you down there in a few."

As his girls headed downstairs, he grabbed his empty Walther and badge from the nightstand and took them to the closet. In the back of the small space, he had a second biometrically-locked, fireproof safe where he kept various important documents and a small store of ammunition for his off-duty weapon. Setting the gun on top of the safe, he quickly dressed for the day in his I'm-just-a-tourist clothing: an old, navy-blue EPCOT Center T-shirt, some worn khaki cargo shorts and a well-made leather belt, to which he affixed the Walther and his badge. From the safe, he withdrew two magazines. After loading the Walther, he chambered the first round and holstered the pistol. On his way to the bathroom, he stowed the extra one in his suitcase.

While Charlie was required to carry a weapon at all times when off-duty, he was not permitted to carry it inside the private property of a Disney park. Upon reaching the main gate, Charlie was required to check in with security, present his law enforcement identification and have his pistol catalogued and locked up. When exiting the parks, Charlie could then sign his weapon out and be free to carry it once more.

This year, Charlie had decided not to bother bringing his weapon with him to the parks. It created an unnecessary extra step, when he could achieve the same results by simply locking the gun away in the wall safe back in their hotel room. Already, the family had to make extra time at the airport so that Charlie could clear his weapon.

In theory, the new process of using identifier codes along with credentials at the standard TSA checkpoints was *supposed* to be faster than the old method of presenting written authorization from the officer's department. In practice, this made the process slower. Unfortunately, many of the TSA agents they'd encountered were not properly briefed on the newer system nor adequately trained in its execution or were simply skeptical of his police credentials. This normally led to a delay as they waited for a supervisor to come along and spout the obligatory, "Let this fine officer and his family through so they can enjoy their vacation; he's already been cleared to carry on the new system, Steven." While not a day-wrecker, anticipation of this event did force the Walkers to allow twenty or thirty additional minutes for the security checkpoint.

§

A half-hour later, the Walkers were fed, clean and packed. Charlie loaded the luggage in the car and led the regal Zeus out first to find him a seat of his own. After locking up the house, Meghan and the kids piled into the car and they were off.

At record-breaking pace, Zeus was checked in at the kennels. The family was at the airport within another half-hour. Charlie encountered the anticipated security blunders—though they were handled much faster than in any previous trip.

The flight was on time and on schedule, the boarding was smooth and everything was going according to plan. Charlie breathed in the air circulating in the cabin, acknowledging the scents of disinfectant and freshly-brewed coffee, and finally felt that his vacation had begun.

He smiled while disembarking, experiencing that telltale 'we're here!' moment when the cool, conditioned air from the plane met the humid Floridian air in the jetway. Charlie didn't even bother to clean his sunglasses when this meteorological event caused his lenses to fog up. *To hell with it,* he thought. *We're home.*

§

His girls squealed with delight from their seats on the Magical Express when the on-board video started with the friendly voiceover thanking everyone and welcoming them aboard. Charlie felt a pang of nostalgic pleasure in his chest upon hearing that all-too-familiar voice.

At this moment, Detective Charlie Walker of the Detroit Police Department's homicide division ceased to exist. In his place, sat the real Charlie Walker: devoted father, loving husband, Disney fanatic and man-child. Gone were any thoughts or concerns about open cases back home.

Vanished were any worries about criminals, killers, thieves or any of the other human trash he dealt with on a daily basis. Even the Walther, holstered on his right hip, beneath his shirt, was nothing more than a mild discomfort.

Along the way, the bus driver pointed out a large alligator sunning himself along the side of the freeway. Violet and Katie had their faces pressed against the glass, giggling as they gazed at the massive reptile from the safety of the bus. Even Meghan leaned across Charlie as far as she could to catch a glimpse. There aren't many gators back in Wayne County; the only time the Walkers had been close to one was in the reptile house at the Detroit Zoo—and they were small and hid beneath logs or foliage. It was just another happy occurrence to add to the already promising vacation.

Charlie had checked in online the day before, and their keycards and Welcome Packet were waiting for them at the desk inside Custom House—the front desk area—at the Caribbean Beach Resort. The Cast Member who presented the packet recognized Charlie, Meghan and the kids from their past visits. She was a middle-aged woman named Lucy and she had the memory of a supercomputer. It seemed that she was at the online check-in desk for every vacation the Walker's had taken in the last three years. She remembered them all and spoke to them as if they were her own family.

"Well, if it isn't Violet and Katie Walker!" Lucy exclaimed, beaming at the two small children. "I was hoping I would see you two sometime soon. Wait here for a second: I have something for you!"

With that, Lucy took off at a brisk pace and disappeared through a doorway. After a few moments, she returned with something clasped between her hands. Lucy presented to the children a familiar pink plastic container with a white handle atop it, roughly the size of a small tackle box. Violet and Katie's names were written on the front in black permanent marker. It took Charlie a few moments to recognize what it was but when it came to him he could hardly believe his eyes.

"Oh my God, Lucy!" shouted Violet, taking the box from her and showing it to Katie. The girls' giddy exclamations drew a few glances, smiles and polite giggles from the others in the building. "How *did* you find this?"

"Oh, I have my ways," she joked, winking at Charlie and Meghan. "I figured I couldn't have two of my favorite princesses staying here without their makeup kit."

"Thank you, thank you, thank you!" the girls shouted as Meghan led them outside to play with their long lost makeup box.

"Lucy, I don't know what to say; that was amazing," admitted Charlie.

"Oh it's nothing, honey. I noticed the girls had left it in the corner over by the benches, but by the time I got to it your bus had taken off. I figured you'd be back sooner or later so I checked to see if you'd made any reservations and—sure enough—today's the day."

"I don't know how to thank you. I thought we'd never see that thing again."

"Never say never, detective. Never say never. Now get on out there; your room's ready and the girls are probably going to explode if you don't get them on Pirates of the Caribbean as soon as possible."

"We owe you one, Lucy!"

"Don't mention it," she said, jokingly shooing him away. "Get out of here and enjoy your vacation!" Charlie smiled and nodded, heading for the door.

"Oh, and Charlie?"

He turned back.

"Yes?"

"Welcome home."

§

This trip really could not have gotten off to a better start. It seemed as if the cosmos was aligning and laying the magic on extra thick to make up for last year's disaster. Charlie had no complaints—you can never enjoy a vacation *too* much.

Just as Charlie had expected, the room upgrade had sent his girls into a euphoric mania. Even Meghan couldn't mask her surprise—Charlie hadn't told her either. He watched as his three loves explored every inch of the gloriously pirate-themed lodgings. The girls had a blast jumping on the pirate ship beds, plotting out imaginary courses using the compass-themed table and discovering the mighty Kraken in all of his towel animal glory.

"I had a feeling you had something up your sleeve," stated Meghan.

Charlie shrugged.

"One day, I just felt like upgrading," he replied, winking at her.

"The place is amazing. Violet and I were checking it out a while back."

"Oh, were you?" asked Charlie in exaggerated mock confusion.

"You noticed that did you, detective?" Meghan shot back.

"I notice everything," he plainly stated, eliciting a laugh from his wife.

As much as he joked about it, Charlie really did have the uncanny ability to notice every single detail. Violet and Katie had learned this long ago; they had no chance of slipping some wrongdoing past him. Recently, the girls had started to adapt to the reality that they'd be caught red-handed no matter what they did, so they had begun running their schemes out in the open, blatantly obvious to any and all who cared to observe. Violet and Katie were very well behaved and their villainous plans were mostly harmless, so it just added another level of fun to Charlie's home life. It entertained him immensely to see what these two creative little monsters could come up with next.

"Well, ladies, where to first?" he asked, already knowing the answer.

"Pirates!" both girls screamed in unison.

"Didn't even need to ask," stated Meghan.

"Tradition," replied Charlie with a shrug.

And so it was Pirates of the Caribbean that would be the first attraction of the Walkers' ten-day vacation.

§

The next day seemed to be right on par with the first. Violet and Katie were, fortunately, entirely immune to the notorious midday meltdown that most children their age experience at some point during long days in the parks. Charlie and Meghan had trouble keeping up but considered themselves lucky that their girls were free from the stigma associated with most small children on vacations.

This second day brought the Walkers to Charlie and Meghan's favorite park: EPCOT Center. Although the park officially dropped the 'Center' in the mid-nineties and became Epcot, Charlie still used its original name. Meghan, having only started coming to Walt Disney World after meeting Charlie, still didn't quite get why her husband felt the need to call it EPCOT Center. Similarly, she didn't fully understand why he spoke of "going to MGM Studios" when the park is now called Disney's Hollywood Studios. Charlie laughed it off every time the question came up but held firm to his roots, leaving his terminology unchanged.

In the mid-afternoon, when the oppressive-yet-welcoming Floridian sun had passed the halfway point of its journey around this side of our planet, the Walkers found themselves outside The Seas with Nemo & Friends.

The girls were eager to ride, but Charlie had indulged in one too many free samples of obscure foreign sodas from Club Cool—smartly avoiding the infamous Beverly—and he found the need to excuse himself in favor of a trip to the nearest restroom. Meghan and the girls agreed to meet him at the nearby benches after their ride. Waving goodbye, he headed off to the nearest facilities.

Feeling much better after his little pit stop, Charlie had a few extra minutes to explore while he waited for his family to finish the ride. He decided to take a stroll into a nearby shop called Mouse Gear—his personal favorite in all of Walt Disney World. Lazily wandering through the near-endless racks of merchandise, he was thankful that he had set a strict budget or he'd have taken half of the store home with him. Checking his watch, he was surprised to learn that he'd been hypnotized by the sights and sounds of the store for much longer than he'd planned; Meghan and the girls were surely waiting for him outside the ride.

Quickening his pace, he left the store empty-handed and made it back to the large area near The Seas' entrance and exit. This being the end of March and the week that most young children had off school, the parks were extremely crowded. The grounds in front of the attraction and the attached Coral Reef Restaurant were no exception. Placing a hand to his forehead to shade his eyes from the sun, he scanned the area to no avail. Once he saw a flash of blonde and mistook it for Meghan but, upon closer inspection, he realized the golden curls belonged to a stranger.

Charlie hadn't checked the wait time for the ride before he'd parted ways with his family, but knew from past experience that there was never much of a crowd—and when there was, it moved along swiftly. He'd been gone for a half-hour; more time than he'd intended. Chalking it up to an unexpectedly long line, he sat on the bench on which he was supposed to meet his family and pulled out his phone to send Meghan a text message.

How's everything going in there? Long wait?

After sending the text, he waited on the bench for another five minutes, checking his phone now and again. With no sign of his family and no reply to his text, Charlie started to become concerned.

Leaving the bench, Charlie made his way to the exit of the ride, finding himself inside an aquatic-themed store. The place was more crowded than he'd ever seen; finding the girls would not be easy.

Traversing the first floor to no avail, Charlie moved on to the second floor, knowing there was a long tunnel with a cul-de-sac at the end. There were never many people in this area, even though it afforded the best views of the aquarium. He remembered this as being a favorite spot of Violet's, who could spend countless hours with her face pressed to the glass, searching for sharks and trying to snap pictures of them with her mother's phone.

Charlie's instincts told him not to worry—that he would find his family—and he was relieved to see flashes of light coming from the far side of the central pillar at the end of the hallway. He was sure that it was Violet being Violet and he relaxed, making his way more casually along the pathway, occasionally stopping to admire the sea life lazily gliding past.

Making his way around the right side of the pillar, he spotted Violet, furiously snapping pictures, with Katie asking if she could have a turn with the phone. Meghan was nowhere in sight, but the area was not very large, so he assumed that she was simply on the far side admiring the sights. Violet and Katie had yet to notice Charlie as he strolled up behind them, enraptured as they were by these creatures of the deep. All of a sudden, Charlie had that feeling in his chest that he occasionally experienced while on duty—that instinct that told him something was not quite right. The only people he'd seen down this entire stretch of hallway and its resulting cul-de-sac were his children. Even though people didn't often come this way, he'd expected there to at least be someone—anyone—but it remained empty save for the girls.

When he rounded the curve, he saw Meghan where he'd assumed she would be, but she was not alone. She had her back turned to Charlie and the children, and she was looking out into the aquarium with a man standing next to her—so close that his elbow was brushing against hers. Meghan Walker, while arguably the nicest and most polite person Charlie had ever met, had an aversion to interacting with people in public, even though she was a professor.

"Bad cell reception?" Charlie asked, causing Meghan to spin around with a start. Her anonymous companion remained with his back turned to Charlie, hands clasped at his waist.

"Charlie!" she blurted with a small nervous laugh. "You startled me. I meant to text you, but I had no reception and then Violet stole my phone to take pictures."

"Who's your friend?" he asked, not masking his apprehension at finding a strange man standing so intimately close to his wife.

The man slowly turned to face Charlie. Upon initial inspection, Charlie sized the man up as being in his mid- to late-twenties; he appeared to be athletically built, with piercing gray eyes. He wore the costume appropriate to this region of the park, and his Cast Member name tag read: Leroy. Charlie also noticed that Leroy's hometown was Auburn Hills, Michigan—forty-five minutes away from where the Walkers lived. Charlie observed that he heavily favored his right leg, leaning most of his weight on it, which betrayed the fact that he suffered from a limp. This was more than likely a hockey injury judging by his build and hometown. A deep scar marred the left side of an otherwise mild-mannered face. Glancing at Leroy's hands, Charlie noted the absence of a wedding ring, but did spy the slight discoloration of the skin-colored makeup that Disney Cast Members often used to hide tattoos in visible areas; it covered the knuckles on both of his hands. The makeup was well done; an average person may have never noticed but Charlie made a living observing and noticing details that others overlooked.

"This is Leroy; he works here. He was just telling me about two injured manatees that have been brought in from the observation center in Fort Pierce. Remember the Manatee Center, babe? We went there a few years back but it was cold and the manatees didn't show up."

"I remember," Charlie acknowledged, still wary of this stranger. Something just wasn't right about this man.

"Your wife and kids have taken a quite liking to the aquarium, Charlie," Leroy stated. "I was telling them about some of the things we do here to raise awareness for the sea life. Violet even said that she wanted to work here when she grew up."

"Yep!" Charlie heard from somewhere behind him, as Violet confirmed Leroy's statement. It made Charlie uneasy to know that, in the few minutes this stranger had been alone with his family, he had been able to learn all their names—including his.

Being a police officer meant that to trust an unfamiliar person was to invite danger to oneself and this situation was no different. Though he rightfully disliked and distrusted this man, he attributed it to the fact that Meghan was a strikingly beautiful woman, and that she attracted nearly every male that made her acquaintance. Many times Charlie had been forced to politely turn away men who were completely ignorant that Meghan wore an engagement ring and wedding band and—in this case—had two young children with her.

Wanting to get his family as far away from this strange man as possible, Charlie broke the heavy silence.

"Come on, girls," he said, eyes still on Leroy. "We've got dinner reservations and we don't want to be late."

Meghan looked relieved to have the opportunity to excuse herself from Leroy's presence. At that point Charlie believed that his initial instincts were right: this man was obviously trying to charm this beautiful woman when he was interrupted by the untimely appearance of her husband. Charlie began to doubt his deductions though, after Leroy abruptly cleared his throat. Meghan halted dead in her tracks with an odd look on her face for just a split second—was it fear?—and stood still while Leroy spoke.

"Thanks for visiting The Seas, guys. And hopefully I'll see you all again very soon. Have a magical day," said Leroy, giving Meghan a look that lasted just a moment too long, lingering on her backside—not well concealed beneath her skin-tight shorts. Grinning, Leroy casually turned on his heel and headed down the hallway, the sound of keys jangling away into the distance.

Pulling Meghan aside, out of earshot of the girls, Charlie decided to get to the bottom of the situation.

"Mind telling me what *that* was about?" he asked.

"I…I don't know. One minute the girls and I were at the window, looking out at the aquarium with a few other families and the next minute that…that *guy* was here and everyone else was gone." She rubbed the back of her left elbow as she spoke, as if trying to rub away the memory of his touch.

"Did he touch you?" Charlie asked, knowing that the first sign assailants tend to display before becoming violent is the urge to put their hands on another person, whether it be a gentle graze on the hand, a pat on the back, or anything more unwelcome.

"He…uh…did put his hand on my back for a second as he was pointing out one of the sharks in the tank. It was harmless though, babe. Really, don't worry about it."

Charlie nodded, sighed and laid the matter to rest for the time being. He made a mental note about Leroy's borderline-inappropriate conduct and decided that he would file a complaint at Guest Relations. It seemed like a harmless scenario, but the underlying feeling of dread remained within Charlie's mind, and he could not get that split-second image of Meghan's face out of his head. He had no doubt that what he saw was genuine fear in his wife's eyes. She betrayed the emotion only for the tiniest instant, but Charlie had seen the look before she could mask it, and he could not let it go.

The next few hours went smoothly until just before dark, when Meghan suggested they leave EPCOT Center and go to the Magic Kingdom. Charlie was a bit confused, considering they'd spent the previous day there. He told Meghan as much.

"I…I just really wanted to catch the fireworks, you know?" she said. "We rarely get to see them. I don't know…I just think it would be nice and I want to get there early to find a good place."

Charlie agreed, but he also noticed that a change had come over his wife during the past few hours. She didn't make eye contact when she spoke to him and it seemed as if she was nervously watching the crowds around her. She was doing her best to mask her feelings—to act normal—but Charlie was just a little bit too keen of mind to be fooled. Still, he knew not to press his wife. Whatever problem she was dealing with would be revealed in time. He became more concerned later in the evening when, emerging from the bathroom, he noticed that Meghan's eyes were swollen and red. It was clear she'd been crying but he couldn't fathom why.

Meghan Walker was a strong woman and the strange event with Leroy in the aquarium, although inappropriate and bizarre, should never have fazed her. Charlie became convinced that something else was worrying his wife and it troubled him deeply. He bit his lip and tried to carry on with as much normality as he could muster.

The longer the night dragged on, the more distant Meghan became until such a point came when it was almost awkward to be around her. Violet and Katie were oblivious, enjoying the joyous sensory overload that is The Most Magical Place on Earth. The pregnant silence that hung between Charlie and Meghan was almost palpable. Charlie could swear that the situation had become so severe that other people were starting to notice the nearly lifeless woman hardly focusing on putting one foot in front of the other.

Darkness had fallen over the Magic Kingdom and the myriad assortments of colored lights basked the park in an entirely different glow. This was Charlie's favorite time in the park, especially in Tomorrowland where the brilliantly placed lighting worked wonders painting the structures every hue in the spectrum.

When they'd reached the futuristic land, Meghan spoke for the first time in almost an hour.

"Let's ride the PeopleMover. It's your favorite, Charlie," she said.

Why? We'll never get a good spot for the fireworks if we ride the PeopleMover, he thought, but decided not to push the issue.

He nearly felt physical pain listening to her speak. Her tone was wooden, hollow, and flat, and chilled him to his core. He had never heard his wife speak in such a way. He vowed that, as soon as they got back to their hotel room, he was going to find out what was wrong. He understood that he should give her time, but something was seriously upsetting her and he was determined to figure it out. "Okay," Charlie replied, glancing at the love of his life, searching her features for clues to this ever-evolving mystery.

The ride was every bit as nostalgic and pleasing as he remembered. The slow-moving train in which they sat was completely empty save for the Walker family. Meghan and the kids sat in a forward-facing seat while Charlie sat alone, across from them in a rear-facing seat. It seemed like an excellent way to relax: the fireworks not far off and the train empty except for his family. He welcomed the serenity and relaxation that the PeopleMover provided. He almost entirely forgot about Meghan's strange behavior, listening to the narrator speak of the various landmarks dotting Tomorrowland's sizable skyline.

They were about to enter the dark tunnel that made its way through Space Mountain when, all of a sudden, Meghan leapt toward Charlie, passionately kissing him, arms thrown wildly around his neck.

"I love you, baby," she cried, tears streaming down her face. "I love you so, so much."

"I love you too," Charlie replied with his most reassuring smile.

Just before entering the darkness of the tunnel, the chilling vision of his wife's face took Charlie's breath away. She had a look of sheer terror spread across her delicate, beautiful features. Her chest heaved with deep breaths as tears flowed steadily from her eyes.

Charlie leaned his head back on the top of the seat, his heart pounding and his mind spinning with theories about why his wife had been so distraught. The brilliant detective's mind failed him for the first time in a long while and he clenched his fists to keep himself from screaming. Meghan's racking sobs were so torturous and so violent that they could even be heard above the sound of the roller coaster cars from deep within Space Mountain.

Just when Charlie felt he could handle no more, the train stopped dead in its tracks and the darkness swallowed them whole.

4

From a small monitor inside a lavish villa, a lone man in his late sixties watched the feed from night vision cameras as the train containing the four people pulled into the tunnel. He waited until the family made it to the darkest possible place in the structure; a spot where ambient light didn't even reach during the day.

Yes, this was the spot.

He pressed a few keys on his laptop and the train came to a full and complete stop. The woman was hysterical at this point but, no matter, it would all be over soon enough.

This was far easier than the man had expected and the costs not nearly as high as anticipated. He waited for a few moments, giving the woman time to calm down. This next part required her silence and the woman knew that she must silence herself—and her children—or face the consequences of disobedience. The man watched as the woman put forth a heroic effort to remain calm. The detective still sat with his head leaned back on the seat and his hands clenched into fists.

The time had come.

"Commence."

He spoke the word into a Bluetooth headset, and leaned back in his custom-made seat to enjoy the show. A few moments later, months of planning began to bear fruit. A growing smile stretched across his meticulously maintained features. He took a sip from an expensive glass bottle of water. *Eighteen dollars a bottle,* he thought. *Worth every damned penny.*

Movement on the monitor caught the man's eye and his smile grew wider. Three of his men slowly appeared out of darkness and approached the train. He had disabled the sensors along the sides of the track to allow his men unhindered access—free of alarm—and he'd looped the cameras in this section using images of an earlier, similarly occupied train coupled with the current timestamp to deter any curious security personnel who may be watching. He could just make out the small syringes the operatives carried in their hands. Only the best anesthetic would do for a glorious occasion such as this, and the man had spared no expense. Fast-acting and entirely nonlethal, these had become the newest craze in most modern medical establishments and triage units. To its less-savory users, the substance was nothing less than liquid gold.

The man watched, lightly chuckling to himself, as his men passed within inches of the brilliant detective—completely unseen.

They had reached the mother and daughters, and their work was nearly complete; the plan executed flawlessly.

The man heard the villa's electronic door lock disengage. A large, clean-cut fellow in his late-twenties entered the room and took a seat beside the man. He was powerfully built, with a scar on the left side of his face and tattoos upon his knuckles. He silently watched the events on the screen, and his smile was almost as wide as that of his older companion. Finally, the drama onscreen was finished, and the man turned toward his companion.

"You have done well, Jeremy," said the man calmly. "The woman has followed your instructions to the letter."

"Thank you, sir," said the younger man, graciously and respectfully.

"But..." said the man equally calmly. Jeremy flinched as if he had been struck. The single word was said no less warmly than the way in which grandparents might tell their grandchildren how much they loved them. Nonetheless, Jeremy tried not to recoil and shrink away from his employer.

"B-but what, sir?" asked Jeremy.

"I am always watching. Listening. I see everything and I *know* everything. However, that is irrelevant. Unfortunately, I was observing you. Do you know what I saw? Could you tell me what has me so perturbed? Or, perhaps, you are uncertain as to any transgressions that have occurred on your part?"

"Sir...I..." stammered Jeremy.

"Yes, I know, Jeremy," he said in a soothing tone, stroking the younger man's cheek with a gentle hand. "I know you didn't mean to. I know you were just being young—oh, how I remember youth! Such an adventurous time in a man's life, is it not?"

Jeremy didn't answer.

"Is it not, Jeremy?" the man repeated.

"It...is," he reluctantly agreed.

"It is...what, Jeremy? Has the education system been so cruel that you cannot speak in complete sentences? It is...*what?*"

Again, the man spoke very calmly and politely, with not a drop of malice to be detected in his voice. His tone did not match his words, though, for it was nothing short of cordial and warm. His words, on the other hand, carried more venom than the boy could bear.

"It is an adventurous time...in a man's life, sir." Jeremy seemed to be nearly on the verge of tears at this point, so fearful was he of this kind, gentle, elderly man.

"That's much better!" admitted the man. "We will make a true gentleman out of you yet, Jeremy! Though not before discussing this little issue."

He paused for a moment, savoring the wave after wave of unmasked fear radiating from the boy. With Jeremy's athletic physique, the man knew that, should the boy assault him, he would be easily bested. After all, a man of his age—while in excellent shape—could never hope to hold his own against a man in Jeremy's condition, but the man took comfort in knowing that a man, even with the fewest of physical capabilities, can be *any* man's intellectual superior. The brain can be a more terrifying weapon than anything a man with three hundred pounds of muscle could ever hope to wield. History has shown, time and time again, that fortune favors the brilliant, and that all men eventually bow before those of a higher intellect. To kill a man is one thing; to destroy him, another. It was the threat of destruction that the man used to his benefit for countless years, awarding him success that grew at an exponential rate.

"Now, Jeremy," the man cooed. "You have played your part perfectly in gaining the woman's compliance. I commend you on your performance—truly splendid. However, you committed one grievous error, which could possibly have ruined everything we worked so hard to accomplish. Luckily, the detective was thinking practically, instead of critically, or right now you would be in a Disney holding room waiting for the Orange County sheriff's department to come for you, and I would be transferring money into a certain law enforcement officer's account to make sure that you were never heard from again."

"Sir, I—" started Jeremy, but the man calmly held up his hand for silence and obedience was immediate.

"I will tell you this one time, Jeremy, and one time only. If you must spend your time ogling the asses of other men's wives, make damn well sure that you choose someone other than the wife of our target." The man's calm was eerily absolute as he continued, "As you know, people who commit such appalling acts of selfishness in my presence—especially those in my employ—are fed through the finest wood chipper money can buy."

"I'm sorry, sir. I'm truly sorry. I didn't know what I was doing; it'll never happen again…" Jeremy's apologies trailed off into silence as he waited for the axe to fall.

Never one to miss taking advantage of a dramatic moment, the man waited, calmly glaring at his subordinate. Jeremy was so thoroughly terrified at this point that he had begun to tremble. The man took another sip from his exquisite bottle of water, savoring the taste of the ultra-purified, mineral-enriched substance. Gently clearing his throat, he decided Jeremy's fate.

"You may go," he declared.

The boy looked up, his astonishment clear. He knew better than to reply, for a single grammatical error could mean the end of his life. He had seen it happen countless times in the past—as the weapon that had taken those lives. Nodding, Jeremy stood and calmly exited the room.

After another few moments, the man leaned back in his chair and allowed himself a small chuckle at the boy's expense. How could he waste such a valuable asset by eliminating young Jeremy? The boy did his job well enough. Jeremy was afraid of his employer, and this fear kept the other subordinates in line. Should he lose poor Jeremy, he would have to assert his dominance personally over anyone he employed. That would not do—that would not do, at all. The older man was above these petty obligations; occupying his beautiful mind with such tedious tasks would dull his senses and muddle his extremely valuable and profound thoughts. No, Jeremy would survive and play a key role in the events to come.

Never before had the man known an intellectual equal as that which he found in Detective Charlie Walker. He'd observed the ingenious detective's methods for many months now and was continually impressed by the results this young man had achieved. Had the older man not been so meticulous and careful in his Detroit endeavors, he had no doubt that young Walker would have discovered his involvement, and the coming battle of the minds would have taken place much sooner. No, the older man was not so easily found. Events that occurred in this life did so on *his* terms, not those of anyone else.

Finally, the time for the man to test the detective's mettle had come. The game was about to begin. The detective's prize: his family's lives. The man's prizes: the glorious death of the promising young detective and the blissful knowledge that there was not a single man left on the planet who could challenge his masterful mind.

Movement on the monitor had caught his eye, pulling him from his sweet reverie. The time to initiate the next phase of the game had come. Cracking his knuckles and smiling brightly, the man leaned close to his laptop and began tapping keys.

5

The darkness was absolute around the Walker family. The air conditioning must have been out of order for quite some time, because the oppressive humidity of the day had remained, leaving the tunnel hot and sticky. When the train had halted in the blackness, Charlie had refused to react. He didn't lift his head; he simply sat in his seat—staring into the empty void above his head—and waited for the ride to commence.

Meghan's cries had almost become too much to bear, Charlie could still hear them over the loud, echoing racket of the roller coaster cars whizzing past unseen. He nearly felt like sobbing himself as whatever his wife was dealing with was beyond his power to fix; he'd never known her like this before. After a few more moments of hysterical sobbing, Meghan began to calm down; her breathing resuming a more natural rhythm until Charlie could no longer hear her at all. Violet and Katie were silent as well and had not reacted to the train's sudden halt. Charlie wasn't surprised by their silence, though. The girls had never been afraid of the dark. They'd been on the PeopleMover in years past when the train had stopped in this exact tunnel; Charlie attributed their lack of reaction to this fact.

After what seemed like hours, but was no more than two or three minutes, the train began its steady forward motion once more through the inky blackness. Charlie closed his eyes, trying to become enraptured again by the sounds and smells of one of his favorite attractions. Serenity began to wash over him for a while, and he enjoyed the cool breeze that he felt as the train exited the tunnel into the night. Charlie decided that now would be as good a time as any to confront Meghan and finally find out what had been bothering her.

Upon opening his eyes, Charlie nearly fainted from an intense attack of vertigo.

Meghan and the girls were no longer seated across from him. They had been just feet from him mere minutes ago: Meghan sobbing, Violet and Katie smiling despite their mother's dark mood. Never had something so heavily disoriented the detective as much as the abrupt vanishing of his entire family.

Frantically, Charlie spun around to search the other cars, irrationally hoping that this was all just some horrible joke and his girls would be sitting a few cars away smiling and giggling at him. He even went so far as to stand up, just to make sure they weren't ducking down anywhere. His family had simply ceased to exist. It was impossible. It was unthinkable. And it was happening. One minute the loves of his life were sitting in front of him, the next they were gone.

And in their place sat a manila envelope.

Noticing the parcel, Charlie lunged forward and snapped it up, quickly pulling out his phone to use the glow of the screen to illuminate the front of the small envelope. There was something printed across the front in dark black lettering. He shook his head and frantically tried to wipe away the pooling tears, some pattering onto the envelope. When he finally regained his eyesight, he read two simple words:

Open Me.

Carefully opening the envelope, he removed the small piece of paper from inside and read it several times. The letter read:

Detective Walker. When your journey on the PeopleMover is complete, you will calmly stand, exit the ride and dispose of this envelope, its contents and your cellular phone, using the trash receptacle near bottom of the moving walkway. Next, you will make your way to the Carousel of Progress and, once inside, you will seat yourself in the back row. You will notice a division between the two seats in the center of the row. It is in the left of these two seats that you will sit. During the show, you will be provided further instructions. Failure to comply with these instructions will result in the grotesque disfigurement of one or more of your beautiful angels.

The terrible letter was unsigned. The plainness of the entire package rendered Charlie's detection skills useless, since the Spartan offering was so barebones that there was nothing which could be used to identify its author. Though not enough to act on, from this purposeful display of neatness and carefulness, Charlie was able to deduce that his adversary was extremely careful. This unknown enemy knew he was dealing with a top-notch detective, so Charlie was certain that all the angles had been covered. Approaching the end of the ride, Charlie knew he had no choice but to comply in the hope that he may be able to offer this person whatever they wanted in exchange for his family.

Charlie did as he was instructed and disposed of the items after exiting the ride. He knew better than to alert a Cast Member or—worse—a security officer. Charlie's hostage negotiation training had made it abundantly clear that, until the situation could be fully defined, anything but absolute compliance with the captor's wishes would lead to casualties. He knew better than to rebel and it was clear that his adversary had known this as well since there was no specific instruction to *not* involve outside sources.

Charlie now had a clearer picture of the entity with which he had become entangled. This person was careful, and also observant. He made dangerous assumptions on Charlie's behalf, which only told Charlie that this person knew him extremely well. He was unconvinced that it was a person that he had known personally, but it was certainly someone who had observed and studied him for some time. This wasn't the average street criminal with whom he had dealt, so Charlie chose to err on the side of caution and play the game exactly as it was presented to him.

In his professional cases, Charlie had never taken risks that would have endangered the lives of anyone but himself. This creed held especially strong in this case—when his family's lives were those in danger. That being said, an unfamiliar rage began to boil beneath the detective's exterior surface of stoic calm. While on his way to the Carousel of Progress, he imagined in the things he would do to this monster if given the chance. The thoughts he had were intense and graphic, not those of a calm and intelligent homicide detective. These more closely resembled the unchecked emotions of the criminals he had spent his career hunting. He took several deep breaths, forcing himself to calm down until he was able to think clearly.

Charlie had made all possible deductions about this person that could be made, and he had no choice but to press on and gather more information. So far, he had no idea what this person even wanted. He could think of no clear motive, therefore he forced himself not to theorize before gaining as much information as he possibly could.

Charlie was still performing his skewed form of Zen meditation as he reached the Carousel of Progress. The Cast Member at the entrance removed the chain and opened the doors.

"Made it just in time, sir," the Cast Member informed him, with a heavy Latin American accent. "Looks like you're the only person here."

"You can skip the safety spiel," Charlie blurted, more forcefully than he'd intended. In an attempt to recover, he told the man, "I mean…I've been here a billion times and could recite it by heart."

"Rules are rules, sir," said the Cast Member sternly, following him into the auditorium.

Charlie quickly located the seat in which he'd been instructed to sit, and made himself comfortable as the other man began to work the PA system. Charlie did recite the entire spiel under his breath, and sighed with relief as the man finally exited the theater and the lights began to dim.

The welcoming and familiar dialogue began to play from the speakers, but Charlie was far too distracted to notice. He simply sat where he was told and waited for the instructions that he was promised. *There's nobody in here*, he thought. *How the hell are they going to give me instructions?*

Charlie waited through the entire introduction, listening to the cheerful song that he loved so much mock him as the auditorium shifted and he was rotated along to the first scene in the show. *There's a Great Big Beautiful Tomorrow, my ass*, he thought. When the auditorium eased to a stop, and the voice of Jean Shepherd began to speak about life in America around the turn of the century, Charlie ignored the Audio-Animatronic and began to worry. He'd been here long enough; why hadn't they contacted him? He began to think that he'd been sent into this twenty-minute show simply to keep him occupied until his family's captor could make a clean getaway. Charlie shortly dismissed that thought since his enemy was clearly looking to gain something. Whatever it was, it had to be something within Charlie's power to provide. Had the object been his family all along, there would have been no note and he'd never have heard from his family or their captor again. No, the instructions would come. They *had* to.

The scene was coming to a close, and Charlie had grown more impatient. As the theater rotated, moving its sole attendant to the next section, Charlie was gripping the armrests of his seat so tightly that he felt and heard his knuckles pop. Why were these people playing these games with him? How much longer did they plan to drag this nonsense out? Charlie felt himself losing control but forced himself to swallow his emotions and remain calm. Logic had always prevailed over emotions; this case would be no different.

On stage, John—the Audio-Animatronic father—was talking about Lindbergh's proposed flight across the Atlantic, Babe Ruth hitting "that old horsehide" and jazz music being "the cat's meow." Charlie was just about to stand up and walk out the emergency exit when—just after Schwartz's car horn honked from outside the window—he heard his name called. At first, he thought he may have heard wrong, but when John didn't tell the audience about the electric starter on his new Essex, Charlie knew something was different—something was wrong. Charlie stood and looked to the stage only to find John looking directly at him, waving his Niagara Falls fan. Rover's head returned to a resting position but John remained silent.

At this point, John should be telling him about their new ability to travel from New York to Los Angeles in only three days, which usually elicits a round of laughter from the audience, but John remained silent. There was no movement aside from the waving of the paper fan.

"What the hell is going on?" Charlie asked aloud, shaking his head slowly and trying to convince himself that he wasn't losing his mind.

"Why, nothing more than progress, detective!" answered John, the gleeful smile permanently plastered on his robotic face.

Stunned, Charlie locked his vision onto the mechanical humanoid.

"Did you just speak to me?" he asked feeling half crazed, wondering if he was hallucinating.

"Of course! You're the only one here, Charlie," replied John cheerfully, still waving his fan.

Charlie was dumbfounded. Clearly, whoever was playing this game had overridden the show's recorded dialogue and was listening to him through microphones planted *somewhere*, but how in the hell did he get that voice to sound just like Jean Shepherd?—it was uncanny, *impossibly* close. Charlie began to wonder what kind of person he was dealing with; this must have taken an unspeakable amount of resources to achieve.

"Where's my family?" Charlie asked.

"Safe and currently unharmed," said John, in a crueler tone, displaying none of the character's jovial, optimistic charm. "And that is all I can say—for now."

"What do I do next?"

"You sit down."

"Sit down?" Charlie asked, incredulously.

"Yes, Charlie. Sit down and enjoy the show."

Confused, Charlie sat down and within a few seconds, John was resuming his usual narrative. The Fourth of July scene finished as planned, then moved through the Halloween scene without interruption. He let out a long, drawn-out sigh as the Christmas scene began. He'd never thought that one of his favorite attractions could depress him, but it was doing a great job of it so far. First, the song—usually so bright and hopeful—now mocked him, taunted him. The Audio-Animatronics themselves had even begun *talking* to him—it almost seemed like some horrible nightmare he couldn't wake up from.

Charlie sank lower in his seat, not expecting any further interactions. He began to doubt that he would ever see his family again, and he was furious with himself for failing them. His mind was full of irrational thoughts and he kicked himself for not being more attentive on the PeopleMover. If he had sat with the girls, would he have prevented them from being taken—or would he have simply prolonged the inevitable? Suddenly, his train of thought was interrupted by a lack of action on stage.

The atmosphere had become eerily quiet and still, and John once again spoke to the bewildered detective: "Are you enjoying yourself, detective?"

"Fuck you," Charlie shot back.

"Language, Detective Walker, language! There could be children around!"

"We both know I'm the only one in this goddamned auditorium. Are you going to tell me why you have taken my family, or did you just bring me here to show off some fancy technological tricks?" Charlie asked, losing his patience completely.

"The reason you are here, detective, is that I wish to test you," John stated plainly.

"What kind of test? What does this have to do with my family?"

"Tests, Charlie. Plural," said John, coldly.

"What do I need to do?" Charlie asked. Any other questions would simply be a waste of time so he thought it better not to waste any more time being rebellious.

"Simply survive. Here's the deal, detective: survive my tests and your family will be returned to you, completely unharmed. Die, and I will be sure to dig a grave deep enough to accommodate four bodies," stated John.

Never before had Charlie thought that this Audio-Animatronic, which has brought a smile to his face so many times and for so many years, could seem so menacing—but he experienced it now, and it made his blood run cold. Something about the familiar voice delivering such horrible threats made an involuntary shiver work its way through his body.

"What do you get out of this?" Charlie asked. "I mean, if I don't succeed, what do *you* have to gain?"

"It's hard for you to turn off being a detective, isn't it?" John asked, his mechanical jaw moving slightly out of sync with his words. "Searching for my motive, are you? Fine, I'll bite. What I gain is simple. Should you complete the tests and survive, then I will have finally found the one mind that can best my own. Should you die…well, then I get to live out the rest of my days, comfortable in the knowledge that no other could successfully challenge me."

"*Challenge* you?" Charlie asked. "I don't even know who you are."

"All things will become clear in due time, detective," spouted John, his hands still mimicking the act of preparing Christmas dinner. "If you're as competent as my studies have led me to believe, you will discover all that there is to know. Trust me—I am on your side. I'm really rooting for you, but I cannot break the rules—the game must be played."

Charlie's head was spinning. First, this maniac threatens him and his family, then—moments later—goes on to say that he hopes Charlie will succeed. Never had he encountered such a personality as this in all of his years on the force.

"Trust you?" he snapped. "How can I trust you when you snatched my family from under my nose not even thirty minutes ago?"

"Well…you can't," stated John. "Not necessarily. I do give you my sincere word on the matter though. I am nothing if not a man of my word."

"Fine," he conceded. "What do you want me to do?"

"Return to your resort and get a good night's rest," said John, simply.

"What? Are you kidding? What about my family?" Charlie shot back, starting to get irritated that he was having this conversation with a robot and not the coward that was controlling it.

"Don't worry, Charlie," John assured him. "Your family is on their way to some pretty swanky lodgings as we speak. Unfortunately, we're running short on time. You will be contacted again before long."

"No!" he shouted. "That can't be it! I want proof that my family is safe!"

"Now is certainly not the time to make demands, detective, but in the spirit of Christmas, I have left a gift behind the seat to your right. See you real soon, Charlie."

Immediately after this sentence, the attraction's signature song blared over the speakers and the theater began its final rotation of the show. Charlie reached behind the seat and, as promised, there was a small box wrapped in Mickey paper with a green bow atop it affixed to the seatback. Shredding away the paper and tearing open the package, Charlie found a sleek new Blackberry inside. As soon as he removed it from the box, the device vibrated. On the screen, there was a notification that he'd received a picture message. Unlocking the device, he found a close-up shot of Katie's face, and she was sleeping peacefully. It wasn't much proof, but it was the best he could hope for right now.

Deciding to explore the phone for anything helpful, he tried to exit the message, but found that he was unable to access any screen save the one he was currently on. He even attempted to shut the device down and power it back up, but it still returned only to the current message window. No names or phone numbers were displayed with the message. This man was careful, resourceful, and clearly well-funded. If he had the technology and manpower to orchestrate all of this, then Charlie knew he must not underestimate him under any circumstances.

Remaining in his seat, waiting for the show to end, Charlie felt helpless for the first time since he had been a child. There was nothing he could do; all he had to look forward to was a night of helpless waiting and intense worrying—and this worrying had begun to manifest itself as physical pain in his chest. How could he be expected to simply return to his resort and go to sleep? He had no idea whether his family was safe or not. The picture of Katie hadn't necessarily been taken recently; his enemy was resourceful enough to have been able to snap that photo any time. The pain of worry in his chest became so intense that for a moment he thought he was having a heart attack. Slowly, he realized these pains were the telltale signs of a panic attack and that shock was setting in quickly.

After the attraction finished, the half-conscious, dazed Charlie Walker meandered out onto the Tomorrowland concourse, worried sick about Meghan and the girls. Within a few minutes, the figure of speech had become a reality and Charlie had barely enough time to make it to a restroom before spewing his expensive Le Cellier dinner all over one of the stalls. After the violent sickness had passed, Charlie stumbled over to a sink where he rinsed out his mouth and splashed cold water across his face. He straightened up and turned to look at his reflection in the mirror.

The Charlie Walker he saw looking back at him looked nothing like the happy, optimistic man he had been just that morning. His world had come crashing down around him and every fiber of his being was stressed to the breaking point. His face was ashen; his eyes bloodshot and glazed. Detective Charlie Walker was a broken man and looked every bit the part. Slowly, he made his way back outside as the fireworks were nearing their finale.

Escaping the park without incident seemed to prove more difficult for the distraught and tense detective than it should have been. Charlie's trek back to the park exit was a long blur of shoving people out of the way and murmuring halfhearted, half-heard apologies. Inevitably, he lost his cool during an instance in which a young man in his late teens came rushing through the crowd and screamed, "Yeah, bro!" directly into his face, then broke into a chorus of loud shouting. Charlie tried to shoulder his way past, shoving the man aside several times, but he was persistent, constantly putting himself in front of Charlie, pounding his chest and screaming, "Come at me bro!" between fits of laughing like a lunatic.

Not himself in the least, Charlie snatched the young man by the wrist, spun his arm behind his back and shoved him to the ground in an artfully executed police takedown, firmly pressing his knee into the man's back and maintaining a hold on his wrist. As soon as Charlie had done it, he regretted it immensely. He saw dozens of people staring at the mild spectacle occurring in the large crowd. This is no way for a park guest to act, let alone an off-duty police officer, and Charlie mentally kicked himself for being so erratic and impulsive.

Thinking quickly, Charlie shoved his badge in front of the man's eyes.

"Undercover police," Charlie declared. "Have you been drinking?"

"No! No, sir, I swear!" the man promised, his attitude entirely changed in a millisecond.

"Do you have any drugs on you or anything else I should be concerned with?" Charlie asked, in the most official tone he could manage under the circumstances.

"No!" the man replied again, his breath short due to Charlie's knee pressing down on his back.

"Any weapons?"

"No, sir! I promise!"

Charlie put away his badge and lifted the man to his feet.

"I suggest you reevaluate the way you interact with other people in public. I wouldn't want to have to have this talk with you again," Charlie warned.

"Of course not," the man agreed, politely. "It'll never happen again."

Charlie nodded and moved away from the man, but not before a few onlookers applauded. The boy's friends began pointing and laughing at him as they disappeared into the crowd. The last thing Charlie needed was to be detained and questioned by Disney Security. He had no doubt he would be released after they ran his credentials, but the delay would not help his situation. He quickened his pace and exited the park without drawing more attention.

Charlie soon found himself waiting at the back of a long line at the crowded bus stop. After three buses had come and gone, Charlie had made it to the front of the line just as a fourth bus was finishing loading. By this point, over forty-five minutes had passed, full of waiting, constantly being slammed into by uncontrolled children and given dirty looks by their parents when he didn't find them to be the world's most adorable little monster. He figured if he didn't make it on this bus, he would either snap or give up and attempt to walk back to the resort.

The heavens momentarily smiled upon him, as it seemed he would get one of the three remaining seats on the current bus. Unexpectedly, the front doors closed and his attention was drawn to where a woman, not much older than him, was approaching the rear door of the bus on a motorized scooter. Assuming she was handicapped, he kept his calm. He watched as the final three seats were folded away to accommodate her scooter. Charlie had a friend on the force who used one of these scooters due to a gunshot wound that had left him paralyzed from the waist down, so giving up his seat to someone in need did not bother him in the least.

Much to his surprise—and ultimately his dismay—once the woman's scooter was secure on the bus, she easily raised herself up and stood next to it, a hand lightly resting on the overhead bar for balance. Charlie could see her casually tapping her foot to the steel drum music as the back door closed and the vehicle pulled away. Sighing, Charlie placed his hands on his head and pressed deeply into his temples, trying to relieve the coming migraine. There was absolutely no way he would rest tonight.

With ever dwindling patience, Charlie waited for yet another bus.

6

The man laughed out loud as he watched Walker's patience wearing dangerously thin; the detective's stress was clearly visible even on the small monitor. The young adult that accosted Walker near the park exit was entirely unexpected, yet blissfully entertaining and fit extraordinarily well into the man's plans. The completely healthy woman on the scooter that had taken the final seats on the bus had played her part perfectly—her timing couldn't have been better. The effect her actions had on the young detective were blaringly apparent and gloriously successful. She had earned her pay and greatly satisfied her benevolent employer.

The current phase of the man's plan was to simply spend rest of the night breaking the young detective's spirit. The older man's mind was sharp as a razor in any situation—especially under stress, annoyance, anger and despair—and he intended to fry the nerves of the detective in order to learn whether the young man could work as well under similar circumstances. Everything was going according to plan—perhaps even exceeding expectations.

For the first time in a long while, the man began to feel a rush of pleasure. Yes, he'd challenged other promising minds but ultimately they'd failed and all were crushed beneath his massive intellect. They were mere distractions as he'd patiently waited for the main event. During his time studying the Walkers, he'd still felt the need to test his mind, and a Rubik's cube simply wouldn't cut it.

For instance, the man had spent time tracking and profiling criminal minds in the Greater Detroit Area and contracting them to help with the minor details involving the surveillance of the Walker family. Little did these men know that if they succeeded, they would die. And if they failed? Well, they would still die, but at least the deaths of those who succeeded were quick and clean. There could be no loose ends.

The man thought back to a specific time when one man in particular had spectacularly failed him, and in turn had met with an equally spectacular end.

§

One morning, a couple of months previous, Detective Walker was working a case away from home and his daughters were at school. Meghan Walker had arrived home early from one of her lectures. Later, the man had learned that the lecture had been canceled without prior notice—something about a water pipe breaking near the classroom.

As it turns out, the man currently had one of his new playthings—a despicable wretch called Eddie—inside the Walkers' house, wiring up a system of extremely small, extremely expensive surveillance cameras in the living room. Seeing Meghan heading for the front door, the man contacted his subordinate by radio.

"Out of the house, back door, now," he said calmly. "The wife has arrived early."

"I'm finished anyway," came Eddie's reply. "Lemme stay and have some fun with her."

"Exit the house via the back door now or forfeit your pay," he demanded.

"Fine," said the gruff criminal.

Within a few moments, the criminal came out of the backyard with a meter-reading device in his hand, and he proceeded to walk down the block and around the corner. The man waited for a few minutes until he was sure that his employee's work had gone unnoticed by Meghan Walker. Finally satisfied, he pulled his van away from the curb and followed the other man's route.

Upon reaching his subordinate, he slowed and allowed the man to enter the van. The younger man sat in the passenger seat, with Jeremy silently in the seat behind him.

"I got a little surprise for ya," claimed the criminal.

"Explain," commanded the man sternly. Jeremy shifted uncomfortably in his seat.

"Remember how you wanted the cameras in the living room?" he asked. "Well, I found a *much* better place for them. I also got us a little somethin'."

From his satchel, Eddie withdrew a small bundle of red and pink cloth and pressed it to his face, breathing in deep. When he unfolded it, the older man noticed that it was actually several lacy pairs of women's underwear. He instantly realized that this criminal had stolen Meghan Walker's dirty laundry. This was absolutely unacceptable. The man pulled the van back to the curb and looked Eddie dead in his eyes.

"You do not understand what you have done," he said calmly.

"Of course I do!" replied Eddie. "Check out the camera placements. You can thank me later!"

The older man removed a tablet computer from his bag and switched to the surveillance feed from the Walkers' house and scrolled through the different cameras. He watched with disgust in high definition as a completely nude Meghan Walker bent over before them and turned on the shower; several different cameras looked upon the striking woman's nude form from every conceivable angle. This imbecile had placed the cameras in the master bathroom. This is the price one must pay for not divulging the purpose of his quest to the ignorant hired help.

"Nice! You really know how to pick 'em boss!" the perverted criminal exclaimed, gazing at the beautiful woman's exquisite form, oblivious to his master's deadly gaze.

The man took a single deep breath.

"Jeremy," he spoke, calmly pinching the bridge of his nose.

Jeremy lunged violently forward in his seat and plunged a needle into the neck of this half-witted criminal. Before Eddie could react, the idiot fell forward in his seat, unconscious, and Jeremy savagely dragged him into the back of the van.

Later that night, Eddie awoke on his back, naked, and bound at the wrists and ankles. It was dark, and he could feel that he had been laid upon cold steel. He was disoriented and couldn't see; his brain was still foggy from the chemical used to incapacitate him. Suddenly, bright lights flashed on and blinded him with searing whiteness. He heard a voice.

"Eddie," spoke the gentle, calm voice. "Eddie, you have failed me."

"No! I didn't re—"

"Silence," demanded the voice. "You will now learn that there are consequences for your actions."

The criminal heard the metallic roar of a massive machine whirring to life not far from where he lay. The surface beneath him began to violently tremble. After a moment, he felt strong hands on his shoulders as he was pushed across the cold metal surface. Suddenly, the hands were removed from his shoulders and he could feel nothing but the white-hot pain in his feet. He could smell blood; he could feel the hot spray splashing his face, yet he refused to believe it belonged to him. The unimaginable pain relentlessly crawled up his shins, past his knees, nearing his waist. The criminal finally and mercifully lost consciousness from shock and blood-loss as his body was dragged ever forward.

Thirty feet away, Jeremy and his cold, calculating employer watched as the pervert was pulled into the spinning maelstrom of steel that was the mouth of an industrial wood chipper. They were unfazed as the pulpy, near-liquefied remains of this disobedient miscreant were sprayed into the Detroit River. When the final bits of the man had been processed through the machinery and there was no trace left of him aside from the grisly scraps left in the end of the chute, the older man turned and walked back toward the van.

"Jeremy, I trust you will take care of this?" he asked, motioning to the machine.

"Of course, sir," Jeremy obediently replied.

"And will you please remove the cameras from Mrs. Walker's shower and relocate them to the living room? At your earliest convenience, of course."

"As soon as the house is next empty, sir," assented Jeremy.

§

The man quietly laughed at this recollection, also remembering Jeremy's earlier discomfort at the strategic mention of the wood chipper. *You'll never work a day in your life if you do something you love,* he thought, and laughed again. This night was turning out to be more glorious than he ever could have imagined.

The man noticed Walker had finally managed to board a bus, thus leaving a few minutes of free time before he would need to initiate the next phase of his plan. As a treat, he leaned back in his seat and pulled out a remote control. Pressing a button, the interior of the villa was filled with the frantic, yet beautiful, music of Franz Liszt. Closing his eyes, gently humming along to the classical piece, the man visualized the things he had in store for the unfortunate young detective.

It brought an even bigger smile to his face.

7

harlie stood near the front of the packed bus. He was leaning against the wall behind the driver and gripped the cool steel railing with both hands, his knuckles white with tension. His imagination ran wild with scenarios of what might be happening to Meghan and the girls. He could only imagine how terrified his family must be, having been abducted in sheer darkness and held captive by a cunning, yet unknown, man. Charlie tried to piece together a character profile on his enemy using the minimal evidence he had from the letter and their brief conversation, but since the details were so scarce, he was left to speculation and guessing to fill in the numerous gaps. He forced himself to think about something else as the trained detective within him was screaming that assumption and speculation were the mortal enemies of true detection. He knew that the majority of the time when one of his fellow officers failed to solve a case—or were simply proven wrong—it was because they went with their gut instinct; their minds subconsciously relating material evidence in order to reinforce their initial instincts. Real detective work is not like in the movies; if you follow your gut, you'll fail. True detection involves Vulcan logic as well as detaching your personality from the case and focusing only on facts presented and how they relate to the matter at hand.

Unable to prevent his mind from speculating, Charlie banged the back of his head lightly against the wall a couple times, trying to shake things up and clear his mind. Just when he thought he'd be forced to succumb to forming theories with no evidence—simply to keep his mind off his family's situation—a loud *bang* came from the front right side of the bus, lifting Charlie off his feet for a split second. The bus lurched and tossed those standing a few inches off the floor. Several people lost their balance and fell to the ground. After settling, the bus listed hard to the right and the driver was forced to pull over and make an emergency stop. Charlie helped a little boy's mother to her feet; she'd lost her grip on the railing and fallen to her knees.

"Are you okay, ma'am?" Charlie asked, concerned.

"Yes, thank you," the woman replied, dusting herself off.

Upon closer inspection, Charlie was relieved to find out that she and the child had indeed emerged unscathed. A quick look around told him that the rest of the passengers—while confused, irritated and tired—were likewise unharmed.

The bus driver stepped outside the bus to assess the damage, leaving behind a chorus of murmurs and whispers from the multitude of passengers. Instinctively, Charlie followed her to provide assistance.

Noticing a passenger attempting to exit the bus during an emergency stop, the driver held out a hand to stop him.

"Sorry, sir. I'll have to ask you to remain on the bus for the time being," she said politely.

"I'd like to help if I can," Charlie offered, displaying his badge. "I'm a police officer here on vacation."

Hesitantly, the woman looked from his face to the badge and back again before sighing.

"Follow me," she said briskly, and quickly made her way around the front of the bus.

When Charlie reached her, she pulled him aside, around the front of the bus and out of earshot of the passengers.

"I'll be honest—I'm glad you're here," she admitted. "It's against the rules to allow passengers to assist, but this is the first time I've had a tire blow out—I'm pretty new—and it kind of has me frazzled. Besides, I don't think the rulebook says anything about not accepting help from police officers."

Charlie nodded his assent and led the driver back around the corner to inspect the damage to the tire. Upon initial inspection, it seemed as if the bus had run over something large. The tire had almost entirely shredded and was hanging loosely on the now-bare rim. Charlie kneeled down to get a closer look and the driver shined a flashlight into the wheel well to help him see.

"Wow," she breathed. "What the heck did we run over? I swear I was paying attention, and I didn't see anything in the road. It must have been pretty big to cause that kind of damage."

Closer inspection revealed something very peculiar to the observant young detective but, if the cause was what he suspected, he could not allow the bus driver to find out. He decided to take advantage of the woman's nerves and inexperience to distract her for a while.

"It looks pretty bad," he admitted. "We can get this replaced soon enough. Do you have a jack and a spare?"

Charlie searched her face while he spoke, and found what he was looking for: absolute confusion. He'd played the right card.

"I—I don't really know," she said. "Like I said, I'm new at this. Let me get on the radio and see if they can provide some assistance."

"Good idea," Charlie agreed. "In the meanwhile, I'm going to take a closer look. I'd like to make sure that whatever we hit back there isn't still lodged under the bus and that there's no other damage. Do you mind if I borrow your flashlight?"

She nodded and handed it over, then quickly made her way back inside the bus. Charlie wasted no time in getting to work. He stuck his head almost entirely inside the wheel well and breathed in deeply through his nose. Earlier he had detected a faint but all-too-familiar scent when he neared the tire. Now he was absolutely positive as to the source of the odor.

Gunpowder.

The acrid, chemical aroma that subtly wafted through the air in the wheel well was unmistakable—Charlie had become intimately familiar with the scent over the course of countless hours at the firing range. There could be no misidentifying that scent. This bus hadn't run over anything at all. The tire had been disabled by a small explosive charge. A gunpowder smell wouldn't be present if the tire had been shot from a distance. A bullet large enough to shred such a massive tire would have passed through and caused further damage to the bus.

Charlie had no doubt that it was an explosive charge, but to confirm his hypothesis, he pulled the shredded remains of the tire free from the rim and inspected it closely. He noted the smooth slice where the wheel had cleaved through the dense rubber after it had been dislodged, but finally the flashlight beam came across a ragged hole with melted rubber along its edge. Charlie ran his fingers around the hole and rolled the residue between his finger and thumb. Observing the black substance, he noted that it was an extremely fine, almost oily powder, similar to graphite shavings from a pencil. The residue was too fine to be rubber, though—it was certainly not a byproduct of the tire. No, this was the exact residue that Charlie had cleaned out of the barrels of his pistols after a long afternoon at the shooting range.

What was the point of this? he thought. *First he tells me to go to my hotel and rest for the night, then he blows out a tire on the bus that's taking me there?*

Charlie, with all of his talents, still couldn't make head or tail of this man. It was obvious that he was careful, and that he was extremely intelligent. He'd known the precise amount of explosive needed to disable the tire, while leaving no traces that the average person could detect. For all intents and purposes, this looked identical to any average tire blowout on any multi-axle, high-weight vehicle. Charlie ran his hand around the rim of the wheel, but he found no residue and could spot no burn marks anywhere. The amount of explosives this man used was beyond close—it was *exact*. Had Charlie not been a police officer, he would have never been able to detect the smell of the explosive agent over the heavy fumes of exhaust and the bitter tang of hot tire rubber.

This unknown enemy knew that Charlie would realize the tire had met with an explosive end. He had known that the detective was too sharp to miss the evidence, however small. Why? What end could this man hope to achieve by allowing Charlie to discover the method? One thing was clear: this man *meant* for Charlie to discover the explosive.

Charlie's mind was left reeling, trying in vain to discover the man's motive. As it stood, it seemed as if there was no motive at all. The entire thing exuded the details of a motiveless act committed by the insane, simply because they knew no better. All of the material evidence lent itself to a crime of passion; something that was done without thinking—without premeditation. Even as he thought this, Charlie knew it was absurd. This man clearly had a goal in mind, and the planning that had gone into this endeavor was extensive to say the least—this was clearly premeditated.

Charlie felt disoriented. His training was kicking in, and because the situation was so painfully anomalous, it seemed as if the two halves of his brain were warring against each other. On one side stood the rational detective: stoic, calm and favoring reason over emotion. On the other was the everyman: passionate, emotional and reasonably confused. The two sides battled relentlessly for supremacy, warring for dominance over the detective's thoughts. He couldn't shake the feeling that he was somehow connected to this man, but he could recall no person he'd ever encountered who fit the bill—who exuded this amount of insanity and ingenuity.

Charlie stood, intending to check on the bus driver and see what progress she'd made when he noticed his surroundings. They had not made it far from the Magic Kingdom before they had lost the tire, and Charlie recognized where they were. To one side stood a small copse of trees with water on the other side, and to the other lay a field through which the monorail track ran. They were on a stretch of World Drive, approximately a hundred yards from the corner of West Wilderness Road, the road that led directly to the Wilderness Lodge. Charlie decided that his best bet would be to make his way to the Lodge, in the hope that he could avoid speaking to anyone who came along to repair the bus or to transport the stranded guests. He stepped inside the bus.

Spying the bus driver's name tag, he spoke to her: "Um, Cathy?"

"Yes?" she asked. Charlie noticed people staring at them, straining to listen in, and it made him uncomfortable.

"The bus should be fine. Whatever we hit must still be back there somewhere. There's no other damage to the bus; luckily it was just the tire. Any news on the jack?" he asked, returning Cathy's flashlight.

"They're sending someone out to repair the tire, along with another bus to get everyone back to the resort. They should be here in about a half-hour."

"If it's alright with you, I'd like to head over to the Wilderness Lodge to call my wife," he lied. "I don't have my phone on me and I've been gone longer than I told her I would be. I'll bet she's worried sick."

"Are you sure?" she asked. "It will be much safer to wait for the replacement bus and I'm certain someone here would let you borrow their phone."

"You don't know my wife," he joked, playing a different character. "It would be safer to swim across Bay Lake than it would be to show up late."

She laughed and nodded.

"Can I at least give you directions?" she asked.

"No need," he shot back, smiling. "I know this place like the back of my hand."

With a few words of gratitude from Cathy, Charlie made his way off the bus, relieved to have been able to get away from the bus without being questioned. Although night had fully fallen, the sky was clear, with a nearly full moon, so Charlie had plenty of light to see where he was headed. Within ten minutes, he had come within eyesight of the great Wilderness Lodge. Powerful fluorescent floodlights illuminated everything within a couple hundred yards of the great log-cabin style structure. Charlie made his way past the parking lot and eventually ended up at the main entrance to the building.

Stepping inside, he smelled the delicious aroma of the fantastic food at the Whispering Canyon Cafe—the restaurant only recently having stopped serving for the night. His mind tried to relax—and it almost succeeded before he remembered that his family was missing, and that at least one brilliant psychopath was playing cruel games at his expense. His mind returned to the present and his shoulders slumped. For the first time since this ordeal began, Charlie realized how exhausted he really was. His eyes hurt, his head was pounding and his muscles ached, even though he hadn't done anything physically exerting in days. On top of everything else, he still had to catch a bus to one of the parks to get another back to the Caribbean Beach Resort.

Charlie Walker was a mess.

The promising young detective stumbled over to one of the chairs in the middle of the massive, high-ceilinged lobby and collapsed within it. Leaning his head back against the soft cushion, he closed his eyes and breathed deeply. His visions were haunted by the image of Meghan's tortured face from just moments before they'd entered the tunnel. The machine that was Charlie Walker was beginning to break down, spurred on solely by the fierce need to protect his family.

Leaning back in his chair, Charlie steepled his fingers beneath his chin and began to plan his next move.

8

Little did Detective Walker know, as he sat feeling sorry for himself in the lobby of the Wilderness Lodge, that he was being watched. The man savored the pain that the young detective had been displaying. He was breaking. The slump of his shoulders, the seeming inability to carry on, and the apparent physical exhaustion—all of these were signs that the current plans were far exceeding their expectations. Charlie Walker was now well within the man's control, but there was much left in store for the detective. He was not out of the woods yet, so to speak.

Much to the man's pleasure, Walker's *mind* still worked like a well-oiled machine after everything he been through and all of the stress he was experiencing. He discovered the existence of the explosive device even quicker than the man had anticipated. The man was impressed; Walker was truly a force to be reckoned with, and it seemed like none of these unfortunate events had any effect on the detective's mental faculties. Regardless, the detective would be tested one final time before he would be allowed to rest this night.

Cracking open a brand new bottle of extravagant glass-bottled water, the man leaned back in his chair and closed his eyes, mirroring the actions of his adversary. He contemplated the actions of the detective so far. The way he'd instantly complied with the man's instructions and his obvious aversion to interaction with Disney Security proved that Walker was doing everything in his power to dedicate himself to the man's game, unhindered. This pleased the man. While he had expected Walker to discover the explosive used on the bus tire, he had not expected him to *actively* cover up its existence. While unanticipated, this development was not unsatisfactory.

The man assumed Detective Walker realized that if he were to be detained by Disney Security, his possessions would be taken from him while his records were pulled and questioning took place. The Blackberry that the man had given Walker was his only link to his missing family, and if he lost that precious device he may lose any chance that might present itself to save his family. Walker would be willing to do anything to keep that phone in his possession.

The man was greatly impressed by Walker's devotion, though he cared nothing for emotional attachment, viewing it as a weakness that could be easily exploited. Those anchored by emotional attachment were simply inviting the keen observer to easily take advantage of their nature. Though the man did not wish to profit from Walker's immense love and dedication to his family, he was overjoyed to have been given such an easy opening to draw the detective in. Had Walker been a solitary person like the man, luring him into this challenge would have been immeasurably more difficult.

The man had never cared for another person in his entire life. He'd once had a family of his own but it was a necessary evil, a tool for advancement and a cover, of sorts. A man with a family is more widely accepted by the public. It allowed him to fly below the radar and execute some of his more legitimate business endeavors with little suspicion as to his true motives and behind-the-scenes actions. Had his family known the actual nature of their patriarch, things might have been different. His wife had known him only as a hard-working, caring person—until her 'accidental' death, when she had outlived her usefulness and her presence had started to complicate matters.

The man had chosen his unwitting wife specifically *because* of the qualities that he detested in her, for it were these traits that would draw unwanted attention away from him. He was young and, at first, it seemed like the perfect cover. What better way to disguise your true intentions than to so closely associate yourself with someone who stood for the exact opposite? For a while, everything had gone according to plan.

The man's wife, Andrea, was a woman of the highest caliber of classic beauty, and had the heart and soul of a humanitarian. He found his wife's physical attractiveness to be an unnecessary but not unwelcome perk, though the person she was inside had only made it all too easy for him to arrange for her untimely demise when this arrangement of theirs had lost its convenience—all beneficial aspects having exhausted themselves.

In their short time together, the insufferable woman bore him twins—a boy and a girl. It was an unexpected occurrence—unwelcome—and it hindered the man's plans for his endeavors, ultimately forcing him to change several plans he had made concerning the immediate future. For a time, he considered raising the children himself after Andrea's death. He had toyed with the idea that they could grow to become tools that he could utilize for his plans. His immaculate genes had undoubtedly been passed along to his offspring, and surely they would come of age bearing his unrivaled level of intelligence. This train of thought was derailed shortly after, as he realized that the traits of the children's mother had also been passed down.

Ever the humanitarian, the children's mother had been considered a 'good' woman, and the man was perpetually mortified by her constant need to help others who were less fortunate. Secretly, the man viewed these less fortunate people for what they truly were: the plague from which the Earth so agonizingly suffered. The only reason these imbeciles were 'less fortunate' was because they had allowed themselves to become so. There was no such thing as luck, divine intervention or a grand plan. A human being's place in life was a direct result of their actions and decisions. The man was nauseated by the state of some of these disgusting people that his wife had so often dealt with. On the outside, he politely listened to their have-pity-on-me sob stories and feigned deep concern, while restraining himself from killing them on the spot and ridding the world, once and for all, of more unsightly pustules.

The man's wife had never known what kind of thoughts truly went through the mind of her husband. She had never known that the man resented her lifestyle. She had access to all the man's money, yet rarely spent a dime on herself. Her charitable nature constantly manifested itself through constant donations to various charities and 'helpful' foundations. Even after so many years, the man was forced to choke down the surge of bile that crept up his throat every time he thought about her. It was an idiotic way to squander such a well-deserved fortune as the one he'd gained for himself—gained *without* the help of these so-called Good Samaritans.

Finally, he had decided that these children—while half his—were also half *hers*. They were tainted by DNA that showed zero promise, and for this reason he rid himself of them. They had the potential to be great but he believed they would never utilize it, held back by their mother's blackened bloodline.

The man did not kill the infants after their mother's death—as he would have liked to. Instead, he gave them up for adoption, citing that his business-heavy lifestyle and constant travelling made him unfit to be a single parent—it was a weak story, but more than enough to convince the agency. He had still kept tabs on his children over the years and he watched them become adults and earn a unique character all their own.

For a short time, his son had shown a small inkling of the potential that he held within. Unfortunately, the boy was amateurish, savage, careless and guided by base passion rather than by logic and reasoning. Therefore, the boy's criminal resume was full of the fruitless labors of small-time morons. The boy murdered in the heat of passion. He kidnapped. He raped. He tortured. He made grotesque displays of human remains simply to gain attention and strengthen his horrible reputation. These crimes were beneath someone of his intellect. Unlike his son, if the man killed or tortured someone, it was simply to further his cause. He didn't necessarily enjoy it, and would avoid it if at all possible, ultimately because murder tended to be a messy and oftentimes irresponsible act. Rape, on the other hand, was absolutely detested by the man. The fact that his son had become infamous for the rape and torture of so many young women physically sickened him. These acts were those of the desperate, the idiotic and the insane. These were not the actions of the offspring of the world's most brilliant criminal mind.

Luckily, the boy's reign of terror had come to an end several years ago when he was thankfully killed. Granted, the boy wasn't sloppy and covered his tracks well, but in some rare cases an individual comes along and is unhindered by these precautions, making the care you've taken unexpectedly inadequate. Ultimately, the boy was beaten, and for that he had disgraced his family name—preserving what little dignity he had left by dying before he could commit more senseless atrocities.

The man's daughter, on the other hand, was an entirely different story all together. She was intelligent—*highly* intelligent—and her prowess impressed the man deeply, but grudging respect was all he had for this girl. She was not unlike her mother: strikingly beautiful, gloriously strong-willed and frustratingly insistent upon using her great mental power to help others—albeit in surprising and unexpected ways. His daughter had, to her father's great surprise and extreme dismay, become a field operative in the Central Intelligence Agency. Imagine that! His daughter, a government agent—it was almost too ridiculous to be real.

The fact that his daughter had found an employer in the CIA had complicated matters extremely. The Company had immense resources along with the time and manpower to fully take advantage of them. The man was not so dense as to think that his daughter had failed to discover his identity. After leaving the orphanage, like her brother, she had retained her given name, as adopted children often do. Using the CIA's resources to find her origins would have been simplicity itself, given even an hour's free time. There was no doubt in the man's mind that the girl knew who her father was, and also the things he had done. The man was sure his daughter had begun to suspect the real cause of her birth mother's death, even if she had no way of knowing for sure.

The man was also positive that the girl had located her brother. The adoption agency had decided not to keep the children in the same household, and so the twins separated and went to different families in entirely different states. The boy went with a family in northern Ohio, while the girl ended up just outside Boston. The girl had, without a doubt, discovered the deeds of her father and brother.

The girl's occupation was a double-edged sword. When she'd joined the Company nearly a decade ago, the man had been forced to cease his surveillance of her for fear of being discovered and apprehended. As it stood, the man had no reliable way of locating his daughter. The girl, however, could track him with ease. It was a loose end that he planned to tie up sooner rather than later.

Jolting himself out of his reverie with an involuntary shiver, the man refocused his attention on the screen, hoping the sight of the tortured detective could alleviate this black mood and return him to his previous state of euphoria. Walker still sat in the armchair with his head back and his eyes closed; he could have been asleep.

Deciding that the time had come to put an end to the night's festivities, the man contacted the head of his operations unit, Brody Kinney, as well as Brent Masters. He'd specifically ordered Kinney and Masters to remain close to Walker throughout the night for precisely this reason.

"Gentlemen," he spoke into his headset. "The hour is growing late. I believe our detective has had enough for one night. What say you accompany him back to his lodgings?"

The two men acknowledged their superior's orders.

"His location should now be available on your GPS," the man added, pressing a few keys to activate the tracking device in Walker's Blackberry.

The man was sufficiently satisfied that the detective was mentally sound, and capable of being a worthy opponent in the oncoming challenge. He had other events planned for the night in the event that he still remained unsure about the detective's state of mind, but he'd come to realize they were no longer necessary. Even after the events that the detective had been through, his mind was still as sharp as ever, matching that of the man stride for stride. While he'd canceled the other plans he'd had for the night, the man still had one event left in place for the detective that was sure to provide the entertainment he so desperately needed after the unwelcome memories of his family had come flooding back to him.

Relaxing in his seat, still listening to the beautiful classical music and sipping the expensive water, the man's eyes were glued to the screen. He waited patiently for his men to present themselves to the detective and bring to him that which he had so desperately hoped to avoid: detention.

Marvelous, thought the man, for he was a virtuoso—and the crescendo of the first piece in his grand symphony was about to be played.

9

"Excuse me, sir. Are you Detective Walker?" asked a disembodied voice.

Slowly, Charlie opened his eyes to see two burly men in brightly colored pastel polo shirts and pressed khakis standing before him, hands clasped behind their backs. They had close-cropped hair and ramrod-straight postures. Ex-military, Charlie guessed. On their chests, they wore Disney Cast Member name tags. Straining, Charlie read their names: Brody from Aurora, Illinois and Brent from Las Cruces, New Mexico. Instinctively, Charlie straightened up in his seat. If these two characters didn't scream 'Disney Security,' nothing did. This was not good.

"Yes, I am. Call me Charlie. What can I do for you gentlemen?" he asked, trying to act as casual as his fried nerves would allow.

"We just have a few routine questions to ask about a recent incident involving a bus," said Brody, evidently the man who had spoken first. "There are some liability issues, and we'd just like to clear everything up and make sure your stay here is as safe and enjoyable as possible."

"No worries, guys. Everything was fine. It was just a popped tire. Not a big deal," Charlie tried to explain, hoping to get rid of these two but knowing he wouldn't.

"If you'll just come with us, detective, we'll handle everything. I promise we won't take up too much of your time," said Brent with an ice-cold smile that didn't reach his eyes.

Charlie had no choice but to comply. Maybe he could talk his way out of the situation quickly. It seemed like they just wanted him to sign some papers releasing the company from any liability. He was sure that this was standard operating procedure for situations like this and Cathy must have told the men where Charlie was headed, along with his physical description.

Reluctantly, Charlie nodded and stood, prepared to follow the men to whatever office they had secreted away in the massive resort. To his confusion, the men on either side of him didn't make their way deeper into the building; they walked him toward the exit, heading for the parking lot.

"Don't you guys have some sort of office in the building itself?" Charlie asked, not having much knowledge of the inner workings of Disney Security past knowing they were always nearby, but often never spotted.

"The resort has its own security," Brody informed him. "Unfortunately, the incident occurred on the roads, which fall under the jurisdiction of the transportation authority. In cases like these, we have to handle everything at the main security hub. Don't worry detective, after we sign a few papers and ask a few questions, we'll take you back to your room at the Caribbean Beach."

Main security hub? Charlie thought. *Does Disney even have one of those? That sounds like something from a bad sci-fi movie.*

As false as it sounded, Charlie had no choice but to follow the men. Any noncompliance on his part would only make finding the girls much harder. With a resigned sigh, Charlie allowed himself to be led into the parking lot where he was ushered into a late-model black Cadillac. Again, this didn't seem on the level. Charlie was not convinced that Disney would give two run-of-the-mill security people a sixty-thousand-dollar car with which to carry out their daily operations.

Charlie had a chance to look around the vehicle during the drive. He was seated next to Kinney in the back of the sedan, with the other security agent in the driver's seat. From his seat, Charlie could spy no paraphernalia relevant to those in the security profession. There was no on-board radio or computer. No clipboard with the day's routine. Not even the stereotypical items were present: flashlights, medical kits, handcuffs, pens—nothing at all. If Charlie hadn't known better, he would swear that he was in a civilian vehicle. The situation grew even more suspicious when neither man acknowledged him a single time throughout the drive. He decided to break the bizarre silence.

"So where's this main security hub?" he asked. "I didn't know there was such a place on property."

"Oh, it's just up here a' ways," replied Brent with an air of nonchalance.

Brent shifted in his seat and revealed a previously unseen bulge underneath his shirt, on his right hip. Charlie mentally kicked himself for not spotting it earlier. The agent clearly carried a concealed firearm, which seemed peculiar to Charlie. He had always assumed Disney had a top-notch security force, armed and ready to handle any emergency scenarios, but this man's dress, civilian vehicle and lack of information on their destination all culminated in Charlie completely distrusting these two men. These were not Disney Security agents; logic and reason told Charlie that these men were, without a doubt, agents of his anonymous adversary.

Deciding he had no choice but to see where this took him, he leaned back in silence for the next few minutes. His thoughts involuntarily turned to Meghan and the girls. Meghan was tough; she always had been—and so were the girls—but no amount of bravado can prepare a person for something as terrible as this. He could only hope that they weren't being mistreated and that this mystery man would keep his end of the deal and release them unharmed, if and when Charlie succeeded. Charlie cared very little for his own wellbeing. He would sacrifice himself for his family without hesitation—and he was fully prepared to do so now, if it meant that they would be safe. Knowing this, he could no longer hold in his suspicions.

"We're not going to any security hub, are we?" Charlie asked.

Hesitating, the two men glanced at each other in the mirror to see if the other had any idea of how to reply to this astute detective.

"Come on, guys," he continued, having noticed the silent exchange. "Do you think you fooled me? You don't work for Disney. Name tags like those can be bought on eBay for under ten bucks. I'm not an idiot. I do this for living. What the hell is really going on?"

"Uh…we…" stammered Masters, at a loss for how to handle this situation. He had clearly not expected the tables to be turned. The two men visibly struggled to find a way to bail themselves out.

"Listen," Charlie firmly commanded. "I know you're working for the man who has my family. Let me tell you this: I'm not going to get you in trouble with your boss—you can still do whatever the hell it was he sent you to do—but you're all complete idiots if you think you can fool me with such a ridiculously thin cover. Now tell me: why am I in this car?"

"Fine," said Kinney. "I'll level with you, Walker, since you're so goddamned smart. I currently have in my possession a syringe that's meant for you. We're not here to hurt you: we're just supposed to drug you and leave you in your hotel room until the boss is ready for you. Honestly."

"Then what are you waiting for?" Charlie asked, with more bravery than he truly felt. "Get this over with and we can call it a night early. I'm not going to fight you. I just want my family back as soon as possible."

Brody and Brent, the alliterative duo, exchanged glances again and shrugged. Finally, Masters casually executed a U-turn and began following the road signs pointing toward the Caribbean Beach Resort. Kinney held up the syringe and the glare from the headlights of the oncoming traffic glinted off the dark amber liquid within the barrel.

"We were supposed to do this at a temporary office the boss set up off-property, but I suppose it doesn't really matter now, does it?" Brody asked, more to himself than to anyone else.

Charlie sighed and waited for the needle to pierce his skin. When it finally did, he barely felt the prick. Within seconds, his vision became a haze before failing him completely. As he lost consciousness, he heard his two captors laughing—congratulating each other on a job well done.

10

Meghan Walker awoke with a start. Looking around, she was caught off guard by the modern elegance of her surroundings. The first thing she noticed when her vision cleared was the massive, sectioned window that was directly in front of her, floor-to-ceiling, wall-to-wall. Twenty feet high and perhaps thirty feet wide, it afforded a breathtaking view of the Magic Kingdom with its legions of colored lights shining bright in the calm Floridian night. The suite she found herself in had the highest ceilings she'd ever seen in a hotel room, two stories high with the massive window spanning the entire distance. Recalling the websites Charlie frequented, she recognized this room as one of the Grand Villas at the Contemporary Resort's Bay Lake Tower.

The view distracted her for quite some time, but eventually the surrealism of her surroundings gave way to the brutal reality of her situation. She remembered everything that had happened before she'd been drugged and taken. She remembered that horrible man cornering her in the aquarium. She remembered being told that she and her daughters were going to be abducted and that she had no choice but to assist the kidnappers in doing so. She remembered Leroy's words of warning: *Do exactly as I have instructed or your entire family will die.* She remembered the terrible and violent plan he had whispered in her ear—the plan to kill Charlie if she did anything other than exactly what she was told.

Fresh tears began to stream down her cheeks. They pattered onto the sofa on which she sat. She desperately wanted to put her arms around Violet and Katie—who were also bound but still asleep on either side of her—and pull them close, but her hands and feet were bound with what seemed like extremely thick plastic cable ties. She studied these restraints for a moment before a smooth, familiar voice startled her.

"Riot cuffs," said a voice from off to her left. "Extremely effective."

Meghan shot him a look of icy hatred.

"You," she hissed. "I'm guessing that you don't work for Disney, then?"

The young man smiled, "Very observant. The detective's wife does a little detective work of her own. I like that." He stood and approached her.

Standing in front of her, he began to stroke her cheek, gently wiping the tears away.

"The real name's Jeremy," he stated, with a predatory tinge in his voice. "And don't you worry, as long as your husband does what he's told, you'll be just fine."

Jeremy's finger traced a teardrop down her face, her neck, and eventually her chest, where he slowly began to draw back the material of her thin tank top.

"Don't you fucking touch me!" Meghan shouted, trying to shove the big man away from her with her bound hands, which elicited a laugh from him.

"Well, aren't you a firecracker?" he laughed, but then his smile suddenly gave way to fiery rage. "You'd better watch yourself, bitch! Disrespect me again and I'll—"

"Jeremy," said a calm voice from behind them, and the big man quickly backed away from Meghan and straightened his posture.

"I didn't expect you so early, sir," Jeremy stated, fear evident in his words.

Meghan turned to see who had frightened this imposing man so thoroughly. Standing in the doorway was one of the most highly-manicured elderly men she had ever seen. He stood just south of six-feet tall, decently built and wearing a dark suit that was clearly tailored to fit him exactly. His perfectly tanned face was framed by a full head of flowing, silvery-gray hair—and not a single strand was out of place. His immaculately straight, fluorescent-white teeth were visible through the terrible grin that stretched across his features. There was something unnatural about this man; his eyes didn't match the rest of his appearance, almost as if he was thousands of years old, his body maintained and kept alive only by the darkest sciences. The air that the man exuded instantly struck fear into Meghan, and she began to tremble uncontrollably.

"There has been a development," he stated. "Get the car. We're needed sooner than we thought."

With one last hungry look at Meghan, Jeremy passed the elderly man and exited the suite.

"Mrs. Walker," said the man, and she jumped. "Jeremy and I will be leaving for a short while. We've left scissors in the kitchen; feel free to remove those awful restraints from yourself and your daughters. Help yourselves to anything the villa has to offer. Feel free to do what you will—enjoy yourselves. You are not a captive here by any means. Should you choose to take your daughters and leave, you may do so with my blessing but there will be dire consequences. If all three of you are not here when we return, we will not pursue you but your husband will die."

That said, he turned and left.

11

When Charlie awoke, his head pounded fiercely—so fiercely that he actually cried out in surprise. His sight had not yet returned and he had no idea where he was, but he could sense people nearby. Eventually, the fog obscuring his vision cleared and he was able to take stock of his surroundings.

Fortunately, taking stock was unnecessary, for he was in his own room at the Caribbean Beach. Unfortunately, he was not alone. In a chair by the compass-themed table sat a striking elderly man in a dark suit, calmly watching him with an almost clinical air, as if studying a lab rat.

"There's a bottle of water on the table to your right, detective," the man spoke smoothly. "Drink no less than eight ounces and the headache will subside shortly. The use of the sedative and subsequent stimulant in so short a time has dehydrated your brain. Do not speak—drink. There will be time for conversation yet."

Seeing no harm in it, Charlie picked up the bottle of water. It struck him as odd, since it was made of glass and capped with stainless steel. Removing the heavy top and tossing it on the table, he swallowed half the contents in one long draught. He wasn't sure whether it was an illusion caused by dehydration, but it was quite possibly the best water he'd ever tasted. A second long draught emptied the bottle, and he set it lightly on the bedside table.

As if reading his mind, the man spoke again.

"Purified glacier water imported from Antarctica," he stated. "Expensive, but it is the single purest, most naturally sweet water on the planet. Perhaps I'll email you a link to the vendor. Unfortunately, I haven't come all this way to converse about beverage preferences. Let's get down to business, shall we?"

"First, tell me where my family is," Charlie demanded, still feeling the effects of the drugs.

"I can't tell you *that,* detective. What I *can* tell you is that they are perfectly safe, unharmed and—quite frankly—currently in better lodgings than yourself," he stated, gazing around the small room with a look of disgust on his features.

"How can I be sure—"

The man held up a hand for silence. He reached into his jacket, withdrew a small photograph from his pocket and tossed it to Charlie. The photograph was a grainy surveillance shot of Meghan and the girls sleeping. It was zoomed in too far for Charlie to deduce anything other than that they were on a vaguely familiar-looking couch, and were indeed unharmed so far. It was better quality than the shot of Katie he'd received on the Blackberry earlier in the night, but only fractionally.

"Keep it," offered the man. "It'll be a good motivator for you. It was taken an hour ago."

The man sat in silence for several minutes while Charlie's eyes remained glued to the photograph. Finally, the young detective looked up.

"Who are you?" he asked.

"Now *that* is the right question, detective. My name," he spoke, pausing for decidedly cheesy dramatic effect, "is Spencer Holloway."

The name sounded *achingly* familiar but Charlie couldn't place it.

"Haven't heard of me?" Holloway continued. "No matter. In fact, I should be proud, for it shows that I've done my work well. I suppose I can also say the same for you. You are also a man who does his job well—correct?"

"What does my job have to do with any of this?" Charlie asked, defensively. "Did I put your brother in prison or something? Is this your way of getting petty revenge?"

"Not my brother, detective…my son. And you didn't put him in prison: you put him in the cemetery."

In an instant, Charlie knew exactly who this man was. Spencer Holloway could only be the father of James Holloway, the only man the detective had ever fired his weapon upon. Instinctively, his hand felt for the scar on his throat. James Holloway had been the one to put the bullet in his neck, though the madman had met a far worse fate.

"James Holloway," Charlie stated, incredulously. "He was your son."

"Yes, but only in blood," Holloway confirmed, dismissing the detective's concern with a casual wave of a hand. "The boy was nearly useless, his crimes unacceptable for one who had such great potential. Don't delude yourself with the romance of the situation, Walker; I haven't come here to avenge my son's death. What you did to James was a blessing. The world doesn't need people like him. What the world needs are people like you and I."

"I'm pretty sure you and I are nothing alike," Charlie stated.

"I beg to differ, detective. Great minds are often inexplicably drawn to one another, and ultimately these minds seek to prove their dominance. They seek to destroy one another—to challenge themselves by hunting down and crushing others. We might not share the same views, and our goals may differ, but the way in which we approach a problem and devise its solution is one and the same."

"You're insane," stated Charlie.

Holloway seemed to ponder this accusation.

"Oftentimes, true genius is mistaken for insanity; an entertaining notion, considering the accusation is thrown around only by the ignorant. I expected more from you."

"I guess you set the bar too high," Charlie countered. "Sorry to disappoint."

"If the past is any indicator, I should say I haven't set the bar high *enough*. You come from a rare breed, detective," said Holloway, calmly. "Your mind chooses logic and reason over passion and emotion. You realize that emotion is nothing but the crutch of the weak and the dimwitted."

"How can you say that?" Charlie asked. "I'm in this situation because I'm trying to save my family."

"In your case, you've detached your personal life from your professional life, something that most people cannot ever hope to accomplish. This allowed me to use your wife and daughters as leverage. I believe that a great mind is within you, and I have come to test you."

"You're wrong—I'm just a normal guy," Charlie said defiantly, hoping to lessen the false sense of grandeur that Holloway was placing on the moment.

"I'm afraid that is where *you're* wrong. Modesty is for the weak, detective.

Recognize your own strengths; celebrate them—do not deny them. I have seen your prowess. It is the reason that I am here. Think back to all those years ago, when you hunted down and killed my son. Reflect on it, and *then* tell me you're *just a normal guy.*"

Charlie tried—and failed—not to think about that horrible ordeal in which he'd shot and killed the man the news outlets had dubbed the 'Hollow Man.' It wasn't a very creative nickname but it fit the bill, and the public lived in fear of the Hollow Man for several months. The apparent lack of a soul within James Holloway made the fantastical moniker more fitting than anyone would have liked. The savage criminal was bold; his actual name was publicly known throughout the entire duration of his spree, as he had left a business card in the mouth of every victim. These usually contained a line of obscure poetry and each was different, though all contained the name James Holloway in bold, embossed print. Giving his real name seemed to be a direct insult to the police force since they had their killer's real identity yet, despite their best efforts, could not apprehend him.

The whole ordeal came rushing back to him in the blink of an eye.

§

For an entire summer, the citizens of Detroit had feared leaving their houses. Special news broadcasts had advised people against going out at night, urging them to travel in numbers. A total of twenty-three people had disappeared that summer—including children and entire families—only to have their bodies found days later in public places, mutilated beyond recognition and posed in grim and suggestive ways.

A particularly horrifying and brutal display occurred when a family of three—a father, a mother and their young son—were found skinned and hanging from a billboard in broad daylight near an exit of the I-94 freeway. The homeless man who had discovered the bodies claimed that one moment he was going about his business and—next thing he knew—the bodies were there, swaying in the summer breeze beneath the sign. The first responders dismissed the statement as the ramblings of a drunk, but the media took the claim and ran with it. Headlines like "Hollow Man Defies Reality" and "Hollow Man Kills in Broad Daylight" flooded the local papers for the next week, even though neither was true.

Charlie, having only recently become a detective, was not asked to investigate any of the Hollow Man crime scenes—he wasn't even considered. The senior detectives in the precinct took precedent on high profile crimes. Charlie was shuffled to the bottom of the stack, forced to question homeowners about break-ins and stolen cars. He gave those cases no less effort than he would any major case, and most of the time he helped find these victims some closure, but greater things were waiting for him, and one day, they found him.

One of the department's most highly regarded senior detectives, Rick Banks, was assigned to the Holloway case after the twenty-second body was found. By this point, the city was in a panic and the killing spree was gaining national media attention. The mayor's office was leaning heavily on the police to find this monster and shut him down quickly—more negative publicity was the last thing Detroit's politicians needed. Banks had a great track record, and the higher-ups were optimistic and hopeful that having him on the case would bring it to a satisfactory conclusion.

When a call came in about the abduction of a woman that bore similarities to Holloway's other instances, the department reacted with haste. Banks's partner was hospitalized with severe food poisoning, so he made his way to the scene alone—an act generally frowned upon. Parking his unmarked squad car in the driveway, he entered the house, officially the first responder. Carefully turning on the lights in all the rooms, he began a methodical investigation of the home while he waited for others to arrive.

After being in the house for no more than five minutes, Banks began to hear noises—voices and footsteps—from outside the front of the house. As he neared the door, a deep male voice called out.

"Who the fuck is in that house?" the voice bellowed.

Choosing not to present himself as a target and remaining safely within the house, Banks answered, "My name is Detective Richard Banks. I'm with the Detroit Police Department."

"Bullshit!" roared the voice. "You're the second stranger I've seen let themselves into this house in the past hour. Now get your ass out here before I put a bullet in you!"

Coolly, Banks crept closer to the front of the house and responded to what he assumed must be a protective neighbor. "Sir, I'm going to have to ask you to remain calm. I am a police officer. Any threat you make toward me is a very serious crime."

Banks leaned out from around a corner and peered toward the front door, trying to get a decent view of the person outside. As soon as he did so, a shot rang out and shattered a mirror just a few inches away; the shotgun blast also tearing up a good chunk of plaster. Reacting quickly, Banks retreated around the corner and drew his radio to call for assistance.

"Shots fired! Shots fired!" Banks yelled, rattling off the address of the house. "Officer under fire, requesting immediate assistance at my location."

Unfortunately for Banks, the annual Fourth of July fireworks were just a few short hours away, taking place down by the riverfront. Recent changes to the event made crowd control an even bigger headache and, as a result, most of the city's uniformed officers were providing extra security for the event. More often than not, it was the yearly scene of a shooting or stabbing. Hearing that backup was a minimum of fifteen minutes away, Banks began to worry.

"Who the hell do we have out this way? Give me anybody with a gun and a car goddamn it," he snapped at the dispatch operator.

"One moment," she responded, and he heard the clicking of a keyboard. "The only officers we have who are even remotely close are Detectives Walker and Harris; they're a few miles away responding to a domestic dispute."

"You've got the new guy and his partner responding to a *domestic?*" he asked, wondering why they were using a detective for what was clearly uniform work. Deciding that the department was stretched thin enough as it was, he decided not to press the issue further. "Whatever. Fuck it. Get the kid on the horn and get him over here, but tell him to watch his ass."

"Understood."

A few miles away, Charlie's radio chirped while he and his partner, Tony Harris, were interviewing a woman who accused her husband of beating her with an eighteen-inch length of hard salami after she refused to go to the store to buy him more beer. They had nearly been forced to feign a coughing fit just to keep from laughing, but they was still determined to help this poor woman—the deli meat had left significant marks on her face and arms.

"Detectives Walker and Harris, an officer is under fire near your location," said the operator, reading off the address. "You are the only officers in the vicinity. It's requested that you cease all further action and assist Detective Banks. You are advised to proceed with extreme caution."

Quickly apologizing to the irate woman, they left the house and hurried to their car. Fortunately, traffic was light on this side of town and they were able to make it to Banks' location faster than anticipated. He could hardly believe his eyes when he reached the house.

On the porch steps laid a large black man, a shotgun lying next to him with a bright red shell casing not far away. Blood soaked through the man's white T-shirt over his left shoulder. Charlie noticed that he was alive: his chest was rapidly heaving.

"What the fuck happened here?" wondered Harris aloud, drawing his weapon and carefully getting out of the car.

"I don't know," admitted Charlie, readying his own weapon. "Stabilize him if you can, then get an ambulance down here. I'm going inside to check on Banks. This doesn't look good."

"Copy that," said Harris, his concern darkening his tone.

Charlie rushed to the house first, kicking the shotgun away onto the lawn and stepping around the injured man. Upon entering the house, he followed a thin trail of blood into the living room. Detective Banks lay at the end of this bloody streak, looking all the worse for wear. He had a close-spread shotgun wound on his upper thigh and hip. Oddly enough, it wasn't bleeding as much as it should have been.

"Walker. Took you long enough," Banks joked, wincing.

"What the hell happened, Rick?" Charlie asked, bending down to inspect the older man's wound.

"It ain't as bad as it looks, kid. I was in the house for a minute...then the fucking neighbor showed up—turns out the asshole had a shotgun loaded with rock salt. Stings like a bitch, but it shouldn't even need stitches. My Kevlar took half the shot anyway. I fired on him after I was hit. I didn't kill him, did I?" Banks asked, genuinely concerned.

"No, he's still kicking," Charlie reassured him. "Through and through on the shoulder, I think. He might not be a great tennis player after this, but he'll live. Harris is out there working on him right now. Ambulance shouldn't be far behind."

"Good, good." He swallowed and sighed, preparing to say something important. "Walker, let me ask you something—you been following this Holloway case?"

Charlie thought for a second.

"Yeah, I've looked over the files. It's a strange thing. We know exactly who he is, but it's like he's invisible—he leaves no evidence other than that card, and even *that* means nothing. It's an interesting case, for sure."

"Right. Well, the house I'm bleeding all over belongs to a woman. And if we don't bust our asses and nail this son of a bitch, it'll be the former residence of the Hollow Man's twenty-third victim," stated Banks. "Now, obviously, the brass isn't going to let me carry on. I'll have to get dragged off to the hospital, but we honestly have a chance to get him this time, kid."

Banks winced and attempted to sit up straight before continuing.

"So, neighbor across the street calls 911 just over an hour ago and says he saw our guy enter the house but never saw him leave. Not two minutes later, the lady next door calls in and tells us she saw some guy in the backyard carrying a tarp. Both callers gave Holloway's description to the letter. There's an alley that runs behind this place and he probably had his wheels parked back there. I'll bet my pension that our girl was in that tarp. No way the neighbors could have seen the alley through those hedges back there to ID a vehicle though."

"Why are you telling me this, Rick?" Charlie asked.

"I'm telling you because this is *your* case now, Walker. Pete tells me you're a bright little fucker, so it's time we stopped wasting your talent on all those B and E's and you catch yourself a headline-maker. You've recovered a lot of stolen stereos, but now it's time to move up to the big leagues."

"Where do I start?" Charlie asked, not wasting any time.

"The way I see it is this: you've got just under five hours, give or take, before he kills this woman. Postmortem puts the time of death of most of his victims at around midnight on the night before they're found. His last four victims died on the night of their abduction and were found on display the next morning. So we have a time. We need a place. What do we know?"

"A place..." Charlie thought aloud. "From what I gather, he *has* to work in the same spot every time. He's not killing them in different places; he brings them to a central location. A lot of his work was done with surgical tools—specialized power saws and drills—not the kind of thing you'd carry around to carve somebody up in an alley. He's got to be somewhere that he can access these tools and also maintain the privacy he needs to do his work."

"Good, keep going," Banks encouraged him, wincing as he adjusted himself once again to find a more comfortable position.

"Contusions on the cranium show blunt force trauma; I'm assuming he knocks his victims out and revives them when he reaches his location."

"Common knowledge," Banks stated. "Also—not relevant right now. Think more specifically. We know what happens *when* he takes them, but what happens when they reach his hideout?"

"Well, postmortems also show that he when he rapes the women, they're alive, and signs of struggle show that they're conscious. We've got friction burns on the wrists and ankles so they're definitely tied down. We can rule out being drugged at any point though; toxicology always comes up negative. The fact that there are no abrasions in or around the mouth tells me that these women haven't been gagged, so they're likely to make a lot of noise. This place has to be somewhere that's isolated—somewhere that these women won't be heard."

"Excellent, Walker. Good shit, but *what else* can we tell from this?"

"It's in the city—his place. These people are found in elaborate positions, sometimes just a few hours after the time of death. It takes time to set something like that up, so he can't be placing these people far from where he's killing them."

"Perfect," grinned Banks. "Unfortunately, that's where I'm lost. I came out here hoping that I could find something that would tell me more, but the place looks clean."

Charlie racked his brain for useful data, kneeling next to the wounded detective in thoughtful silence. There had to be a way to narrow down the area, but how? Just then, Charlie spied an old, antique-style map that was a decoration on the wall nearby.

"A map," he said.

"A map?" questioned Banks.

"Yes, a map! Let's paint a picture of where this asshole has been. Sometimes you can know all this information, but when you actually *see* it, everything comes together."

Charlie pulled out his cell phone and called Pete Valdez.

"Captain, it's Charlie Walker," he said. "I need you to do me a favor. Pinpoint every location where one of Holloway's victims was found on a city map, scan it and send it to my car's laptop."

"What's this about, Charlie? You're not on the Holloway case," scolded Valdez.

"I am now," Charlie declared. "Listen, I don't have time to explain. Get me the map as fast as you can."

Charlie hung up his phone without another word.

"Damn, Walker, did you just steamroll the Captain?" Banks asked, with a small chuckle.

"He'll get over it," he said, dismissing the notion. "We can get this guy— we *will* get this guy."

"What are you on to?" Banks asked, as a siren neared the house and the red and white lights of the ambulance lit up the room.

"My theory is this: the guy is smart—we'll give him that. But what is the one thing that can pull the rug out from under even the most on-point genius?"

"You got me..." Banks replied with a shrug.

"The subconscious, Rick. The shit he doesn't even *realize* he's doing. If I'm right, then this asshole doesn't realize that he's literally drawing us a search perimeter. If this map looks like what I think it's going to look like, the location of every victim he's left on display will draw us a circle around where this guy is."

"I see," Banks agreed. "Put all the locations on a map, connect the dots, and we've got ourselves a narrow region where he could be hiding."

"Bingo," Charlie exclaimed. "The paramedics are on their way in. Take care of that leg, Rick."

"Don't worry about me. I'll be fine. Walker, go catch this idiot, will you?"

"You got it, boss," Charlie said, making his way outside.

A couple of squad cars had shown up alongside the ambulance and uniformed officers were now cordoning off the area with yellow tape. Charlie ducked under the tape and hurried to his car. Harris was waiting for him inside, his face lit by the laptop screen he was looking at.

"Cap sent you a map," he said.

"Show me."

Harris handed the laptop over and Charlie nearly gasped when he looked at the screen. His map idea had worked like a charm. Right on the northeast side of the city, near the river, was a blob of twenty-two pinpoints, heavily concentrated. The perimeter wasn't much more than a mile in diameter. It just goes to show that sometimes the brightest minds overlook the most obvious details.

"Son of a bitch," Charlie exclaimed.

"What?" asked Harris.

"James Holloway. We're going to find him," Charlie said as he fired up the car and started to drive.

"James Holloway?" Harris asked, incredulously. "The fucking *Hollow Man?* Nobody can catch that guy and, even if they could, he's dangerous. He'd never go down without taking a few of us with him."

Harris looked at Charlie, who ignored him and stared straight ahead, a look of furious intensity painted across his features.

"You're serious?" Harris asked.

"Deadly serious, Tony. He's just taken another one—we can save her. Get the Captain on the phone and tell him to use that perimeter as a search area. Have him find us a list of every vacant building within it."

Harris did as he was told and Charlie sped through the streets of Detroit, heading for the area on the map. When he was just a few miles away, the Captain's search results returned showing only three vacant buildings in that area. Two of them were small stores, but the third was an apartment complex.

"The apartments," Charlie asked. "Where are they?"

"Right here," Harris pointed to a spot on the map that was almost dead center of the cluster of pinpoints.

"He's there. He's in that complex."

Charlie was sure of it. The shops were too small and too close to operating businesses, but the apartment complex was tall—twelve stories. The sound of a person screaming inside the complex from one of the upper floors would never reach the streets below. It was the perfect location.

When the two detectives had reached the building, Charlie's suspicions were reinforced. Charlie circled the structure using the alleys that surrounded it. The place had only recently been abandoned. The windows were still intact and all the doors hung firmly in their frames. No vehicles were present, but that didn't mean much. A smart criminal wouldn't park his vehicle nearby in case it was identified. Then again, a smart criminal wouldn't leave his victims in a near-perfect circle around the place where he killed them all.

"Lemme get SWAT on the line," Harris said as Charlie slowed the car to a stop by the front doors.

"Do it, but we have to go in *now*," Charlie said, with an air of urgency.

"Charlie, we should really wait for the team. It might get dicey in there."

"We've got to go in, Tony. SWAT will take thirty minutes or more to gear up and get here. This woman can't wait that long. He could be torturing her while we sit down here waiting—a half-hour could make all the difference. No, we're going in."

Sighing, Harris nodded. "Go get the front door open. I'll meet you there."

Charlie ran to the glass double doors while Harris called in the cavalry. Charlie wanted to take a look at them before they made their way inside. Upon closer examination, he noticed small scratches above the keyhole. The brass on all sides was tarnished and darkened, but it was shining just above the lock. This told Charlie that someone had recently used a well-made lock picking on the door and the device had scratched the top of the lock, scraping away the layers of wear.

For the sake of science, Charlie tried the door handle—and it opened. Something was wrong. Holloway had left this door open, but why? He was more careful than any criminal in the city's memory; locking a door behind him would have been second nature. Holloway must have been in a hurry. Had he known that the neighbors had seen him? No, that wouldn't make a difference. His name was known and there had been witnesses to his past abductions. Clearly, Holloway didn't think that the police could trace him, so he wasn't worried about being followed.

As far as Charlie was concerned, Holloway's reason for haste didn't matter. All that mattered was that there was only one act that he could be hurrying to complete, and that was the torture and death of his latest victim. He was in a rush to kill this woman, and Charlie needed to get to her—now. Deciding to leave Harris to follow alone, he dashed in through the open door and drew his service pistol.

The lobby of the complex was free of furniture, and a healthy layer of dust covered every surface of the building. The place still had power, but it was just the basic amount; small security lights bathed the floor immediately beneath them, and dim red exit signs shown off in the distance, but other than that, the place was dark. Charlie turned on his flashlight and tried to decide which direction Holloway had gone.

Shining his flashlight on the floor, the layer of dust was disturbed and the young detective bent down to inspect the footprints: size eleven work boots by the look of it. The toe of the left foot dragged on the ground from time to time. Initially, Charlie thought it was from a limp, but then realized that, when headed inward, Holloway would have been carrying an adult in his arms. Assuming Holloway was part of the right-handed majority, he would naturally carry a body with the heavier trunk on his left-hand side, bearing the initial full weight of the person upon his right arm when picking the body up. Charlie was now absolutely positive Holloway was in the building. There were many footprints, most covered in varying thicknesses of dust, but the faux-limping trail he had observed was brand new.

Following the trail, he went straight past the elevators—which had no power—to the main stairs. Unfortunately, the glossy linoleum floors of the lobby and hallway gave way to porous concrete in the stairwell, and Charlie lost the visible dust trail he'd been following. Taking the stairs two at a time, Charlie stopped at each landing just long enough to check the doors for any recent signs of use. Winded after hitting the eighth floor landing, he paused for a moment to catch his breath. That was when he heard it—a woman's voice. More specifically: a woman's *scream*.

The cry had come from far off, possibly two or three floors up. Charlie tapped into a reserve strength he didn't know he had, and flew up the stairs three at a time. Pausing at the tenth floor landing, he heard the scream again, this time much closer.

Taking a deep breath, Charlie pocketed his flashlight and waited for his eyes to adjust to the darkness. Slowly, he eased open the door and took a look at his surroundings. He was in the standard apartment hallway, with doors to the rooms on his left and windows overlooking the city on his right. It wasn't difficult to discern his next destination. One of the doors was open, and bright light spilled from within.

After silently making his way to the doorway, he paused, listening for anything that could give him the location of the occupants within. The only noises he heard were those of a woman, quietly sobbing and praying. He smelled blood, and something else—but he couldn't quite place what it was. Able to wait no longer, Charlie entered the room low; his pistol leading the way.

The room beyond was something out of a cheap horror movie and had no place in a rational world.

The room was lit by several workmen's spotlights that were mounted atop bright yellow industrial stands and attached to car batteries. Along the walls were various medical tools—scalpels, bone saws, clamps and spreaders—as well as modern power tools like drills, jigsaws and chainsaws. Blood, fresh or dried, covered almost every surface of the horrible room. Some of it was so faded and black that it must have been there for months. How many people had died in this room? Charlie shuddered at the thought.

In the center of the room stood a crude operating theater. A woman in her mid-thirties lay shackled to a wooden table. Clearing the room, satisfied that Holloway was not present, Charlie holstered his pistol and rushed over to the victim, releasing her from her bonds. He helped the sobbing woman into a sitting position.

"My name is Detective Charlie Walker," he told her. "Everything is going to be okay."

"No!" she whispered hoarsely. "He's still here! He's still here!"

Before Charlie could look away from the terrified woman, he felt another presence in the room. Turning slowly, he found himself face-to-face with the infamous Hollow Man—the big man's frame entirely filling the doorway.

"Welcome," Holloway spoke.

James Holloway was exponentially more terrible than the reports had ever made him out to be. The man was more creature than human: his black hair wild, his massive beard unkempt and tangled. The ice gray eyes that looked upon the detective with such hunger nearly broke his resolve. Charlie was terrified, but he would never let this monster see it. His chance to prevent the Hollow Man's latest massacre was handed to him on a silver platter, and he would die before he gave up.

"Holloway, you slipped up," Charlie said.

"Did I, detective?" Holloway asked, his tone so neutral that he could have been goading Charlie or he could have been dead serious.

"Let me see your hands," Charlie demanded.

"I'd like to see yours first," the wild man replied.

Charlie didn't like the look in Holloway's eyes: it was dangerous and clearly foreshadowed violent intent. Charlie decided not to take any chances, and he quickly reached for his holstered weapon with one hand while pulling the defenseless woman behind him with the other. Unfortunately, Holloway had been ready; a silenced nine-millimeter held behind his back. The killer raised the weapon and fired once, catching Charlie in the neck, but the detective had already drawn his pistol and fired three shots. One found its mark and sent the infamous killer crashing backwards to the floor of the hallway, dead.

The few minutes before Charlie passed out were a blur. He recalled the woman screaming at the top of her lungs. He recalled Harris entering the room, removing his coat and pressing it onto his partner's wound. Shortly after, Charlie lost consciousness. He awoke the next day with a tracheal tube down his throat and his pregnant wife looking down at him, holding baby Violet. Meghan's eyes were red from crying, but she smiled brightly when she noticed he was awake.

After his recovery period, Charlie was honored by the mayor and the woman he'd saved, along with the families of Holloway's other victims, in a special award ceremony held on the steps of the city hall. He graciously accepted the key to the city—which, until this point, he thought existed only in the movies. For the next week, he couldn't look at a newspaper or turn on the TV without seeing his own face staring back at him. One headline, "Hero Cop Stops Hollow Man," made him blush, perhaps because Meghan insisted upon framing it and hanging it in their living room.

Never had he thought that his actions that day could lead to an event as terrible as the one that was occurring now.

§

Charlie shook his head, trying to clear the memories, and looked straight into the eyes of the elder Holloway.

"Your son was a monster," Charlie claimed. "I did what any cop would have done in my place. It doesn't make me different."

"I suppose there's no convincing you," said Holloway. "Regardless, your actions have brought you to my attention. His case was only the tip of the iceberg. Since then, I have watched you. I have studied your methods. You *are* different. Your mind operates on a whole other level."

Holloway paused, deep in thought.

"Sadly, you dedicate your life to the protection of other people," he continued. "These disgusting commoners don't *deserve* your help."

"They deserve more than that," Charlie declared.

"Again, you refused to be swayed. No matter. Perhaps I am wrong. Perhaps the obnoxious do-gooders like yourself are destined to rule the world. Maybe you people are right. We will soon find out; you will be tested. The time has come to prove yourself, detective. Beat me at my own game and you will have won. I will be a scourge upon the world no more."

"Why test me?" Charlie asked.

"For years I have looked for individuals with a talent for using their minds to achieve great ends. Some like you. Others less savory, like my son. I have tested them in a similar manner. None have survived. Do you not understand? I'm searching for the person who can defeat me. I can't live forever but my legacy can. I've devoted the twilight of my life to scouring this planet for its greatest minds. None, so far, have even stood a chance.

"*You,* on the other hand, are exceptional. All the events that have occurred tonight, these seemingly random happenstances that have affected your psyche so profoundly, were all fabricated—by me. The PeopleMover, the Carousel of Progress, the bus tire, the false security agents—you saw right through all of these things. Your mind, though stressed, functioned as precisely as ever—perhaps more so. You are different, detective. Yours may be the mind that I've searched all these years for."

Charlie stared at the man in bewilderment for a few moments before speaking.

"I'd call you insane again," he said, "but you've already talked your way out of that one."

Holloway laughed and stood, setting two Blackberry batteries on the table and then made his way toward the door.

"Get some rest, detective. You have a long day ahead of you tomorrow." He paused before leaving and turned back toward Charlie. "One more thing. Your angels are safe but, should you decide to leave this room before you are told to do so, they will learn the true meaning of pain—my son was not the only creative sadist in the Holloway family. Goodnight, detective."

Holloway gently closed the door behind him and Charlie heard his footsteps fading steadily into the distance.

12

Meghan found the scissors as quickly as she could and released Violet and Katie from their bonds. Not being able to free herself from her own restraints, she entrusted the still-groggy Violet with the task. Luckily, the girl did her work well and Meghan's hands were freed quickly and without injury.

After making sure both of her girls weren't experiencing any ill effects from the drugs, Meghan slowly looked around at the enormous, two-story villa in which they found themselves. In any other situation, she would have loved being in this place. It was beautiful. The furniture, the decorations, the *view*—all of it was beyond anything she'd experienced before. It pained her that her first experience in so gorgeous an environment was such a terrible one.

"Mommy, what happened to us?" Violet asked, her tone more somber than any seven-year-olds' voice had any right to be, especially given that they were in Walt Disney World, staring at this breathtaking view of the Magic Kingdom.

"Nothing," she lied, trying to keep up a strong front for her daughters' sake. "We've just got to stay in this big room for a while, baby."

"Really, Mommy. What *happened*?" Violet prodded, rubbing her wrists where the bonds had so tightly been.

Sometimes Meghan forgot how mature her daughter was. Little white lies and misdirection rarely worked on Violet Walker. Katie was happier being a normal child and, while fiercely intelligent, had no interest in skepticism—to her, the world was a beautiful place and there was no better time than now to live in it. Violet, on the other hand, had a firm grasp on the world around her and when something seemed out of place, she questioned it.

"Well, we've gotten into a little bit of trouble with some scary people. I don't really understand what's going on yet," she admitted.

"What about Daddy?" Violet asked.

"Daddy's coming to get us," Meghan said firmly, knowing Charlie would stop at nothing to free them.

Katie stood silently at the large window, forehead pressed against the cool glass, looking out at the Magic Kingdom. Meghan and Violet joined her and all three of them stood in silence for a while, absorbed in the magnificent view of one of their favorite places on Earth; not even the terribleness of the moment could tarnish their love for this place of wonder. Meghan put her arms around the girls and knelt for a while with them in silence, taking in the view, trying not to think about the current situation.

"Are you guys okay?" she asked, gently.

"Yeah," the girls both agreed in unison.

"Are you scared?" Meghan prodded.

"A little," Violet admitted. "But not really. Daddy will get us, and he'll send all of the bad guys to jail after he does."

"Daddy's stronger than they are," added Katie.

Meghan smiled, thankful that she had such brave and strong daughters. They were right too—Meghan was sure of it. Wherever Charlie was, she knew his mind was racing a million miles an hour, working out every possible way he could get them back. She knew all too well Charlie's protective nature and his unyielding need to keep those he loved safe and happy. He'd put his life on the line without a second thought to save a stranger; Meghan knew that he would die to save his family.

She worried about him, though. She didn't want Charlie to get hurt, but she had faith that—out of everyone in the world—her husband was the one man she could trust to get them all through this horrible ordeal unharmed.

"I love you guys," Meghan told the girls. "You know that?"

"We love you too, Mommy."

After a few more moments of silently gazing out the window, Meghan heard the door to the villa gently open behind her. The strange elderly man had returned.

"Mrs. Walker, I've just come from a little meeting with your husband," the man stated.

"Did you hurt him?" she asked angrily.

With a resigned air, he admitted, "I have tried, but he is a refreshingly resilient man."

"He will come for us," shot Violet from a few feet away.

"He won't have to, Violet," replied the man.

"I don't understand," Meghan said.

The man—whose name, he revealed, was Spencer Holloway—pulled Meghan aside, out of earshot of the girls. He explained to her their entire situation.

He told her all about the cruel tests Charlie would face and the very real danger that he was in. He explained that, if Charlie succeeded, none of them would be harmed. Meghan seethed with unchecked rage, never hating a person more than she did Spencer Holloway. Deep inside her mind, she hoped Charlie wouldn't arrest Holloway when he beat him; she hoped he would *kill* him—even *that* was still more than this monster deserved.

"Do you believe your husband will succeed?" asked Holloway.

"He'll do more than that," Meghan promised.

"Oh?" chuckled the old man.

"He'll kill you," she rasped. "Just like he killed your worthless son."

Meghan spoke quietly yet viciously. She wanted to make sure Holloway understood how much she loathed him. She wanted him to know how badly she wished he would fail. And most importantly, she wanted him to know that taking Charlie Walker's family from him was the biggest mistake he would ever make.

"I assure you that I share your opinion of my son. I feel no pity for the boy; he was useless and now he is dead. That is all. Your husband will get his chance at revenge, Mrs. Walker, but only if he passes my tests."

"You're wasting your time," she declared.

"Is your opinion of him so high that you think these tests unnecessary?" Holloway asked, interested in the effects emotional attachment had on facts—whether or not love could override factual observation.

"No," she said, surprising him. "My opinion doesn't matter. *Facts* matter. Charlie is the most intelligent, inventive man I have ever known. My first impression of you has already told me that you couldn't even *dream* of being a match for him. If you allow him a fair chance—and don't try to cheat—he *will* win. *These* are facts."

"I hope you're right. I've waited a long time for someone like him to come along," Holloway admitted, sadly.

"You're insane," Meghan stated.

Holloway laughed, "I feel as if I have heard that somewhere before. Now, Mrs. Walker, I must leave you. I will send in Jeremy to make sure your stay here is comfortable."

He stood up to leave, but Meghan stopped him.

"Don't you *dare* leave that monster in here with us."

"And why not?" Holloway asked, genuinely concerned.

"Let's just say that he's not exactly the type of person that should be left alone with a woman."

Holloway considered this for a moment.

"He has made…inappropriate advances?" he asked, objectively.

"More than one," she stated bluntly. "I imagine it will happen again if you let him in here. If he touches me again, I'll kill him. I'd rather my daughters see that than anything that coward might do to us."

Holloway nodded his assent. "Worry not, Mrs. Walker. Get a good night's rest and enjoy yourselves the best you can. The three of you will be left in peace. Jeremy will be dealt with."

With that final statement, he glided out the door, closing it gently behind him, leaving Meghan and the girls alone once more. This time, though, they were left with the knowledge that Charlie was okay, and that their safety hinged on him besting this psychopath in a battle of the minds—a battle Meghan knew her husband couldn't lose.

Meghan began to feel hope for the first time since this nightmare scenario had begun.

§

"Follow me, Jeremy," Holloway said calmly, exiting the villa and walking briskly toward the identical room that he occupied next door.

"What's wrong, sir?" Jeremy pried, but Holloway remained silent. *This isn't good,* Jeremy thought. His mind raced with possibilities as they entered the old man's villa.

"Sit," Holloway commanded, motioning to the couch.

Jeremy did as he was told and Holloway stood before him, towering over the younger man.

"You have disappointed me again, Jeremy," explained Holloway, pinching the bridge of his nose and sighing.

"What have I done, sir? Did that bitch next door—"

"Shut your mouth!" Holloway snapped, staring daggers at Jeremy. Actual rage showed itself for a split second on Holloway's face. Almost immediately, his characteristic calm returned. "*Mrs.* Walker has reported to me some inappropriate actions on your behalf, Jeremy. This, coupled with what I have already seen, troubles me deeply."

"Sir, I—"

"I am beginning to think I have misjudged your character, Jeremy. Do you remember what became of Eddie after his less-than-savory decisions regarding the respect of Mrs. Walker's intimate privacy? *Of course* you do," Holloway paused to clear his throat. "You cleaned his leftovers out of the wood chipper. Still, allow me to refresh your mind: Eddie was nothing more than a brainless pervert. You, Jeremy—I must admit that I had higher hopes for you. As it seems, my hopes were all for nothing."

"Sir—"

"Speak another word and it will be your last. Listen with your ears, look with your eyes, but *do not speak*. While those three young women are under our care, they will *not* be touched. They will be respected. They are not playthings for you and your sickening carnal desires. They are the prizes that Walker will play our game to win. Do you understand? No. Don't answer. You are dumber than the couch upon which you sit; whether you understand or not is irrelevant. If you retain anything at all from this conversation, remember this: you are no longer permitted to set foot in their villa, nor are you permitted to interact with them in any way. This is your final chance, Jeremy. I believe I have given you a fair number of warnings and have allowed you to bear witness, firsthand, to what happens to those who disobey me. From this second on, you will obey me. This time, you may answer: do you understand?"

Jeremy seethed beneath the surface—furious and terrified—and Holloway noticed but could not let this young man disrespect or harm the detective's family while they still had a key role to play.

"*Do. You. Understand?*" Holloway snapped.

"I understand, sir," Jeremy sulked, staring intensely at the floor between his feet.

"Good. Now get out of here. Get some rest and be at your position in the morning ready to initiate the next phase."

Holloway stepped around the couch and made his way up the staircase, leaving Jeremy to let himself out.

13

Charlie glanced at his watch but his vision was so blurred that he could no longer read the roman numerals just a few inches from his face. After rubbing his eyes, he learned that it was just before eight in the morning. He'd not slept for an instant. He thought about the torturously long night he'd had.

For an hour or so after Holloway had left, Charlie had gone to the window every few minutes and cracked the blinds just wide enough to see outside. He searched everything in his field of vision, but he couldn't spot the agents of his enemy—or any signs of life at all, for that matter. He had no reason *not* to believe that there were men hidden outside, or cameras, or sensors, or *something* that would alert Holloway if he exited, though he could spot nothing with his naked eye. Perhaps the old man had people in adjacent rooms—hell, he could've even had men hiding in the landscaping. It was possible that Holloway could have been bluffing, but Charlie refused to take the risk. Besides, where would he have gone? To the pool for a brisk swim? To the Banana Cabana Pool Bar to drown himself in watered-down whiskey?

No, there wasn't any *reason* for Charlie to leave his room. He had no course of action—no plan, no way to begin his search—until Holloway contacted him. Charlie knew that he had no hope for sleep: a man whose family has been taken hostage cannot possibly be expected to simply relax and doze off. He'd begun to wonder if this was part of Holloway's plan. If Holloway was trying to gain an advantage then sleep deprivation was definitely a good place to start.

Charlie had spent a large portion of his night sitting on the edge of his bed, trying to clear his mind and stop his heart from beating so fast. He worried intensely about his family. The fact that he had no control over their safety increased his anxiety exponentially. Knowledge was power, and Charlie Walker had made it his life's work to gain as much as possible. Having no knowledge as to the whereabouts of his family chipped away at his composure like a hot icepick.

At one point, boredom had led him to the wall safe where he removed his Walther. He stripped the weapon and spent a few minutes checking every component to make sure everything was in order, even though he already knew the gun was in perfect shape before putting it back together. He disassembled the pistol and then reassembled it again for no reason. Just for good measure, he ran through the process a few more times. After the fourth time, he began to time himself to see how quickly he could fieldstrip and reassemble the weapon. Checking his watch, he was dismayed to learn that he had only wasted twenty minutes. Sighing, he returned the weapon to the wall safe and resumed his place on the edge of the bed.

At another point in the night, Charlie had turned on the TV. No matter what you had been watching before shutting it off, Disney's in-room TVs always returned to the channel running *Must Do Disney*. Charlie leaned back against the headboard of the bed and watched the familiar fifteen-minute loop over and over again. Aside from a few minor changes, it was the same program as the previous few years, and many times he had watched it over and over again while waiting for the girls to get ready, but it never really got old.

The host, a woman named Stacey, generally got on his nerves, but nonetheless he couldn't stop watching. He still cringed every time he heard the hideous and awkward shriek she let out every time the Expedition Everest segment came on. That scene was so horrible and memorable that Charlie had once even had a nightmare in which she chased him screaming, "Yeti! Ahhh!" continuously until he had run off a cliff and died, mercifully waking himself up. The thought had made him laugh aloud.

For hours, he watched the loop on endless repeat, until he had seen it so many times that he had nearly every line memorized. Glancing toward the window, he noticed the sun starting to peek in through the gaps in the blinds; he sat up, finally shutting off the TV.

It had been a terrible, tedious night.

Snapping himself out of the memory of the previous night, Charlie checked his watch once more, just to make sure he'd read the time right, and decided to go to the bathroom and clean himself up. Setting the Blackberry on the sink counter, he changed clothes and washed up, waiting for some form of communication from Holloway.

When the time neared nine o'clock and he still hadn't heard from Holloway, Charlie once more became restless. He rhythmically began pacing the room, hoping for a sign—*anything* that would let him take action instead of waiting and worrying.

At precisely nine o'clock, there was a firm knock on the door. Quietly, Charlie made his way to the peephole and looked outside. Bathed in the golden light of the Florida morning sun stood a pretty girl in her twenties, decked out in the unflattering floral shirt and khaki shorts of a Cast Member at the Caribbean Beach Resort. In her hands she held what seemed to be a cellophane-wrapped gift basket. Intrigued, Charlie opened the door to greet her.

"Good morning," she said. "Delivery for a Charlie Walker?"

"That's me," he declared casually.

"Awesome! If you could just sign right here for me." She handed him a clipboard and pen. "And if I could also see your ID, that would be perfect."

Charlie obliged and as he traded the clipboard and ID for the gift basket, he asked her, "Do you have any idea who this is from?"

"No, sir," she stated, handing him his ID. "The only information attached was the delivery info. It's not uncommon. We deliver a lot of anonymous gifts."

"Thank you," he said, nodding graciously as he closed the door.

Charlie placed the item on the table and sat down to investigate it. He noticed that the gift basket was pirate-themed. Upon closer inspection, he found that it contained several different types of beer, along with a bag of tortilla chips, a small pirate hat, an eye-patch and a collapsible cooler. Tearing away the cellophane, he removed the items one by one. Beneath all of the items was a piece of heavyweight cardstock. Disregarding the other items, he read the short message printed on the card: *Abandon all hope, ye who enter here.*

Charlie recognized the quote but it didn't make much sense to him. What did it have to do with his current situation? Clearly the gift basket and its contents pointed toward Pirates of the Caribbean, but he'd been on the ride several times this trip—what more was there for him to see? Turning the card over, he noticed a smaller message printed on the back, near the bottom. *You seek treasure, detective. This should be an easy beginning.*

If Holloway had wanted Charlie to simply ride the attraction, he would have sent the note alone. The fact that it was buried beneath all of these items in the gift basket told the detective something crucial. It wasn't merely a random assortment of items—it was a message. The items pointed toward something specific—a goal or a location. Very quickly, Charlie came to the conclusion that Holloway had intended for him to go to the gift shop at the exit of Pirates of the Caribbean, and not the attraction itself. He almost kicked himself for not realizing it at first sight—this random assortment of novelty *gift* items had made his path all too clear. Finally, he had a starting point. He didn't know what he would find when he arrived, but he knew there was something in that store that was meant for him. But why the shop? After all of Holloway's drama, it seemed as if the attraction itself would have been his destination—instead, the strange old man had chosen the gift shop.

Not concerning himself with more fruitless speculation, Charlie stood, prepared to leave, when the quote on the front of the card popped up in his head, nagging at him. While it seemed playful and harmless at first glance—a joke like the beer and the other gifts—there was something sinister about that quote; some hidden meaning that Charlie *should* have known, but couldn't quite put his finger on. *An easy beginning. Abandon all hope.* The two lines bounced around in his head before finally clicking into place. Their meaning appeared from the foggy recesses of his mind.

Hell.

The quote was from Dante's *Inferno* and was the final line of the inscription on the gates of Hell. Charlie knew that there must be something more to it, but he couldn't remember the full inscription, so he quickly located Meghan's iPad and brought up the Internet app. Typing the line into the search engine, the second link brought him to the original quote, translated in its entirety. He read the terrible text over and over again:

Through me you pass into the city of woe:
Through me you pass into eternal pain:
Through me among the people lost for aye.
Justice the founder of my fabric mov'd:
To rear me was the task of Power divine,
Supremest Wisdom, and primeval Love.

Before me things create were none, save things
Eternal, and eternal I endure.
Abandon all hope, ye who enter here.

"Son of a bitch," he breathed, not believing his eyes. The impact of those grim lines of poetry hit Charlie like a truck, and sent his mind reeling. He'd read the *Divine Comedy* years ago and recalled that this inscription over the gates of Hell was meant to inform the doomed souls that passed through of what awaited inside. The ghostly guide, Virgil, informed Dante that this did not apply to him, for he was not yet damned. Charlie took a deep breath, trying to understand what Holloway had meant by this. Was he to be Dante? Would he experience Hell and escape to be reunited with his beloved? Or was he destined to burn, without hope, like the countless damned souls that had read this inscription on their way to oblivion?

One thing was certain: he wouldn't find his answer sitting in this room worrying about a centuries-old quote. Something waited for him in that shop, but how would he know what it was? He figured his time would be better spent trying to answer that question in the shop itself. He stood and retrieved the Blackberry from the sink counter. A message awaited him.

Better get moving, detective. Time is wasting.

Pocketing the device, he glanced at the wall safe and considered taking his Walther with him. Deciding against it, he left the room and headed for the bus stop. For the second time this trip, a journey was to begin at Pirates of the Caribbean. Would he truly be entering Hell?

Only time would tell—and Charlie Walker had yet to abandon hope.

14

harlie arrived outside Pirates of the Caribbean a few minutes after ten. Adventureland was swarming with people—people like himself—who began their Magic Kingdom day by heading for the leftmost spoke and working their way clockwise around the park.

He slowly but steadily made his way through the crowds and finally reached the entrance to the gift shop. The Plaza del Sol Caribe Bazaar was modeled after a sixteenth-century Spanish fort; the shop itself open to the elements in the center, as if in an old courtyard. Many people milled around inside, yet it wasn't as claustrophobic as it would surely be in a few hours' time.

Charlie leaned against a pillar, pondering where he should begin his search. He didn't have much to go on; all he knew was something was in this store that required his attention and would allow him to further progress in this cruel game. He decided to meander through the store and hope that some fortunate cosmic magnetism would eventually take him where he needed to be.

Picking his way to the rear of the store, he started searching for anything that seemed out of the ordinary, but nothing caught his eye. He waded through racks upon racks of clothing, toy weaponry, plastic treasure and books about pirates—historical and fictional—still nothing jumped out at him. After what seemed like an eternity of aimless wandering, Charlie had begun to think he'd misinterpreted the morning's delivery and had come to the wrong place.

Charlie was heading for the exit, planning to go back to the hotel to see if there were any details from the gift basket that he could have missed, when something caught his eye. A flash of blonde to his left made him stop dead in his tracks. When he turned to look, he saw nothing but a shelf of decorative pieces, but atop it sat an item he was sure he'd never seen in the store in any of his past trips—or even just a couple of days earlier. It was a digital picture frame. Generic photos of Disney vacationers would be displayed and then change every ten seconds or so and one of them had been the source of the blonde that had caught Charlie's eye, but the image had disappeared before he'd had a chance to see it clearly. Determined to be sure that it was just a coincidence and that he'd simply glimpsed a random picture of a blonde woman, Charlie waited, staring intently at the screen as the images changed.

After a couple of minutes, he'd still not seen a picture of anyone with blonde hair. He watched more meaningless pictures scroll by and began to get discouraged. He rested his hands on the shelf and waited, not taking his eyes off the screen. Sensing a presence to his right, Charlie glanced over to see a Cast Member standing a few feet away from him, politely trying to see if there was anything she could assist with. He smiled and nodded, returning his attention to the screen.

"Is there anything I can help you with, sir?" the young girl asked, apparently not satisfied with Charlie's polite, yet dismissive nod.

"No, thank you. I'm just checking out this cool picture frame. I've never seen one of these here…"

Charlie's words cut off mid-sentence as an image of Violet appeared on the screen. It was a picture that Charlie had taken with his own phone just the day before of Violet standing in front of Spaceship Earth, her arms reaching up to give the illusion that she was holding the massive geodesic sphere. This was the object he had come to find.

"Is something wrong, sir?" the Cast Member asked, concerned with Charlie's abrupt silence.

Knowing he could not let the woman learn the truth, he turned away from the picture to face her. He placed himself in front of the digital frame to prevent her from seeing any images—images he may be in.

"No, no. Everything's fine," he promised. "How much is this digital frame?

I'd like to take it with me."

"Unfortunately, that one is a display model that we just got in this morning. The frame itself is a prototype display and the actual for-sale units won't be in until next week. We *are* taking preorders though, if you'd like to have one shipped to your house."

This was not good. Charlie knew that this frame contained information he desperately needed to know.

"That's too bad," he said. "Oh well, I'll just have to hope you guys have it on my next trip. Thanks for your help."

He slowly wandered away from the Cast Member and the picture frame, keeping his eye on both of them. Charlie knew he needed to get that frame out of the store. If he couldn't buy it, then he would have to steal it. Being an officer of the law, stealing was against every principal that he held but, if he didn't take this frame, his family was as good as dead. Charlie knew that Holloway had done this on purpose—he knew it would entertain the old man to see the valiant police officer break the law to save his family. He was sure that there was a camera nearby trained on him. He imagined Holloway watching, probably sipping his expensive water and laughing as Charlie worked up the nerve to steal a hundred-dollar digital frame.

Charlie dismissed the thought and turned his mind toward the current situation. If he were caught stealing the frame, he would certainly be arrested by Disney Security—*actual* Disney Security—and detained, condemning his girls to death. On the other hand, he was confident that it wouldn't be terribly difficult to get the frame out of the store.

Standing fifteen feet away, Charlie feigned interest in a book about Blackbeard while surveying the area that the frame was in. The Cast Member that he'd spoken to was currently assisting a mother and young son in picking out a hat, but she was still too close to the area for him to make his move. Charlie was thankful that no security lock had been placed on the device; it would be easy enough to secret away the frame when the area was clear.

Finally, the boy had chosen a hat and the Cast Member had moved away to go on break. Charlie set down the book and began slowly making his way toward the frame. Halfway to his destination, he had to stop and quickly pretend to be deeply interested in a barrel of plastic cannonballs as the woman with the little boy found the picture frame and were apparently mesmerized by it.

You've got to be fucking kidding me, Charlie thought. *What are the odds these two would head straight for the frame?*

"Look at the magic picture frame, Jimmy!" the mother said to her son.

"I can't see! Too high!" the boy exclaimed.

The mother lifted her son and both watched as pictures appeared and were replaced by others. Irritated, Charlie tapped his foot, counting the seconds that these people stood between him and his only means of rescuing his family. He knew that they were just vacationers, and that they were simply enjoying their time in the park, but he couldn't help the frustration that bubbled up within him.

It's a digital picture frame, he thought. *They're forty bucks at Target. Get the hell out of the way and pay for your hat.*

He mentally kicked himself for his inappropriate thought, but any amount of internal scolding couldn't solve the very *real* problem that these people were still impeding his progress. The Cast Member that had helped them earlier was gone, but Charlie was sure that her replacement would arrive soon. His only opportunity to get this frame was to get these two out of the way quickly and make his move as soon as possible.

Trying to think of a way to distract the woman and child, Charlie searched his surroundings. Finding nothing that could be of use, he decided to apply some simple trickery. Eagerly, he sidled up to the duo, as if he were as enchanted by the device as the family. After a few seconds, Charlie noticed the hat the boy had chosen.

"Ah, Jack Sparrow," Charlie said good-naturedly. "He's my favorite too."

"Jimmy just can't get enough of Captain Jack!" the mother stated enthusiastically, taking a breath for what was surely going to be a long-winded speech about her beloved Jimmy. "Isn't that right, Jimmy? Oh, he's got all the action figures at home. You should see his bedroom—pirates everywhere! Last Halloween, he even went trick-or-treating dressed up as Jack Sparrow! My husband Carl got a spare set of keys from his work, and we had our dog carry them around all night. Let me tell you, it was the darndest sight you ever did see! Later on, after he came home..."

Charlie tuned out, disinterested in Jimmy's adventurous Halloween, searching for an opening in which to unveil his plan.

"There's this really cool Jack Sparrow show just outside the shop," he interjected. "It starts in five minutes. Jimmy could probably swordfight with

Jack Sparrow if you get there early enough."

Charlie had no idea if *Captain Jack Sparrow's Pirate Tutorial* was performed this early. Still, he decided to roll the dice.

Lying and *stealing,* he thought. *This is what I'm reduced to?*

"No kidding?" she asked. "You hear that, Jimmy? We'd better pay for your hat and get you over to meet the Captain! Thanks for the tip, sir."

"No problem at all. You guys have fun," Charlie smiled, watching them hurry to the counter.

Wasting no time, Charlie grabbed the frame and searched for the power button. Locating it, he shut the frame down—it wouldn't do to have a bright LCD screen drawing attention to you while trying to escape unnoticed. Charlie made his way to the most remote corner of the shop and quickly scanned his surroundings. There were no guests nearby and all the Cast Members were still at the checkout. Smoothly, Charlie lifted his shirt and tucked the frame into the waistband of his shorts. Satisfied that nobody had seen the move, he made his way toward the front of the store and successfully reached the bathrooms that were just outside without capture or accusation.

Finding an unused stall, Charlie locked the door behind him and withdrew the frame. He sat on the toilet seat and powered up the device. Upon closer inspection, he found other buttons near the power switch—a menu button, a select button and two arrow buttons. Charlie pressed the menu button and a small blue square appeared on the screen displaying various options. He scrolled down to an option labeled 'Thumbnail View' and pressed the select button. The screen changed to show small thumbnail previews of all the pictures contained in the frame's memory. Atop the screen was a counter; the numbers telling him which photo he was viewing and how many there were in total. There were currently one hundred forty-two images on the frame.

The Blackberry vibrated in his pocket and he quickly withdrew it and checked the screen. The text contained only numbers, but their meaning was instantly clear to the detective:

41, 58, 76, 95.

As fast as he could, he located image forty-one. As he'd suspected, it was the picture of Meghan he'd seen in his peripheral vision in the store. In this image, she was sitting in the airport reading and Charlie had taken the picture without her noticing. She'd never looked more beautiful. Image fifty-eight was the photo of Violet that he'd seen in the store. Seventy-six was a picture of Katie jumping on the bed in their hotel room.

Finally, Charlie made his way to image ninety-five. It took him a few seconds to realize what he was looking at. After focusing, Charlie realized he was looking at a bright green circuit board with a set of batteries at the bottom. In the center of the circuit board sat a silver key. *Why a circuit board?* he thought.

A few more moments of studying the image led him to believe that the picture was actual size. The key and batteries were the same size they would be if he held them in his hand. He needed this key, but where was it?

Flipping to the next image, Charlie saw a stock photo of a random family riding Splash Mountain—not relevant to his quest. He returned to the photo of the key on the circuit board. Something about returning to the image after viewing another had changed his perspective of the picture. For a moment, he forced himself to imagine that the screen was missing and he was viewing the circuitry of the device behind it. There was no doubt in his mind: he was looking at the interior of *this* device.

Prying the device apart using the plastic attachments on either side, he saw the key neatly placed on the board. Upon closer inspection, he noticed that it was soldered into the circuitry at each end. He would have to break the solder joints to free the key and, as a result, render the device inoperable. For a while, he thought about the situation, leaving the key in place.

Charlie needed this key, but he didn't know what it opened. Why provide a key with no indication as to what it unlocks? He searched his memory, but couldn't think of any doors that stood out. He was sure that this key opened a door he hadn't seen before; therefore, Holloway must have already given him the clue he needed to locate it. Where? All he had was this digital picture frame and a gift basket full of nonsense back in his room. The gift basket could yield no location—it was a direct reference to Pirates of the Caribbean and Charlie doubted that the door in question was in this building. This frame, however, could possibly still show him the way.

He had only been given the numbers of four images. There were far too many pictures in the frame's memory to analyze them one by one and he'd already seen doors in the background of several images. Surely there were other doors in other images but he couldn't be sure which would be the right one. He lacked the time necessary to locate and test them all. Holloway knew this and therefore must have already given Charlie the location.

For some reason, Charlie couldn't get the numbers from the text message out of his head. Something nagged at his mind; some connection between those numbers—possibly a pattern, but what kind? He looked at the numbers once more, hoping this visual stimulus would trigger something in his brain and gain him some insight into their connection.

41, 58, 76, 95.

Suddenly, the pattern emerged. It was so simple that he scoffed at himself for not noticing it earlier. Forty-one was seventeen places from fifty-eight. Fifty-eight was eighteen places from seventy-six. Seventy-six was nineteen places from ninety-five. It was a simple logic puzzle where the interval between numbers increased by one each time. If his theory was correct, image one hundred fifteen would show him the location of the door.

Carefully, so as not to dislodge the key, Charlie turned over the frame and found the image that he was looking for. It was a stock photo of a small child standing proudly in line for Space Mountain. The image was dark, but Charlie knew the spot well; it was in the queue's long tunnel, right where it flattens out and begins to ascend. Behind the little girl stood a door with a bright red exit sign above it. This was the door.

For some unknown reason, Holloway intended for him to enter the bowels of Space Mountain. Nothing good could possibly await him there.

Satisfied that his next destination was clear, Charlie turned the device over and pried the key from the circuit board. Sure enough, the key was a part of the circuit and the device was rendered useless once the key was removed. Holloway was clever. He'd tested Charlie to make sure that he was worthy. Had Charlie not figured out the second part of the test and simply removed the key without recognizing the numbers as a puzzle, the location of the door would have been lost forever and Charlie would have failed.

He had passed this test with flying colors.

Dropping the digital frame in the garbage can on his way, Charlie headed outside and began his hike toward the other end of the park and the mysterious door inside Space Mountain.

15

Spencer Holloway sat alone in his villa, enjoying the luxurious air conditioning and tracking the progress of the determined young detective. Charlie Walker had so far failed to disappoint, and Holloway was thoroughly entertained. He'd thought that installing the key to act as a *functional* part of the digital frame's circuit was an extremely elegant touch on his part—if just a tad cruel. Still, Holloway knew that any amateur detective worth his salt would never have removed that key before being absolutely positive that the device yielded no further information.

Watching the detective *steal* the picture frame was a reward in and of itself. It was a priceless moment, watching Walker lurk in the back of the shop, battling his own personal values and trying painfully hard to overcome them. Reducing a renowned hero and upholder of the law to a common shoplifter was supremely entertaining, and the plan had worked like a charm. Holloway had laughed aloud when Walker had secreted the device away and casually made his way out of the store. The detective was a talented thief— perhaps *too* talented. It had always been a pet theory of Holloway's that all the hours detectives spent studying criminals would make them the most efficient and effective criminal agents of all.

Walker had reached Tomorrowland and made his way past Stitch's Great Escape. He had no doubt found the image of the door, but he did not know that Space Mountain was not intended to be his next destination—the door was part of an event planned for much later. Holloway had many other plans for the young detective before the grand finale in the darkened roller coaster. He called up the application on one of his computers that would allow him to send text messages to the detective's Blackberry. He began to type.

Heading to Space Mountain so soon, detective?

Onscreen, he watched the feed from a distant security camera as the young detective stopped in his tracks and withdrew the phone from his pocket. Holloway watched as Walker typed out a reply. Within seconds, the words appeared on the computer monitor.

I found the key. I know where the door is.

Holloway chuckled; this was *his* game and the detective would do what he was told, when he was told.

Tsk, Tsk, detective. I made no mention that Space Mountain was your next destination. It is but one of many.

The detective looked toward the sky in frustration, as if the gods had somehow forsaken him. Eventually relaxing, he casually sat in the shade on a nearby bench and began typing.

Fine. You've got me, Holloway. You're a genius. Where next? snapped the frustrated detective.

Sarcasm does not become a man of your talents, Walker. You should try being serious.

Holloway saw the detective laugh and then politely wave as a family of four sharply glared at him for his impulsive outburst.

Maybe when I get my family back, you and I can sit down and have a serious chat, Charlie offered.

Confidence, on the other hand, suits you. You've done well thus far. Have some lunch. Ride a few rides. Now is not the time to worry about the door in Space Mountain. You'll be contacted with further details on your next destination this afternoon.

The detective showed no emotion onscreen, but Holloway was certain he was disappointed and frustrated. Exactly as he should be.

This afternoon? Why the hell are you wasting time?

Ah, yes. The frustration came through quite clearly in his reply.

Like I said, enjoy the morning. You haven't slept or eaten. Eat. Rest. Then find a Cast Member named Eduardo. He is working the locker rentals. He has recently been given a key, reported lost, for a locker rented under your name. That is all.

Holloway severed the connection with the detective and sat back. Walker would, indeed, be contacted, but it would be much sooner than the afternoon. The old man leaned back in his chair, relaxing as he waited for the detective to claim his reward.

Holloway was savoring this game. In the past, during each man or woman's first trial, he'd always set the game up to be lethal upon failure and he'd watched most competent challengers perish as a result of their own ignorance. In this case, Walker simply would have had no way to find his family and Holloway would have disposed of the girls in a timely fashion and never contacted Walker again.

Sometimes death wasn't the worst consequence. Walker was a man who cared little for his own wellbeing; the fear of death would not motivate him. Walker was selfless, unlike all of the others that Holloway had challenged. If the detective lost his *family*, he would be utterly destroyed; Holloway knew it would be a fate much worse than death for that particular man.

Holloway felt a sense of relief rising within himself. He had not wanted the game to end this early. How droll it would have been to have Jeremy execute the detective's family so soon. The old man also felt another emotion—one alien to someone such as himself: hope. Holloway truly wanted the detective to claim victory. He wanted to see someone exceed his own vast intellect during his lifetime. Never had he been bested in the many years he'd lived on this planet, but he'd always held out hope—glorious, unreasonable hope.

He knew that his time on Earth wasn't infinite, and that he was in the twilight of his life—though he wasn't ill and had many healthy years left in him. Still, he'd searched the planet for generations for the one mind that could surpass his own, and had been repeatedly disappointed. Something was different about Charlie Walker: a determination and a presence of mind that Holloway had not seen in any of his previous challengers. There was a spark in that young man which might finally ignite the flames of victory.

If his instincts were to prove true and the detective finally bested him, Holloway's time on this Earth would finally expire. The old man's death was the price that was to be paid for the detective's victory.

For as many years as Holloway had longed to find the person that could finally challenge him and prove themselves superior, he had also known that the two great minds could never coexist. Holloway knew that, should a challenger ever claim victory, he could no longer survive—his own brilliant mind, the mind that had *longed* to be defeated, would turn on him and torture him to the point of insanity. It was for this reason, vain as it may seem, that Holloway planned to take his own life should a challenger emerge victorious. The old man could not live with this defeat, even though he'd spent his entire life searching for it. Besides, he'd never planned to die in a hospital bed, sick, miserable and vegetative.

After a few more moments of reflection, Holloway's mood darkened rapidly with the striking realization that he may only have hours left to live. From a cabinet in his villa's kitchen, he removed a bottle of Scotch and an ornate glass. This was not just any bottle of Scotch, it was a 1926 Macallan that had been bottled in the mid-1980s, making this particular whisky nearly ninety years old. Holloway had been saving this fine spirit for the special occasion when a challenger finally claimed victory. His recent thoughts had driven him to realize that he wouldn't be in much of a mood for this elegant whisky when he was finally bested.

Removing the stopper from the old bottle, Holloway poured himself two ounces of the dark amber liquid. In a single gulp, the old man swallowed three-thousand-dollars' worth of Scottish pride.

Watching the monitors, Holloway poured himself another round as an entirely new emotion began to creep up in the back of his mind, something much more alien than hope.

Fear.

For so long, Holloway had wanted to find that one mind that was his equal—his superior, even—and now that this mind had potentially presented itself, he began to fear the end. The whisky had a calming and clarifying effect, allowing Holloway's mind to wade through the thick fog of irrational fear and emerge upon the precipice of a harsh truth: Holloway was not yet ready to die and he was certainly not prepared to lose. All these years, he had expected to be beaten, yet he had never once thought that he would be ill-prepared to meet his end. He'd always thought that when the day finally came, he would be at peace—fulfilled and prepared to leave this unjust world.

Even though it was too early in the game to be backed up by factual evidence, Holloway could nevertheless not shake the inexplicable feeling of foreboding and dread; the unreasonable conviction that Walker was going to succeed. He could not rationalize this feeling—could not explain it—but he knew that he was finally going to be beaten at his own game. Never had he even *entertained* the notion that a challenger could succeed until just this very moment.

This simply should not come to pass, for Spencer Holloway was the master of this game. *He* made the rules and *he* decided the outcome. *He* could not lose.

The time had come to stack the deck against the detective.

16

Violet Walker stood barefoot in front of the massive window, staring out at the wondrous Magic Kingdom bathed in the glory of the late morning sun. She sighed wistfully, longing to be *in* that beautiful place instead of looking at it.

Her family's horrible situation aside, this villa that the strange man had left them in was incredible. She wished that she could *live* in it. There were high ceilings and giant windows. There were multiple bedrooms, countless beds, couches and chairs. There were more bathrooms than one villa could possibly ever need—even if someone threw a *huge* birthday party. The kitchen was big, sleek, futuristic and fully stocked; although she wasn't sure that this place was supposed to come fully stocked. More perplexing was the fridge, containing near-identical contents to their fridge at home. Thinking of the fridge made Violet decide to head over to the stainless steel appliance and investigate its contents more closely.

If this refrigerator was *really* stocked with all of the same contents that they had at home, then they absolutely *must* have her super-special delicacy. Rifling through the fridge, she shoved aside the more mundane items in search of her quarry. Finally, after moving aside a massive jug of apple juice, Violet finally found what she was searching for. Carrying her spoils over to the wooden chair that sat near the colossal window, she pulled on the bulky piece of furniture until she had turned it around completely to face the window. After tossing the back-pillow to the floor, she threw herself down onto the comfortable leather cushion, sliding all the way back until she was leaning against the curved wooden slats. She placed her feet on the cool glass of the window and popped the tab of a shiny, dark red can.

Dr Pepper was just *too* good not to have on hand any time of the day. Checking her trusty Hello Kitty watch, Violet noticed that it was eleven in the morning. She smiled mischievously—it was never too early for the Doctor. Sipping the delicious beverage, she looked out over the park like a goddess watching over her people.

Exhausted as the three Walker ladies had become, Violet was wide awake—she never really required much sleep. Meghan and Katie were still asleep in the downstairs bedroom. Violet wasn't surprised; she always arose before her Mom and sister. She tended to enjoy the hours of solitude that being the earliest riser afforded. Even in a situation as terrible as this, she found herself relaxed and enjoying herself—maybe even more than she would at home, since she had such a breathtaking view to keep her company.

Rubbing the spot on her neck where, just the night before, a needle had punctured her skin, Violet thought about the events that had taken place. She didn't remember much—not even if the needle had hurt—but she very vividly remembered waking up in this room the previous night. She remembered Leroy—or Jeremy, whoever—and she'd watched him very closely. Her mother had thought she was still under the effects of the anesthetic, but Violet Walker wasn't just the earliest riser *sometimes*—she was the earliest riser *all* the time. She had lain awake undetected, feigning unconsciousness, and she'd seen how violently Jeremy had reacted when the older man, Holloway, had suddenly appeared in the room.

Violet had known precisely the moment when the older man had entered. She had heard the gentle noise of the door swinging open preceding the slight click of the lock. Violet didn't have particularly keen hearing, yet she'd easily heard Holloway enter so she figured Jeremy's ears must not work so well. She remembered her Dad telling her that sometimes people went sort-of deaf from shooting so many guns without wearing ear protection—and she had spied a gun beneath Jeremy's jacket when he came close—so she assumed that he was very violent, and that he had used a gun many times.

Jeremy's startled reaction to Holloway's not-so-stealthy entry said something very specific to Violet. Well beyond her years, Violet understood the intricacies of intimidation. She knew all about her Dad's work—he had always answered her questions with the unabridged truth—as well as the kind of people he dealt with, and she could tell when someone felt threatened by another person.

She knew that her Dad was coming for them, but she was always making contingency plans—it was part of who she was and how she was raised. Her Dad had always told her that there was nothing you couldn't accomplish with the right amount of brainpower. She had taken this advice to heart, memorizing the details of everything, everywhere, all the time—no matter how obscure—because more often than not, the smallest details were the ones that made the biggest difference. Violet thanked God that she had such a smart Dad.

After a few minutes of mindlessly relaxing and staring at the place she loved so intensely, she began to think about home. She didn't think of it in that melancholy 'I'll never see home again' type of way, but in that she missed certain things about the place. This ultimately led her to thinking about Zeus.

Oh, how she missed the great and powerful Zeus. Aside from Katie, Zeus was Violet's best friend. She could always count on the big, beautiful German shepherd to be there for her, no matter what. Zeus, Violet and Katie were a team, and they could never be stopped as long as they were together. She wished that she had Zeus with her now. He would tear the bad guys apart in a flash and still find time for one of his beloved handshakes.

Violet figured that her situation wasn't too different from that of her beloved Zeus. Both were held captive—though neither of them in a terrible place—and neither of them could be free without the help of their Dad. She couldn't wait until he came for her.

A noise from the downstairs bedroom caught Violet's attention and she realized that she'd sat for almost a half-hour, thinking about things while zoning out and staring at the Magic Kingdom. She didn't look behind her, but she sensed a presence—light footfalls on the wooden floor and then eventually on the rug. She recognized the timing and gait as that of her other best friend and partner in crime.

"Morning, Vi," Katie said with a yawn, settling into the other chair.

"Morning, Kay," Violet replied, smiling at her sister.

"How long have you been up?" Katie asked.

"Not long. I've just been thinking about stuff."

"What sort of stuff?" Katie asked.

Not yet ready to talk about the situation with Katie, Violet decided to steer the conversation in a different direction.

"There's more Dr Pepper in the fridge," she said, motioning to her can on the table between them.

"It's never too early for Doctor P," stated Katie, lightly making her way to the fridge and grabbing herself a can. Returning to the chair and opening the can, she pressed the issue again. "What sort of stuff?"

Violet gave in. "Just…everything. I'm worried about Mom. She's really scared."

"There's gotta be something we can do," Katie offered.

"That's what I've been thinking about. I noticed some things. Things about the guy who faked being a worker at the aquarium," Violet stated.

"He limps, but tries to pretend he doesn't," Katie proclaimed, adding to Violet's mental databank.

"And he has bad hearing," Violet agreed. "He didn't hear when the old guy came in."

"I know, even *I* heard when the old guy came in," Katie laughed a little.

"Wait—you weren't asleep either?" Violet asked, incredulously.

"No, I was already awake for a little while. I just acted like I wasn't 'cause Mommy was crying."

Violet smiled, full of pride. Her sister was just as crafty as she was, and she'd never loved a person more.

"Is Mom still asleep?" she asked.

"Yeah, I snuck out of there. She looked real tired. I didn't want to wake her up. What now?"

"Well…" Violet began, thinking deeply before finally making a decision. "For now, we just have to wait. You heard what the old guy said; if we leave, he hurts Daddy. So until we know for sure that Daddy will be okay, we can't do anything."

"Okay," Katie agreed.

Never ones to sit idly, the girls immediately searched for some way to occupy their time—some new scheme for nothing but entertainment value and a little bit of personal gain. Violet and Katie were *never* above a little bit of personal gain.

"I'm hungry," Violet proclaimed, standing up from her chair. "Are you hungry?"

"I'm *starving*," Katie admitted.

Violet had an idea—an *excellent* idea. She quickly located a room service menu. Luckily, it had the room number printed on it so she wouldn't have to risk going outside to find out. After heading upstairs with Katie in tow, the girls sat on a bed in one of the bedrooms and Violet picked up the phone and dialed the number that she found on the menu for the room service people.

"Hi," she said, cheerfully. "I'd like to order some food. Charge it all to the room, please."

Violet and Katie may not yet be able to defeat the bad guys, but that wasn't going to stop them from *royally* pissing them off. Violet ordered almost everything on the menu.

Then, being a virtuous and benevolent soul, she added a one-hundred percent tip to the bill.

17

Jeremy was briefing Eduardo near the front of the park, when suddenly he received a strange, hurried call from Holloway. He hadn't expected the old man to call for at least an hour. *Something must be wrong,* he thought.

"Jeremy, listen to me closely. Scrap everything for the day. Circumstances have changed," Holloway ordered, almost frantically.

"Everything? What do you mean? What's changed?" Jeremy asked, sensing a strange and unfamiliar emotion coloring his employer's words. Was it fear?

"I tire of these games. This place is far too cheerful. It grates on my nerves. This detective is not worth our time. I was wrong in my initial evaluation. I am ready to leave. I'm forwarding a new plan to your PDA. Set it up, make sure it is executed and then regroup with me and we will leave—sans one worthless detective and his far-too-optimistic and aggravating family. These Walker ladies are proving to be more trouble than they are worth."

Jeremy thought he heard the elderly man sigh. How strange that he would be this off-put by them so shortly after defending them against Jeremy the previous night.

"What are you trying to say, boss—are you giving up?" Jeremy asked, confused as to why they needed to change a perfectly good, ingenious trial in favor of something new—Jeremy hadn't even known there *was* an alternative trial until now. Many months of meticulous planning and deep research had gone into this operation; Holloway *never* made incorrect evaluations, especially after so much work gathering data on a target. Jeremy's mind began to race with possibilities, sure that Holloway wasn't being straight with him.

"I am not *giving up*, Jeremy! I am trying to say that, this time, it's a no go. I was wrong about this detective. He is unworthy. He has no chance. He will most certainly fail—I have no doubt. Therefore, we are wasting our time here and I cannot stand to be in this horrid place for another minute."

Jeremy knew, right then, that something was absolutely wrong. In no conceivable way had their research, planning or experience ever once implied that this detective was unworthy. He seemed the complete opposite—Jeremy had never seen a challenger quite like him.

"Then why change anything at all?" Jeremy asked, testing the waters. "*Let him fail. This plan is flawless.*"

"When I give you an order, Jeremy, you carry it out—regardless of whether you *agree* with it or not!" Holloway nearly yelled the last part, giving Jeremy further evidence that something had gone wrong with their plan. It seemed Holloway was attempting to end this quickly and make a hasty exit for some reason that he wasn't apt to share.

"Fine," Jeremy agreed, grudgingly. "Why don't I just take care of this asshole and then we can get out of here? I can take him out in fifteen minutes. We can be at the airport by one."

"We can't simply kill him ourselves. It is not how we operate. He must fail the trials. This is how it has always been and will remain to be. The document should now be in your email. Check it, execute it, and call me when it's done."

With that, Holloway severed the connection, leaving Jeremy alone with his thoughts.

§

Who the fuck does Spencer Holloway think he is? Jeremy thought, making his way toward the Hub, dodging numerous guests as he picked his way down Main Street. Jeremy stewed over this new development and the resulting conversation. What could Holloway have been thinking? What could possibly have gone wrong? Sure, Jeremy was hired muscle, but he wasn't *brainless*. Did Holloway think of himself as some sort of king? Sure, the guy was smart and filthy fucking rich, but he was still a human being and Jeremy fumed over the way he'd been repeatedly talked down to.

Sometimes it seemed as if Holloway had forgotten that Jeremy could think for himself. He couldn't seem to remember that Jeremy was a sentient being and thought of him as a tool, most times treating him as such. Usually, it was a simple case of Holloway looking down on Jeremy and sending him on menial tasks. This was one of those occasions, but the implications of his employer's current lapse in judgment seemed direr than ever before. Jeremy thought that he had heard the haunting tinge of fear somewhere in the old man's venomous words, but what could have scared Spencer Holloway enough to have made him act so rashly?

It didn't take Jeremy long to realize that only one thing could strike any amount of fear into Spencer Holloway—defeat. Never had Jeremy seen the old man lose at anything. The aging genius had always emerged victorious— and not just by a fraction. Spencer Holloway utterly *destroyed* all opponents. Not satisfied with simply winning, he *ruined* these poor souls, eventually allowing them to die by their own hand during one of the trials—but not before fully realizing that they were inferior to Holloway in every way. Could Holloway be afraid that the detective was going to beat him?

The entire time that Jeremy had worked for Holloway, he'd known not only that the old bastard was out of his mind and *beyond* super-genius, but also that he was bat-shit crazy. The guy spent obscene amounts of money challenging really smart people to ridiculous trials—sometimes against their will. The craziest part about it all was that the old man wasn't setting up these challenges for entertainment; he was actively looking for someone to *beat* him.

Initially, it had seemed to Jeremy that Holloway thought he was some sort of god and that he searched for these challengers in a "nobody could possibly defeat me" vulgar display of power. Recently, that line of thinking had begun to change as he'd watched Holloway while various people passed their early trials—he had seemed genuinely happy for these people. Still, everybody eventually failed and the old man seemed to glean just as much joy from their failures as their successes. All of these occurrences had compounded themselves inside Jeremy's mind, never quite allowing him to get a clear picture of who his boss really was.

Maybe that's what crazy really means, he thought. *You can usually understand a person after watching them for long enough, but maybe the crazy people are the ones who can never be understood, because something inside them is broken and there is no sense to be found.*

Jeremy had always had a strange feeling that once a challenger finally beat Holloway, his life would be forfeit—as though the old man wouldn't be able to carry on after such a monumental defeat. Could it be possible that

Holloway sensed the end nearing and feared his inevitable downfall, even though he'd been searching for it for so long? Jeremy had always found it ridiculous and pointless how the old man had challenged so many people searching for the one person could *beat* him. Regardless, he had kept his mouth shut because he enjoyed the work and he was paid more than enough money to put those concerns well out of his mind. He'd always known that Holloway couldn't possibly win forever and he'd wondered what it would be like when the old man finally met his match.

Jeremy thought back to the previous day, when he'd come face-to-face with Detective Charlie Walker in Epcot's aquarium. He had evaluated the detective upon first glance and was surprised that he'd found the man to be more impressive than any specimen that Holloway had pitted him against in the past. Walker was athletically built, clearly strong, but not massive or overtly muscular. Jeremy had been confident that he could easily best the detective in a physical confrontation. Strangely, this thought did not reassure him as thoroughly as it should have, for Jeremy had learned the value of a cunning mind.

There was something else about the young officer that was unsettling to Jeremy and he'd been unable to shake the feeling or to identify it entirely. The detective had a relaxed yet calculating stare that unnerved him, almost as if he could see deep inside someone with ease and read their thoughts like a book. Jeremy had seen the detective give *him* the once-over and was sure that the man had learned a great many details that weren't readily apparent to Jeremy himself. There was a confidence in the way the detective stood and spoke— shoulders back, hands held in loose fists at his sides, words deliberate and clear—that made Jeremy feel like a smaller man. Jeremy was never uneasy around Holloway's targets, but for the first time, he felt his usual confidence waning when Walker had been near.

It was simple enough for Jeremy to see why Holloway had feared the detective—if that was indeed the case. Jeremy, while not feeling *physically* threatened by Walker, felt apprehension at the thought of having him as an adversary. He was most definitely intimidating, especially to someone in Jeremy's field of work. Couple this with the young detective's legendary track record as an absolute bloodhound and you had the real-world equivalent of a superhero. This was definitely Holloway's most capable and worthy opponent to date. There could be no doubt about that.

Jeremy was enraged. Holloway had turned into a coward precisely when he had found a challenger worthy of him. He was sure that whatever new plan Holloway had sent to his PDA was an unwinnable, impossible scenario—a trap that would give Walker the illusion of hope where there was none and then it would kill him. He opened the email application and deleted the message from Holloway without reading it.

In the past, the old man had had a few close calls with challengers and Jeremy had decided that if the outlook ever seemed too grim for his boss, he would intervene and make damned sure that Holloway emerged victorious.

What if the detective somehow found a way to pass the impossible test? What then? Did they simply flee for their lives and hope he never tracked them down? No, Walker and his family knew names. They knew faces. There was no way Jeremy could leave this to chance. There wasn't an opportunity to cut their losses and run if Holloway's new plan fell through. Jeremy would be damned if he let Charlie Walker put down *two* Holloways in his lifetime.

Fuck that.

Jeremy decided to take matters into his own hands, as he'd imagined so many times in the past that he would one day be forced to do. He felt the comforting weight of the suppressed .22 caliber pistol in the shoulder-rig under his arm, beneath his hooded sweatshirt. This weapon's suppressed report was no louder than a small balloon pop and was more than deadly enough in the close quarters in which Jeremy did most of his wetwork. A pair of .22 caliber rounds fired with Jeremy's surgically precise aim into the back of Walker's head at close range would finish the detective off as effectively as a shotgun slug.

Jeremy had lost sight of the detective nearly an hour earlier in Tomorrowland—leaving while Walker had been sitting on a bench, texting—and had made his way to the front of the park before the call had come in. Now, Jeremy intended to reacquire a visual on Walker, tail him until he made his way into any secluded area, eliminate him quickly and quietly, and make a swift exit before anyone could be the wiser.

Using a GPS tracker, he followed a small beacon marking the location of Walker's Blackberry. Eventually, he stopped outside a place called Casey's Corner at the end of Main Street and leaned against a pillar. The GPS indicated that the detective was inside an ice cream shop across the street. Jeremy finally laid eyes on Walker as he exited the building. Jeremy watched from fifty yards as Walker stepped aside and held the door open, allowing an attractive, dark-haired woman in an out-of-place canvas jacket to exit. She turned to face Walker and said a few words—most likely thanking him for holding the door.

What the hell's with the coat? Jeremy thought. *It's like ninety out here. Whatever.*

He never thought about the woman again after she disappeared into the crowd and his view of her ass had been interrupted.

For a while, Jeremy tailed Walker, eventually ending up near a restroom in Tomorrowland. To Jeremy's surprise, no guests were milling about outside the facility for at least thirty yards. The detective entered the restroom calmly, casually and without looking back—he suspected nothing. Jeremy laughed aloud at his good fortune. This was turning out to be one of the easiest hits he'd ever performed. The detective had actually *cornered* himself in a secluded area of the park that was devoid of people. It was as perfect a location as he could ever hope to find.

Jeremy waited for a few moments to give Walker time to start doing his business before he made his move, making it that much easier to catch him off guard. To pass the time, he thought about Walker's unreasonably beautiful wife and the things he would do to her before putting a bullet in her head, followed by those two know-it-all brats of theirs. He smiled, thinking about how fantastic a day he was about to have. First, he'd execute a famous detective in The Most Magical Place on Earth and then he'd have his way with the detective's Victoria's Secret model wife, kill her and then fly off into the sunset on Holloway's private jet.

Where Dreams Come True, indeed.

He shoved those glorious thoughts aside and placed his hand on the custom ivory grip of his weapon as he made his way toward the restroom, preparing to do what he did best. He quietly yet casually made his way into the opening of the restroom, not bothering to remove his sunglasses as he stepped fully into the well-lit area near the sinks.

Unexpectedly and seemingly out of nowhere, a rock-solid fist crashed into the center of his face with devastating force, shattering his sunglasses, crushing the cartilage in his nose and lifting him off his feet. The last thing Jeremy saw as he fell, through the shards of broken polarized glass and copious amounts of his own blood, was the face of Detective Charlie Walker staring down at him.

Then his head smacked against the floor with a sickeningly wet *thud* and the world went dark.

18

Charlie's right fist throbbed with intense pain worse than ever before, threatening to go numb. He'd been in some world-class scuffles, especially being a member of Murder City's brave men and women in blue, but never before had he landed a haymaker with such destructive power in his entire life. He picked a small shard of glass from the skin between two knuckles as he looked down upon the unconscious body of his bloodied and broken victim.

Leroy—or Jeremy, as Charlie had recently learned the man's actual name was —laid flat out on the floor, blood from his ruined nose pooling in the bottom of his eye sockets. Inspecting the man's face more closely, Charlie learned how devastating his punch had actually been. Not only had the man's sunglasses and nose been shattered, but his left cheekbone was also misshapen—crushed beneath the force of the powerful blow. Charlie could already see the shape of a bruise starting to spread outward from the epicenter of the savage impact to the further regions of his face. He was willing to bet that this was the worst shiner that Jeremy had ever received and almost laughed at the thought. The man would live, but his face would be disfigured forever without some top-notch reconstructive surgery.

After shaking the pins and needles out of his hand and giving it a few flexes to make sure he hadn't broken a finger, Charlie grabbed the big, unconscious man by his shirt and quickly dragged him into the large handicap-accessible stall. He patted the man down, finding and removing a small-caliber, ivory-handled chrome pistol outfitted with a suppressor and relieved him of it. Jeremy also carried with him a flat-black, razor-sharp, out-the-front switchblade knife called a Microtech Halo. The ridiculously expensive knife was illegal to purchase by all but law enforcement and military personnel, but was commonly found on wealthier criminals and other less-than-savory types. He also located the man's phone, taking that as well. Charlie searched, but could find no wallet or ID, only a sizable wad of cash, which he left in the man's pocket.

Leaving the unconscious man on the floor near the toilet, he grabbed some paper towels and quickly began to clean the floor of any blood.

As he scrubbed the tiles, Charlie thought back to the strange and unexpected yet welcome turn that his day had taken.

§

Just minutes after his text conversation with Holloway had ended and he'd begun his trek to find Eduardo, he was intercepted by a pretty woman who appeared to be the same age as him. She was dressed in dark skinny jeans, a thin gray tank top and a fitted olive drab canvas jacket that had no place in this type of heat. Being no stranger to plainclothes officers carrying weapons, Charlie instantly recognized the telltale bulge beneath the woman's left arm. Her raven hair was pulled into a tight ponytail leaving loose only some short bangs that were swept across her forehead. Her voice was like velvet when she spoke to him and something about her ice gray eyes struck him as achingly familiar, yet he couldn't quite put his finger on exactly what.

"Charlie Walker?" she asked, quietly—so quietly that he almost didn't hear her.

"Yes," he replied, apprehensive.

"Do you have a moment to talk?"

"Not really," he admitted. "I'm kind of in the middle of—"

"This concerns your current situation, friend. I'm here to help, and I've got some *seriously* vital info that you should know. Do you have a moment to talk *now?*"

Hearing this, Charlie had instantly nodded his assent and eagerly followed this strange woman into the gloriously air-conditioned yet frantically crowded Plaza Ice Cream Parlor. Somehow, a spot of real estate near the window was mysteriously vacant—even though every other conceivable place in the building was swarming with vacationers. It was to this space that they made their way.

Standing, surrounded by the cacophony of a hundred noisy guests, Charlie was the first to speak. "Who the hell are you?" he asked, bluntly.

Her reply was equally blunt, and exceptionally shocking. "My name is Victoria Holloway, and I'm a Senior Field Agent with the CIA."

Charlie laughed aloud, drawing a few odd glances from bystanders but the woman withdrew a credential case from her jacket and presented him with her identification. Sure enough, her Central Intelligence Agency ID confirmed that she was indeed Victoria Holloway. Charlie looked from the ID to Victoria and back again, completely dumbfounded. Now he understood what was so familiar about those eyes—they were the icy eyes of both Spencer and James Holloway. Could it be true that Holloway had a daughter?

"What the fuck?" he breathed in a whisper, unable to form a coherent sentence.

"Let me explain—don't speak, just listen, okay? You're a really bright guy, Charlie, so I'll just assume that you have already figured out who I am. I'm not here to hurt you or your family—the opposite, actually—but yes, I *am* Spencer Holloway's daughter. James Holloway was my twin brother."

She spoke matter-of-factly, but it wasn't in a rude or unfriendly way. Her voice was edgy yet smooth, warm and almost sarcastic in a way that was not at all characteristic of how one would assume a CIA Senior Field Agent would sound. Her large, bright eyes radiated warmth as she spoke and Charlie felt a strange trust brewing, even though she was the kin of the two most terrible criminals he'd ever encountered. Her mannerisms, dress, style and speech all bespoke an air of youth and intelligence that Charlie found intriguing. She called him Charlie, which was a refreshing respite from all of the "Detectives" and "Walkers" he had experienced as of late. First impression: he liked this woman.

"I'm sorry—" Charlie began, but he was interrupted.

"Don't you *dare* apologize, Charlie," she warned in that playful, mock-angry way that old friends did when ribbing one another. Then her tone became a fraction more serious. "We were given up for adoption as infants.

I never knew James. We grew up in separate homes. I only learned of his whereabouts after his first publicized killing in Detroit. When you killed him, it was a relief. I'd have done it myself if I'd gotten the chance. So if you want to be sorry about anything, be sorry that you robbed me of the chance to pull the trigger."

"I—"

"Don't speak, Charlie—just listen. Remember?" She winked. "Neither one of us has much time. Now, for years I have been tracking my father using the agency's resources and for years I hadn't been able to locate him in time to prevent any of his ridiculous murders—hadn't been able to locate him at all, if we're splitting hairs. I've only been able to learn where he's *been,* never where he *is.* He has killed *many* people with his clever traps and games or trials or whatever the hell else he calls his sick perversions. And I always seem to be one or two huge steps behind the old bastard.

"Anyway, to make a long story short, I found that a few federal files had been accessed remotely—files concerning the events in Detroit surrounding my dear brother's killing spree. Files were also accessed concerning *you.* The intruders accessed everything they could find about you—even from as far back as your early days in the academy. Whoever broke into our system was good, but not good enough—and someone from Dad's organization should never have fucked with our system. Still, it was ballsy and they got their data. Anyway, they tried to rewrite the software to disguise its intrusion, but it was detected during the attempt and traced by our cybercrimes unit. Can you guess where the trace led?"

"Um, I—" Charlie started.

"It doesn't even matter. It was a dead end like most of these things turn out to be," she shot back with a little laugh. "What matters is that it was an *exact* match for an old rerouting path that my old man had used on several previous digital invasions. It was *that* easy to learn that he was researching you, and I already knew why. So then, naturally, I researched you. Found out who you really were and learned what it was that my father must have learned."

"And what was that?" Charlie asked, finally able to speak a full sentence, but bracing himself for the inevitable interruption during all four words.

"That you're a goddamned genius, man!" Victoria exclaimed, loud enough to draw a few glances from the guests in line for ice cream. This woman spoke so fast and fluidly, and with such enthusiasm, that Charlie was enraptured by her, powerless to do anything but listen to every word she said. "I saw exactly why he chose you, and because you were still *alive* I knew that I had found you in time to prevent whatever the old man had planned. Finally! Finally I had found one of his victims *before* he made his move. Finally I'd gotten the chance to intervene and prevent disaster." Suddenly, her enthusiasm drained from her body and her wide bright eyes became very sad. "But then I messed up."

"How?" he asked.

"I was stupid—*so* fucking stupid, Charlie. I learned of your vacation and I assumed that dear old Dad would wait to hit you until *after* you got back. Boy, was I wrong. It's just like him to go after you in broad daylight in one of the most heavily-crowded vacation spots in the country. I should have known!" Her fist pounded lightly against the window and it was clear she was genuinely frustrated. Deep worry lines appeared around her eyes and mouth, and she turned away from Charlie for a few moments.

"You couldn't have known," Charlie said. "Nobody could have figured out that he would do something like this."

"I'll bet *you* could have," she stated. Charlie searched her face and tone for signs of spite or sarcasm, but she was entirely serious. She'd researched his work; she was an admirer.

Charlie became mildly self-conscious. He reached out and put his hand gently on Victoria's arm.

"Victoria," he said gently. "We both know that's not true. If I could have figured it out, we wouldn't be having this conversation."

"You're being unreasonably hard on yourself," she said with none of her usual feistiness. "Let's just agree that neither of us could have prevented this. But we're both here now, and we have a chance to do something about it. We *will* get your family back, I promise—but something has changed," she admitted, not able to meet his eyes.

"What do you mean?"

"Charlie, my Dad isn't planning to give you a chance to win your family back anymore. He's going to kill you."

This news was disheartening, but Victoria proceeded to fill him in on everything she knew—then the glimmer of hope slowly began to reignite itself deep within him. She was able to learn that her father was in Walt

Disney World; security cameras had captured one of his men's images and facial recognition software had sent up a red flag. So, with this knowledge in hand, she convinced her superiors to authorize the use of a company bird to fly them down to Orlando International Airport as soon as possible. She and her team had only arrived a few hours ago, but they'd already made staggering progress in piecing together the scenario.

Charlie was impressed by everything that she'd achieved in such a short amount of time. She had amassed a great deal of useful intel on her father and his confederates, and had already learned key details about their plans.

"As far as my team was able to learn, my old man's here with a skeleton crew. He has approximately ten hired hands with him, including his right-hand man, Jeremy O'Neill, and any Cast Members he may have been able to bribe or blackmail. This Jeremy asshole is a special case. He's a ruthless bastard, convicted rapist and remorseless killer—at least seven deaths in the last three years are thanks to him, and one of them was someone close to a member of my team. Jeremy's a muscular guy, walks with a bit of a limp, scar on his face. You'll know him when you see him. He is not to be underestimated," she informed him. "But…if he somehow doesn't happen to come out of this alive, nobody in Langley will shed any tears."

"I think he and I have met," Charlie said, his suspicions confirmed about 'Leroy.' "I found him speaking to my wife yesterday at EPCOT Center dressed as a Cast Member, but I didn't really buy it. Does he have tattoos on his knuckles?"

"That's the guy. I'd have nailed him long ago for all those murders but he's as much of a ghost as my Dad. They've always been together, and always been invisible—until now."

"How can I find them?" Charlie asked, intensely.

"You can start by looking out the window," she offered, nodding her head toward the glass.

Sure enough, across the street, leaning against a pillar outside Casey's Corner, stood Leroy, AKA Jeremy O'Neill. Charlie watched him intently as he looked down at a phone screen in his hand and then across at the ice cream parlor. Charlie was sure Jeremy couldn't see them through the crowds, but he still felt uncomfortable.

"He's got you tracked," Victoria informed him. "The bug is in that phone you've got. About an hour and a half ago, one of my guys got close enough to the big dummy to run a scanner. The device scans for the SIM card in a phone, transmits the information to the Company's nerds and gives us the information we need to tap the line. We listened in to a conversation earlier between Jeremy and my Dad. Something's got the old man spooked and he's ready to cut and run—I'm thinking that you've got him worried. Whatever he originally had planned for you has been eighty-sixed and he sent that big idiot out there something new in an email.

"We've got a shiny, new spy satellite floating overhead sporting one of those fancy super-cameras that all the conspiracy-theory nuts freak out about on internet forums. It's currently watching old Jeremy and recording every move he makes. Not long ago, it watched as he deleted my Dad's email without even opening it. Yeah, the camera is *that* good," she said, noting Charlie's bewildered expression.

"I can guarantee you that hothead Jeremy has decided to take matters into his own hands and eliminate you himself," she stated. "Right now, he's wiping his ass with hundred-dollar bills and never wearing the same pair of boxers twice. If you take out my Dad, Jeremy's out of a job—and I can assure you that high-class hitboys do not qualify for unemployment or student aid for trade schools." She let that hang in the air while Charlie thought the matter over.

"I've got to get him first," Charlie deduced.

"Bingo," she said with a snap of her fingers. "And we're here to help you. This is what my boys and I do best and I've got an idea that just might work."

In as few words as possible, Victoria laid out her idea. She told Charlie that the assassin would most likely follow him until he made his way to a relatively secluded area. This being a ridiculously busy day in the parks, Jeremy may never have gotten the chance to find an opportune area—and that was, as far as Victoria's plan was concerned, *not* a good thing. Victoria explained that her team was already at work clearing the area in and around the restrooms near the Carousel of Progress. They would be able to confidently keep the area clear for a half-hour in conjunction with trusted park management and maintenance personnel. The plan, as it stood, was to have Charlie use himself as bait and enter the area with Jeremy hot on his heels. Once inside the restroom, Charlie would get the drop on Jeremy, overpower him and apprehend him. He would then have just over twenty minutes to extract the information he needed from Jeremy and make his exit to meet with Victoria and her team to formulate the next stage of their plan based on the information he was able to gather.

"Do you think you'll be capable of handling Jeremy alone?" Victoria asked, visibly concerned for Charlie's wellbeing.

"There's no doubt in my mind," Charlie reassured her confidently. While not the biggest man in the world, Charlie was in excellent shape. He was fit, athletic and highly trained. Alongside his hand-to-hand training in the academy, he was an eight-year veteran of Krav Maga training: a visceral, brutal and extremely effective form of tactical-defense street-fighting originally used by the Israeli Defense Forces. This hybrid style of martial arts is the polar opposite of honorable combat and would never be considered fair. There was only one object: to disable and obliterate your opponent quickly and efficiently before they found an opportunity to do the same to you. Krav Maga awards the deciding advantage to anyone who practices it, rather than the biggest and the strongest. With this knowledge at hand, and the rage he felt toward this man for abducting his family, Charlie knew there was no possible way he could lose.

"Good," she said, handing him a set of nylon riot cuffs and a small syringe, both of which he pocketed. "Because, unfortunately, none of my team can be with you. They need to remain anonymous to him. If Jeremy gets away, he can't see their faces or my Dad will execute your family. He has to believe that you are still working alone and that you don't know what he's up to. He's smart, so there's no way in hell he will kill your family unless he's absolutely sure that you're dead.

"That being said, once you've learned all you can, stick this syringe in his neck and give him the full dose. It's a fast-acting but short-lasting tranquilizer. Once you've got Jeremy knocked out, step outside for exactly four seconds and dry your hands with a paper towel. Do *not* forget the paper towel—that is the go-code. If you do anything other than come out with a paper towel, we'll know something is wrong and will take appropriate measures. Got it?"

"Absolutely."

"Good. Charlie, you'll see your girls again. My guys are the best and I'm even better. We're here for no other reason than to make sure that you and your ladies get back to Detroit safe and happy. I give you my word as an agent of the United States government and—more importantly—my word as a human being, and one of the good guys, that we'll get your family back."

"Thank you, Victoria," Charlie said, nearly at a loss for words. He was stunned that the daughter of his enemy was so passionate about helping him. It was almost overwhelming.

"This is the part where I'm supposed to tell you that I'm just doing my job," she said, eyes downcast. "But I can't. It's personal. The fact that the country is safer because we take out the bad guy is just a bonus."

"I understand," Charlie told her. "Listen, Victoria. Even though your Dad and your brother are straight out of hell, you've got a lot of good in you—and I trust you."

Her glossy eyes stared into his as if what he'd said had meant more than he ever could have known. She was clearly haunted and damaged by her birth family being full of monsters.

"I'm a hell of a judge of character," Charlie stated. "And I give you *my* word that you've got my trust, no matter what your last name is. Actions are a result of choices, not a result of heritage."

Then, a tear appeared in the corner of one of her eyes, but she wiped it away quickly and regained her composure, masking her emotions.

"Thank you, Charlie," she said, offering her hand. Charlie shook it firmly and without hesitation. For better or worse, they were a team.

With a few more words of encouragement, Victoria and Charlie started for the door, each prepared to head their separate ways.

Charlie exited the building first. He held the door for Victoria and she turned to face him.

"Good luck, Charlie. I know it's weird, me being the daughter of the bad guy, but you're right to trust me—and it means a lot to me that you do. I meant what I said—we will win this," she stated warmly and with a bright smile.

Charlie nodded and headed off back toward Tomorrowland.

§

Having mopped up all of Jeremy's blood, Charlie returned to the stall, noticing the unconscious man finally starting to wake up. Charlie stepped over to him and lifted his torso up onto the toilet, positioning him facedown so that his bleeding face dripped into the bowl and his shoulders rested on the seat. Quickly, Charlie secured Jeremy's hands around the back of the toilet with the riot cuffs, tightening them *far* too much—perhaps even cutting off circulation—and not giving a damn about it.

"How...?" Jeremy mumbled as Charlie heard more blood dribble into the toilet.

Charlie drew the silenced pistol and ground the cold chrome suppressor into the back of Jeremy's head.

"Alright, motherfucker. Let's talk," he snarled.

19

The overwhelming smell of delicious food filled the entire suite, pulling Meghan from her wonderfully deep slumber. Hearing the high-pitched *ting* of metal clanking against porcelain and even higher-pitched devilish giggles coming from the other side of her door, Meghan stood with a yawn and a stretch and went to investigate. She didn't even bother herself with the knowledge that her girls were no longer in the room with her. Those diabolical laughs could only mean that her girls had started their schemes early. This came as no surprise.

What did surprise Meghan was the time. It wasn't early at all—it was nearly noon. Had she really slept so long? She checked the bedside clock again, just to make sure she'd seen correctly. Yawning once again, Meghan padded into the massive living room to see what the girls had gotten themselves into this time.

Upon entering the cavernous living space, Meghan was unable to prevent her sudden outburst of laughter. The girls were sitting at the large dining table, flanked by not one, but *four* wheeled carts that were piled high with every manner of edible delicacy imaginable. Her girls had truly outdone themselves this time. They had plates full of a variety of different foods in front of them and they were digging in with reckless abandon.

The smell of all of this food, coupled with daughters shoveling bite after bite into their mouths, reminded Meghan of how hungry she was. She hadn't eaten since lunch the previous afternoon. They'd had dinner at Epcot's Le Cellier, but she had been too distraught to touch her food.

"What have you girls done this time?" Meghan asked.

"Oh," Violet said innocently, swallowing her current mouthful and looking up at her mother. "We got some food. Have some."

"It's good food," Katie assured her, not bothering to look up. "Except for the shrimp. There's like three different kinds of shrimp here." Katie hated shrimp.

"I see that. Thank you for clearing everything up, ladies," she stated, sarcastically. "I suppose I should have asked: *how* did you girls manage this one?"

"Um, remember last year when we were all sick and we had to order room service because we couldn't go out?" Violet asked.

"Yes…"

"Well, I heard Daddy tell them to charge it to the room. I charged this to the room," Violet stated, casually and plainly.

Meghan seated herself at the lead of the table, near her two brilliant, villainous daughters, and grabbed herself a plate.

"They let a seven-year-old charge this much food to the room?" Meghan asked, not believing that it was possible.

"They weren't going to," said Violet.

"Then?" Meghan prodded.

Violet grinned the wicked, lopsided grin that meant she'd recently experienced a stroke of genius. "I told them that my name was Violet Holloway. Then I told them that my Dad said I could order whatever I wanted for my birthday party and charge it to the room. Oh—and I said he couldn't talk because he was in a business meeting."

All Meghan could do was stare at her daughter for several long moments. The girl was an evil genius. This was easily her daughter's grandest plan to date.

"I'm going to let this one slide," she said, shaking her head and smiling, reaching for a Cuban sandwich.

"We figured you would," offered Violet with a little wink. "That old guy paid for the room, so he can pay for this too."

Meghan laughed at the hilariously vindictive nature of her daughters. She'd never seen this side of them before.

"I have never loved you guys more than I do right this moment. I'm *starving*," she stated, and dug into what turned out to be an absolutely amazing Cuban sandwich.

For the next little while, the three Walker women ate in silence, enjoying more food than they'd ever even seen in one place before. Meghan truly felt blessed to have been given the priceless gift of these two little angels—or demons. The situation was unthinkable and the outcome was still uncertain, but—even so—the girls were unafraid. They were still Violet and Katie Walker, scheming masterminds of the highest order, and they were still able to enjoy themselves—even at the expense of their captor. The deep fear that Meghan had been feeling all night started to dull to a more manageable level. She could not remain so terrified in the presence of such genuine courage.

Violet spoke up, "When Daddy comes and gets us and the bad guys go to jail, I want to ride Splash Mountain first."

"Are you sure?" Meghan asked. The entire time they'd been in captivity, Meghan had believed that, once this ordeal was over with, they would return home. "You want to *stay* here?"

"Yeah. I mean, all last night and this morning I've been staring out the window, looking at the Magic Kingdom. I really want to ride Splash Mountain. We never got the chance last night."

"You don't want to go home?" Meghan asked, still not certain why Violet would want to remain here after everything that had happened.

"No, this is our vacation," Violet stated, defiantly. "Disney World didn't kidnap us—that old guy and that other big jerk did. It's not Disney World's fault we're here. I've been thinking all morning about how excited I was to go on more rides and how annoyed I am that I have to sit in this room instead—even though it's a *really* cool room."

"Yeah, Mommy. I want to go on the Haunted Mansion. We didn't get to do that yet, either," Katie added.

"Or the new *Little Mermaid* ride; we've never been on that," Violet supplied. "It's brand spankin'."

"And I haven't even had a turkey leg yet," stated Katie, matter-of-factly. "*And* we haven't even been to Animal Kingdom this year."

Meghan was speechless. Her daughters were, quite possibly, the strongest people she'd ever known. After all the terrible things that had occurred—that may *still* occur—Violet and Katie were only frustrated that their vacation had been interrupted. It was almost supernaturally mature of Violet to dissociate the events that had happened with the place. This told Meghan two things: that her girls were stronger than she'd given them credit for and that their faith in Charlie's ability to rescue them was absolute.

She thought about her husband and the situation that they were in. It was a live-action Disney story for the ages. If ever there were a hero capable of saving the day, it was Charlie Walker. Meghan and the girls were in a real-life damsels-in-distress scenario, complete with an actual villain and an honest-to-God tower in which they were held captive. Charlie was the valiant prince, fighting against all odds to rescue the princesses. Meghan knew, in her heart-of-hearts, that Charlie would stop at nothing to save them.

"You girls have a deal," Meghan announced, her strength bolstered for the second time in as many minutes. "When we get out of here, Splash Mountain it is. Then the Haunted Mansion and the Little Mermaid. And—if we're not still stuffed from this feast—it'll be turkey leg time and then off to Animal Kingdom. You have Mom's solemn promise."

The girls cheered enthusiastically between bites of food and sips of Dr Pepper.

"Well, I definitely need a shower," Meghan said, finishing her sandwich. "Will you girls be okay by yourselves for a few minutes?"

Violet stopped chewing and made an overly dramatic show of looking around at all of the carts of food. "Oh, I think we can handle it," she stated. Meghan laughed and stood. Now came the tough decision.

Which of the four bathrooms should she choose?

20

Blood dripped steadily into the toilet, rhythmically alternating between hitting porcelain and water. Pain dominated Jeremy's world. Stars danced in the periphery of his vision. Nausea overwhelmed him. And there was something else too. The left side of his face felt unnaturally tight and hot.

Still, Jeremy O'Neill shows weakness to no man.

Defiantly, he spat a sizable amount of bloody saliva into the water that was inches from his face.

"You hit like a bitch. That all you got, Walker?" he challenged, though his words were hard to form and his mouth difficult to move.

"We'll see," came the calm and measured reply from the man he couldn't see. He felt the cold steel barrel of a suppressed pistol digging hard into his scalp. Son of a bitch.

"Well," Jeremy began, "we've both got things to do. So why don't you just tell me what it is you want so we can both head our separate ways?"

"What I want," Walker paused for dramatic effect, "is my family back. But that's not why you and I are here."

"Then why are we here?"

"You were going to kill me just now, Jeremy. I want to know why?"

Somehow, Walker had learned his real name. Jeremy couldn't understand how he could have possibly come across that information, since he carried no identification of any kind and his phone held no clues as to his identity. Walker definitely had something up his sleeve, but Jeremy hadn't yet decided whether that should worry him or not.

"Can't a guy just take a piss without this kind of harassment?"

"Don't bullshit me. You follow me in here, carrying this serious hardware—this can't be a coincidence. So let me ask you again: why are you here to kill me? Did Holloway send you?"

"I don't know what you're talking about," Jeremy lied, hoping it would piss off the detective. "I just had a few too many Dole Whips this morning and I—"

Jeremy froze as he heard the sound of his own knife opening—that telltale, solid *clack* of the wickedly sharp blade snapping into position.

"Okay," was all Walker said before Jeremy felt the barrel of the pistol pull away from his head. He heard Walker moving around, but was stuck in a position where he couldn't see anything. Could Walker really be that crazy? Would he truly torture a man in a public restroom? Jeremy had no idea. He had no family—nobody that he cared for more than himself. Suddenly, the feared killer became fully aware that he had no idea to what lengths a normal man could be pushed in order to save the ones he loved. He felt the first pangs of fear surge through him.

Jeremy had been in many confrontations in his life—more than he could count or even recall. He knew what signs to look for when an opponent was about to attack. He also knew the truth behind most people's misconceptions regarding physical confrontations. You didn't have to worry about the massive, raging, angry guy, stomping around and yelling; they were transparent and predictable. You could read their every intention like a picture book and act accordingly. The ones you had to worry about were the sleepers. The calm ones were always the most trouble. *Always.* The cool, collected manner in which these unpredictable opponents usually conducted themselves made Jeremy have a healthy and useful respect for their kind. And never before had Jeremy encountered so calm and calculating an individual as Charlie Walker. It was a scary thought, almost as if the mind of Spencer Holloway were placed in the capable body of an athlete—a deadly combination. Jeremy began to sweat. He struggled against his bonds to no avail.

"I'm a good guy, Jeremy," Walker informed him calmly, still moving around unseen. "You can talk to me."

"Fuck you," Jeremy shouted, but with much less conviction than he'd intended. He mentally chided himself for this display of weakness, sure that the detective had picked up on the initial note of fear that had crept into his tone.

Unexpectedly, Jeremy felt the cold steel of the knife pressing against the inside of his wrist. He braced himself for the inevitable. It wasn't the pain that worried him; the knife was so sharp that there would be little or no pain. What worried him was the rapid blood loss and swift death that would surely follow any slash to so vulnerable an area. Instead, he realized that it wasn't the razor-sharp edge of the blade that pressed against his skin, but the flat, blunt side. With one smooth stroke, Walker cut away the nylon riot cuffs that bound him.

With a confident strength, Walker lifted Jeremy to his feet and turned him around, shoving him into a seated position on top of the toilet. His head smacked solidly against the wall but he couldn't feel it. He closed his eyes, feeling instead a grinding sensation beneath his left eye—a feeling of bone grating against bone. *Yep,* he thought, *the fucker broke my cheekbone. Fantastic.*

Opening his eyes weakly, Jeremy got his first real glimpse of Walker. A much different man stood before him than the one he'd seen less than twenty-four hours earlier in the aquarium. This Charlie Walker was much more intimidating than his past self. His unmasked confidence worried Jeremy. The .22 was tucked into the waistband of his shorts, and he stood with his back to Jeremy for a moment, almost as if taunting the beaten man to try his luck at taking the weapon.

When Walker turned around to face Jeremy, he held the Halo in front of him. Instead of impulsively leaping forward and cutting Jeremy's throat, the detective calmly and slowly pulled on the spring-loaded rod that would retract the knife blade. Clicking the safety catch on, Walker stuck the knife in his pocket.

Jeremy didn't want to look into the man's eyes—it was too much for him to bear, and he liked none of what he saw there. The detective was a haunted man. His eyes shone with a darkness and a ferocity that Jeremy had never before seen in anyone. There was pain there, but also hope—and determination. The determination was what worried Jeremy above all else. He knew that Walker would do anything to rescue his family—including carving off parts of Jeremy that he was literally and figuratively attached to. He felt his resolve breaking and he hated himself for it. Walker knelt before him—a better angle for looking Jeremy directly in his eyes.

"What?" Jeremy asked defiantly, even though he felt his walls of rebellion crumbling under Walker's icy stare. He found it hard to hold the detective's gaze.

Walker said nothing; he simply knelt there, staring up into the bigger man's eyes. That worried Jeremy deeply. The tables had turned. He was essentially unarmed, in front of a dangerous prisoner whose bonds he had just cut. Jeremy was free to attack him at any point in time—and Walker didn't seem worried about that one bit. It was either a crazy man or a confident man who could remain in such a position without worry. Jeremy finally knew that the detective was not crazy.

After what seemed like an eternity, the detective spoke.

"Talk to me," he said simply, gently and quietly. No creative threats of violence. No dramatic brandishing of any weapon. No fist crashing into Jeremy's ruined face a second time. Just "Talk to me." It was enough.

And talk he did.

§

Jeremy was ashamed. He had poured out everything that there was to know. The truth was: he was not ready to die. His imagination raced with rational and irrationally creative scenarios, in all of which the detective found some new way of torturing and killing the infamous assassin. Jeremy knew, deep down, that Walker would never do any of these things—he was, like he'd said, a good guy—but something in the man's stare promised possibilities far worse than mere torture and death. It was a hard truth to admit but Jeremy did not want to cross this detective again. His chance of survival greatly increased with absolute compliance, so compliance it was.

He told Walker everything there was to know about Holloway, in as few words as possible. He told him what the original plan was, and that it had been canceled. He told him that he'd ignored the new plan in favor of killing the detective himself, and he also told him his reasons for doing so. Jeremy even went so far as to give Walker his take on the scenario; that he figured Holloway had secretly begun to fear the detective and that he was attempting to cut and run. Most importantly, he told Walker where his family was being held.

"They're in a suite in Bay Lake Tower. Not far from here. You know the place?"

"Well enough," he stated.

Jeremy told Walker the room number.

"But you can't just walk in and get them," he added.

"And why not?"

"Because Holloway has the hotel and its grounds under surveillance by an entire team. If you even so much as ride past in a bus, one of our guys will know and Holloway will kill your family."

"There's no way around this?" Walker asked, the gears clearly turning in his mind.

"None that I know of," Jeremy stated, honestly. "Even *I* couldn't get them out. Holloway's in the room next door. He would kill us all. They're not to leave the room until you either win or lose—well, that *was* the plan, anyway."

"Damn it." Walker shook his head and looked at the floor. "How many men do you have with you? Total."

"Including me and the old man? Fourteen."

"Where are they positioned?"

"He's got four guys in Bay Lake Tower but they're always on the move with no concrete patrol. The rest are somewhere else—and I'm being honest when I tell you that I don't know where. Holloway doesn't tell me and I don't ask."

Jeremy watched as Walker processed this information. He was silent for a few moments, thinking everything over. After a few moments, he reached into his pocket and for a split second Jeremy thought he was going for the knife again. Instead, he held up a silver key.

"What do you know about this?" he asked, his eyes looking up and practically boring holes into Jeremy's.

"Oh, the key…"

Jeremy fidgeted uncomfortably.

"It's to a door in Space Mountain. Holloway mentioned it was his grand finale. What did he mean?"

Jeremy hesitated before answering, trying to decide whether telling Walker the truth or lying to him would upset him more.

"That's part of his final test for you. Or it *was*. I don't know anymore. He's, uh…he's got something planned for tonight."

"What?" Walker prodded, impatiently. "What was this test?"

"He meant to test you with much bigger consequences than just the lives of your family."

"Quit fucking around! Tell me already," Walker demanded, his face suddenly inches away from Jeremy's and his fist knotted into the man's shirt.

Jeremy decided to tell him directly, since there was no sense in sugarcoating it. "He's got a bomb on one of the coaster's structural supports, set to detonate at nine tonight should you fail any of his tests. It's only on one of the tracks, it's not big and the blast itself won't kill anybody."

"So?"

"So, after it goes off, the tracks will separate and point in a new direction."

"And?"

Jeremy sighed, swallowed, his eyes downcast. He couldn't bring himself to face Walker for the next part.

"And the cars on the tracks will fall directly into the queue at the busiest time of the night."

21

This was an entirely new game. Not only did the lives of his family hinge on his success, but now the lives of countless men, women and children would end if he couldn't find a way to prevent this unreal disaster in time. Holloway had changed his plan after implementing the explosive and Charlie had no idea whether he had since disarmed the bomb or simply abandoned it, leaving it to explode when the timer ran out. Hundreds of innocent lives depended on him. He could not fail them.

It took him a few minutes to come to terms with this shocking realization, but finally he stood and checked his watch. He had only a couple of minutes left before he needed to signal Victoria. Quickly, he pulled the syringe from his pocket and turned to face Jeremy.

"I assume you recognize this," he said, showing Jeremy the small instrument; the barrel filled with a dark amber fluid.

Jeremy remained silent, but his eyelids seemed to grow heavy with defeat—he knew that he had no further part to play in this drama. He smiled, sadly.

"It probably looks a lot like the ones you assholes must have used on my wife and daughters last night. Anyway, this one's meant for you. I trust you're not going to fight me on this?"

Jeremy cocked his head to the side to allow Charlie to give him the injection. Wasting no time, Charlie stuck him roughly with the needle and depressed the plunger hard. It must have hurt, but the big man betrayed nothing and within seconds was slumped against the wall.

Quickly, Charlie hurried out of the stall and grabbed a paper towel. Stepping outside, pretending to dry his hands, Charlie hoped that Victoria saw the signal. After a four-count, he returned to the restroom to wait for Victoria's response. While he'd been outside, the area had still been mysteriously clear, but he'd seen nobody preventing guests from entering; they'd simply stayed away. These CIA spooks were scary good. He made a mental note never to underestimate a Company man.

After just a few seconds, Charlie heard heavy footsteps entering the restroom mixed with what sounded like heavy wheels rolling over the tile. When he looked up, he saw a gigantic man of Pacific Island descent wheeling in a large trash cart piled high with black bags. Admittedly, the cart was the most bizarre part of the scene, since you rarely or never saw them in the park due to the underground AVAC trash disposal system.

The man behind the cart was impressive, to say the least. Charlie stood a solid six foot tall, but this man must have been six-five, minimum. He was one of the most heavily muscled people that Charlie had ever seen. He guessed that the man weighed roughly three-hundred pounds—without an ounce of fat. He wore a dark gray T-shirt under a flamboyant green Hawaiian shirt that fit him extremely tightly over his massively muscled arms. Charlie noticed that the shirt was unbuttoned, hanging loose to accommodate his shoulder holster. His arms were almost fully covered by intricate tattoos. When Charlie looked up at his face, though, he saw nothing but kindness and warmth. The man smiled at him from beneath his close-cropped black Mohawk.

"Detective Walker?" he asked, smile plastered on his face.

"That's me. You one of Victoria's guys?"

"Yep. Name's Kalani. Good to meet you, braddah. Heard a lot about you." Kalani offered his hand and Charlie shook it, finding it surprisingly gentle.

"You must be the team's muscle," Charlie implied, jokingly.

"Nah, I'm a scientist. Computers and crap," Kalani shot back, followed by a big, booming laugh. He slapped Charlie on the back and stepped past him, headed for the back of the room. "So where's this big, scary Jeremy *moke*, eh—he somewhere back here?" he asked, pointing toward the handicap stall then quickly poking his head into the others to make sure they were empty.

"Yeah—in the handicap stall," Charlie agreed with a nod, watching the big man struggle to fit into the small space.

"Good God, *haole!* You really fucked this big-timer up, didn't you?" Kalani asked rhetorically, with a sharp whistle of appreciation. He leaned his head out of the stall, "What'd you hit him with, a wooden bat?"

Charlie smirked, holding up his bruised right hand. Kalani's eyes widened and he smiled.

"Much respect for you, braddah. Remind me not to get on your bad side," he offered with another quick flash of a smile, disappearing back into the stall. "Would you mind grabbing those trash bags out of that cart, detective?"

"As long as you promise to call me Charlie from now on."

"You drive a hard bargain, *haole*. But you got a deal," he said, chuckling to himself.

Charlie grabbed the trash bags and threw them on the ground just as Kalani approached, dragging Jeremy's unconscious form by the leg as if he weighed nothing. Kalani leaned over the side of the cart to check that it was empty and, once satisfied, lifted Jeremy like a ragdoll and tossed him haphazardly inside. Without even a second glance at the unconscious man, Kalani started piling the trash bags on top of him. Charlie decided to help.

"So, Charlie, you get some good information out of him?" Kalani asked.

"I got info," he acknowledged. "But none of it is good."

"No worries, braddah. We're going to get your girls back."

"That's the least of our worries right now, Kalani."

"Is it that bad?" asked the big man with genuine concern on his face.

"It's worse," Charlie admitted, truthfully. Kalani lowered his eyes and respectfully decided not to say anything. "So what's the plan? Are we going to meet with Victoria?"

"Yep. My partner, McCoy, is outside. He'll take out the trash while you and I go see Victoria and the rest of X-ray Team."

Charlie nodded. "How many of you are there?" he asked.

"Me, Victoria, McCoy, Mason and Jen-Jen. So, uh...five."

"Thought you were the scientist?" Charlie joked, razzing him on the slow count.

"I do not consider math a science," he stated as he threw the last of the trash bags into the cart.

"Six of us against fourteen of them. I don't like those odds," Charlie told him.

"Six of us equals sixty of them," stated Kalani, confidently. "I love those odds."

Charlie couldn't argue with that logic. If the rest of the team were as capable as Kalani seemed to be—and Victoria definitely was—then Holloway's men had their work cut out.

Charlie followed as Kalani wheeled the large cart out of the restrooms. Guests were beginning to return to the area and it looked as if nothing strange had occurred—as if this piece of Tomorrowland had been vacant merely by chance. It was bizarre, but effective and it spoke to the level of orchestration and skill displayed by Victoria's clandestine unit.

A short, well-built, red-haired man with a thick beard, who was no doubt McCoy, stood just outside the entrance to the restroom. He was dressed similarly to Kalani—unbuttoned shirt, shoulder rig and loose cargo shorts— but his shirt was a more modest dark brown. He nodded to the pair of them and took over the cart without a word, swiftly pushing it away until he rounded a corner and disappeared from view.

"McCoy's a quiet character, eh?" Charlie asked as he walked casually through the park with Kalani.

"He sure don't talk much," Kalani agreed. "But he's a good guy and he's always got my back in a fight."

Just then, a detail struck Charlie that he couldn't help but remark upon.

"Kalani, what if Holloway's got his men in the park watching me?"

"No doubt he does. But it would be hard for them to believe you were getting help from a big-ass Hawaiian scientist like me. I'm just too good looking for them to think I'm anything but a cool cat on vacation. Hell, they can think whatever they want. It doesn't matter."

Charlie laughed at Kalani's jokes, but the thought of being watched as he trudged along with a CIA operative made him uneasy. Still, there was nothing he could do about it, so he shelved the thought and walked on with his new companion. After a while, Charlie found himself following Kalani into the Liberty Tree Tavern.

The restaurant was a colonial-style eatery that reminded Charlie of the Mel Gibson movie *The Patriot*. The atmosphere was quiet and private, and Kalani led him to a table in a dim corner where Victoria sat with two other members of her team. Kalani pulled out a chair and lazily threw himself down before kicking the final chair toward Charlie.

"Take a load off, braddah. Meet the family," he said.

Charlie took his seat and looked around at the others. To the left of Victoria sat a rail-thin man named Mason that had slicked back hair and thick-rimmed glasses of a Hubble telescope prescription. He nodded politely but nervously as he was introduced to Charlie.

On the other side of Victoria sat a woman who looked more like she belonged on a beach volleyball team rather than a highly specialized team of CIA operatives. She was very attractive, with golden blonde hair and a deep almond tan. She was almost the polar opposite of Victoria and her raven black hair and ghostly pale skin. Charlie assumed that this was Jen-Jen.

The blonde offered her hand and Charlie gently shook it. "Jennifer Jennings," she stated. "My parents had a sense of humor. But these idiots call me Jen-Jen, which I guess is okay by me."

"And what should I call you?" Charlie asked, releasing her hand.

"Anything you want…" she replied, alluringly.

"Stow it, Jen-Jen. This one's happily married," Victoria said, backhanding the blonde lightly on the shoulder. Jen-Jen looked mildly disappointed. "So, Charlie, now that you've met my weird little family, we can get to work. What did we learn from Jeremy?"

Kalani cut in, "We learned that this *haole* has one wicked right hook! You should see the other guy. Look at this monster's hand!" He grabbed Charlie's battered right hand from the table and shook it at the rest of his team. Victoria and Mason looked impressed. Jen-Jen looked infatuated. Charlie felt self-conscious.

"Thank you, Kalani, but I meant what did we learn about the situation?" Victoria said, smiling at the massive Hawaiian.

Charlie laughed as he heard Kalani mumble in mock-sadness under his breath, "That *was* part of the situation."

Charlie recounted the conversation he'd had with Jeremy in the restroom, finally revealing the existence of the key and the location of the door that it unlocks. He expected his revelation to be earthshattering, but it surprised no one at the table. Mason even looked a tiny bit excited.

"This doesn't surprise you?" Charlie asked, trying to mask his own emotions so that he wouldn't be the odd man out.

"Bombs never really surprise us," Victoria claimed. "In a post-9/11 world, assholes with bombs are as common as assholes with guns or assholes with knives. We see them all the time. In fact, we see them so much, that Mason's main role is being a walking Bombcyclopedia. He knows all there is to know and if someone can build it, he can disarm it."

That explains why he looks so damn excited by a bomb in a fucking theme park,

Charlie thought. "So what's the plan?" he asked.

"First—give me that key you found."

Charlie took the key out of his pocket and tossed it to Victoria. She caught it and inspected it closely, turning it over in her hands. After a short while, she spoke.

"This key is not for the door you saw in the picture."

"What?"

"Who's the famous super-detective here, you or me?" she joked. "From what you've told me, that door has an exit sign above it—what does that tell us?"

"Damn," Charlie said, recognizing his own ignorance. "It tells us that we're looking at an emergency exit."

"Or a door that *leads* to an emergency," Victoria added. "Which means that, by law, it cannot ever be locked. Therefore, this key belongs to another door—one that no doubt leads to the tracks or somewhere equally vital. Dear old Dad didn't mislead you, but he did rely on you figuring this out at some point."

"I should have known right off the bat," conceded Charlie, frustrated that he'd overlooked so huge a detail.

"Don't kick yourself—it's a stressful situation. Anyway, I'll have McCoy look into it and tell us what this key really unlocks. In the meantime, we've got to get your girls."

"No," Charlie said.

"No?" Victoria asked, taken aback. "What do you mean?"

"Not yet. We've got to deal with the bomb first. Like you said earlier, your old man won't touch my family unless he knows I'm dead, right? Well, that buys us the time we need to take care of the bomb."

"Charlie, I've got some bad news," she said, with a somber tone. "We may have to make a choice. If we disarm the bomb, it's possible that my Dad will kill your family. Alternatively, if we go for your family and he or any of his men spot us before we get to them, it's possible that he will detonate the bomb. I hate to say it but we might be forced to make that decision."

"Maybe not," Kalani offered. "We can hit them both at the same time."

"He's right, Vee," added Mason, doing his best to convince Victoria that an alternative was possible. "McCoy can handle the rundown on the bomb by himself and, as long as there's no heavy resistance, he and I can disarm it. That leaves the four of you to assault the Tower. Depending on if you're successful or not, we can disarm the bomb or boogie out of there."

"A head-on assault?" said Jen-Jen, licking her lips. "I fucking love it."

Victoria sat still for a moment with her palms on the table, lost deep in thought, and Charlie watched her closely. Finally, she spoke. "It might be possible," she admitted cautiously. "But not in a full-frontal assault. Sorry, Jen-Jen. We've got to be smart about this. We need to even the odds. My Dad has still eight of his operators unaccounted for, and four more at the Tower. We've already removed Jeremy from the equation, but if we can't locate these eight unknowns, then we won't be able to confidently pull this off."

"What do we need to do, *wahine?*" Kalani asked Victoria.

"I hate to say it, because we're in such a beautiful and happy place, but there are twelve hostiles that need to not be alive anymore."

"I'm still loving it," Jen-Jen added.

"Charlie, did you get any names from Jeremy? Anything that can help us find out who these assholes are?" Victoria asked.

"No, it didn't really occur to me at the time to ask," Charlie replied. "You don't have access to a list of your Dad's known associates or any of that other spy stuff you see in the movies?"

"We might. Maybe I can trade it to you for coffee and donuts," she shot back.

"Point taken," Charlie laughed. "I do have two names for you to run, though they're only first names and I don't think they'll turn out to be legit."

He gave her the names of Brody and Brent, the two clowns who had picked him up from the Wilderness Lodge the night before.

"It's a start," she said. "We can run a search similar to your Hollywood-style approach. Even with first names alone, we can cross-reference them with my Dad and see what comes up. Maybe we'll get lucky and find a connection. Mason, get on that, will you?"

"Aye," he grunted and pulled a small laptop from a bag hanging on the back of his chair.

"I can almost guarantee that these two idiots were ex-military," Charlie added.

"Good. Mason, add that to the parameters and try to refine it," Victoria ordered.

"On it," was Mason's reply, as he began rapidly tapping keys.

Charlie turned to Kalani, "I thought *you* were the scientist, big guy," he joked.

Kalani leaned back in his chair, hands clasped behind his head, and smiled. "Nah, you pegged me right off the bat, braddah. I just hit things and shoot things."

"You had me fooled; you CIA spooks are excellent actors," Charlie grinned.

"You think *I'm* good, you should see some of Jen-Jen's…acting," he quipped.

Jen-Jen simply smiled, winked and shrugged.

"Ease up, kids. Did you forget we have a situation?" Victoria prodded.

"Just blowing off some steam, boss," offered Kalani.

Mason's eyes narrowed as he leaned in closer to his screen. All attention was on him. Everyone waited for the little man to speak.

"Fucking bingo!" he blurted.

"What is it, Mason Jar?" Victoria asked, using the pet name she'd created for him. "Don't keep us in suspense."

"Brody Kinney and Brent Masters. They used their real names. Fucking morons!" He laughed loud, drawing glances from other patrons.

"These your guys?" Victoria asked Charlie.

Mason turned the screen so the rest of them could see.

"That's them, alright," Charlie confirmed.

Mason brightened. "This is big."

"Elaborate," Victoria ordered.

"This is it, Vee—the key to everything. Check this out. These two bozos have been seen with your father not once, not twice, but on *six* different occasions over the past five years."

Victoria whistled.

She gestured toward Charlie and together they leaned in to look at Mason's display.

"It gets better," Mason promised. "Charlie was absolutely correct: they're both ex-military, alright. And I can do you one better."

"Hit me."

"Kinney and Masters belong to a rogue unit of Blackwater mercenaries. A unit of *twelve* men."

22

Ninety-year-old Scotch, be damned—nothing was working!

Spencer Holloway was in exceptional physical shape for a man of his age, in no small part due to medicinal remedies and tonics of every variety. One such elixir was a glorious dietary potion that supercharged his metabolism and left his body without even an ounce of fat. The downside was that if Spencer Holloway wished to get drunk, he had to try—*hard*. His body burned off the alcohol nearly as fast as he could drink it. He would have loved nothing more than to upend the bottle and empty it down his throat in one long draught, but he just couldn't bring himself to disgrace such a fine spirit. And so he sat, in the villa next to the one he'd reserved for the Walker women, sipping the dark amber liquid and savoring the deep burn of the ancient single malt.

The burn reminded him that he was still alive, but eventually this train of thought led him to the realization that he was in a situation he desperately needed to be freed from. The nerve-crushing, earthshattering truth that what he'd searched for his entire adult life was not the thing he'd truly desired was cruel and demoralizing. He'd spent years being sure that his end would be his greatest and most glorious moment, but now he knew how foolish he'd been. How could his failure and death be his crowning achievement? There was no logic to it. It was as if a dam had been holding all of his stupidity at bay and, over the course of many years, the walls had been eroding until they'd finally failed and the flood consumed him. Who searches for the person who could bring about the end of their life? Had he really fooled himself into this pursuit with such a thin and idiotic premise?

Holloway knew the answer, but his surgically precise and supremely logical mind could scarcely believe that it had been tricked for so long by such idiocy.

He knew the truth stemmed from retaining and following the overwhelming arrogance of his younger self. When he'd first begun challenging other highly intellectual people—back in his early thirties—it had been a hobby: a way of exercising his power and displaying the greatness of his beautiful mind. After so many decades of crushing victories and not even a hint of defeat, his mind had slowly decided for him that this would no longer be a pastime, but his life's work.

Spencer Holloway had always been a shrewd businessman and his endeavors had made him more money than the average person could make in twenty lifetimes. Still, he was a man who never stopped at good enough. Finding legitimate business to be far too easy, he began testing his hand at less-than-legal schemes and found this to be a much more interesting way to spend his time and amass further fortunes. By his late forties, Spencer Holloway knew that he would never again have want of money. It was during this time that his hobby finally evolved into an obsession.

He started spending countless dollars creating clever traps and ingenious scenarios designed to test the world's greatest minds—all in order to prove to himself that there was no mind more brilliant in existence. Some of these challengers came to him willingly, hoping to achieve such petty rewards as money or fame. Others had to be challenged against their will. One thing remained constant throughout, and that was the undeniable fact that none of these people ever showed the slightest possibility of victory.

It wasn't long before Holloway had known—truly *known*—that he had the world's greatest mind. Who could dispute it? Everyone who could have laid claim to the title fell before his feet, unable to best the aging genius.

Until now.

Something in the detective was forcing Holloway to finally believe that his own defeat was a possibility. His confidence had been shaken and, knowing that defeat would surely befall him if he stayed his present course, he realized that he'd been lying to himself all these years. He'd fooled himself into believing that he was searching for his superior. In actuality, he was simply destroying brilliant mind after brilliant mind in order to prove his prowess and so reinforce himself as the world's foremost mastermind. He'd tricked himself into believing that his search was to find a greater mind only to give his *real* quest a skewed sense of purpose.

Spencer Holloway's mind had fractured somewhere along the way and he'd finally learned this brutal truth.

For so many years, Holloway had believed he was looking for that one truly great mind that *must* exist. Hiding deep within his subconscious was the *real* truth of his life's work—the truth that perpetually guided him under the guise of something entirely different. The *true* Spencer Holloway— unbeknownst even to his conscious self—sought to dominate. To overpower. To *destroy*. This entity sought to prove to others that he was as close to godhood as a human being could ever hope to be. No one on this young planet could take from him what he had so rightfully earned.

This twisted subconscious puppet master pulled all the strings. This guiding spirit that kept his gears turning was relentless in its pursuit of domination and with every mind it defeated became exponentially more destructive and empowered. The *true* Spencer Holloway had no desire to be defeated. Perhaps the other half of Holloway's mind really believed that he was searching for his successor, but it was simply a reality carefully crafted by the more malevolent aspects of his mind to trick its more sensible counterpart into doing what needed to be done.

For so long, these two sides had warred within the old genius. He was appalled by the notion. He was being controlled; his actions were his own but his intentions were those of another. Spencer Holloway was mortified to realize that he'd never known who he really was. He'd never believed that schizophrenia had any place in his great brain. How could two things share the same space inside his head yet remain unknown?

Holloway had been manipulated for years by an unknown aspect of his own persona, and it terrified him. He had never entertained the notion that he might be crazy. Eccentric? Maybe. Impulsive? Definitely. Sadistic? Absolutely. But crazy? Never. Not once in all his years had insanity ever crossed his mind.

Was this necessarily a bad thing though? People only needed treatment for insanity when they couldn't control it—when they couldn't make two halves whole again. Holloway was the most intelligent of all—he could control anything he damn well pleased. If he were truly insane, then he would use it as a tool—a weapon—to turn this scenario around. Perhaps, instead of a disability, he'd found a new advantage.

Holloway stood, slowly made his way to the large window and then gazed out over the Magic Kingdom. Somewhere below him, among the sweating, writhing masses of ignorant vacationers, was the detective that had come to be his finest opponent: the man who had brought such enlightenment and clarity to his previously clouded mind. The detective had brought something else too—something much more important. Healing. Holloway's mind had begun to heal itself; the fracture that had been mistakenly created so long ago was knitting itself back together along jagged edges. Holloway welcomed this entity and became one with it. If this detective were to be his greatest opponent, then Holloway would not disappoint his true nature—he would destroy this man.

Two halves had finally become one. A monster was reborn.

23

Jeremy awoke with a start and a strangled gasp. Panic set itself upon him when he realized that he couldn't breathe—or move. Something soft, slick and pliable pressed hard against his face, wet from the condensation of his panicked exhalations. The darkness that surrounded him was absolute. He thrashed and clawed frantically, hoping to free himself from his mysterious entombment. For a few terrible seconds, Jeremy irrationally thought he was dead and that this was the afterlife—a personalized hell of suffocation and blackness.

Relief surged through his body as heavy black trash bags were lifted from his face, sunlight spilled over him and he saw the face of a red-haired, bearded man staring down at him. Confusion overrode his emotions and instinctively he began to sit up. The bearded man casually placed a pistol to his forehead and pushed him back down. Jeremy's face ached and throbbed with deep pain made worse by the pressure of the man's weapon.

"Don't," said the man.

Jeremy was unsure of where he was or who this mysterious man could be. He could see sky above him, but no other landmarks. The man's face disappeared and then Jeremy sensed himself being moved. He felt the grinding, rumbling sensation of wheels beneath him. Finally, he realized that he must be inside some sort of trash cart. The man had only moved the black bags away from his face so that he could breathe; the rest of his body was still buried beneath them.

"Where am I?" he asked.

"Quiet," replied the man in a monotone.

"Who are you?" Jeremy asked, worried.

"Quiet," came the reply once more.

The voice was not fierce, nor menacing, but it worried Jeremy all the same. Where was he being taken? Who was this man and what was his connection to Charlie Walker? The last thing Jeremy could remember was the detective plunging a hypodermic needle into his neck. The pain had been intense— and he had almost instantly lost consciousness. Now he was here—wherever *here* was.

For several more minutes the cart moved on, its pilot deathly silent. Jeremy could hear the faint sounds of traffic, but nothing else. Thanks to his broken nose, he could discern no scents other than the sterile plastic of the trash bags sitting on his chest. Jeremy became so disoriented that he thought he might lose consciousness once more. The sky seemed to spin in circles above him and nausea crept its way up his throat.

Finally, when Jeremy felt as if he could take no more, the cart halted. The bearded man's well-muscled arms descended into the cart. In his hands, he held something amorphous and black that Jeremy couldn't quite make out. The object descended further and further until it obscured Jeremy's vision entirely. He felt warm cloth on his face and realize that a hood had been placed over his head, cinched tight at his throat.

Without warning, he was lifted easily from the cart and tossed effortlessly. For a split second he was airborne before landing hard on his back, a cry escaping his lips. Excruciating pain blossomed once more through his ruined face as the back of his head connected with the ground resulting in a surprisingly hollow thud, as if the floor were a thin sheet of material rather than solid earth. Whoever had thrown him—he assumed it was still the bearded man—grabbed hold of his legs roughly and spun his body ninety degrees. He heard two doors slam shut and realized that he had been thrown into the back of a vehicle. The engine roared to life, the drive gear was engaged and the vehicle smoothly rolled forward.

Jeremy noticed that he had not been bound. He laid flat on his back and realized that, should he get the urge, he could simply reach up and remove the hood. The confidence with which this man—as per Walker—had carried himself had intimidated Jeremy into inaction. It almost seemed as if they knew something he did not and that this mysterious information led them to be unconcerned about Jeremy's freedom.

The wounded assassin had no concept of time in his hooded world. The only two sensations which he experienced—darkness and the dull vibration of the road—gave him no indication as to how long he had been in this vehicle. After an eternity, the motion finally ceased. He heard the driver's door open and he heard footsteps crunching on gravel or asphalt outside. The back doors open and he felt the van shift as the big man entered and closed the doors behind him.

"Up," commanded the man quietly, and Jeremy did as instructed.

The hood was pulled, surprisingly gently, from his head and Jeremy was finally able to take stock of his surroundings. He sat on the floor of a large panel van. There were no windows in the compartment in which they sat and a metal partition separated the driver's area from this one. The quiet man sat on top of a blue plastic milk crate and motioned toward an identical crate for Jeremy.

Carefully, not taking his eyes off the strange fiery-bearded man, Jeremy took a seat atop the second crate. He studied his captor in silence for a while and felt that something about him seemed horribly familiar. The man stared at him from beneath intense green eyes that never blinked. It was unnerving, to say the least.

No longer able to bear the close scrutiny, Jeremy turned away from the man and began to look around the van. The compartment contained nothing, save for the two crates upon which they sat. The floor was covered in a layer of plastic or rubber, and the walls were painted steel. Upon closer inspection, Jeremy noticed small dents and stains in various places on the walls that were a sickly shade of faded brown. Jeremy knew the sight all too well: spilled blood that had been shoddily cleaned—no doubt on purpose.

Having nothing left with which to busy himself, Jeremy looked back at the man. On the man's lap sat a large manila folder and a small-caliber suppressed pistol much like his own. Carefully, the man opened the envelope, leaving the pistol sitting neatly on his thigh. Jeremy could easily have lunged forward to snatch the pistol and put an end to this strange scenario. Again, the confidence and casual nature of the man stayed his hand; the man's careless disregard for the weapon cowed Jeremy into inaction.

From the envelope, the bearded man removed a stack of glossy, high-resolution color photographs. They appeared to be photos from various crime scenes. Slowly and silently, the man turned and showed Jeremy the photo on the top of the stack. His heart leapt as he realized who the subject of the photograph was. He gazed at the picture deeply, noting every familiar detail.

A man in his late forties sat dead in an office chair, his hands resting on the armrests and his head down. Two small red holes had been punched through his shirt, just over his heart. Another was neatly bored through his forehead. There was very little blood in this photo. Jeremy recognized this man—there was no way he would ever forget. This was the first man that he had eliminated in the service of Spencer Holloway. He was surprised, and it must have registered on his face because the bearded man silently nodded and placed that photo on the floor beside him.

The next photo was that of a young man, lying dead in the parking lot of a dive bar outside Chicago. His body had been outlined in white and there were several yellow, numbered evidence markers in various places around the body, some next to patches of blood, another near half of a footprint in the dust. In this instance, Jeremy had not killed for Holloway but in a fit of rage he'd beaten the man to death with a gloved fist.

Setting the photo on the floor, the silent bearded man began to show him more pictures of atrocities that were Jeremy's work. A photo of an elderly man with his throat cut ear-to-ear, executed after the man was caught trying to sell Holloway out to a rival. Another was of a woman he'd raped and beaten to death years ago. Holloway had never learned the cause of death or her horrible treatment beforehand. Following that came a photo of a man slumped against the steering wheel of a car, parked beneath a bridge—two familiar holes over his heart and one in his head. Jeremy had killed him for refusing to take part in a challenge and attempting to flee the country. The next: a photo of a young woman, naked and dead on a hotel bed, a telephone cord wrapped around her throat—another victim whose fate was still unknown to the assassin's employer. Jeremy recognized every single body and he prided himself that not a single shred of evidence was left at any scene to connect the killings to him.

The bearded man stiffened then, not immediately moving on to the next photo. He looked Jeremy deeply in the eyes and slowly let the current photo fall to the floor instead of neatly placing it on the pile with the others. Only one photograph remained and Jeremy studied it closely.

There, in brightly colored high-resolution, gracefully laid the body of a seventeen-year-old girl, fully clothed and free from blood or any other signs of violence. Jeremy had found her one night at a concert in Washington, D.C. Before long, he had convinced her to leave the venue with him and had attempted to drug her and take advantage of her unconscious form. His intent had not been to kill this girl, but she had unexpectedly succumbed to a violent reaction to the drug, resulting in her death. He'd panicked and left her body in an alley in Alexandria, which was where this picture was taken. He looked from the photo to the man holding it.

There it was—the connection. That familiarity that he'd noticed earlier. The girl had the same deep red hair and the same intense green eyes.

It couldn't be.

Jeremy's eyes widened with shock as he looked at the bearded man. The man slowly exhaled.

Casually, the bearded man lifted the pistol and fired two rounds, punching neat holes in Jeremy's chest—the hollow point rounds entering but not exiting his body. Jeremy looked down in horror to see the two small holes staring back at him like the red eyes of the devil that he was on his way to meet. He'd never thought it would end like this—the young, red-haired girl's death was a rare mistake, and it had cost him dearly. He felt himself start to fade, his ruined heart no longer able to pump oxygenated blood to his vital organs. With his last ounce of energy, Jeremy looked up into the eyes of his killer—just in time to see the suppressed barrel of the gun pointed at his forehead.

With one bright flash and a small *pop*, Jeremy O'Neill's world was cast into infinite blackness.

24

"Son of a bitch," breathed Jen-Jen.

"That's one hell of a find, Jar," complimented Kalani with a low whistle.

Charlie was astonished by what he'd heard. Holloway was using ex-Blackwater mercenaries as his operators—this was above and beyond anything he could have ever imagined. There were ten men who had remained nameless until now, when this gift of clarity had so conveniently fallen into their laps. A child could have put together that Spencer Holloway had lured Brody Kinney, Brent Masters and their brothers in arms away from the infamous private military contractor. Holloway had the funds to take care of these men—luxuriously—for the rest of their lives, which was much more than Blackwater could have ever offered them.

"What other info do we have on them?" Victoria asked, not missing a beat.

"Says here that these guys were the biggest pieces of shit you could possibly ask for," began Mason. "They were mostly stationed on security detail for embassies in war-torn nations where political assassinations and other really scary things were a part of everyday life. These fellows are not nice people. Apparently, their unit is nicknamed 'Chaos Squad.'

"One report says that while protecting a South African diamond mine from militia forces, one of the day laborers was caught trying to smuggle a diamond out in his mouth instead of turning it in. I guess the worker was new and didn't know that the security checkpoint at the single exit ran cavity searches as well as pat-downs. Anyway, standard procedure—hell, *common sense*—is to turn a thief over to the local police. Right?"

"Well, the Chaos Squad boys don't like that way of thinking, and they decided to take the law into their own grizzled, apelike hands. Says here these maniacs lined up all of the remaining laborers outside the mine and beat the thief to death in front of them to set an example."

"Jesus," breathed Jen-Jen.

"That's pretty messed up," Kalani agreed, raising his eyebrows.

Charlie remained silent, but felt a simmering rage coming to a boil within his chest. These animals had taken his wife and daughters. It seemed like Holloway—truly a monster in his own right—had surrounded himself with creatures cut from the same psychotic cloth.

"They weren't brought up on charges?" Victoria asked. "Even Blackwater has to be held accountable for some things."

"Well, the foreman tried to do the right thing—called the American embassy and reported them. He was found dead in his office the next morning—gun in his hand and a good part of his head decorating the wall next to him."

"You think Chaos did him in?" Kalani asked.

"The local constabulary didn't think so," offered Mason. "But the Company *knows* Chaos did it. Turns out we had a guy who happened to be in the area, and he went to check out the scene. He found fibers and friction burns on the foreman's gun hand, neck and head. Sound familiar?"

"Sounds like Portugal all over again—an amateur version, anyway," offered Jen-Jen.

"What happened in Portugal?" asked Charlie.

"It's a long story—and a matter of national security—so I've got to be really vague," Victoria explained, "but one man we were after was trying to kill *another* man that we were after and make it look like suicide. He'd rigged up a pretty clever contraption: a system of fishing line that held a gun in place next to a victim's head and, once the loose end of the line was pulled, forced the victim's finger to pull the trigger. After that, you cut away the string, take it with you and not even Gil Grissom could tell you it wasn't a suicide."

Charlie had never heard of anything like it in his life—it was insane. He realized that the Detroit Police Department and the CIA, while both law enforcement agencies, were two very different entities. Charlie dealt with grisly crimes of passion while the Company seemed more accustomed to ingenious, premeditated assassinations.

"Right," agreed Mason. "But the Chaos guys have more muscle than brains, so they used twine instead of fishing line. You see, the smart killers used fishing line because it glides easily along skin, and leaves no fibers or burns. These dummies used twine and when it slid across the foreman's skin it left both. The local guys didn't catch it—probably because they've never seen anything like it. Right after that, our guy got in touch with Blackwater and found out that Chaos Squad had vanished from the face of the Earth. How convenient is that?"

"So," Victoria cut in. "We're dealing with idiots—*tough* idiots, but idiots all the same. I know for a fact that everyone at this table is as smart as they come, so we shouldn't have any trouble. What do we do?" she asked, but it was a challenge to her team rather than a request for help.

"Run the names into the computer, hack into Disney's cameras and find these assholes using Mason's facial recognition software. Should give us a pretty good idea of where they are," Jen-Jen offered.

"Exactly," Victoria nodded. "And then?"

"Then, we make 'em dead," ventured Kalani.

Charlie spoke up, "Wait. We can't just kill these guys. I'm a cop, for God's sake. I *save* lives."

"Charlie, they gotta go," added Mason, darkly. "I'm sorry, man. They're carrying out terrorist activity on American soil. We don't take that shit from foreigners and we sure as shit ain't taking it from our own."

"But we're in *Walt fucking Disney World!* How can you kill twelve people here?"

Jen-Jen laughed, "Babe, we can kill twelve people *anywhere*."

"That's enough, guys," Victoria barked. She stood. "Charlie, come take a walk with me, alright?"

Charlie nodded.

"Get a hold of me as soon as you learn anything," she said, flashing her phone at them before shoving it into her back pocket.

Confused and a little irritated, Charlie stood and followed the daughter of his enemy out of the restaurant.

They wandered for a while, silently and lazily, dodging screaming kids and exhausted parents while Charlie stared at the ground, his overwhelmed mind making it difficult to focus on anything. Suddenly, Victoria pulled Charlie aside as he nearly collided with an energetic, bearded, tattooed man in a trucker hat and sunglasses. He was speaking animatedly into his phone's camera but Charlie didn't register much of what he was saying. He thought he heard the phrase, "Join me...shall you?" before the man hurried off.

Soon, Charlie found himself approaching It's a Small World. He hadn't been on the ride in a while. The girls had always tended to like rides with a higher thrill factor. They always mentioned in passing that they'd like to ride it again, but somehow it had been continually, although Charlie had always had a soft spot for the classic attraction.

Victoria placed a hand on his shoulder. "Be right back," she said with a wink and disappeared into the attraction's exit.

A couple of minutes later, she reemerged and motioned for him to follow. Right on Victoria's heels, he made his way along the exit walkway to a Cast Member who was standing next to an empty boat. Victoria stepped past the man and into the second row, sitting down and casually putting her feet on the seatback in front of her. She motioned for Charlie to join her. With a quick glance and a nod at the smiling Cast Member, he took a seat next to Victoria.

"Thanks again, Shane," she said, smiling at the Cast Member. He nodded courteously as their boat departed.

"He sent out some empty boats ahead of us and he'll send a couple more behind us, so it'll be safe to talk once we get a little deeper inside," she whispered to Charlie.

After the boat had moved away from the Cast Member—and the frustrated stares of the people waiting in line—Charlie ventured to ask how Victoria had gotten them such special treatment.

"A CIA badge can get you far in this world, child," she replied. Then she teased, "Much further than a police shield."

"Mine has deer on it," Charlie offered.

"Mine has an eagle," Victoria stated, triumphantly.

Charlie smiled the humble smile of the lowly police officer and nodded in defeat. Victoria remained quiet for the next sixty or so seconds until their boat had made its way deep into the cheery bowels of the attraction, finally speaking as they neared the Eiffel Tower section.

"So," she began, "now might be a good time to let you in on what we really do—before things start getting real and I don't get the chance."

"It's pretty obvious what you do," Charlie replied, honestly but respectfully.

"That's what you think," she said, "but you aren't seeing the whole picture. We aren't action heroes, we're regular people too. We've never fired guns while driving cars or jumped out of helicopters—well, Kalani fell out of one once, but it was on the ground with the engine off, so I refuse to count it."

Charlie laughed at the thought of the big Hawaiian falling out of a chopper door. Victoria smiled too, enjoying the opportunity to bond with her new friend. After a moment though, she became serious—or as serious as she could manage.

She sighed lightly. "We've killed people, but it's never been anyone who didn't deserve it. And let me tell you a secret: we hate it. It really fucks us up. I've killed three people, and I've thrown up each time after the shock has worn off. It's something that nobody likes to do, ever. Kalani's takes it especially hard—sometimes I won't hear from him for days after we get home from an op. I guess he deals with it in his own way too. We all do. But we won't stop—we *can't* stop—as horrible as that sounds. We do the things that good people shouldn't have to do. We do it to *protect* good people. You're a good person, Charlie. Meghan? The girls? Good people. You don't deserve to be in this situation, and you need people like us to help you out of it."

"I understand. It's just hard to come to terms with," Charlie admitted.

"Listen, I know you hate it—"

"That's not it," he interrupted. "Not entirely."

"What is it, then?" she asked, genuinely perplexed.

"I've killed too," he stated, but he couldn't look at her.

"My brother had it coming. He murdered so many people. He was the worst of the worst, and you did the world a favor—you're a hero. Look at me, damn it."

He looked into her eyes and saw a fierce intensity.

"James was a fucking monster. My Dad is a fucking monster. Good people—people who haven't done anything wrong—have suffered and died because of those two. Who deserves to live, Charlie? People like James and my Dad—or Meghan and your daughters? Does Chaos Squad deserve to keep running around like barbarians, killing whoever they please—or do the innocent families in line for Space Mountain deserve to enjoy their vacation without a goddamn roller coaster train falling on their heads?"

"It's not my—" Charlie began.

"That's just it, Charlie," she continued, not allowing him to finish. "It's not a decision a good person like you should ever have to make. That's why there are people like X-ray Team. It's *our* job to make these awful decisions and act on them so that the rest of the country can still be pure."

For once, Charlie didn't respond. He simply looked into her eyes and saw once more the fire that had always been burning. Her face was a stone mask of fierce conviction. She'd done terrible things to make sure people like her father never got the chance to prey on more innocent people. Charlie felt a deep sadness for this woman just then. She'd spent her entire adult life making up for the horrible deeds of a father she'd never met—making up for acts of terror that she'd never been a part of. She'd taken the burden of guilt upon herself and made it her life's work to right every wrong that she could. Charlie was convinced that Victoria would do anything in her power to stop her father and rescue Meghan and the girls.

He realized, then, that the world still had a place for true heroes. The men and women of X-ray Team were relentless in their selfless crusade to protect the good people of their country. Charlie had only a small idea of the sacrifices that these people had made to become who they were, and if they'd cast aside their innocence to place themselves between the good and the evil, then he had no right to stand in their way. Regardless, he believed that there must be another option.

"Chaos Squad," he began. "What would happen if we took them in?"

"You mean arrest them?" she asked. "Well, I suppose it would depend on whose office got ahold of them. If the police took them in, they'd sit in a country club prison for a couple of years while cases were built against them and trials were held. Truth is: they'd probably end up getting out within three to five after some money exchanged hands. Blackwater wouldn't want these guys' names tarnishing their image. They'd most likely buy them out and make them disappear. Probably to twelve unmarked graves somewhere in a forgotten country."

"Shit," Charlie breathed. "And if the Company got them?"

Victoria hesitated before speaking, but then continued with a sigh.

"There would be no trial. There would be no public mention that these mercs ever existed. The Company has zero tolerance for terrorists who are American citizens. The first couple of weeks would see them spending their time in blackout rooms deep inside Langley. They'd be stripped of their clothing and left to rot in pitch-black rooms. There's no sense of time or space in there and, after a while, it starts to erode the mind. When the blackout rooms have done their job, the real shit will begin. There's a guy down there, a Compliance Specialist named Weaver." She made air quotes with her fingers when she spoke Weaver's title. "He has a lot of tools, a lot of free time and a lot of fucked up brain cells. He'll wring those twelve mercs for every drop of information they could possibly have retained in their entire lives. After Weaver's treatment, they'll disappear—same as the other scenario. Either way, these guys aren't going to make it to retirement age. No cashing Social Security checks or playing golf in Boca Raton for them."

Charlie sat quietly for a moment, thinking. He could tell from Victoria's tone that she hated the endgame as much as he did, and that she wouldn't consider taking these men's lives if it wasn't the best possible course of action. There was no hope for these men, and so the police officer within Charlie's mind finally took a step back in favor of the more savage instincts of the primal man within. Regardless of the fates of these men, one constant remained: they had abducted his wife and his daughters, and would not hesitate to harm them if Holloway gave the order. The thought of these animals anywhere near his family caused fresh waves of rage and anxiety to wash over him. Victoria, while ruthless, was absolutely right. If the one true way to save his family was killing these men, then that was what they must do. His family had so much to offer the world, while these savages simply detracted from it. No harm would befall his family if he had the opportunity to prevent it. His decision had finally been made.

"You're right, Victoria," Charlie said finally, with a slight air of resignation. "I'll do whatever it takes."

Her intense gaze softened and she smiled her characteristic bright smile. "Good. We could really use that brain of yours on this one, detective."

§

They finished the ride in comfortable silence, Charlie finally at peace with the fact that he may be forced to go against his morals. It was easier to deal with the consequences knowing that whatever he may be forced to do was in defense of hundreds of innocent people who'd done nothing to deserve the hell that Spencer Holloway was planning to rain down upon them.

Victoria seemed more at ease, as well. She appeared looser and more relaxed throughout the rest of the ride, leaning back against the seat with her feet crossed at the ankles on the seatback in front of her. Charlie had even spied her lips moving in sync with the song a few times and she'd laughed when she'd noticed him looking.

Upon exiting the ride, Victoria's cell phone rang.

"It's McCoy," she told Charlie, before excusing herself to take the call.

Charlie stood just out of earshot and absently watched the seconds tick away on his watch. In no time, Victoria appeared in front of him, a solemn look darkening her otherwise cheerful features.

"What is it?" Charlie asked as they began making their way back toward Liberty Square.

"Jeremy's dead."

"What? Was it because I—"

"No, it wasn't you," she held up a hand to reassure him. "Remember when I told you that Jeremy killed someone close to one of my team? Well…she was McCoy's daughter."

Charlie nodded but remained silent, urging her to continue. Victoria put her hand on his back and steered him toward the waterfront, out of earshot of any passersby.

"Last year, poor McCoy lost his only daughter—a pretty little girl, only seventeen. Toxicology reports say she was drugged in an attempted date rape. She had an allergic reaction to the drug and didn't recover from it. A jogger found her body in an alley in Alexandria. Footage from local businesses' security cameras gave us the lucky break in finding out who did it. Only one car had turned into that alley between the time the jogger found her body and the last time she was seen alive. It was a rental car registered to a Jeremy O'Neill…"

She trailed off, allowing Charlie to process the information on his own. He didn't know what to feel. That coward had killed McCoy's only daughter and dumped her in an alley. It was something Charlie saw all too often in his profession, and he'd also seen the effect it had upon the family members of the victim, most often their reactions had been violent. These were civilians; McCoy was a hardened combat operative working for the Central Intelligence Agency.

Charlie had seen fathers swear death upon the killer of their child in front of multiple uniformed police officers. These men were regular people—all they had was hurt and rage and confusion to fuel their vendetta—so most of the time it began and ended with that single painful outburst. McCoy, on the other hand, was a trained killer. He had the skills and resources necessary to track and find the person responsible. Finally, it appeared, he had brought some form of closure to that painful chapter of his life. Charlie didn't fully disagree with his actions, even though the lawman within him urged him otherwise.

"I'm guessing you didn't turn that information over to the locals," Charlie said, thoughtfully.

"Local PD would have needed warrants to access the cameras near the scene, but the Company doesn't waste their time with that sort of thing—don't need a warrant if nobody knows you were there. We knew that, without the footage, the locals' case would have gone cold and stayed that way. I left it up to McCoy whether he wanted to hand it over or not. He chose not to," she stated.

Something changed within Charlie, then. He put himself in McCoy's shoes. He thought deeply about what he would do if someone had ever taken the lives of one of his girls. His first notion had been that he would do the right thing, make the arrest, testify at the trial—put the bastard away forever. But now…now he wasn't quite sure what he would do if faced with that kind of pain. Maybe he would have made the same choice as McCoy. He decided to bury the issue.

"We should go," he said, still haunted by the changes taking place so rapidly in his mind.

"Let's head back to the restaurant, see if Mason has anything for us," Victoria offered.

§

Not far away, in his villa in the Contemporary Resort's newest addition, Spencer Holloway sat deathly still. He watched the silent security feed as a beautiful, raven-haired woman leaned in close and spoke intimately with

Walker near the water's edge. The woman had been facing away from the camera, but any doubt Holloway may have had as to her identity evaporated when she turned.

Victoria.

25

H olloway trusted his eyes, but he nearly refused to believe them. His own daughter had come to the aid of his enemy.

Isn't this adorable?

He'd known, even a decade ago, that leaving his daughter alive and well and working for the CIA would one day come back to bite him, but this couldn't have come at a worse time. His child must not be allowed to continue her rebellion. He cursed himself for his oversight.

Frustration soon gave way to speculation as he began to wonder how long Victoria had been involved. He'd not seen her before, but he'd been tending to other matters and had ceased his surveillance on the detective after their previous conversation. When had his daughter first shown her face?

No matter; she must be dealt with.

Refusing to take his eyes away from the screen again, he grabbed his phone and dialed Jeremy, intending to have the boy dispose of pretty little Victoria once and for all. To his extreme dismay, his young assassin didn't answer and after several rings the call went straight to voicemail. Holloway hung up and instantly tried the number again. Once more, he reached Jeremy's voicemail.

Frantically, he pulled up a GPS application on another laptop and tracked Jeremy's phone. When the ping came back, and he was able to see the location of the pulsing blue dot, his breath caught in his throat. Jeremy's phone was right on top of Walker's location.

Looking back to the surveillance feed, he could still see Walker standing with Victoria, but he couldn't see anyone else nearby—no Jeremy. Where could the boy possibly be? Closer inspection of the scene showed him that Walker had a cell phone in his hand and was speaking quickly to Victoria. The detective no doubt held Jeremy's phone. Holloway sighed and pinched the bridge of his nose.

How could this have happened? Holloway had sent Jeremy to carry out his new task hours ago. How could Walker have possibly obtained his phone?

Rage building within him, he dialed Jeremy's phone a final time. Onscreen, he watched as Walker reacted to the third call, quickly exchanging words with Victoria—surely asking her advice whether or not to answer the phone. Finally, the detective answered without a word.

Silence greeted Spencer Holloway on the other end of the line, but he managed to remain calm.

"Hello, detective," he breathed.

"Holloway," declared the detective in a venomous tone. Holloway could see Walker slowly pacing, holding the phone in a white-knuckled grip. "Are you wondering what happened to your errand boy?"

"I *am* a bit curious," Holloway casually admitted.

"First, let me tell you what *I'm* curious about. I'm curious as to why you sent that asshole to kill me. I thought you were in this for the challenge. I play *one* game and you decide that you've had your fun and it's time to kill me?"

Holloway was confused. He hadn't sent Jeremy to kill Walker. Granted, the new challenge he'd sent Jeremy to initiate would have surely proved fatal for the detective, but Walker couldn't have known a thing until he was dead.

Come to think of it, he also didn't recall hearing from Eduardo—Walker had not gone to retrieve the contents of the locker as planned.

Holloway figured that Jeremy must have taken it upon himself to kill the detective—and must have failed miserably. Regardless, he must not allow the detective to know that this wasn't part of the plan.

"All in due time, detective—"

"No," Walker interrupted in an enraged snarl. "No more of your enigmatic blow-offs. You're stalling for time. I want my fucking family, and I want them *now!*"

"Speaking of family members, how is my little Victoria?" he ventured.

"She hates you as much as I do."

"Hate is a strong word, Walker. Let us reserve that for special occasions. May I speak to her?"

Onscreen, he watched Walker mute the phone and have a short exchange with Victoria. Reluctantly, she nodded and accepted the device.

"Still hiding behind your technology, I see," she stated.

He dramatically feigned a painful gasp. "My dear Victoria, is that any way to speak to your father?"

"My *father* is a retired electrical engineer in Massachusetts. *You* are a maniac. You are not my father."

"If only wishes came true!" he retorted. "You remind me too much of your mother. Perhaps I'll introduce you to the same strain of curare that ended her life," he threatened, hoping to goad her into divulging any useful information in her anger.

Unfortunately, she was either well prepared or perpetually well-guarded because all he got for his trouble was a fierce "You won't get the chance."

He could feel himself gradually losing the upper hand. He had no idea whether Victoria was alone, or if she had brought a team. He didn't know the fate of Jeremy, nor what damaging information the young man had given them.

Still, he had the twelve boy scouts and they were standing by, awaiting his command. He hoped that Victoria hadn't learned of their involvement, but his daughter was intelligent so he couldn't dismiss it.

"Let me give you some advice, dear," he said in a gentle tone. "Slowly draw your sidearm and execute Detective Walker. He will not survive the day anyway, so you might as well make it easy for him."

Holloway watched his daughter turn toward the detective, looking the man in the eyes as she replied, "I've got a better idea. Bring the detective's family to me, and I'll make sure you end up in a nice maximum security prison for the rest of your life."

He saw Walker give her a mischievous grin.

"Tempting…" Holloway joked. "But, I believe I have an even better plan. Pack up your operation and leave, or I will execute the detective's family myself."

The truth was: he couldn't execute Walker's family. Not until the detective was dead and his escape route was clear. If Holloway were to kill Walker's family, then—assuming Victoria had brought a team with her—she would have no reason *not* to lead an assault on his position and kill him. He was confident in Chaos Squad's ability to protect him, but only four of them were on the hotel's grounds; the rest were in various other places throughout Disney property.

Much to his rage, she called his bluff without hesitation. "You could," she offered, "but then I'd kill you myself. We know exactly where you are."

We. She wasn't talking about herself and Walker; she'd meant it in reference to her team. It was exactly as he'd feared; she'd brought a team with her. He had no current way to discover how many operatives she'd brought with her, nor their positions. He'd normally have used Jeremy for such reconnaissance, but he was currently unavailable—which reminded him....

"Where is Jeremy?" he asked, needing to know for sure.

"Dead," came her simple reply.

"You're a terrible liar," he managed, but he already knew it was true. Jeremy would never let himself be relieved of his possessions.

"Your pet had a thing for underage girls," she told him, venomously. "He killed one of them—drugged her."

"Jeremy did have his peculiarities," Holloway admitted.

"Well, the father of that poor girl happens to work for the Company. He just put three rounds into your boy. Wrong guy to fuck with."

Holloway's rage was almost too unbearable to keep in check. He heard the plastic of the phone creaking beneath his grasp as he squeezed it with every ounce of his strength. It took all of the self-control he had to keep from hurling it across the room. Jeremy was dead, as a result of his emotions overriding his logic in not one, but two different situations. Holloway kicked himself for allowing the boy to live after making such costly mistakes.

"That's what the Company hires these days, then? Common assassins?" he shot back.

"Yes," she said, surprising him. "And that was personal. Are you prepared to see how we operate under more professional circumstances?"

He was losing control of the situation—of himself. This was not good. *He* was the true genius here, so why didn't he feel like it? Why was he losing to a Detroit detective and his own bitch of a daughter? They'd taken his right-hand man from him. They'd foiled his secondary plan to eliminate Walker. But he still had cards left to play.

"It's an interesting proposition, but if you allocated all your resources to killing me, then who would be left to save all the innocent guests?" In an attempt to gain her curiosity without giving anything away, he'd purposely failed to mention the bomb.

"Oh, you mean the bomb?" she asked. "We've got that under control, thanks."

And it was at that moment that Holloway knew he still had a glimmer of hope left. Victoria knew about the bomb, but she didn't have the situation under control. She couldn't. He'd made sure of that.

"Really?" he asked. "That's interesting. So you've disarmed it? Congratulations."

"We will—"

"Save your breath, Victoria, and listen to me," he commanded, not waiting for her to finish whatever weak threat she was starting in on. "You clearly have no idea what you've gotten yourself into. That bomb cannot be disarmed by anyone but me. In fact, the bomb cannot even be *accessed* in the time before it detonates. I have the only device capable of disarming it."

"You're lying," she snapped, but she didn't sound convinced.

"I invite you to have a look. Detective Walker has the key, which I'm sure he's given you. There is only one way to prevent the detonation of the bomb, and that is to give me exactly what I want. And what I want," he paused, "is the man standing in front of you dead."

She didn't respond, but he saw as her body language shifted. He could tell he'd struck a nerve with his ultimatum. It was clear that she was determined to rescue the detective and his family, but her duty was first and foremost to the innocent citizens of her country—hundreds of which would perish if she failed. He smiled, watching her struggle with the weighty decision. Finally, she spoke.

"I'll have the park evacuated," she threatened.

"Tsk, tsk, dear. I was under the impression that you were more experienced than that? Has the Company taught you nothing? The moment an evacuation begins, I'll simply detonate the weapon. In fact, more guests will die during the panic than they would otherwise. Not to mention the trampling and rioting that will surely follow such a horrendous announcement." He was enjoying this.

Then, much to his surprise, the line went dead. He watched onscreen as Victoria removed the battery from Jeremy's phone and tossed it into a trashcan. She barked a few words at Walker and then stalked off, with the detective hurrying quickly to keep up.

This had not gone as Holloway had hoped. True, he still had the bomb and Walker's family, but if he used either of those pieces of leverage he would surely fail. With the execution of the Walker women, or the detonation of the bomb, his death would most certainly follow.

He had to think of something else—some other way to win—but how? What did he have left? His two remaining options were only thinly veiled bluffs that would end in his death if he executed either one of them. Jeremy was dead, Victoria was here with a team of her own and it seems as if she knew more of his operation than he knew of hers.

Things were falling apart and, even with his newly united mind, he couldn't foresee any way out of this situation. He could simply leave, but how long would it be before Victoria and Walker caught up with him? Besides, his dangerous levels of pride would never allow him to leave a job unfinished—death before dishonor.

Fed up with the circumstances, Holloway quickly stood, toppling his chair in the process. He gripped the bottle of Scotch and brought it to his lips. After three or four swallows, the burning in his throat became too painful to continue. He let his arm fall to his side, the dark amber liquid dribbling down his chin and staining his shirt. Had he consumed enough to overwhelm his metabolism?

The room began to spin—just a bit, but it was plenty. Still, for good measure, he took three more sizable draughts. He'd successfully gotten himself drunk and broken his unspoken oath to the near-antique spirit, but for what purpose? Confusion wracked his once-great mind before mutating into blinding rage. Suddenly, he hurled the Scotch bottle at the window before him. The windowpane cracked—the fissure spider-webbing its way to the edges of the frame. The window bowed out slightly in the middle, held together only by the anti-shatter film that coated it.

Holloway stumbled away from the scene, eventually finding himself in a bedroom. He attempted to make his way to the bed but found it increasingly difficult due to the blackness on the edges of his vision closing quickly in upon him. When he felt himself begin to pass out, he tried to aim for the bed.

Misjudging his landing, he found nothing but the floor to welcome him into unconsciousness.

26

"What's going on?" Charlie asked, as he hurried to keep pace with Victoria.

"Something's changed. The old man's not playing games with you anymore, Charlie. He wants you dead."

"Is that all?" Charlie joked, but Victoria wheeled upon him.

"This isn't a joke, Charlie. If the past is any indicator, when my Dad wanted someone dead, they ended up dead. He's not looking to test you again."

"He didn't really *test* me in the first place," Charlie said. "That key wasn't hard to find. Now what's his angle?"

"I don't know," she admitted. "But he says he wants you dead, otherwise he's letting the timer run out and he's blowing that support on Space Mountain."

"Do you believe he'd really detonate it?"

"I've got to give him the benefit of the doubt. If I roll the dice and call his bluff, I could be condemning innocent people to their deaths. I couldn't live with that."

"Neither could I," Charlie agreed, darkly. "That being said, we're going to have to be open to the idea of an endgame contingency plan."

Victoria looked into Charlie's eyes, fear washing over her.

"You don't mean—"

"If it comes to that, you've got to hand me over," Charlie told her.

"No! We can find another way," she managed desperately.

"I know—and we *will* try. I have no desire to die today, but if all else fails, you need to do what's logical. My life isn't worth condemning all of these families for; it's not worth losing Meghan and the girls for. Listen to me, Victoria. If we can't figure out how to finish this, then you know what you have to do."

Victoria seemed too distraught to speak. She raised a hand to her brow and paced in a small circle, clearly searching the deepest recesses of her mind for any plan that would save her new friend's life as well as the innocents in danger. After a moment, she sighed, stopped pacing and gazed out over the waterfront, facing away from him. Charlie made his way over and stood next to her, but remained silent, watching the *Liberty Belle* lazily cruising the Rivers of America. A monumental decision had been made, and the impact it had upon the two valiant upholders of the law was immense.

Slowly, Victoria turned to look at Charlie, whose eyes remained focused on the large paddlewheel ship.

"You'd really do it?" she asked, still trying to get her mind around what this detective was willing to do to save his family.

"Yes," he replied, without hesitation. His voice did not waver and was filled with a steely determination. Finally losing interest in the ship, Charlie turned to face Victoria.

"The world needs more people like you, Charlie," she said, quietly.

"I'm just doing my job," he declared.

Victoria threw her arms around him and squeezed tightly—for a lithe and slight woman, she was surprisingly strong. Startled, Charlie fumbled clumsily for a moment before returning the gesture. She held onto him for a few moments and Charlie could feel her body gradually stiffen. When finally she pulled away, Charlie could see that she'd erased all vulnerability. Victoria Holloway—the brave intelligence agent—had returned, complete with attitude and sense of humor.

"You're a goddamned real-life hero, Walker," she said with a grin, punching him lightly on the arm.

"If I agree with you, will you promise not to crush my spine again?" he joked. Victoria's laughter was a welcome respite after the somber mood recent events had left them in. Her laughter was cut short, however, by nearby voices shouting in complaint.

Looking toward the source of the commotion, they saw Kalani barreling toward them. The massive Hawaiian clumsily dodged guests as he maneuvered his sizable bulk through the dense crowd. Several more people shouted at him in frustration before he finally skidded to a halt before Charlie and Victoria.

"Guys!" he shouted, before taking a few deep breaths and wiping the sweat from his brow. A few people nearby glanced at the large, out-of-breath giant.

"Uh…yeah?" Victoria prodded, urging him to continue.

"I've been looking everywhere for you! We've got an idea. I think you're gonna like it!" He smiled wide. Victoria glanced at Charlie—who shrugged—before returning her attention to Kalani.

"I don't know why you didn't just call," Victoria said, gesturing to her phone. Kalani simply stared at her. After a moment, she realized that he wasn't about to offer any explanations. "Lead on, then, Big Kahuna," she said with a sweeping gesture of her hand.

§

"So check this out," Mason said, when Charlie, Victoria and Kalani had made their way back to the Liberty Tree. "While you nerds were out riding rides and eating churros, *we* were doing research. McCoy just returned from his…uh…trip, and we sent him to check out Space Mountain."

"He never mentioned being back," Victoria said.

"I didn't know if your Dad had your phone tapped, so I told him to leave it out. Anyway, we were listening in on your phone call and when your Dad said that there's no way we can disarm the bomb, he wasn't kidding. McCoy found the device and managed to send a picture. It's washy because of the flash and bad autofocus, but you'll get the idea."

Mason spun his laptop around so that Charlie and Victoria could see the screen. Attached to one of the support beams was a steel box. It had no visible openings or seams except for a small hole from which jutted a short antenna.

"What am I looking at, Jar?" Victoria asked.

"You're looking at the world's most gangster unidirectional explosive charge. That box is welded straight to the beam. The charge is inside, so we can't access it to physically disarm it—at least not in time. McCoy checked it out and that box is filled with water."

"What's the water do?" Charlie asked.

"It acts as a focusing agent—kind of a makeshift way to aim the explosion. Instead of allowing the blast to discharge its energy equally in all directions, it forces most of the energy into the direction without water—in this case, straight into the beam. The angle of the blast and the height at which the support would be cut would break the track and aim it directly at the queue. Your Dad must have had a seriously badass engineer come up with this."

Victoria straightened.

"If we can't disarm it, why am I sitting here listening this useless information?" Victoria barked, still clearly on edge from Charlie's decision to sacrifice himself.

"Because there's an upside, Vee. The bomb itself isn't very powerful, since it's in such a small enclosure. It'll take out the support, but that's about it. The good part is that there's no danger of anyone being injured from the blast itself."

"How does this help us?"

"Because if we can get those trains to stop running, then we've effectively neutralized the threat—the trains are the real threat, not the bomb. Worse comes to worst: he detonates the bomb, and Disney has to build a new section of track. No loss of life. I think we can all live with a little loss of property as a consequence."

"We already went over the evac option—he'll blow the ride as soon as he knows. You listened in, you've heard this already."

"No, not an evac, Vee."

"Then *what?*" she demanded, impatiently.

Kalani offered the solution, and it was ingenious. "We break the ride."

Charlie laughed aloud. It was so simple a solution that he was shocked nobody had thought of it earlier. If Holloway was as thorough as Charlie believed him to be, then he knew that rides and attractions experienced downtime due to mechanical difficulties and other unfortunate events almost daily. He'd have to have anticipated the possibility that the ride could experience a technical malfunction and need to be repaired. Therefore, he wouldn't detonate the bomb simply because the ride was down for fifteen minutes or so. If they could manufacture some 'technical difficulties' then the ride would have to go down for maintenance. At that point, even if Holloway detonated the bomb, nobody would be hurt and the damage would be purely structural.

"You guys are on to something," Victoria said with a smile.

For a split second, she turned to Charlie and he caught her eye. He saw relief brightening her features and imagined that his expression mirrored hers. There would be no reason for self-sacrifice today. X-ray Team had come up with the solution that could finally give them the edge they needed.

With the bomb neutralized and the members of Chaos Squad identified, it would simply be a matter of taking them out and bringing the fight to Holloway's doorstep. Unfortunately, that meant that Meghan, Violet and Katie had become Holloway's sole pieces of leverage. The old man was ruthless and clever, so Charlie assumed that when he found out about the loss of his bomb, he would do everything in his power to stop Charlie from reaching his family.

What Holloway did not know—could *never* know—were the lengths a man would go to in order to rescue the ones he loves. Charlie was willing to move Heaven and Earth and fight his way through Hell to save his girls and was fully prepared to ruin the day of anyone that tried to stand in his way. The time for playing fair had come and gone. Now Charlie was prepared to play the game on Holloway's terms—smart and ruthless.

Charlie and X-ray Team were about to become a serious thorn in Spencer Holloway's side.

27

Brody Kinney's head throbbed something fierce from all of the goddamn squinting he'd been doing. This was definitely a three-Excedrin headache. He fished around in the cargo pocket of his pants for the small bottle of migraine relief medicine and shook three pills out into his hand. Short on water and fresh out of patience, he chewed the caplets so that the medicine could work its way into his system faster.

Cupping a hand over his brow to block out the fierce glare of the relentless Floridian sun, he scanned everything in his field of view. He stood uncomfortably on the hot pavement near the main entrance to Bay Lake Tower—purposely far from the welcoming shade of the large portico, where his continued presence would be easily noticed. His usual strain of bad luck had caused his sunglasses to fall from his face and into the dark waters of the Seven Seas Lagoon earlier in the day when he'd bounced over another boat's wake while using one of the Sea Raycers to zip around the lake.

He'd sped around the lake aimlessly for the half-hour he'd paid for. He'd made up a halfhearted excuse about wanting to survey the land with his own eyes and he'd fed the boss some bullshit along the lines of: "I never rely on technology; I only trust what I can see." The entire thing was fabricated. In reality, he relied on technology most of the time; he trusted it more than his own eyes. Fortunately, the boss had been strangely distracted and had waved him off without objection. The old man seemed distant, as if something had been on his mind—but Brody was paid far too well to pry.

Regardless of his boss's mental state, he was still furious that all of the squinting he'd been doing had given him a seriously bad fucking headache, and he'd been wasting his time standing in the sun all day for no real reason. The boss must have been punishing him for his mishandling of the situation the previous night. How was he supposed to know that Walker would be able to see through their cover? Brody wasn't a goddamned Jedi. He couldn't just wave his hand and make the detective forget. Walker was a smart little fucker. He didn't waste *any* time in figuring out who they really were. Brody and Brent had played their parts well, but it just wasn't good enough.

Next time I see that asshole detective, I'm going to beat him to death with my bare hands.

All day, he'd wished agonizing death upon the clever detective for making him look bad in front of the boss. After all, this guy was the reason Chaos Squad was here in the first place. Brody wished that the detective would magically materialize before him so he could break the little fuck's teeth out of his stupid skull.

Brody may not have been the sharpest knife in the drawer, but he was fully aware of this and he embraced it. Fortunately, people didn't hire guys like Brody Kinney for their massive intellect; they hired guys like him for their ruthlessness, their muscle and their confirmed kill counts.

Brody was in his early forties, his age bolstering his abilities with a wealth of brutal experience. For almost two decades he'd made a living out of conflict, shipping off to wherever the fighting became too much to handle for the average foot soldier. Brody may have been the hammer of God with a firearm, but he was an absolutely unstoppable killing machine in hand-to-hand combat. Anyone could kill with a bullet, but few had the prowess to overcome an armed and trained opponent using nothing but hands and feet. He longed to pit himself against the detective. Walker was fit and capable, but he was still just a detective—a puzzle solver, not a fighter. Brody Kinney, on the other hand, was a machine, conditioned and programmed to kill efficiently and without remorse.

Just as he was fading into his fourteenth consecutive daydream about beating Walker into a thick red paste, his cell phone vibrated. Glancing at the screen, he instantly answered. It was the boss calling—and nobody ignores the boss, no matter how tough they are.

"Kinney," Brody answered.

"Kinney, recall your team immediately," ordered Holloway. "Meet me in my villa in thirty minutes. There have been new developments that we need to discuss and there are plans that must be made. We may have been compromised."

Compromised? But how?

This was unbelievable. Walker was clearly smart, but how in the world could one man compromise the cover of an entire highly trained unit? That kind of thinking was above Brody's pay grade, yet he couldn't help but wonder. Still, he held his tongue and remained calm.

"Affirmative," was all he said, when he wanted to say: *Compromised? What the hell are you talking about? You said this was going to be easy.*

Holloway disconnected the call instantly and left Brody alone with his thoughts. Refusing to waste time with inefficient and fruitless thinking, Brody contacted his team using a secure communications channel. Tapping the small button on his earpiece that would connect him to the other eleven men, he spoke.

"Hi kids, it's Dad. Grandfather has requested a family reunion ASAP. Put in your two-weeks' notice and catch the nearest ride to the estate."

Affirmatives all around. Chaos Squad was efficient, brutal and ruthless yet still retained a healthy respect for the chain of command. When Brody spoke, they listened and acted. As light and absurd as their call-signs and radio chatter were, they took their work very seriously with responses as quick and professional as possible. Brody said nothing else, expecting each of his men to follow their orders and report back.

Hand once more raised to his brow, Brody turned his gaze toward the upper floors of the Tower. Scanning the windows absently, he pondered what the meaning of this recall could possibly be. Beginning his walk inside, his mind raced with possibilities.

§

Brody was the first member of Chaos Squad to arrive, being the closest to the building when the recall order was given, and he entered his boss's villa while the old man was fastening the buttons on what appeared to be a new shirt.

"Hello, Kinney. Please, have a seat," Holloway said, motioning to a high-backed chair at the dining table. "Since you're here ahead of the others, I'd like to speak with you alone for a moment before they arrive."

Brody nodded and made his way toward the proffered seat, noticing as he did so that one of the window sections in the great glass wall was severely cracked; the remnants of a glass bottle lay nearby in a puddle of dark liquid. He smelled alcohol.

What the hell happened in here?

Taking a seat, Brody sat with his practiced ramrod-straight posture and looked toward his boss, eagerly awaiting whatever it was that the old man had to say.

Sighing, Holloway placed his palms on the table and kept his head down while he spoke.

"We have a very serious problem, Mr. Kinney," he stated, his voice still a bit strange.

"How serious?" Brody asked.

A pause. Holloway took a sip from a mug of coffee sitting on the table in front of him

"My daughter," Holloway stated.

"The Fed?"

"Central Intelligence," Holloway corrected.

"What about her?"

Holloway looked up, his eyes narrowing as if the light hurt them.

"She's here."

Brody scowled. "Now we've got the Company to deal with—on *top* of Walker?" he asked, mildly annoyed.

"Not on top of—in conjunction with," Holloway corrected again. "She has come to the aid of the detective, and she has brought a team along with her. I do not currently know the size of their force. So, not only do we face Detective Walker but my daughter and her confederates, as well."

Brody thought about this for a moment—the girl's presence certainly did complicate matters, but they still had cards left to play.

"Well, we've still got Walker's family," Brody offered. "And the bomb."

"Not really," Holloway countered. "We can't execute the family or detonate the bomb. Those are the only reasons Company agents haven't stormed this room already."

"Let them come," Brody challenged, his words laced with bravado. "Chaos will destroy them."

"You have good intentions, but you're failing to think. My daughter and Detective Walker are two of the most fiercely intelligent people on the planet, rivaled only by myself. No amount of muscle can stop them, should they wish to eliminate us. The mind is a dangerous weapon, Kinney. Never underestimate it."

Brody's hands clenched into fists as he leaned forward in his seat, gritting his teeth. He respected Holloway, but did the old man really think some egghead could outthink a bullet to the face? It was absurd. Charlie Walker was a human being, not some deity; he could—and *would*—be killed.

"Boss, just let me take out Walker. I could do it in no time at all."

"Sadly, Jeremy thought the exact same thing—and attempted to do so against my wishes. He is no longer breathing." Brody's surprise must have immediately shown on his face. Holloway arched an eyebrow at him.

For the first time, Brody began to feel a bit of apprehension at the thought of facing Walker. Brody had seen Jeremy in action and, while not a military man, the kid had top-notch abilities. Jeremy O'Neill had been a world-class combatant and if *he* had failed while trying to eliminate Walker, then perhaps Brody was dangerously underestimating the detective's abilities. Brody had no doubt that he was the more highly skilled fighter, and therefore could succeed where Jeremy could not, but he still had a newfound grudging respect for the detective and he took a mental note not to underestimate him again.

"So, what's the plan?" Brody asked.

"The plan is to wait for the rest of the team. However, I wanted to run over a few things with you before they arrive."

"Shoot."

"The coming hours are certain to test Chaos Squad to their limits. It's a definite possibility that there may be casualties on our side. Are you willing to accept this?"

"I never accept casualties on my side, but I am prepared for the worst—if that counts for anything."

"A well-spoken answer," Holloway said, thoughtfully. "Truth is: we are facing an enemy unlike any we have crossed swords with before. With Victoria and Walker at the helm, even a small team of trained operatives can deal heavy damage to our organization." Holloway looked somber, but still spoke with hope.

"Are you trying to tell me that a cop, a half-assed spy and a team of Company muscle can stand a chance against Chaos Squad?" Brody asked.

"That's exactly what I'm trying to tell you. Understand this, Kinney: if you do not abandon your ego, it will be the death of you and your team. I understand the need for confidence in your line of work, but an overinflated ego can only be detrimental to your success. Assuming you have won any battle before you've begun to fight is the surest way to fail."

Still irritated, Brody sat in silence for a few moments, thinking about the implications of what his boss was telling him. His team had been together, training and operating, for nearly two decades. In that time, they'd never lost a man and they'd always come out on top. It was tough for Brody to ignore eighteen years of constant successes—successes that were a direct result of his team's training and hard work.

"Then what do you suggest I do?" he asked.

"I suggest you go about this differently. Smarter. Brute force alone cannot win this for us. We must think, and then act."

The sound of the door opening drew their attention and they watched as the other members of Chaos Squad entered the room. Brody caught Masters' eye and told his old friend everything he needed to know with one look: the situation is bad—get pissed. Brody eagerly awaited Holloway's reveal as the remainder of his team found various seats throughout the villa.

When everyone was settled in, Holloway cleared his throat and began.

"Gentleman, thank you for making such excellent time in arriving. I've called you here due to some unfortunate developments that I regrettably must inform you of."

Holloway went on to explain the circumstances surrounding Jeremy's death, as well as the news about Victoria's presence and the threat she presented. Eventually, he'd filled Chaos Squad in on all of the recent developments.

"This brings us to our course of action," Holloway began, taking a seat and gazing at his mercenaries. "As I've already explained to Mr. Kinney, a brute force assault will be exactly what they're expecting. We must fight their cunning with an equal amount of guile.

"It is not my intention to offend, but I feel as if you've all been with me long enough to know that I do not insult. I merely deal in pure facts. The fact of the matter is that Victoria is more intelligent and resourceful than any man in this room, save myself. Detective Walker—even more so. The threat that these two present is very real."

One of the men on Brody's team, Purefoy, spoke up during this pause. "What's the big deal? We're in good shape. We have Walker's wife and kids. We own him."

"Is that what you think? Do you have children, Mr. Purefoy? A wife? Anything?" Holloway goaded.

"No, sir."

"Then you do not understand what it is to have your family taken from you. I admit that I also do not fully understand the emotional attachment that a man has to his family, but I have studied the human condition long enough to know that a protective father is as dangerous as any cornered animal. We cannot wait him out—Detective Walker will not simply give up and go home. He will pursue us until his family is safe or until he is dead. All of you know that Walker killed my son, but do any of you know why?"

Heads shook all around.

"Walker put himself between my son and the woman that he was about to murder. The detective took a bullet in his throat and nearly died to protect a perfect stranger. Can you fathom, now, what he would be willing to do to protect his wife and children? Gentlemen, our bargaining chips have now become our greatest threat."

"Why don't we just let the wife and kids go?" asked another merc.

"A reasonable idea, but they *are* still our bargaining chips—the Company team would assault our location the moment they confirmed the Walker women were safe. His family is both the reason we have yet to be attacked *and* the reason that we are certain to be—if that makes any sense. Victoria and Walker *will* come for them, have no doubt in your minds, but the detective is clever, and he will surely have a strong plan. This is the reason why we must think, and *then* act."

Brody spoke up, losing his patience for his boss's theatrics. He was ready to finally confront the detective.

"So, what *is* our plan?" he asked.

Finally, Holloway laid out his plan.

The old man had really thought of everything.

28

Meghan was sitting at the dining table with Violet and Katie, drawing pictures on hotel stationery, when the three large men rapidly entered the room and began shouting. Instinctively, she leapt from her seat and put herself between the men and her daughters.

"Step aside, Mrs. Walker. We don't want to have to hurt you," commanded a large man in a brightly colored polo shirt and cargo khakis. He looked tough, sunburned and frustrated, yet Meghan refused to budge.

"No," she stated, crossing her arms. "Why are you here?"

"Those girls are coming with us," said the big man, gesturing toward Violet and Katie, but offering no further explanation.

"Over my dead body," Meghan snarled, staring daggers into the giant's eyes.

The big man gritted his teeth then suddenly lashed out at Meghan with a vicious backhand, catching her square on the cheek and sending her stumbling away. Stars danced in her vision and she tasted blood in her mouth.

"Brody! Come on, man!" shouted one of the other men. "You weren't supposed to touch her."

"You'll keep your mouth shut if you don't want to be next, Addams," threatened Brody, pointing a finger at him before stepping toward Violet and Katie.

The girls shrank away from him, but they did not run—Meghan was proud of their courage in the face of danger. Brody grabbed Violet by her shirt and lifted the girl to her feet, roughly shoving her toward Addams, who grabbed hold of her wrist. Meghan lunged toward her daughter in an attempt to prevent these men from taking her away. She'd almost made it to Violet when a hand knotted itself into her hair and violently pulled her back. Brody spun her around and struck her again, this time with a closed fist. Meghan felt the skin on her cheek split as she screamed from the pain. Even though the force of the punch was crushing, she could tell that the man had held back, careful not to cause any permanent damage.

Dazed and off balance from the savage attacks, Meghan fell to her knees as the other men dragged Violet and Katie, kicking and screaming, from the room. The door closed behind them and she was left alone in the villa with Brody. Meghan's tears mixed with the blood from her cheek before dribbling to the floor. Still, she refused to let this man gain any satisfaction from these attacks. She dried her eyes with the back of her hand and stood once more.

"What are you going to do with my daughters?" she asked, her voice shaky yet firm.

"The boss wants them. It seems your beloved Charlie is attempting to rescue you," he said with a sarcastic laugh. "But we have a plan of our own. Divide and conquer."

Meghan's spirits lifted at the sound of her husband's name. He was still alive! She'd heard no news on Charlie's condition since the night before, when Holloway had told her what had been in store for him. She'd known that Holloway could never stop her husband, for Charlie was the truest of heroes—one of the few truly selfless individuals left in the world. Even though the situation was grim, she smiled. Brody noticed.

"What the fuck are you smiling about?" he asked, glaring at her.

"Charlie," she replied, her smile growing wider. "He's coming."

Brody stepped so close that she could smell the pungent aroma of sweat mixed with sunscreen. He looked directly into her eyes before speaking.

"Do I look worried to you?" he asked, in a near whisper. "Does it look like your runt of a husband has me running scared? No. Do you want to know why?"

Meghan crossed her arms once more and held his stare, but remained silent. Brody continued his display of masculinity.

"Because I've killed men like him before—lots of them. He's just another notch on the stock of my rifle. Let me tell you about men like your husband. They think that just because they're well educated and can solve a few Sudoku puzzles that they're invincible. Well, before the day is through, I'll show you just how wrong you both are."

"You have no chance," Meghan laughed. "You think you're so tough. Let me tell *you* about my husband, you fucking Neanderthal. Charlie is the finest man you will ever come into contact with. He's smarter, he's stronger and he's *better* than you. He will come for us, and he will kill you for what you've done." She stared defiantly into Brody's eyes, but the big man simply smiled.

"Just for that, I'm going to beat your husband to death with my bare fucking hands, and I'm going to make you watch. Oh—and as a consolation prize—you and I are going to have some fun before your hero gets here." Brody's hand found its way to the small of Meghan's back and his fingers began to slide beneath the waistband of her shorts.

Shocked and disgusted, Meghan threw her fist into Brody's unguarded nose as hard as she could—pivoting at the waist and following through, twisting her hips to add extra force to the punch. She felt the cartilage in his nose crush beneath her knuckles, even as something gave way in her right wrist with a sharp *crack*. Brody recoiled from her, clutching his broken nose and trying to staunch the flow of blood. She ignored the pain in her wrist— surely broken or sprained—and stared at the big man, waiting. He began striding toward her, blood already coating the front of his shirt. He stopped just outside of her reach, clearly wary of another attack.

"You fucking bitch! Try that again and I'll—"

Meghan gave him no chance to finish; she lunged forward and attempted to throw another haymaker with her uninjured hand. Unfortunately, Brody was prepared for this second assault and he batted away her swing even as his other fist came rocketing toward her face. For the third time in as many minutes, Brody struck the same part of Meghan's cheek with devastating force, knocking the slender woman from her feet.

Meghan lost consciousness during her fall, but her last thoughts were of her beautiful daughters and loving husband, hoping they were happy and safe.

She hoped she would survive to see them again.

29

harlie and Kalani were seated next to each other on a bus bound for Hollywood Studios. According to Mason's facial recognition software—which had so far only located four members of Chaos Squad—as of ninety-six minutes ago, two mercenaries were near the Tower of Terror, and records showed that they'd been in the same place all day near the entrance to the queue. Charlie and Kalani had no plan of attack once they acquired a visual of the enemy, but Kalani assured him that improvising was 'kind of his thing.' All Charlie could do was shrug, grin and offer up his mind as a resource to his gigantic new Hawaiian friend.

§

Earlier, before leaving the Liberty Tree, Charlie had handed over Jeremy's weapon to Mason for disposal. After leaving the Magic Kingdom, Kalani had thought it would be a good idea for Charlie to remain armed, so they'd returned to the Caribbean Beach to pick up his Walther. Kalani had remained at the bus stop while Charlie headed for the room, just in case Holloway was running surveillance on the place.

Entering the room, he found it much the way he'd left it, although housekeeping had clearly made their daily visit. A rabbit-shaped towel animal sat on the bed nearest the door. The pirate-themed gift basket still lay on the table, although it had been neatly repacked. Ignoring the tidy room, Charlie quickly made his way to the safe and unlocked it.

Over the years since he'd purchased the black Epcot T-shirt he was wearing, he'd filled out with muscle, so the shirt fit him more snugly. Still, it adequately covered his holster and spare magazine—so he didn't bother to change. Looking at himself in the mirror, he noticed how terrible he looked. His eyes were ringed with the dark circles that come as a result of a lack of sleep, his five o'clock shadow had made an appearance and his shoulders slumped with the heavy burden and stress of the crisis at hand.

He placed his hands on the counter and leaned in, staring his reflection straight in the eyes and having a silent conversation. As he looked into his own bloodshot eyes, he steeled his nerves for what was certainly to come: violence—and lots of it. As an officer of the law, Charlie had never been a proponent of violence, having seen firsthand the results of such passionate releases. He'd seen the bodies of countless victims of violent crimes and they'd affected him deeply. He'd become a detective to put an end to these things, not to add to the number of casualties.

All of his training told him to search for a peaceful resolution to this crisis, but his brain and his instincts told him that peace was no longer an option. The primeval man that lived within his mind—that lives within the minds of *all* men—was taking charge, telling him that peace was an illusion, and that this had escalated into an all-out war.

Wars were fought and won at the hands of the most powerful and violent combatants. To emerge victorious and save his family, he must become that which he worked every day to defeat: a killer. To be the savior that his family needed, Charlie knew that he must adopt the mindset of X-ray Team. Meghan, Violet and Katie were good people—pure, innocent people—who weren't able to help themselves out of their situation. They needed someone who was willing to match the evil that held them, stride for stride. One last glimpse in the mirror revealed a changed man. A ferocity that he'd never before seen had washed over him. He looked hardened. More determined. Stronger.

He looked *ready*.

Sighing, Charlie loaded the Walther and chambered a round before holstering it. He looked around the room one final time, praying that it would be the last time he would ever see the place without his arm around his wife and his giggling daughters jumping across the beds.

He grabbed one of the Blackberry batteries Holloway had left and installed it in the phone.

Finally, he left the once-cheerful room and headed straight for the frontlines.

§

As a testament to Disney's security forces, Charlie and Kalani walked straight past the bag search with their firearms concealed beneath their shirts while elderly security guards picked through the diaper bags of mothers and the fanny-packs of toddlers. Charlie shook his head in bewilderment as he and Kalani passed by unhindered, never glanced at twice, while innocent senior citizens were having their oxygen tank carriers searched.

Thankfully, we're the good guys, Charlie thought.

Kalani already had a Park Hopper ticket so they made it inside without delay. Wasting no time stopping to see the sights, Charlie led Kalani directly toward the Tower of Terror. The huge faux-hotel lived up to its namesake, towering over the masses, visible from almost any place in the park. The crowds seemed strangely light for the time of day, but Charlie was just thankful that Kalani was able to keep up with him in his haste to reach the attraction.

Stopping halfway along Sunset Boulevard, Charlie and Kalani bought turkey legs from a nearby stand and sat at a table near Fairfax Fare affording them a clear view of the entire area. Charlie wasn't hungry, and he'd only bought the slab of meat to keep up his cover, but Kalani eagerly set to work, ravenously devouring his. Charlie laughed while watching the big Hawaiian and shook his head lightly.

"What?" Kalani asked, powering through another mouthful of turkey.

"Nothing, man," Charlie said. "Pull out your phone. What do these guys look like? Mason sent you pictures, right?"

"Oh, yeah," Kalani replied, setting the turkey leg on its foil wrapper and fishing around for his phone. He pulled up the pictures and handed the phone to Charlie.

Before Charlie could get a good look at the Chaos Squad boys, Kalani's phone began to ring. Victoria's name flashed on the screen, along with a picture of her wearing a black bikini and holding an assault rifle—clearly taken while on what would seem to be a very interesting vacation. Charlie pointed to the screen and showed it to Kalani.

"What's *that* all about?" he joked.

"Inside joke, braddah. Answer it, will you? I'm sure it's for you anyway."

Charlie did as he was told while Kalani fought a losing battle with some flimsy napkins.

"Victoria, it's Charlie," he said.

"Good, Charlie, I was hoping you'd be nearby. An opportunity has come up, and I've made a decision," she informed him.

"Talk to me."

"Ten minutes ago, a kid threw up on Space Mountain. And I'm literally talking about *on* Space Mountain. Splashed the people behind him. Huge mess."

"There's our opening," Charlie said, seeing where she was heading with this.

"You're damn right it is. I've already moved on it. I've got Jen-Jen and McCoy heading down to City Hall to get Space Mountain evacuated *before* they get that mess cleaned up."

"Wait—you're calling in an evac order on the ride?" Charlie asked.

"Yes. It's the only way to be completely sure. They're not telling them why, they're just telling them who we are and that the attraction needs to be empty and offline ASAP. But Charlie?"

"Yeah?"

"All hell is possibly about to break loose. My Dad will know as soon as the place is evacuated. That means that he and his boys will be on high alert from this point on," Victoria warned.

"This is our only chance to take the bomb out of the picture. It's the only way. Do it."

"I'm glad you agree. Have you and Kalani had any luck finding the Chaos guys at the Tower?" she asked.

"Not yet, but we just got here. The area is not that crowded, though. I've scanned it, but I haven't seen anybody who looks like they could be a merc. You called before I could look at the pictures."

"Okay," she acknowledged. "Keep up the search and call me if you find anything."

"Likewise," Charlie said before terminating the call and looking at the photos.

"So, Vee's evacuating the Mountain, eh?" Kalani observed. "Good call. Might make some trouble for us back at the Company, but she's saving a lot of lives—it's worth the extra paperwork."

"Agreed," Charlie said, absently, his focus still on the two men in the photographs. He didn't recognize either of them, but he was absolutely certain that they were not here. He'd scanned the area several times in the ten minutes they'd been there and he hadn't seen anyone who came close to resembling the two mercenaries. It was discouraging and frustrating.

"So, you find our guys yet, Sherlock?" Kalani asked, finishing his turkey leg and stealthily reaching for Charlie's, which he'd abandoned after getting his hands on Kalani's phone.

Noticing Kalani's slowly encroaching hand, Charlie slid the turkey leg toward him before replying. "No, Kalani. That's the thing—I don't see these guys anywhere. The facial recognition software had shots of them every five minutes since right around nine this morning. Where the hell did they disappear to?"

"Are you sure they're not here?" he asked, shrugging and picking up Charlie's turkey leg. "Maybe they just went to take a piss or something."

"A ten minute piss?" Charlie shot back. "No, something isn't right. Let's check the area by Rock 'n' Roller Coaster, just to be sure, but I have a feeling that these guys bugged out."

They stood and quickly hurried to the adjacent area, standing on the knee-high brick wall in front of the giant red guitar to get a better view. Still, the area wasn't very crowded and it didn't take more than a couple of minutes for Charlie to realize that the Chaos Squad mercs were nowhere to be found.

"Damn it, Kalani. Those guys are gone," Charlie breathed, frustrated.

"You sure, braddah?" Kalani asked, even though he knew the answer. He took a bite of the turkey leg.

"I'm positive. Where the hell did they go? Get a hold of Mason for me. We need to track these idiots down."

Kalani pulled out his phone and, once again, Victoria's name and picture popped up on the screen before he could do anything. He answered the call and Charlie listened to his side of the conversation. He watched the big Hawaiian's joviality slowly disappear from his face and be replaced by steely determination as the call went on.

"Hey, Vee…Yeah…What? When?…Do you know where they went?… Okay. Here, tell Charlie." Kalani handed the phone to Charlie, his expression grim.

"What's going on, Victoria?" Charlie asked, worried that something had happened to his family in retaliation for Victoria evacuating Space Mountain.

"My Dad's cooking up something new. We just received facial recognition hits on all twelve members of Chaos Squad."

"What?" Charlie exclaimed, incredulous. "Where?"

"They were all captured in less than a half-hour by a camera in the lobby of Bay Lake Tower."

"Jesus," Charlie breathed.

"Charlie, they've turned that tower into a goddamned fortress."

30

The room was *full* of bad guys. Violet and Katie were seated on the couch, surrounded by menacing villains of all makes and models. Every one of them had a gun. The old man, Holloway, was there too. He seemed really unhappy and was being noticeably quiet, but Violet couldn't figure out why. The old man never spoke to Violet or Katie; he'd simply watched as two of his men led the girls into the room and made them sit on the couch. He kept checking a little computer that sat in front of him, sighing every time when he didn't see whatever it was he was looking for.

Violet sat forward and craned her neck to take in the surroundings. A small sigh escaped her lips when she realized that this room was identical to the one she'd been in with her mother and Katie. However, one interesting detail piqued her interest. She noticed that one of the panes in the giant window was cracked. A large puddle of something dark pooled on the floor nearby. It was interspersed with shards of broken glass—maybe from a vase or a bottle. The window worried her; it was bowed out and looked like it could easily break if touched.

On impulse, Violet stood and walked across toward the chair by the window—much to her captors' surprise. She ignored the strange stares from the bad guys and continued on her way until one of the men stepped in front of her and blocked her path.

"Where do you think you're going?" the man asked, trying to sound scary.

Violet wasn't impressed. She stared up at him and crossed her arms, like she'd seen her mother do when she was really mad at somebody or when she needed to say something important.

"I'm going to sit in the chair by the window. I want to look outside," she stated, still staring at the man defiantly. She could see confusion written all over his face. At one point, he even looked toward Holloway for a suggestion. Violet was losing patience. "Don't look at him! I'm on vacation. You ruined it. I want to look out the window at the Magic Kingdom. Now be nice and turn that chair around so that me and my sister can sit in it."

Violet almost giggled at the bewildered look on the man's face. It was so funny that some of the other men in the room laughed aloud at him. He turned bright red and looked over at Holloway one more time for direction.

"Be nice, Masters," said Holloway, with a nod toward the chair in question, before returning his eyes once more to the small computer.

The man, Masters, looked from Holloway to Violet and back again before finally shaking his head and turning around. Violet was forced to stifle another laugh as he turned the chair around and then angrily stalked off to another room.

"Come on, Kay," Violet said, and waited for her sister to join her before taking a seat by the window. The two girls easily fit in the large chair; Violet did not want her sister anywhere near that broken window—it looked like it was ready to give way at any moment.

The view from this room was as stunning as the view from the villa next door. The park looked different in the mid-afternoon light; a little less bright but warmer—even more welcoming than it had looked earlier in the morning. Violet sighed lightly again, wishing she and her family could be down there. Her mood had darkened considerably in the few minutes since she'd been in this room. She'd almost been able to trick her mind into believing that she was still on vacation when she was in the room next door. Violet remained strong, because she knew it took an iron will to make it through any difficult situation, but she worried about her Mom. After a while, she could no longer keep quiet.

"Mr. Holloway," Violet called, without turning around. She could see him in a reflection in the glass. Her voice seemed to startle him, and he jerked his head in her direction before answering.

"Yes?" he said, slowly and with mild irritation in his voice.

"Why did you bring me and my sister over here, but not my Mom?"

Holloway hesitated before answering. "It's all a part of things to come. You girls and your mother have different roles to play. Everything will be over soon."

Violet didn't understand the way he spoke—so mysterious and enigmatic—but she thought that she must not be meant to understand. "Is my Daddy coming?"

Again, Holloway hesitated.

"Yes."

Violet knew she wouldn't get any more answers out of the old man. She shared a smile with her sister at the mention of their father coming to rescue them.

§

The next while went by in almost complete silence, with only passing conversations happening between the few men who were still left in the room. Earlier, Holloway had sent away all of his men, except for Masters and two others, to 'take up positions'—whatever that meant. He'd even told two guys to ride the monorail and wait for orders. Violet didn't mind; fewer scary guys with guns was never a bad thing. She was finally able to relax, and Katie had fallen asleep next to her. Although Violet still worried deeply about her mother, she could not take her eyes off the Magic Kingdom—so close, yet so far away. The view greatly helped to distract her.

The sun was just beginning to set, and Violet noticed another change in tone for the park. As lights gradually came on throughout the property, Violet found the place as irresistible as ever. She'd always enjoyed the Magic Kingdom at night, sharing her father's love of the colorful lights of Tomorrowland after dark. It was only the night before when they'd taken their fateful ride on the PeopleMover, but it felt like an eternity had passed since she'd last set foot in the park.

Needing to stretch her legs a bit, Violet slowly stood, careful not to wake Katie as she gently eased her into a more comfortable position. Satisfied that her sister was still asleep, Violet decided to head to the nearest bathroom. She felt the eyes of the bad guys upon her, but nobody said anything as she made her way across the room.

Finally, some privacy.

After Violet finished, she was washing her hands at the sink when she heard voices from the other room. It sounded like Holloway and Masters were concerned about something. She quickly dried her hands and left the bathroom, eager to make it back to Katie's side and watch over her.

When she opened the door, Violet noticed that lights had been turned on throughout the villa. Holloway and Masters were hunched over the small computer, speaking in quick hushed tones. Violet couldn't make out much of what they were saying, but Masters kept pointing to different places on the screen and asking "What about that one?"

Violet rushed back over to the chair by the window just as Katie was waking up, rubbing her eyes and yawning.

"What's going on, Vi?" she asked.

Violet made a shushing gesture with her finger and spoke to her sister in a whisper.

"I don't know. They're interested in something on that computer. Something's going on, though."

"They turned all the lights on—woke me up," Katie complained.

The sun had almost completely set outside as Violet looked down upon the grounds before her. She scanned the ground below for anything of interest, but nothing seemed to catch her eye. After a few moments she'd begun to grow disenchanted with the view, and had decided to find a pen and paper so that she could draw. Just when she shifted to stand up, something amazing happened.

Three cars in the parking lot below suddenly and inexplicably exploded.

Clouds of fire and smoke climbed toward the sky. Katie let out a startled yelp as the shockwave from the blasts rattled the windows in their frames. Impossibly, the broken pane held strong, though Violet couldn't believe that it remained in place. It looked as if it could fall away at any moment.

Ignoring the commotion caused by Holloway and his men following the explosions, Violet gazed out at the scene and noticed that she could still see the monorail smoothly gliding in for its stop at the Contemporary's main tower. Something wasn't right about the train. She couldn't make out any details through the tinted windows but, from one of the compartments near the front, she saw several bright flashes of light coming from within. She leaned closer to the window for a better view, but the flashes had stopped almost as soon as they'd started and the monorail had pulled entirely inside the main building.

Before she could even begin to speculate about the source of the flashes or the cause of the explosions, a man burst into the room, clenching a squawking radio in his fist.

"Sir, they're here!" he yelled, before disappearing back into the hallway.

"Masters, it's time. You know what to do. Go," the old man commanded.

Masters nodded, drew his weapon and exited the room, leaving Violet and Katie alone with Holloway and the two other men—who had taken up positions on either side of the door. Holloway looked tense, and the other two looked nervous—exchanging worried glances with each other. The explosions outside seemed to have rattled more than just the windows.

Something was *definitely* happening.

Violet checked her watch; the time was just before eight o'clock. Deep within her heart, she knew—absolutely *knew*—that her Dad was coming. These men were on the defensive; they were excited—maybe even afraid.

Violet looked at Katie and smiled the characteristic all-knowing grin of her father. If there was one person on this Earth who could strike fear into guys as scary as these, they knew it could be none other than Charlie Walker.

31

At ten minutes past seven PM, Charlie and Kalani met up with Victoria and the rest of X-ray Team inside Tomorrowland, near a few benches that had a good view of Space Mountain's entrance. Their fruitless search at Hollywood Studios had frustrated the detective, and Kalani had been required to crack a handful of bad jokes before he could finally snap Charlie back to the present. The big Hawaiian was absolutely brimming with positivity and was relentless in his quest to infect everyone else with it.

Charlie sat down on one of the benches, taking an open spot between Victoria and Mason, who had a satellite laptop resting on his thighs.

"What's going on?" Charlie asked Victoria.

Without taking her eyes off the entrance, Victoria told him, "They're just finishing up the evac. If you take a look at the entrance, you can see it's already chained off. There should only be a handful of guests left inside and we should see them exit the arcade any second now."

"That's a relief," Charlie agreed. "What about the bomb—do you think he'll blow it?"

Victoria didn't hesitate before answering.

"I don't think so. The old man is definitely pissed off, but I don't think he's that petty or spiteful. The bomb is useless now and I don't think he'd waste his time just to force Disney to fix a section of track. I'd say the bomb is safely neutralized."

"What about disposal?" Charlie asked, concerned for any maintenance workers who might come across the explosive.

"I've notified Langley and Disney of the threat, as well as its current status. Disney has agreed not to reopen the ride, and to remove all personnel from the vicinity until further notice. I've also warned them to keep everything else operating as usual—with the exception of the PeopleMover due to its close proximity. They were hesitant, so I had to tell them the truth. They're definitely worried—a bomb on an attraction is no laughing matter—but I think I've made them understand that the threat is confined to the Mountain and that evacuating the entire park would be an unnecessarily dangerous decision. A Company disposal crew is en route and, after the old man is taken care of, they'll head inside and dismantle the weapon."

Charlie nodded and breathed a sigh of relief. It seemed as if he'd been holding his breath for the last day and he was finally able to breathe again. It was a great relief to know that the bomb was no longer a threat to anyone. He felt reinvigorated, able to devote all of his focus, effort and brainpower to saving his family. The threat of the bomb had torn him, and he'd been forced to spread his resources thin in an attempt to solve both problems simultaneously, but now he could breathe a little easier knowing that his focus was whole once again.

"So what's the plan?" he asked, eagerly. Normally, Charlie was the decision maker, the master planner, the chief tactician and the bloodhound, but he was absolutely fine with letting this remarkable woman take the reins. Victoria was beyond intelligent, and Charlie was thankful for her support.

"Let me expand a little on what we talked about on the phone," she began, finally taking her eyes off Space Mountain and turning to face Charlie. "The way I see it is this: when the ride went down, my Dad must have noticed. A standard Code V doesn't take long to clean, so he put two and two together and figured out that we'd taken the ride offline. I'm guessing that as soon as he saw that his bomb was useless, he recalled his dogs to the Tower. He knows we're coming, and he's setting up one hell of a welcoming party."

"What kind of resistance are we looking at?" Charlie asked.

"Mason, laptop," Victoria requested, extending an open hand across Charlie, toward Mason. When the thin agent handed over the computer, Victoria moved closer to Charlie to allow him to see the screen. "When I said they've turned Bay Lake Tower into a fortress, I meant it quite literally.

My Dad and your family are on the fourteenth floor, occupying two large villas."

Involuntarily, Victoria glanced in the direction of the Tower while she absently pulled up a floor plan of the villa. Returning her attention to the screen, she went over the layout of the rooms with Charlie and showed him a few interior pictures so that he knew what to expect when they finally made their way inside.

"He's rallying his knights and barricading himself in his castle," she continued. "I assume he knows that we're prepping to hit him hard, so he's trying to use his Chaos boys to stop us before we can reach him."

"That's either a hell of a gamble, or some epic confidence," Charlie offered. "Why not just cut and run?"

"Because I have him and he knows it," Victoria stated, directly—the most intense Charlie had ever seen her. "If he bugged out now—sure, he would survive the day—but I have his scent and I'd follow it to the ends of the Earth to find him. He knows that I've picked up his trail and that it would only be a matter of time before I followed it straight to him."

"But that would mean…" Charlie began, absently making the obvious connection.

"Yes. He's going to be gunning for me too. He knows he'll never be safe until all of us are dead. While the old man seems to be on the defensive, he is very much on the offensive."

"Son of a bitch."

"I know. It's hard to come to terms with, but this is the way it has to be, Charlie. I can't let him go, and he can't let you or I live. We are far too great a threat to each other. This ends here, one way or another."

Charlie nodded, slowly. He knew that the end was near, and he'd been steeling himself for the inevitable showdown for the better part of the day. He now found himself looking forward to the moment in which he would stand toe-to-toe with the enemy. It was sure to be dangerous, and a detective against a unit of militarized special operatives didn't seem like a promising scenario, but he now had a clear path to his objective. These mercenaries stood between him and his family and, for that, they'd signed their own death warrants. Charlie wondered if Victoria and her team felt this way before every operation. In the short time he'd known them, he couldn't imagine Victoria or Kalani actively looking forward to the things they had to do in the line of duty. He attributed his uncharacteristic feeling of malice to the fact that this situation was deeply personal. Holloway had transformed him from a lawman who took pride in his job to a vengeful entity that would do anything it took to save the ones he loved. It would be the last mistake that Spencer Holloway would ever make.

"We need to plan," Charlie stated.

"That's why I called you here—this is your operation, now," Victoria stated.

"What?" Charlie exclaimed, taken aback. "I'm a detective, not an operative. I don't know the first thing about planning something like this."

"I think you do, Charlie. You know the layout of the entire Disney property better than anyone on my team. You know the inner workings of an evil mind better than detectives twice your age. You're a *genius*," she winked. "You are absolutely our number one resource right now, whether you like it or not."

Charlie took a deep breath, considering what she'd said.

"Where do we start?" she asked him.

"The monorail," he said.

"Is it safe?" Victoria asked.

"It's the best option," Charlie told her. "If the Chaos guys are in Bay Lake Tower, then they'll be lax on security at the main Contemporary building. The resort loop heads from just outside the Magic Kingdom to the main building of the Contemporary. From there, we have the best chance of making it to Bay Lake Tower unseen. Any other approach is too exposed; they'll literally see us coming. There's a bridge between the two buildings, though it seems like an excellent place for an ambush—or at least a sentry—so I think it would be safer to avoid it."

Victoria took a moment to consider Charlie's suggestion.

"Smart," she agreed with a shake of her head. "You seem to have a knack for the subtleties of covert operations planning. Beginner's luck?" she joked.

"I read a lot of books," Charlie said with a shrug.

Victoria let out a light laugh before moving on. "So, we have a way in. What else do we have?"

"We know our enemy," Jen-Jen offered.

"Bingo," Victoria said with a snap of her fingers. "We know exactly what we're up against. There aren't going to be any surprises on the personnel front.

Jeremy is done for, and all that remains are twelve idiot mercs and my Dad. We've been up against worse."

"Prince Edward Island!" Kalani blurted, with a pump of his fist.

"Prince Edward Island, indeed, old friend," Victoria acknowledged with a slight bow of her head. "We've eliminated two variables—Jeremy and the bomb—but many remain, so it's important that none of you let your guard down."

Just then, Mason spoke up. His eyes were locked on his laptop, which Charlie had returned to him moments earlier.

"Vee? I just noticed something...uh...not good."

"Hit me," she ordered, with a sigh.

"Cameras have stopped picking up Chaos Squad."

"What?" Victoria asked. "Why? Figure it out."

"Already did. The cameras are being looped. It was a well-done job, but they can't slip that shit past me. The feeds are all running in a constant thirty-second loop. I spotted the seam where the loops restart. Smart, because the shots are either devoid of people, or contain stationary people who don't move enough to ruin the continuity."

"Does this mean what I think it means?" Victoria asked, looking irritated.

"Yes," Mason said. "It means that we don't know where these fuckers are anymore. They could be anywhere."

"Goddamn it!" Victoria barked. "Well, at least we still have the photographs. We'll just have to memorize them and do it the old-fashioned way."

"Uh, Vee?" Mason asked, apprehensively.

"What."

Not a question.

Mason sighed and swallowed.

"Those are gone too," Mason said, holding up his phone, the screen displaying just one terrible number and a single word:

0 images.

32

Mason's revelation had been unsettling, to say the least. Charlie, while not technologically savvy, still had a firm grasp on the limits of what people could accomplish with modern devices. He understood very well that to digitally break into a cellular phone—a Company agent's encrypted device, no less—from a remote location and wipe clear its contents was digital wizardry of the highest order. They'd grossly underestimated Holloway and his men, and their lack of precautions had not only robbed them of the element of surprise, but also of the intel they'd had—essentially making them unaware of the physical descriptions of their enemy. Charlie could recall the faces of the two men whose photos he'd studied on Kalani's phone, but the other ten men were completely unknown to him, and it caused him great discomfort. Anyone could be a hostile, and that made their operation exponentially harder.

As the final fiery glow of the dying sun dipped below the horizon, casting the Sunshine State into welcome darkness, Charlie stood at the Magic Kingdom's monorail platform with Victoria and the rest of X-ray Team. Victoria stood near Charlie, but she remained closed off; arms folded across her chest and a look of dissatisfaction on her face. She'd taken the loss of the photos—and the looping of the security cameras—personally, and blamed herself for the lack of preparation. Charlie had tried to reassure her that there was nothing she could have done, but after fifteen minutes, he resigned himself to the realization that Victoria would not be swayed. He decided to let her harness the anger, no matter how irrational, to use against her enemies. Still, something occurred to him and he felt compelled to share it with the team.

"Guys," Charlie called, in barely more than a whisper. "I don't think all of us should take the monorail. I think it would be smarter to split up."

"What makes you think that?" Victoria asked.

"Well, it's probable that your Dad has men watching the station," he offered, sure that Holloway had covered all the bases. "We'll be slaughtered as soon as we exit the monorail if that's the case—the station is wide open and has little to no cover. There are walkways on every floor that overlook the platform and could provide excellent high ground for even an amateur shooter. I think it might be well worth it for half of us to *walk* to Bay Lake Tower—it's not far: ten minutes, maximum—and maybe even cause a little trouble along the way. If we can create a distraction, it might draw any lookouts away from the station and give us an opportunity to slip in unnoticed."

Victoria thought about this for a few moments before responding.

"You're right," she admitted, with a small nod. "It might also be a good decision for you and I to split up, as well. If my Dad really does get the drop on us, I'd rather both of us not be in the same place."

Charlie nodded—Victoria had a point. She and Charlie were Holloway's primary targets and if they ended up walking into a trap, they'd both be killed. At least they stood more of a chance if they separated.

"Who's going with who?" Charlie asked, eager to begin.

"Mason, McCoy—you're with me," Victoria ordered. "Kalani and Jen-Jen—you're going with the detective."

Nods and murmurs of assent all around—the team clearly trusted Victoria with their lives and none of them opposed the plan.

"Well, we'd better be off, then," Victoria stated. "Need to get the ball rolling over there before you board the monorail."

Charlie nodded, steeling his nerves for what was sure to be a difficult confrontation. Before leaving, Victoria stepped over to him and wrapped her arms around him, squeezing him tight. Charlie returned his new friend's gesture and wondered if he would ever see her again.

"Good luck, Victoria," Charlie said.

"Damn it, Walker. You're not getting soft on me, are you?" she teased.

"Of course not," Charlie said with a smirk.

Victoria grinned and turned away, heading back down the entrance ramp with Mason and McCoy in tow. After a few steps, she looked at Charlie over her shoulder and said, "Godspeed, Detective. See you on the other side." She added a little wink for effect and disappeared out of sight.

§

Charlie had decided to let the first monorail pass to buy Victoria a little bit of time to create a disturbance and lure any hypothetical scouts away from the Contemporary's monorail platform.

"Charlie, I'm going to sit a few cars back," Jen-Jen declared, eyeballing a family waiting near the opposite end of the station.

"Why?" he asked.

"Same reason Vee left—too many of us in one area just makes us a bigger target."

Charlie didn't like the idea of splitting up again, but he couldn't deny that her logic was sound.

"Be careful. Keep your eyes open," he said as she turned to leave.

"Always do, boss," she said with a laugh. "Always do…"

When the next monorail glided to a stop in the station, Kalani chose to remain with Charlie instead of finding his own car. They'd been waiting alone on the platform outside of the car at the front of the train; the closest family was several cars back. The Main Street Electrical Light Parade would start soon, meaning that the crowds in the park were surely searching for prime viewing real estate, leaving the monorail station nearly empty as a result.

When they were able to board, Charlie and Kalani found that they were not alone in their chosen compartment. Two men already sat in the rear-facing seats. It wasn't an uncommon occurrence: every day many resort guests rode the monorail loop for the experience alone. Wary of these strangers, Charlie and Kalani took the seats opposite them as the doors automatically closed and sealed.

As the monorail departed the station, Charlie tried to observe the two men in the dim light. The pair were dressed nearly identically: pastel-colored polo shirts and khaki cargo pants. The outfits seemed entirely out of character for men of their size. Both men were large—muscular and fit—though one was several inches shorter than the other. Something about these men bespoke a familiarity that Charlie could not quite place. The lack of sleep, coupled with an overabundance of stress, was taking its toll on his memory and focus. During the ride, Charlie noticed that their cabin had been momentarily cast in an intense white light that faded to orange, but he refused to take his eyes off these two strange men.

Charlie finally looked over at Kalani and noticed that the big Hawaiian was gazing intently at the taller of the two men—who returned the stare with equal intensity. Judging from his tense posture, Charlie deduced that Kalani had also sensed something sinister about these two men. One of the men had a bewildered look on his face, almost as if feeling the strange sense of familiarity that Charlie had been experiencing. It seemed as if the two men were equally wary of Charlie and Kalani, and the staring contest continued—both pairs of men quietly observing the other. After a few moments, the smaller man shifted uncomfortably in his seat and leaned forward to get a better view.

Finally, Charlie solved the puzzle that his foggy memory had placed before him. The smaller man's movement had momentarily flattened his polo shirt against his hip and Charlie had seen—just for the smallest fraction of a second—the telltale bulge of a concealed firearm. It was this clue that had given his memory the clarity that it had so desired. While not the men from the photographs on Kalani's phone, the outfits they wore were definitely variations of the clothes the men had been wearing in the surveillance photos. This data, coupled with the definitive presence of a sidearm, told Charlie exactly who these men were.

Evidently, Kalani had made the same connection, for he shifted his position and freed up his left arm, a maneuver specifically designed to allow him quick access to his sidearm that was holstered in his shoulder rig. Kalani feigned an itch and scratched at his left armpit—outside of his shirt—and Charlie could hear the faint *snap* of the shoulder holster's button being disengaged.

Clever, he thought. Kalani was preparing for war.

"Is there a problem, gentleman?" Kalani asked the men, with a friendly smile plastered on his face that never reached his eyes. The two men seemed stunned into silence, clearly having made the same connection that Charlie and Kalani had made just moments earlier.

Charlie felt his fight-or-flight instinct kick in as both mercenaries made a rapid grab for their weapons. Charlie and Kalani, having been ready for this moment, were equally quick on the draw. Within a fraction of a second, all four men had brought their weapons to bear.

Without any hesitation on either side, all hell broke loose.

Time seemed to slow to a crawl as four triggers were pulled simultaneously.

Volleys of hot lead tore into the walls and punched through the seats of the compartment as four handguns spat fire, and a deafening thunder roared through the tiny space. None of the four had time to aim their weapons after drawing them from holsters on their waists; they simply fired from the hip like gunslingers in a Spaghetti Western.

Charlie heard sizzling rounds pass within inches of his head, like the sound of a swarm of furious killer bees buzzing past his ears. Two of his first rounds found fleshy new homes—one in the upper shin of the bigger man, the other directly in the gut of the smaller man. The remainder of his wildly fired shots punched harmlessly into the wall and seat. From his right, he saw that Kalani had fired several rounds into the chest of the bigger man—the big Hawaiian being the only one able to properly aim his weapon, having drawn it from the shoulder rig.

In his distraction, Charlie felt a searing hot pain tear into his right side, just outside his ribcage. The overdose of adrenaline allowed him to ignore the pain and, as the man across from him attempted to eject the magazine from his empty weapon, Charlie leapt from his seat—causing an all-new wave of burning agony to stab his side—and lunged toward the smaller man. Startled, the man attempted to raise his arms in defense, but Charlie was simply too fast. Swinging as hard as he could, but sacrificing precise aim, Charlie brought the handle of his Walther down hard on the man—missing the head that he'd been aiming for, but shattering the man's collarbone in the process.

The Chaos Squad mercenary screamed in pain, but it was short lived. The soldier had been trained and conditioned to deal with pain, and within an instant his arms were wrapped around Charlie's torso. The muscular man stood, lifting Charlie from his feet and driving him to the floor with devastating force. Charlie felt the air burst from his lungs as the man slammed him to the floor of the compartment. Gasping for air, Charlie struggled to free himself from beneath the big man. The mercenary was prepared and he stymied all of Charlie's attempts to escape. Raising a meaty fist, the man brought it down hard, aiming for Charlie's face. Luckily, Charlie's Krav Maga training kicked in and he was able to deflect the blow while at the same time bringing up a fist that caught the man square in the jaw. Charlie wasn't able to put adequate force behind his punch due to his position, but the connection was solid and it stunned the man just long enough for Charlie to buck him off and scramble away.

Finally free, Charlie lunged for the man once more. The mercenary had somehow found an opportunity to draw a knife which he jabbed toward Charlie's midsection. Again, he was prepared, grabbing the man's wrist and leaning away from the wickedly sharp blade. He latched his right hand onto the man's throat and squeezed, still firmly grasping the man's wrist. The mercenary tried with all of his might to free himself, but Charlie held fast with all of his strength. The man weakly clawed at Charlie's hand but the detective would not be moved.

Just then, a single shot rang out, resonating in the small space like a bomb blast.

Blood, hair, bone shards and brain matter decorated the window of the compartment and he finally released his grip. The dead mercenary fell limply to the floor among the countless shell casings and spatters of blood. Charlie turned to see Kalani holding his smoking pistol in the classic shooters' grip. Luckily for Charlie, Kalani had been able to reload his weapon during the struggle and it had saved the detective's life.

Charlie gasped for air and struggled to combat the shock that was attempting to set itself in.

Soon after, the train glided to a stop in the Contemporary's main building and the heavy, acrid smoke wafted out into the clean air of the platform as soon as the doors opened. Charlie stumbled out of the monorail, drenched in sweat and dripping blood from his wound. Kalani followed close behind.

Catching sight of the slaughterhouse that was Monorail Red's front passenger compartment, a woman on the platform began to scream in terror at the horrific sight. Quickly, Charlie and Kalani hurried away from the monorail without looking back and made their way to the ground floor where they took refuge in a nearby restroom.

"Fuck!" Charlie gasped as he stumbled over to the sink and checked his reflection in the mirror. He had been lucky—extremely lucky—that the wound was only skin deep, the bullet having simply grazed him along the ribs. The laceration would certainly require stitches, but Charlie was in no immediate danger.

"Is it bad, braddah?" Kalani asked, weapon still drawn and trained on the door in case any unexpected visitors decided to join them.

"No," Charlie replied firmly, slapping a fresh magazine into his weapon and chambering a round. "What about you—are you hit?"

"Negative. Close call, but I ain't dead yet, *haole*."

"So much for a stealthy infiltration," Charlie pointed out, his words laced with frustration.

From outside the restroom door, a voice spoke up.

"Charlie, Kalani, let me in quick! It's Jen-Jen!"

Kalani quickly opened the door and ushered the blonde into the room. Catching sight of Charlie's bloodied shirt, Jen-Jen gasped.

"Charlie, are you okay?" she breathed.

"I'm fine—just a scratch," he said, dismissing her concern with a wave of his hand. "Did you hit any resistance on your way here?"

"No, but what the fuck happened? I heard the gunfire. People are screaming and running all over the fucking place. It's complete pandemonium out there."

Kalani answered, "Two Chaos Squad guys were waiting for us. Well, not *waiting* for us—I definitely think we surprised them. They drew down and we returned fire. Bad news: white boy took a bullet. Good news: bad guys took a lot of bullets. Chaos Squad is now short two assholes."

"Jesus," she breathed. "You guys have some seriously strange luck."

Charlie interjected, "We need to get moving. If we were hit this hard, I can't imagine what the others must be up against out in the open. We need to get over there now to bail them out."

Kalani and Jen-Jen exchanged nervous glances. Charlie took notice.

"What?" he asked.

"They're on their own, Charlie," Jen-Jen answered, eyes downcast.

"It's protocol," Kalani added. "Our first priority is to complete the objective. We need to get in the Tower as fast as possible."

Charlie was taken aback. He understood chains of command and the importance of following orders, but it was possible that Victoria and her guys were facing heavy resistance and were in great danger. He wasn't about to throw them to the wolves—not after everything they'd done for him.

"Fuck your protocol," he said. "I'm going to get them. You can come with me, or you can go to the Tower—but she needs us, and I owe it to her to help."

For a moment, Charlie stared intensely at his friends. Nobody spoke. Finally, Kalani broke the heavy silence.

"You've got some big iron balls—and it's probably suicide—but we're with you all the way. Lead on, *haole.*"

Jen-Jen reluctantly nodded in agreement.

"Thank you," Charlie breathed and headed for the exit.

Weapon at the ready, Charlie threw open the restroom door and hurried toward where he assumed Victoria would be. Jen-Jen and Kalani followed, eyes constantly scanning their environment for threats.

Heading into enemy territory, with almost no idea as to the identity of their adversaries, Charlie felt no fear. What he felt instead was a boiling rage that washed away his pain and honed his focus. It would sustain him until he either resolved this situation and rescued his family, or died trying.

Charlie had become a machine.

33

As Victoria made her way toward Bay Lake Tower, flanked by Mason and McCoy, she quickly pulled up a satellite image of the property on her phone. Even while she hurried toward the tower at a brisk pace, she studied the map intensely. Luckily, there was not much to memorize. Charlie had been spot-on: a sidewalk led directly past the bus stops and beneath the monorail tracks until it met the road, at which point she and the others would be able to cross and take cover between the numerous cars in the resort's large northern parking lot.

For the first time in Victoria's career, she had no plan—she was simply winging it. It pained her to know that countless variables stood in her path. She had no idea where the Chaos agents had been posted, no clue what they looked like and no plan for what to do if and when she found them. All she knew for certain was that Charlie's life—and the lives of his family—relied solely on her ability to buy the detective the time he needed to make an unopposed entrance. Kalani and Jen-Jen would be doing everything in their power to keep Charlie safe, but two extra guns would mean nothing if they were caught by a sniper's bullet in the exposed section between the two buildings. Even a semi-competent sharpshooter could put a swift end to their mission before it had truly begun. She *had* to think of something.

Reaching the road, McCoy took point and rushed across the lanes, halting on the far side as Victoria and Mason followed suit. The three moved on together and when they reached the edge of the parking lot, McCoy and Mason stopped, turning to Victoria for orders. After a few seconds of empty silence, Mason spoke up.

"Vee, we need to think of something. Fast," he said.

"I know," she replied, pinching the bridge of her nose. "For the first time in as long as I can remember, I don't have a plan."

McCoy remained silent, but Mason continued.

"They need us, Vee. We don't have much time before their monorail heads this way."

"Mason!" Victoria snapped. "A minute of silence, man. Jesus. I'm working on it."

Mason raised his hands in a mock apologetic gesture, but seemed unable to stay quiet.

"I'm sorry. These Chaos guys worry me. They—"

"That's it!" she blurted, startling him. "Chaos."

Mason cocked an eyebrow at her.

"Chaos," she repeated. "We're going to get into some serious shit back at HQ for this, but it's a surefire way to get things moving."

"What have you got?" asked Mason, cautiously.

"A ridiculous idea, but it's simple and it'll work. Do you still carry that low-yield det cord with you everywhere you go?"

"Of course I do. Never leave home without the stuff," Mason scoffed, lifting one leg off the ground. Reaching for a spot near his knee, Mason grabbed at the seam of his pants. Within seconds, he'd withdrawn a three-foot length of the explosive cord from a cleverly concealed sheath. "Will this do?"

"Perfect."

Quickly, Victoria separated the explosive cable into three equal one-foot lengths and handed one to either team member. Mason removed three small devices from his pocket, and clamped them to the ends of each piece of cord.

"Remote blasting caps," he stated. "I can detonate all three of these at once using an app on my phone. What's the plan?"

"Find a car, then drop these fuckers into the gas tank and run for your life," Victoria told them.

"Holy shit! You really weren't kidding about that whole chaos thing, were you?"

"Not in the least—things are about to get wild. But it'll work, I guarantee it. Once these go off and we've got three smoking carbecues, panic will set in. Guests will be running wild and it should bring any nearby Chaos members running to the scene."

"You do realize that there is a *massive* downside to this, don't you?" Mason snapped. "I mean, we wanted to distract Chaos Squad, not to lure them into an uneven firefight on their home field. It's suicide."

"If we don't do this, Charlie and his family could die. We're still far enough away to be sure that they haven't spotted us yet, but if they see Charlie getting off that monorail, the heat will be entirely on him and he'll be exposed, surrounded and overwhelmed. We have the element of surprise and a fair amount of cover. We don't need to beat them, Mason. We just need to keep them occupied as long as we can."

"And what happens when we run out of bullets and ideas?" Mason asked, voicing a solid concern.

Hesitating, Victoria sighed and told him, "We'll worry about that if and when the time comes. For now, let's blow up some fucking cars. Meet me back here after you've planted the det cord and get ready to scratch that itchy trigger finger."

Mason and McCoy nodded before the three split up to decide which three unlucky families wouldn't have a ride home in the morning. Victoria chose a large black Hummer with massive chrome wheels—a scourge on the face of the Earth and a monument to environmental ignorance if ever there was one. *Fuck it,* she thought, *they're clearly rich, and the insurance money will buy them a Prius or two.*

The owner had replaced the standard fuel hatch with a cheap, gaudy carbon fiber model that came complete with a lock that required a key. Irritated by this inconvenience, Victoria snapped open her pocketknife and broke the flimsy lock with a quick pry. She removed the cap, dropped the det cord inside and made her way back toward the road to regroup with the others.

Mason and McCoy returned just seconds after Victoria, and Mason fished his phone from his pocket in preparation for detonation.

"You sure about this, Vee?" he asked.

"It's the only way," she said. "Now flip the switch, draw your damned sidearm and get ready to engage a dozen armed and highly trained mercenaries."

She spoke in an ironic, comical tone, but neither Mason nor McCoy laughed. Mason closed his eyes and let his thumb touch the onscreen detonation button.

For several full seconds, nothing happened. Victoria glanced at Mason, hoping he could fill her in. He shrugged.

"I don't know what the problem is. Maybe the blasting caps weren't waterproof? I could have sworn that when I—"

The sky lit up a brilliant white.

Three massive pillars of smoke and flame rose up to meet the night sky and the shockwave from the trifecta of blasts ruffled clothing and bent blades of grass. Windows rattled in their frames hundreds of yards away. Windshields and mirrors shattered on cars near the explosion—some of which were even thrown several yards away. Victoria felt the pressure of the blast in her ears and sinuses. When the percussive thunderclap of the explosion had faded, Victoria could hear the sound of dozens upon dozens of car alarms shrieking away into the night. People screamed and ran toward the three massive pyres.

Well, this is definitely a spectacle.

As Victoria had expected, nobody was injured by the blasts. She trusted her team to know that both men would have chosen vehicles specifically for their isolation and distance from anyone who could possibly get hurt. Assured that all innocents were safe for the time being, she surveyed the area and searched for any signs that would betray Chaos agents who should be closing in on their location. She spied many vacationers and Cast Members gawking; some corralling children away from the scene, others on cell phones most likely dialing 911. Unfortunately, none seemed to be the Blackwater type. Victoria could tell the difference between a vacationer and an operator, and all of these onlookers were clearly tourists or employees.

Violently, the side window of a car burst just a few feet to her left, followed by a sharp *crack* from off in the distance. Ducking behind an SUV, Victoria drew her sidearm and checked to make sure Mason and McCoy were okay. Spotting them unscathed and behind cover, she tried to discern from which direction the shot had come. She was certain that she'd heard the report of a sniper's rifle, but the suppressor had done its job well. It had not masked the shot entirely, but instead made the intended target unable to locate the shooter by sound.

A hundred yards to her left stood a dark copse of trees that would provide excellent cover for a shooter, but the angle of the shot that had shattered the car window wasn't possible from that position. The shot had come from the direction of the tower, or the parking lot between. The most likely position for a shooter, she knew, would either be from one of the tower's windows, or from an automobile in the lot. Still, she had trouble believing that a shooter—an ex-Blackwater mercenary, even—could miss a shot from such a short distance. With all of this in mind, Victoria was able to piece together the most viable location that their assailant was in.

The sniper wasn't in the tower, nor were they in an automobile or the trees next to the lot. He was mobile. The fact that the first shot had missed—by a large margin, for a professional—revealed this truth. A shooter in a comfortable and stationary position would have put two rounds through her chest before she could have even realized it was happening. This meant that he was in motion. He'd stopped, lined up a quick shot, fired, and moved on. Victoria sighed as she felt the rush of adrenaline pumping through her veins. A mobile shooter, while likely to be less accurate, was in fact *more* deadly. They were unpredictable and hard to track. Not only were they dangerous, but they also provided an excellent distraction—drawing their target's focus while other assailants closed in on their prey, unnoticed.

"Fuck," Mason snapped. "Runner?"

"Runner," Victoria agreed.

"That means a sweep team isn't far behind," Mason added. We need to burn this motherfucker before they get here or we're as good as dead, Vee."

Looking around, Victoria glanced toward the trees once more. The most logical decision would be for the shooter to head for that darkened area. It would provide optimal cover for moving and shooting, and he could essentially force Victoria and her team to turn away from the resort—the direction from which the sweep team would surely come. It was a cleverly lain trap, and it would essentially catch X-ray Team in the crossfire between the shooter and the flanking team. Mason was right—their survival hinged upon the removal of the shooter—their odds of success would greatly increase with him out of the picture.

"McCoy," Victoria called. "Mason and I are going to draw his fire. Find him, flank him and put him to bed. Understood?" She pointed to the tree line so McCoy would have the best idea of where to start.

With a grunt and a nod, McCoy crawled toward the rear of the car he was concealed behind and set himself in a position to move as soon as he was covered.

Victoria glanced at Mason and then back to the tree line. The two of them would need to break cover and fire blindly to provide McCoy with the distraction he would need to slip away.

After a mental three-count, Victoria burst from cover, staying low and firing wild shots high in the direction where she thought the shooter would likely be. Mason also opened fire in the same general area. Their haphazard volley of shots was answered almost immediately by three high-caliber rounds that ricocheted off the pavement near Victoria's feet, showering her with fragments of asphalt. Miraculously, she made it to cover behind an SUV just as three more rounds hit the automobile, shattering a side window, bursting a tire and puncturing a fender.

"Did you get a location?" Victoria yelled, but McCoy was already on the move, nearly halfway to the tree line. "Mason! Think you can make it across?"

"Yeah, I'm pretty sure I can. Cover me."

Victoria leaned out from behind the SUV, staying low, and began taking more precise shots toward areas where the shooter could be concealed. Mason broke from cover and fired again, sprinting as fast as his legs could carry him. To Victoria's horror, a dim muzzle flash lit up far from where she'd been aiming and Mason went down hard on the pavement, ten feet from the SUV and still very much out in the open.

"Mason!" she shrieked. "Mason, tell me you're okay!"

Mason coughed once, still facedown on the asphalt. Victoria could see the puddle of blood slowly spreading from beneath him.

"Mason, please!"

She heard her gravely injured friend attempt to inhale, and it sounded grotesquely unnatural—broken and ragged. He gasped—each inhalation a struggle, each exhalation wet and bubbling. Victoria couldn't see Mason's wound, but she knew from the sound of his breathing that the round had punctured one of his lungs. He was dying—slowly.

Victoria was close to panicking. Tears rolled down her cheeks as she leaned out from behind the SUV to try to reach her friend, but two rounds slammed into the tailgate of the vehicle and forced her back into cover.

"Goddamn you—fucking coward!" she screamed, even though she knew the shooter was too far away to hear.

She collapsed to her knees and leaned against the rear wheel of the SUV. Just a few yards away, her friend lie suffering, dying in a pool of his own blood, and she was powerless to help him. She buried her face in her hands and openly wept—firearm discarded and all but forgotten on the ground next to her.

Victoria had never been this terrified or hurt in her life. A natural born protector, she never gave a moment's thought to her own wellbeing and she did not fear death, instead fearing the loss of those close to her. She had led these people here, and now one of them was dying and it was her fault. What if she'd made the wrong call? What if her team were to be slaughtered here in such close proximity to The Most Magical Place on Earth? How could she live with herself?

Suddenly, five shots rang out in the distance—loud, not from any suppressed rifle. Victoria could only pray that McCoy had found and eliminated the shooter—Mason deserved that much. Justice and retribution were all that could be done at this point. Even at a glance, it was clear that the poor man had lost too much blood to recover. Fresh waves of agony washed over Victoria and she found it difficult to focus on the moment. Never before had she lost a teammate in the line of duty. Still, the world was a cruel place and it refused to give Victoria the time to mourn her friend.

Three sets of footsteps were rapidly approaching from the far side of the SUV. It was surely the sweep team coming to finish her off.

Fuck that, she thought. *I'm taking one or two of these assholes with me if it's going to be like that.*

She lay on the ground and raised her pistol, aiming straight ahead, toward the front of the vehicle. She relaxed her shoulders and drew in a deep breath to steady her aim. If this was to be her last stand, then she refused to fail. She would kill at least one of them before they took her life.

Finally, right on cue, the first mercenary cautiously stepped around the corner and into her iron sights. He was a large man wearing a bright blue polo shirt, and he carried a large-caliber handgun held low, but ready. Without hesitating, she pulled the trigger with practiced smoothness and her weapon jumped in her hands once. Twice. Three times. Bright red splashes of blood erupted from the mercenary's chest and neck. His momentum carried his dead body forward where it collided hard with a parked car before finally falling to the ground.

Too late to change course, the second mercenary skidded around the corner and she fired three more times. Each round found a home deep within the man's chest and he collapsed atop his fallen comrade.

Still aiming for the corner of the vehicle, waiting for the third and final mercenary to appear, Victoria noticed something that made her breath catch in her throat and her hopes dissolve before her eyes. The slide on her weapon was locked back—out of ammunition. There was no time to dig a fresh magazine out and reload, for she was lying on top of her extra magazines.

And then the mercenary showed his face, raised his weapon and took aim.

Victoria closed her eyes as a wave of serenity overcame her. She was going to die, there was no doubt, but she was unafraid. She had succeeded in buying Charlie the time he'd needed to get inside, and it was more than enough for her. She laid down her weapon and kept her eyes firmly pressed shut, awaiting the deafening roar of a high-caliber handgun to cast her into oblivion.

Finally, the sound came—it was quieter than she'd expected.

But why could she still hear? Why did she feel no pain? Was this what dying felt like?

Realizing that she was in fact not dead, Victoria's eyes shot open to reveal the last thing she had expected to see: her attacker lay dead, slumped against the side of the SUV with a bullet hole above his eye and the contents of his head splashed across the vehicle. To her right, smoking gun still in hand, stood Detective Charlie Walker of the Detroit Police Department, flanked by a large Hawaiian and an attractive blonde. The detective lowered his weapon and rushed to her side. Gently, he lifted her to her feet as Kalani and Jen-Jen hurried to check on Mason.

"Charlie!" Victoria shouted and threw her arms around his neck. She squeezed him harder than she'd ever squeezed anything in her entire life—she'd never been so glad to see another person in all her days. After a few seconds, she felt a light tap on her back and realized that she'd probably been cutting off his supply of oxygen. Pulling away, she noticed the bloody hole in his shirt and the way he favored his left side. He'd been shot. "Are you okay?"

Charlie dismissed her concern with a wave of his hand. "It's okay, Vee. It's nothing. Jesus, what the hell happened to Mason?" he asked, stepping quickly past her to get a closer look at their fallen comrade.

"There was a shooter. McCoy went after him." She wiped a fresh tear from her cheek.

From behind them, a man cleared his throat and everyone turned around to look. Before the group stood McCoy, dragging a bloodied, bullet-ridden— but very much still *alive*—mercenary with him. The merc looked defiant, but it was clear that he was fading fast.

"This our shooter?" Kalani asked, all traces of joviality gone from his voice. McCoy nodded.

"Was he alone?" Victoria asked.

"No. He had a spotter," McCoy stated.

"Dead?" Kalani ventured.

McCoy nodded gravely and shoved the wounded mercenary toward the big Hawaiian. Kalani caught the man by the collar, lifted him and slammed him onto the hood of a nearby car. Withdrawing a knife from his pocket, he snapped open the blade and turned to the team. The mercenary began to hyperventilate.

"I think it's time we asked a few questions," Kalani stated.

34

Victoria wiped the final tears from her eyes as she lightly stepped toward the wounded Chaos soldier. Jen-Jen and McCoy held the man's arms, not allowing him to move even an inch. Kalani loomed over the bloodied man, combat knife still in hand. The mercenary's breathing was erratic, but the big Hawaiian refused to relent. Victoria had to put a hand on his to calm him down.

"What's your name?" Victoria asked the mercenary, calmly and with no emotion coloring the tone of her words. It was almost as if she were having a normal conversation with a stranger. Still, the man refused to speak, rewarding her instead with a look of the purest disgust. "Again I'll ask you: What is your name?" Again, nothing but defiant silence.

Victoria was far too exhausted to play these kinds of games. She'd interrogated men like him before—they always played tough. Normally, she'd go through the entire song and dance and, after a few hours, she'd be able to leverage some answers out of her subject. This time her patience had worn thin, and the man who'd killed her friend would give her the answers she needed—and he would give them *immediately*. She turned and cocked an eyebrow at Kalani.

"Cut him," she said softly, before turning her back on the grisly scene.

Kalani did as ordered, digging the blade an inch into the mercenary's abdomen. The man bucked and thrashed, but the two Company agents held him firmly in place and he screamed in agony. A consummate professional, Kalani only penetrated the muscle and fat, causing excruciating amounts of pain, but no damage that couldn't be reversed.

Kalani removed the blade from under the skin and Victoria waited a few moments for the man to calm down before speaking again.

"Your name," she demanded, her voice calm.

The mercenary coughed, but this time he obliged, not wanting to face the wrath of the knife-wielding Hawaiian for something as trivial as a name.

"Moran," the man said, finally. "You crazy bitch. I hope you don't think—"

"Cut him," she said again, wasting no time letting this man talk tough. Kalani moved quickly, but the mercenary screamed once more.

"No! Wait! Don't cut me again, damn it!"

"Then I suggest responding to the question I'm going to ask with an answer I'll like," Victoria demanded. She saw Charlie's reflection in the windshield of the car and, while the brutal torture of their enemy clearly unsettled him, he still had his characteristic grin.

"What do you want to know?" the mercenary asked, deflated.

"I want to know where the rest of you assholes are positioned."

"It won't make a difference. You'll never get those girls."

"Then it'll do no harm for you to tell me, will it?"

The mercenary looked conflicted, as if trying to decide whether to answer. Kalani showed him the knife once more—and it did the trick. The man's reply was exactly as Victoria would have preferred it—short and to the point.

"Two in the Tower lobby. Two in Holloway's room with the little girls. Our Captain is in the room next door with the wife. Two more riding the monorail. The three you just killed. Then there's me and my spotter."

"That's twelve," Victoria stated. "It adds up, but you'd better not be lying to me."

The man shook his head and swallowed. "Is that it?" he asked.

"That's it," Victoria informed him and turned on her heel, grabbing Charlie gently by the elbow and leading him away from the scene. Charlie just caught a glimpse of McCoy withdrawing a suppressed pistol from his shoulder holster before he was led out of sight. Still, he heard two muffled gunshots and knew that Chaos Squad was now seven members short.

Ignoring the feeling of nausea creeping up in his stomach from the overabundance of violence he'd witnessed in such a short period of time,

Charlie stopped walking and faced Victoria.

"Vee, I'm so sorry about Mason. He was a good man."

"He knew what he was doing. We all did," she managed, trying to look detached. Charlie could tell she was hurting. Losing Mason had really cut this poor woman deep and Charlie couldn't help but feel responsible for Mason's death—after all, nobody would be here if it weren't for him. He decided not to voice his concerns, realizing it wouldn't help to ease Victoria's troubled mind. Instead, he chose to direct her anger toward justice for their fallen comrade.

"Where do we go from here?" he asked. He had already come up with a few ideas of his own, but he knew that allowing Victoria to plan their route would help to get her mind off Mason for the time being.

"We're sticking together. I don't know how you took that bullet but it won't happen again. It might seem like a bad idea, but we're heading straight through the Tower's main entrance. The plan is simple: we storm the lobby and kill the two assholes stationed there. Then we take the elevators to my dad's floor, and keep shooting until your girls are back in your arms. We're so close, we can't fail."

The plan was risky but Charlie knew it was their only option. Normally, he'd try to formulate a new plan, but he simply went with the flow. He was exhausted, he was bleeding and he was in a hurry to finish this nightmarish scenario and be reunited with his family.

"Then let's finish this. I'm not getting any younger," he joked and put his arm around Victoria's shoulders. Victoria gratefully returned the gesture and then the pair joined the remaining members of X-ray Team around Mason's body.

One of the team had rolled Mason onto his back and closed his eyelids. Charlie spied a bloody rag nearby; someone had cleaned the blood off the fallen agent's face. Hands folded neatly over his chest, Mason looked at peace. Charlie could see that Victoria was thankful that Mason hadn't suffered long. Even though she tried to act tough for the sake of her team, Victoria still couldn't suppress the tears that came once more upon the sight of her friend's body. She wiped clumsily at her eyes until Jen-Jen led her away.

No words were spoken for the fallen operative, just a moment of silence as each man found their own personal way to harness the pain that they felt from their loss. Finally, they'd all found a place to bury their emotions and they moved to follow Victoria and Jen-Jen.

As the five armed combatants made their way toward the main entrance, fire trucks pulled into the lot and furiously set to work on the blazing cars. The landscape, so full of violence and wreckage, more closely resembled a war zone than a vacation resort.

War.

Charlie tasted the word—savored it—for it was war he was about to bring to his adversary's doorstep.

35

"This is a terrible time for jokes," Spencer Holloway declared, eyes locked on the mercenary who'd just delivered some rather unacceptable news.

According to this man, seven out of the twelve members of Chaos Squad were inexplicably unreachable. This meant that either seven communicators had malfunctioned simultaneously—or that these men were dead. Either scenario seemed unlikely. Seven highly trained mercenaries could not possibly fall before a mere detective and a handful of CIA operatives. Still, Victoria was smart—Walker, doubly so. Perhaps the men of Chaos Squad had underestimated these people. If so, it had no doubt been their last mistake.

"I'm completely serious, sir. I can't reach any of them."

Holloway stood and turned his eyes toward Walker's two children, still sitting together in their chair near the window. Their eyes remained locked on the destruction laid out below them: cars ablaze, emergency vehicles scattered about, guests gawking and Cast Members panicking. It was truly a spectacle; one no doubt concocted by his clever daughter. Absolute mayhem was the perfect bait for unwitting mercenaries. Holloway had no doubt in his mind that Victoria had lured these five ignorant men to their deaths.

"Whom do we have left?" Holloway asked.

"Masters and Ramirez are down in the lobby, sir. Captain Kinney is in the room next door, and you've got me and Addams here with you."

"Would you please not refer to Mr. Kinney as Captain? You are civilians, now," Holloway snapped, clearly agitated by the sparse number of soldiers left at his disposal. "Get back to your post and try not to die like your colleagues."

Unsure of what to do, Holloway settled back into his chair as the dejected mercenary made his way back to his partner near the door. The old man leaned his elbows on the tabletop and laid his head in his hands. This entire night had become a disaster. Nothing was going according to plan and nearly half of his men were dead, captured or too severely wounded to speak. Deciding against detonating his now purposeless bomb, he pulled up the computer program that controlled the bomb's timer and detonator. With a deep sigh, he deactivated the mechanism.

The collateral damage the bomb would have caused was pointless and, if this were to be his last stand, he would not allow himself to be seen as nothing more than a vengeful amateur.

Struggling to rein in his frustration, he focused his attention on the knowledge that his own daughter was on her way to his location, backed up by the ingenious young detective and a team of highly trained Company operatives. What could be done? How could they be stopped?

In a fit of rage, Holloway swept his laptop computer off the table and it landed hard on the wooden floor with a loud crash. Startled, the two Walker girls turned their attention from the window and gazed at their captor. Holloway gave them a cold stare until they turned away and shrank low in their chair. The last thing he needed was to be judged by these two children.

All night he'd observed these two girls and they'd made him increasingly uncomfortable; their courage had filled him with a growing sense of unease.

For children, they were irritatingly resilient. As much as he hated to admit it, Holloway respected these two children very highly. After all they'd been through, the two seemed entirely unaffected by the circumstances. More than once Holloway had heard the girls giggling or humming *Grim Grinning Ghosts* and he didn't at first understand where their energy and mood had come from. It was only just moments ago he'd realized these girls were optimistic because they knew their father was coming to rescue them, and they held the detective in the highest possible regard—to the girls, Walker was a superhero. Holloway felt a momentary pang of regret for his own children—until he remembered his daughter.

The girl was coming to stop him. To arrest him. Possibly to kill him. Holloway threw away any sense of regret, and hardened into his usual self when he envisioned his daughter slaughtering his hired hands. The bitch would not survive the night. Tonight, Spencer Holloway would finish the job he should have done more than three decades earlier. Victoria Holloway was as good as dead.

"Brooks, come here for a moment," Holloway ordered in a soft tone.

The mercenary did as he was told.

"Yes, sir?" he asked.

"Your sidearm, please," Holloway requested.

Brooks removed his .45 caliber pistol and placed it gently in his employer's hand without argument.

"Now, take Addams with you and meet Masters and Ramirez downstairs in the lobby. They will require your assistance."

"But sir, you'll be alone. You need protection if they come for you."

"*Think*, Mr. Brooks. If your unit does its job as well as it should, they will not *make* it this far. The lobby is where you must make your stand, else all is for nothing."

Brooks looked uncomfortable, but he reluctantly nodded and headed for the door. After exchanging a few words with Addams, the pair left the room, leaving Holloway alone with the Walker girls.

Standing, Holloway grabbed a chair and dragged it to face the door.

Spencer Holloway was not a stupid man. He understood that if Walker and Victoria made it to his room, he would be finished—regardless of how many men were present. His only chance at survival was to rely upon the four men now stationed downstairs in the main lobby.

The tower he had chosen for his base of operations had now become a trap. Holloway had understood that the building was a risk due to its shortage of escape routes, but he'd been so confident in his abilities and the strength of his mercenaries that he used it anyway. Finally, his vanity and overconfidence had come back to bite him. He sighed deeply at the horrific lapse in judgment to which he'd fallen victim.

Even though the situation looked grim, Spencer Holloway still had fight left in him. He racked the slide on the weapon, chambered a round and dragged his chair across the room to face the door. He was prepared to fight—not for his life—but for the sake of justice. The world didn't need people like his daughter, and he was fully prepared to remove her from it.

If I am to die today, then I will drag Victoria and the detective to Hell with me.

With this conviction in mind, Spencer Holloway did the only thing left in his power to do.

He sat and waited patiently.

36

The glass doors of Bay Lake Tower's main entrance glistened before Charlie and X-Ray Team—noticeably free of fingerprints or smudges. The lobby beyond was not deep, but afforded many opportune places for an assailant to take cover. There were several pillars near the center of the room, as well as desks immediately to either side of the entryway. Luckily for them, any civilians that had been in the lobby had been drawn toward the scene of carnage at the rear of the parking lot—it seemed as if even the Cast Members had abandoned the place. Several police cars and fire trucks were present, but few were near the building so none of the team needed to hide their weapons.

Taking cover on either side of the doors, the team quickly planned their entry. Breaching the lobby itself would be the most dangerous part. The team would essentially be forced into a bottleneck upon entering. Even worse was that any place they may choose to take cover could possibly already conceal a member of Chaos Squad. Charlie had a strange feeling in his gut that the shooter they'd interrogated had been wrong. Why would only two mercenaries be guarding the most opportune place for an ambush? Charlie warned the team to proceed with extreme caution and was met with affirmatives all around.

From what little he knew of the lobby's layout, Charlie recalled a hallway branching off to their left containing the elevators that would take them to the fourteenth floor, where Holloway's twin villas were located. The hallway itself provided no cover whatsoever, so Charlie knew that if any mercenaries were on the ground level, they'd already have positioned themselves in the lobby itself.

"These doors are going to be a problem," Victoria stated, also recognizing the threat that this natural chokepoint posed. The team agreed and everyone seemed to be wracking their brains for a way around the issue.

Sometimes, the best solution is also the simplest.

Thinking quickly, Charlie blindly stuck his Walther around the corner and fired off two rounds. He heard the staccato sound of shattering glass, but dared not risk looking around the corner until the noise died down. Poking his head around the corner, he jerked it back nearly instantly as two bullets ricocheted off the wall next to his head, peppering his face with shards of stone. Even though his glance had been brief, he saw what he was looking for—as much as he'd hated the sight.

The two sets of windows next to the doors had been completely destroyed, leaving a clear and direct path to the lobby. Unfortunately, four armed men were in position in the lobby—not two, as originally specified. He spied one of the alliteration duo—Masters—among the enemy inside.

"Well," Charlie said, "the doors aren't a problem, anymore—but the four assholes with guns definitely are."

"We'll handle it," Victoria assured him.

"Why don't we just use a different entrance?" Charlie offered, knowing there must be more ways into the building than just this inopportune area. "There has to be something."

"Because we need to take these guys out. If we sneak in another way, then we run the risk of being flanked by mercenaries. That's not a good thing at all—if you were wondering."

"This won't be easy," he said.

"It never is," Victoria agreed, pain lacing her words—her thoughts clearly still with Mason. "Which is why *you* are going to find another entrance, and *we* are going to handle these clowns."

"You can't be serious," Charlie exclaimed. "They'll kill you on the spot."

Victoria gave him a small wink. "Trust me, Sherlock—these guys won't know what hit them. Besides, there's only one merc left upstairs and with these idiots out of the picture, you shouldn't have any trouble getting to your family. Once we've dealt with this," she made a sweeping gesture toward the lobby, "we'll join you upstairs."

Charlie locked eyes with his friend for what seemed like an eternity, trying to read everything he could from her expression. He expected to see that she'd already admitted defeat and was mentally preparing her mind to cope with the sacrifice she was about to make. Instead, he saw something that lifted his spirits and made him know—actually *know*—that everything would be okay. He saw hope. He saw the fierce intensity, intelligence and determination that had come to be Victoria Holloway's defining characteristics. Above all else, he saw the knowing gaze of the victor—Victoria *knew* that she and her team would defeat these morons.

After a while, Charlie nodded slowly. Holstering his weapon, he put a hand gently on her arm.

"Thank you for everything you've done—all of you," Charlie said, turning to the team. "I couldn't have—"

Victoria punched him in the chest, solidly, but playfully.

"Detective," she said, her voice full of mock annoyance. "Shut the hell up and get upstairs. Don't get emotional on us. Let *us* kill these motherfuckers, then we'll go get your girls and finish this." She finished the statement with a wink and a smile. From her jacket pocket, she fished out a blank white card with a black magnetic strip and handed it over to Charlie.

"What's this?" he asked.

"Dummy master key," she replied. "You'll need it. It'll get you access to any door that requires a magnetic key."

"Thanks, Vee. I—"

She cut him off again, this time telling him the room numbers of Holloway's villas.

"Now go!" she barked.

A sharp, clumsy laugh burst out of Charlie as Victoria roughly shoved him off in the direction of the north wing. As he searched for an entrance, he heard the first sounds of gunfire from the lobby and he prayed that his friends were okay.

§

Finding an entrance and making his way to the elevators had been child's play for Charlie, but he'd not encountered a single soul during his entire trek. He'd occasionally heard gunfire, but it was sporadic and he was unable to discern from which side the shots were fired. Anything could be happening to his friends and it pained him to know he was powerless to help them. Still, he refused to let his regret have any negative effect on his current objective. He was finally close to reuniting with his family, and nothing would stop him.

The elevator steadily made its way to the fourteenth floor, and Charlie found himself drumming his fingers on the wall in anxious anticipation. He knew the room numbers, and that he'd find these rooms on his left. Unfortunately, he didn't know which rooms contained his wife and the final mercenary, and which contained Holloway and his children. Truth be told, Charlie was uncertain as to the possibility of an ambush. The final mercenary may not still be in the room with Meghan. He might be waiting for Charlie outside the elevator—he couldn't know for sure. Still, the safe assumption was to believe the mercenary was with Holloway—or near him, at the very least—since he would be the old man's last line of defense. Charlie guessed these things, but he didn't truly know anything—nor did he care. He'd search every room in this tower if he had to—he would not be stopped.

Before reaching the fourteenth floor, Charlie ejected the magazine from the Walther to see how many bullets he had left. Four rounds remained. He'd emptied an entire magazine during the firefight on the monorail, and he'd put two more rounds through the lobby windows. Four bullets remained with which he could dispose of this final Chaos Squad soldier. It wasn't much, but it was enough.

Exiting the elevator into a small, modern atrium, Charlie quickly rushed to his left and took cover with his back against the wall, just before entering the hallway. He risked a quick glance and found the hall completely deserted. Allowing his weapon to lead the way, Charlie all but sprinted the distance between the elevators and the first of Holloway's two villas. Taking a deep breath, Charlie pulled the master key from his pocket but hesitated before unlocking the door. He needed time to steel himself for what was to come.

After a few more deep breaths, Charlie felt himself centering. He felt his focus honing to previously unknown levels. He felt the now-familiar rage simmering in his chest when he thought of Holloway and the Chaos soldiers holding his family hostage. Charlie was ready, and God help any poor, unfortunate souls who got in his way.

Inserting the key, Charlie heard the small *click* of the electronic lock disengaging. He dropped the card in his pocket, and relaxed his grip on the Walther. He was prepared for anything that may await him inside.

Finally, Charlie entered the room and was utterly taken aback by what he saw.

Meghan Walker, bruised, bloodied and unconscious lie in a chair near the massive window, her fragile form framed by the breathtaking view of the Magic Kingdom far below. Charlie felt his heart sink and his rage start to boil at this horrible sight. In the chair next to Meghan's sat one of the men who'd accosted him at the Wilderness Lodge the night before. Charlie remembered this man's name: Kinney, Brody Kinney.

Slowly stepping into the room, simmering rage threating to boil over, Charlie pointed the Walther directly at Kinney's head. The man was big, but a .40 caliber round through each eye socket would stop even the most enormous of men.

"Walker," Kinney scoffed, taking a sip from a glass of clear alcohol—perhaps vodka or gin. Noticing the fierce snarl on Charlie's face, Kinney gestured to Meghan's unconscious form and said, "What—not a fan of my work?"

"Fuck you," Charlie barked, taking another step closer. So far, Kinney didn't seem to have a weapon—his hands were free.

The big man stood. He was a full six inches taller than Charlie and perhaps fifty or sixty pounds of muscle heavier. He was imposing, intimidating, but Charlie felt no fear—only intense, nearly blinding rage.

"If you think what I did to this whore is bad, just wait until you see what I'm going to do to you." Kinney drained the contents of his glass and threw it across the room.

"You *do* realize that I have a gun pointed at your throat, correct?" Charlie shot back.

"You won't use that gun." Kinney smiled.

"And why not?" Charlie challenged.

"Because you're a coward. And cowards constantly feel the need to prove themselves. Let me tell you what you're going to do. You're going to drop that weapon, and you're going to try to beat me, man-to-man. Trust me—I've seen it all before."

Kinney drew his own weapon but, instead of firing on Charlie, ejected the magazine, racked the slide to eject the chambered round and dropped the pistol to the floor before kicking it toward Charlie.

"Oh! I forgot. You're also a cop. 'Protect and Serve!'" he mocked. "You won't fire on an unarmed man. It's unethical!"

For a moment, the rational man within Charlie took full control. He had fully intended to shoot Kinney—unarmed or not. Why would any rational person risk their own life in this situation? The confrontation could be ended before it began. Who could possibly pass up this chance?

"I'm going to have a lot of fun with this cunt after I kill you," Kinney taunted, gesturing to Meghan. "I wanted her to see your corpse before I finally put her out of her misery."

The rational man within Charlie was abruptly shoved over the precipice of reason by the primal beast deep within—his ferocity overruling rationale and logic with purified bloodlust. Charlie tossed his weapon aside. He fully intended to kill the arrogant mercenary with his bare hands. Charlie Walker was no coward and this situation was not destined to end the way that Kinney had predicted.

"Good," Kinney cooed, making a show of loudly cracking the joints in his neck. "Do your worst, detective," he taunted with a wide grin.

Abandoning self-control, Charlie charged the mercenary; every muscle in his body tensed and prepared to kill.

37

As Charlie headed off to find an alternative entrance, Victoria met the eyes of each member of her team in turn. She looked at her closest friends— her brothers and sister—and smiled. They had been with her through thick and thin, and they'd follow her to the ends of the Earth. These were some of the most dedicated people she'd ever met—not to mention the most skilled. It was for this reason that she knew her team would succeed. Four mercenaries stood between her team and victory, and X-Ray refused to be stopped. They would do anything in their power to make sure that Mason had not died in vain.

"Ready?" was all she said.

Her team nodded their assent and checked their weapons. They knew *exactly* what they were doing and they knew how to do it better than anyone else in the world. X-ray Team was widely known for their success, and the Company paid them well to be the best.

"Let's do this," she said, before breaking cover and running directly through the frame of the shattered window. Gunfire erupted from multiple weapons in front of her, but she was able to take cover behind a large potted palm, free from injury. Weapon in hand, she looked back toward her team. Kalani and McCoy were still outside, but Jen-Jen had made it to cover behind the potted palm opposite hers. Thankfully, she made it without being hit. She flashed a quick thumbs-up at Victoria before refocusing herself.

Thinking quickly, Victoria leaned out from behind the palm and fired off five quick shots, giving McCoy and Kalani the support fire they'd needed to reach cover next to Victoria and Jen-Jen.

"We're in the shit now," Kalani pointed out as a volley of return fire slammed into the planter and surrounding walls.

"Only way out's through 'em," Victoria sighed, before slapping a fresh magazine into her pistol.

Kalani grinned and lifted his left pant leg. Attached to his ankle was a small cylindrical object, roughly four inches long and about the diameter of a D battery. He removed it and held it out to Victoria. She recognized it instantly, but had not known that he'd brought it along.

"Flashbang!" she whispered, laughing aloud in triumph—this was *exactly* what they needed to turn the firefight in their favor! "You big, beautiful Hawaiian bastard—I love you!"

Victoria energetically kissed Kalani on the forehead as she graciously accepted the small stun grenade from him.

Strangely enough, aside from the volleys of gunfire that had erupted from the Chaos mercenaries when X-ray Team had forced their way into the room, the lobby was eerily silent. There was no heavy breathing, no metallic clatter of weapons being checked or shouted threats—just deafening silence. Victoria found it slightly intimidating that her enemies could operate so smoothly under pressure; they had supreme self-control and a remarkable amount of training and experience.

X-ray could—and would—handle them; these mercenaries were still only mortal. Sure, Victoria's team was loud, brash and unorthodox, but they always got the job done. Chaos Squad had been doomed from the moment they'd taken up arms against her team—they were just too confident in themselves to know it.

Jen-Jen and McCoy looked toward Victoria for orders and she held up a closed fist—the signal to remain in place for the time being. Victoria gestured again, indicating she would flank the enemy from the left after throwing the flashbang. Kalani would provide covering fire and McCoy and Jen-Jen would cut down the soldiers stunned by the blast—she didn't need to explain this part; it was something her team had been trained to do. It was a tactic that had worked countless times in the past, and Victoria was confident that it would work this time—even against such well-trained opponents.

Taking a deep breath to steady herself, Victoria pulled the pin from the flashbang and held it in her hand. She knew that this particular nonlethal weapon had an internal five-second fuse, so she cooked the grenade for three seconds before throwing—a dangerous but effective way of guaranteeing that the intended targets wouldn't have time to clear the area. After an internal three-count, she lobbed the grenade over the potted palm and it landed directly next to a pillar that she'd seen a Chaos mercenary take cover behind. Covering her ears and closing her eyes, she waited for the deafening blast of the stun grenade.

It came almost instantly—a loud *bang* resonating off every surface. To the unsuspecting victims, the concussive blast and blinding flash would effectively stun anyone within fifteen feet.

With no hesitation, Victoria shot to her feet and launched herself from cover, just as her team members opened fire on the mercenaries. Sliding across the smooth floor, she made it behind the lobby's leftmost desk unscathed. It concealed a single mercenary, and his attention had been momentarily drawn away from her, toward the blast. Raising her weapon, Victoria put two rounds into the center of his back, knocking him from his feet and causing him to land face first on the hard floor. She heard her team's weapons continuously barking from behind cover—and also heard the intense cry of agony as another Chaos member went down under the heavy fire rained down by her allies.

Sticking her head out from around the desk, she noticed that no attention was on her—the team had been successful at diverting the mercenaries and her flanking maneuver had, as far as she could tell, gone unnoticed. From her position, she could only see one Chaos member, but she couldn't risk a shot from this distance—a miss would surely draw attention to her—so she decided that she needed to move closer. Suddenly, Kalani was at her side—taking cover behind the same desk.

Ignoring the big Hawaiian, Victoria once more took flight from cover, staying low and heading for the lone mercenary. At the last moment, the mercenary wheeled upon her and brought his weapon to bear. Fortunately, she was prepared for the move. Her sidearm already held before her, she squeezed off three shots mid-run—two missed wide to the left but the third punched a neat hole through the man's upper chest. Dropping his weapon, the man clutched at his wound futilely, even as Victoria put a final round through his eye. Wasting no time, she slid into cover behind a pillar near the dead man. Ten feet from her new position, she spotted another mercenary lying in a pool of his own blood. Jen-Jen and McCoy had racked up at least one kill.

The lobby was silent aside from the sound of her final shell casing rolling to a stop on the floor. Had the four mercenaries all been killed? It was a possibility, but something made the hair rise on the back of Victoria's neck. Something just didn't feel right. She decided to hazard a look in the direction in which she assumed the final mercenary must be. What she saw caused her stomach to churn and bile to rise into her throat.

The final mercenary stood next to one of the potted palms with a pistol placed firmly to Jen-Jen's temple. A second pistol swept the area, pinning Kalani and McCoy behind their respective covers. Jen-Jen looked livid, infuriated that she'd been caught. Looking closely, Victoria recognized the mercenary. It was Masters, one of the men who'd abducted Charlie the night before. Slowly, Victoria rose to face him. She leveled her gun at his head, the iron sights hovering over his eye.

"Everyone drop your weapons," Masters demanded.

"Can't do that," Victoria called back.

"I'll paint these fucking walls with her brains," he threatened. "You want to lose another one? Drop your weapons. *Now*."

From behind nearby Victoria heard Kalani and McCoy set their pistols on the floor. She knew that these men were determined to protect their friend, but she had no intention of letting this asshole gain any leverage. She kept her weapon raised, leveled directly at Masters' head.

"She knows the risks," Victoria bluffed. "Shoot her. But if you do, there will be no way out for you. It'll be just like signing your own death warrant. You don't want that—there are other options."

"Fuck you," he shouted, and cocked back the hammer on his pistol, pressing the barrel harder into Jen-Jen's temple. "I ain't rotting away in fucking Gitmo. Now, for the last time, drop your—"

Victoria shot him.

Masters' head snapped back violently from the destructive impact of the .45 caliber slug and he went down hard on the floor, pistols skittering away in either direction. Jen-Jen looked shaken, but completely unharmed—Victoria's gambit had paid off.

"Jesus, Vee!" Jen-Jen breathed, an involuntary shiver running through her body. "You could have shot me, you know that?"

"He could've shot you too," Victoria offered, inserting her final spare magazine into her pistol. "Though I'd imagine that you like this outcome a little better."

Jen-Jen sighed with great relief. The mercenaries in the lobby had been dealt with, and the conclusion was nearing. A great weight was about to be lifted from their shoulders, and the anticipation was so great that it was nearly palpable.

After making sure that all of the mercenaries in the room were dead—and that her team was not—Victoria hurried everyone to the large elevator that would carry them to their final destination. Victoria prayed that Charlie had survived his inevitable encounter with the last remaining mercenary. She willed the lift to move faster as the seconds ticked away at an agonizingly slow pace.

38

Charlie lowered his shoulder and slammed into Brody Kinney with the force of a professional linebacker. Even though the mercenary was much larger, Charlie easily lifted the man from his feet and drove him hard to the floor. The impact was severe for both men, but Charlie refused to let something as finite as pain interfere with his relentless pursuit of vengeance. The force of the impact violently forced the air from Kinney's lungs.

Charlie managed three viciously hard blows to Kinney's face—one opening up a deep gash on the mercenary's cheek—before the large man recovered enough to throw Charlie from atop him and scramble to his feet. Refusing to allow Kinney to gain even a slight advantage, Charlie shot to his feet and slammed into the man again, but this time the big mercenary was ready. Charlie absorbed a crushing underhanded blow to the abdomen and was knocked back a step.

It was at this point that Charlie realized what kind of fighter he was dealing with.

Kinney decided to close the gap with a well-placed roundhouse kick, and this was enough to tell Charlie everything he needed to know about the man. A kick during any fight—especially one as flashy as a roundhouse—was one of the worst ideas a fighter could have. Kicks expose vital areas and leave the attacker open to counterattacks from almost any direction. For this reason, Charlie deduced that he fought against a man who'd spent his time studying the flashy mixed martial arts techniques that were so popular these days. On television, in a ring with a referee and safeguards against serious injury, kicks look impressive and usually make audiences cheer. In a fight to the death, a kick does no good—only gives an opponent the opportunity to unleash a devastating counter.

With this in mind, Charlie dropped his left shoulder and absorbed the blow with his forearm. The block was successful and it threw Kinney off balance long enough for Charlie to close the distance and use the mercenary's mistake to his advantage. The failed kick had left the bigger man open to almost any attack Charlie wished to deliver, and he chose the one that was sure to have the most beneficial effect. Open hands cupped, Charlie clapped his hands as hard as he could over Kinney's ears and the big man screamed in agony as his eardrums burst from the dirty but effective technique.

Blood dribbled from Kinney's ears as he struggled to maintain balance; Charlie's attack had seriously hindered his equilibrium. Relentless and tireless, Charlie charged back in for another attack. Kinney, however, seemed to have a good amount of fight left in him and was not yet ready to quit. As Charlie threw another powerful haymaker, Kinney sidestepped the blow and delivered two solid body shots, followed immediately by a fierce uppercut that Charlie was barely able to avoid. As Charlie leaned away, the blow only glanced off his chin, but it was enough to make stars dance in his vision and put him off balance. If that punch had fully connected, he would have certainly been knocked unconscious. He couldn't afford to let Kinney unleash another attack like that.

"Not bad, Walker," Kinney offered, wiping the blood from his ears. "You fight cheap, though."

"I fight *smart*," Charlie corrected, circling his opponent—matching Kinney's each step with an identical one of his own.

"You're in over your head. You can't win," the big man taunted.

"Big talk coming from the guy with blood pouring out of his ears."

Kinney snarled in anger, but he did not charge as Charlie had suspected he would. Instead, Kinney looked over Charlie from head-to-toe, appraising him. Although Charlie desperately wished to end this fight, he was grateful for the chance to catch his breath. The violent exchange had taken a lot out of him and he wasn't certain how much longer he could last. His chest heaved with every breath but he noticed that Kinney was having a harder time than he let on—sucking in wheezing, labored breaths. Charlie decided to capitalize on the mercenary's barely-masked exhaustion.

Stepping in and throwing another hard punch toward Kinney's already injured cheek, Charlie was surprised when the mercenary moved faster than expected and swatted the blow away with his left hand. Just as quickly, Kinney's right fist crashed into Charlie's gunshot wound, sending white-hot spikes of searing agony throughout his entire torso. Charlie cried out, feeling his ribs cracking from the impact of the well-placed blow. The detective staggered back several steps before regaining his balance.

Kinney had an evil glint in his eye, and Charlie at once knew what the break in the action had been for. Kinney had been searching Charlie for any signs of weakness, and he had found a winner in the gunshot wound—his labored breathing had been nothing more than an act. Satisfied with himself, he studied the wounded detective—smiling as he watched Charlie struggle to draw breath.

Charlie tried to overcome the crushing agony that was beginning to dominate him. He could not lose—not now. No amount of pain would stop him from avenging his wife's assault and rescuing his family. Drawing in the largest lungful of air that he could, Charlie stood and faced his attacker one last time. He knew that he couldn't withstand another one of these clashes—he needed to end the fight. Fortunately, the mercenary was smiling—satisfied with himself. His overconfidence would lead to his downfall.

"Let's get this over with so I can get back to your wife," Kinney taunted. "I haven't had my fun with her, yet."

Fueled by rage, Charlie raised his fist once more, feigning the act of throwing the same punch as he had just seconds ago—and Kinney fell for the bait. Exactly as Charlie had predicted, Kinney took a step forward with his left leg in an attempt to shift his center of balance forward in anticipation of the blow. At the last moment, Charlie shifted his weight, lifted his right foot and stomped as hard as he could on Kinney's leading knee.

The mercenary didn't stand a chance.

Charlie's foot drove the mercenary's kneecap backward—past the natural angle—and hyperextended the joint as far as possible. Kinney cried out as his shattered knee gave way beneath him with a sickening *crunch*, and he fell on his back on the floor, still screaming from the torturous agony of his obliterated knee joint.

Pain further fueling his rage—and rage driving his strained muscles to their limits—the vengeful detective fell upon the massive mercenary.

Charlie rained down one devastating punch after another directly into Kinney's face. Each consecutive punch connected more solidly and achieved more satisfying results than the one before. He felt the cartilage in Kinney's nose give way; heard the mercenary scream more intensely; watched the blood flow freely from several places—yet he did not relent. The hardened soldier cried out in vain, seeking mercy, shrieking syllables that his ruined mouth could no longer form into words.

Three more blows and Kinney lost consciousness. Four blows after that, the monster's face was no longer recognizable—and three more blows after that, the mercenary finally ceased to breathe.

Charlie's right arm hung limply at his side, completely numb from overexertion. He was certain he'd broken bones in his hand, but he could neither feel nor see any injuries—his right fist was coated in a thick layer of Kinney's blood and he stared at it in horror as he still straddled the dead mercenary's chest. Until this moment, Charlie hadn't realized that he'd been screaming.

Recoiling in horror, Charlie scrambled away from the dead man and sat for a moment with his back against the couch, trying to regain a shred of composure—he'd just beaten a man to death! His mind was having trouble coming to terms with what he had done. Never had Charlie Walker believed that he was capable of killing a man with his bare hands, but the threat to Meghan's life had brought out a whole new aspect of himself that he'd never known existed. He'd known that he would do anything it would take to protect his wife, but he hadn't realized that he could ever be pushed so far.

Staring at the grisly sight of the mercenary's corpse in complete shock, Charlie cleaned off his hand using a blanket that had been draped over the arm of the couch.

A slight moan issued from somewhere nearby and he jumped, momentarily startled by the irrational thought that Kinney was not actually dead. After a split second, he remembered that Meghan still lay in the chair by the window. He shot to his feet and leapt over the couch, rushing across the room to Meghan—all thoughts of his recent actions forgotten for the moment.

He dropped to his knees on the floor before her and stared at her angelic face as he gently took her hands in his. He leaned in close.

"Meghan," he said, softly. "Baby, it's me—it's Charlie. Please wake up. Everything's going to be okay. I'm here now."

For a moment, Charlie worried that his wife was not going to regain consciousness, but much to his relief, she stirred and slowly opened her eyes. She was bruised and bloodied, but he'd never seen such a beautiful sight as the bright smile that spread across her face when she recognized him.

"Charlie!" she screamed, easing herself to her feet.

Charlie struggled to his feet and the two embraced tightly. Even though it had only been twenty-four hours since he'd last seen her, it felt like he'd not laid eyes on his wife for an eternity. He'd fought his way through hell and finally reached his love.

Abandon all hope, ye who enter here.

To hell with Dante, and to hell with Spencer Holloway—Charlie had never once given up hope—not for a moment. He *knew* that he would be reunited with his wife, no matter what it took.

His face inches from hers, Charlie wiped away her tears and kissed her forehead, her cheeks, her nose, her lips—anywhere he could. A great weight had been lifted from his shoulders. He pulled Meghan to his chest, squeezed her tight, once more. He never wanted to let her go—never again.

"You came for me," she sobbed. "I knew you would come for me."

"I'd die before I let them have you," he said. "I love you."

She echoed his words and buried her face into his shoulder, sobbing uncontrollably. Charlie remained silent; simply holding his wife and feeling his spirits lift with every breath he took. He wished that he could remain here with his wife forever.

But....

Violet and Katie were not in the room. Abruptly, he pulled away from Meghan, mentally kicking himself for not realizing that his daughters were not present.

"Baby, where are Violet and Katie?" he asked, his words rushed and frantic.

"Holloway took them," she said, her voice shaky. "He took them next door several hours ago. We've got to get them!"

"No, you're staying here. I'll handle this." He turned and retrieved his Walther from the ground.

"Charlie, you can't do this alone!" Meghan cried.

Suddenly, a female voice arose from the opposite side of the room, startling both Meghan and Charlie.

"He won't have to," the voice stated.

Charlie spun around and looked toward the doorway at the source of the voice.

Framed by the gentle light from the hallway, Victoria Holloway stood with her arms crossed, flanked by the remaining three members of X-ray Team.

The cavalry had come.

39

None of X-ray Team commented on the grisly scene inside the villa. They'd all seen the gruesome condition of Brody Kinney's remains and the bloodstained and bruised knuckles of Charlie's right hand—it was all too clear what had happened. Still, the sight of Charlie with his wife brought a smile to their faces, despite the situation. He'd fought hard to come this far, and they were all grateful that he'd finally been rewarded—if only partially.

Meghan reluctantly agreed to remain behind in the villa and Jen-Jen volunteered to stay and watch over her, promising to tend to her wounds and explain just who these strangers were and how they'd come to know her husband. Before leaving for Holloway's villa, McCoy and Kalani dragged Kinney's body into one of the bedrooms and wrapped it up in a comforter so that Meghan didn't have to see. Meghan graciously thanked the two men as they followed Charlie and Victoria from the room.

§

A few minutes later, outside the door to Holloway's villa, Charlie stood shoulder-to-shoulder with Victoria, mentally preparing to face the elder Holloway. On either side of the door were Kalani and McCoy, who had agreed to stay out of sight until they were needed. This final confrontation was deeply personal for Charlie and Victoria, and the two other X-ray operatives had made the decision to let the pair handle it on their own. Kalani and McCoy would only intervene in the event of an emergency.

"You ready for this, Vee? Charlie?" Kalani asked, genuinely concerned for his friends. Neither Charlie nor Victoria had spoken in the last few minutes. Charlie hadn't even said goodbye to his wife, only hugged her tight, kissed her atop her head and left without a word. Kalani hadn't voiced his opinion aloud, but he believed that Charlie couldn't bring himself to say goodbye to her again—it seemed like he was promising Meghan that he would be coming back.

For a tense few seconds, neither of them responded. Charlie slowly glanced to his right and caught Victoria's eye. To Kalani, it seemed as if a silent conversation was happening between them. Finally, Victoria gave a small nod.

"Ready as we'll ever be," Charlie said simply, his voice hoarse.

Charlie gently inserted the master key into the lock, waited for the bolt to disengage and then traded the card to Kalani for his newly reloaded Walther. Taking a deep breath, he slowly eased open the door and let his weapon lead the way into the room. Victoria stayed close at his heels, her pistol also at the ready. Strangely, what awaited them inside was far from what Charlie had been expecting.

No scene of carnage awaited them. There was no room full of computer equipment or a command center with weapons and gear strewn about. The atmosphere seemed almost peaceful—or it *would* have, if it weren't for Spencer Holloway sitting in a lone armchair facing the door, his hair disheveled and his hand atop a pistol on the armrest. He smiled uncomfortably at the pair as they slowly and cautiously entered the room, weapons trained on the aging criminal mastermind. Oddly, Holloway didn't lift the gun; his hand simply rested atop it loosely, almost as if he'd forgotten about it entirely.

"Good evening, detective," he greeted. Overdramatizing a gasp when he turned to look upon his daughter, he said: "And Victoria, how beautiful you have become. You remind me so much of your mother."

Victoria took a quick step forward. "Don't you *dare* speak another word about my mother!"

Charlie placed a gentle hand on her shoulder. "Vee, it's not worth it. *He's* not worth it. He's just trying to get a rise out of you."

"*Vee?*" Holloway sneered. "Pet names, detective? How adorable!"

Charlie was finished wasting time. He scanned the room for Violet and Katie, but couldn't see them anywhere. Irrationally, Charlie began to worry—

even though they could have simply been in one of the villa's numerous rooms.

"Where are my daughters?" he asked, calmly taking a step forward and letting his gun hand fall to his side, so as not to obstruct his view of Holloway's eyes.

"Little Violet and Katie?" Holloway mocked, in a bizarre, singsong voice. "Oh, you didn't hear about them?"

"Tell me where they are," Charlie demanded in a deep growl, growing ever more furious with each wasted second. "Now."

"They're dead, detective," the old man leaned back in his chair and grinned wide, looking at both the detective and his own daughter in turn. "You have failed."

Without warning, Charlie leveled his weapon at Holloway and nearly pulled the trigger—but something stopped him. He'd seen something in the old man's eyes and it had stayed his hand, if only momentarily.

Pleasure.

The impulsive urge to gain instantaneous revenge upon the person who had brought harm to his family was exactly what Holloway had wanted to inspire in Charlie. It was another test—Holloway had been bluffing. His daughters were still very much alive—there was no doubt in his mind. Grimacing, Charlie lowered his weapon once more.

"Try again," he challenged.

Holloway laughed. "Very good, detective. I am impressed," he commended.

Holloway stood and picked up the pistol but held it loosely in his hand, hanging limply at his side, still giving off the impression that he'd forgotten he even had it. He turned his back upon Victoria and Charlie and began to lazily wander toward the seating area at the far side of the villa. The pair exchanged wary glances before cautiously following him, weapons once more leveled at the old man. Holloway stopped on a large rug not far from the massive window, and turned to face them.

"You saw right through me, didn't you, Walker? I should have known you wouldn't be fooled so easily. You haven't made things easy on me these past twenty-four hours."

"I haven't made things easy on you?" Charlie barked, not believing the arrogance of this psychopath. "Do you think I've spent the last day trading pins and eating fucking turkey legs? I've been through hell—and *you* put me there."

An insane glint worked its way into Holloway's eyes. "You call this 'hell', detective? You aren't fooling me. You aren't fooling *anyone*—so stop trying to trick yourself. You enjoyed this! Playing these games with me. Finally getting the chance to show the world your gifts, thwart the villain and save the girl—you live for this!"

Charlie was finally beginning to understand the deep-seated insanity that had taken hold of Spencer Holloway's mind. The old man was intelligent, but he was also lost in a fantasy world—a world where epic heroes and villains clashed and the lines between the two were black and white. Holloway obviously considered himself the villain; his sole purpose in life was to challenge the people he considered to be heroes. In Spencer Holloway's book, no one in existence qualified for the opposing role more than Charlie Walker: the man who'd gone through a terrifying ordeal to stop Holloway's only son—nearly sacrificing his own life in the process to save a woman he'd never even met.

"You think that this is why I'm a police officer—for the fame and the glory? For the thrills?" Charlie asked, incredulous.

Holloway cleared his throat. "The world is a shallow place, detective. No matter what lies people choose to believe, there are only three motivators for human actions: wealth, attention and pleasure. Your salary is a pittance compared to the money you could make—so you don't do it for the money. What else, is left, then? I watched the news reports after you killed James. I saw you standing on those steps, shaking hands with the mayor, smiling for the cameras. You enjoyed it—you enjoyed your fifteen minutes of fame. Attention *and* pleasure! My, how deep the rabbit hole goes…"

"I do what I do because I'm fortunate enough to have been given gifts that can help better the lives of others. Innocent people don't deserve to be victims of sadists and psychopaths like you. *That* is why I do what I do—I stand between people like you and the rest of the world."

Holloway laughed aloud—a frantic, terrible sound. "Excellent speech. For a moment, I almost believed you! In reality, you are no different than I. In fact, we are one and the same. We are a different breed of monster—and we use what we have solely for our own advantage. There are no more *good* people left in this world. There are only those who can admit to what they really are and accept it—and those like you, who lie to themselves."

Charlie knew that he'd never be able to convince the lunatic of anything else, and any more attempts to do so would be in vain. Every second he wasted speaking to this maniac was another second that he was apart from his daughters. This had gone on long enough. Victoria had remained silent the entire time, letting Charlie handle the situation whichever way he decided was best.

Ignoring the ramblings of Spencer Holloway, Charlie shifted gears. "Call me a liar. It doesn't matter. I'm not here to argue about moral standings with you. Where are my daughters? Tell me now, or I will shoot you and search this place, myself."

"Everything in due time, detective," Holloway sneered.

Losing his patience, Charlie closed the distance between himself and Holloway in a heartbeat. Before the old man could react, Charlie batted the pistol from his hand and grabbed him by the lapel. Roughly, he jammed the barrel of the Walther into Holloway's forehead. Victoria gasped, but did not intervene—her weapon held firmly in a two-hand grip, aimed directly at her father. She waited patiently to see what Charlie would do next.

"Where are my fucking daughters?!" Charlie yelled, inches from Holloway's face.

"Daddy!" breathed a small voice from behind him.

Charlie's eyes widened, his grip on Holloway loosened and his gun fell to his side, all but forgotten. His heart beat faster than it had at any point in the last twenty-four hours, and he could barely hold onto his pistol as he slowly turned toward the source of the tiny, fragile, beautiful voice.

Violet's voice.

When he turned, he saw his daughters—the older girl holding the hand of the younger, watching over her, as any big sister should. Charlie gasped and fell to his knees. His girls were safe. They were unharmed, and they were *here!* The three people he loved most in the world were finally safe and he could breathe easy at last. The girls rushed to him and leapt into his outstretched arms.

He squeezed his girls tightly; his mind overwhelmed by the relief flooding through his body. After all of the obstacles he'd overcome—the pain he'd experienced and the terrible things he'd done—he didn't regret a thing. Everything had become worth it in a fraction of a second. Meghan and the girls were worth everything he'd been through and everything he'd done—

and he'd have done it all a million more times if it meant that they would be safe. Charlie felt a lone tear roll down his cheek as he held his children.

For a while, he refused to let go of his girls—they held him just as tightly and didn't mind the contact. He couldn't help but smile at the simple fact that these two miracles were unharmed after everything they'd been through. All of his worries—everything that had been eating away at him—vanished, and he was finally whole once more.

"Are you guys okay?" he whispered, gently.

"We're okay, Daddy," Violet reassured him in an equally soft whisper. "Did you find Mommy?" she asked.

"I did. She's waiting for us next door with a friend of mine. She's safe. We're all going to be just fine."

That was when he heard the shot ring out—a single thunderous roar that caused him and his daughters to jump. A lone shell casing bounced onto the rug as the shot reverberated off the walls and ceiling of the cavernous villa.

Charlie looked up to see Victoria standing in the same place she had been, gun smoking in hand, still aiming somewhere over Charlie's shoulder. Reflexively, he stood and wheeled around, shoving his girls behind him. Directly before him, Spencer Holloway stood, his face ashen with a dark spot of blood spreading through the fabric of his shirt—directly in the center of his chest. Somehow, Holloway had retrieved the gun that Charlie had swatted from his hand and Victoria had shot him to prevent him from using it.

For a brief moment, Charlie and Holloway locked eyes. The old man looked shocked, devastated and afraid—he knew he was dying. Charlie's gaze was intense, filled with anger and free from any traces of mercy— Spencer Holloway had dragged him through hell; he harbored no regret that this man was about to die. The detective held the man's stare for another few moments, until something abruptly changed in Holloway's eyes. A malevolent expression overcame the dying genius and it was almost too late before Charlie realized what was about to happen.

As Charlie had anticipated, Holloway was bringing up the weapon that he still held. Charlie, not realizing what he'd done, had stood between Victoria and her father, effectively blocking her shot. Doing the only thing he could, he lashed out with a devastating kick, catching Holloway in the chest just beneath his bullet wound and staggering him backward, off balance. The old man stumbled a few steps until he came into contact with the massive window that was behind him.

"No!" he screamed, slamming directly into the window with tremendous force.

Unfortunately for Spencer Holloway, the windowpane against which he fell was the very same one as he'd thrown his Scotch bottle at. Already severely damaged and lacking any structural integrity, it easily gave way beneath the elderly man's weight. Losing his hold on the pistol, Spencer Holloway disappeared through the shattered window with a crash and fell away into the night.

§

Strange, he thought. *This is how it ends.*

Time slowed to a crawl as Spencer Holloway suddenly found nothing beneath his feet save for fourteen stories of open air. In the last few seconds of his life, he gazed skyward, knowing that this would be his last glimpse of the heavens before he began his infinite incarceration in the deepest bowels of Hell.

Nobody saw the elderly man plummeting from the top floor of Bay Lake Tower among a downpour of shattered glass. Refusing to give into fear during these precious final moments of his life, Spencer Holloway simply stared toward the heavens with a smile on his face and awaited the inevitable end. He was finally at peace—his defeat had come at the hands of his most worthy opponent and there was no shame in it.

When the crushing impact came, it was nothing short of apocalyptic. The aging genius' frail body was no match for the ground with which he collided so forcefully. His gruesome end came so violently and destructively that not even his smile remained recognizable upon his obliterated face—a gruesome end for the monster named Spencer Holloway.

Death had finally come to collect the bounty on this damned soul.

Serenity.

§

Charlie was thankful that the riotous noise of the numerous emergency vehicles masked any possible sound of impact that the girls may have heard. More chaotic cacophony added itself to the atmosphere as Kalani and McCoy burst into the room, clearly drawn by the sounds of the confrontation that had just taken place.

Violet and Katie had gasped in shock after witnessing their captor plunging to his death, but Charlie and Victoria merely remained silent—both of them viewing the old man's death as the conclusion to a terrible chapter in their lives. Victoria no longer had to live with the knowledge that her father was a threat to the people of the country and Charlie was finally able to relax—his family alive and safe from any threat that Holloway had posed.

Kalani and McCoy approached, but remained deadly silent. Along with Charlie, they turned to face Victoria, but none had any idea what her reaction would be. She'd just witnessed her biological father fall fourteen stories to his death—but he had been a monster and she'd spent years hunting him. When Charlie caught her eye, she looked back at him and did the last thing he would have expected.

She smiled. She laughed. She came to them and knelt before the girls, making sure they were okay. She asked if they were hungry or thirsty. She distracted the girls from the current situation—made them feel comfortable and happy and within moments had them laughing and talking as if nothing bad had happened at all.

Spencer Holloway had been dead wrong—there were still good people left in the world and his own daughter was one of them. Victoria Holloway was one of the finest people that Charlie had ever known. He couldn't find the words he needed to express his gratitude toward this remarkable woman and her team. Before he could speak, Victoria beat him to the punch.

"Let's get these angels back to their Mommy," Victoria suggested, looking into Charlie's eyes with a bright smile.

Speechless, Charlie took one last look toward the empty window frame and followed Victoria and the others from the room.

EPILOGUE

Two and a half days later, Charlie was released from Osceola Regional Medical Center and, along with Meghan and the girls, driven by an Orange County sheriff's deputy back to the Caribbean Beach Resort. He'd been treated for several injuries, receiving eighteen stitches for the gunshot wound on his torso, as well as having been diagnosed with three broken ribs. Due to his confrontation with Brody Kinney, he had to undergo surgery on his right hand to repair two broken metacarpals—requiring two plates and four screws.

Needless to say, Charlie Walker had been in better shape.

Throughout the duration that he'd been admitted, Meghan and the girls had stayed with him at all times. The staff had given the Walkers a room to themselves—Charlie hadn't wanted to be away from his family again. The hospital was very accommodating, allowing the newly minted "national hero" almost anything he desired. Charlie, not one to take advantage, simply requested privacy from any visitors other than X-ray Team.

§

Immediately following the ordeal at Bay Lake Tower, Victoria had the Walkers taken to the hospital while she stayed behind with her team. She needed to coordinate with the local authorities and make sure that Mason's body was treated with the respect he deserved. The man had given his life in the line of duty and she was determined to see that he was recognized and respected.

The following day, Charlie had just woken up from his surgery when Victoria had come to see him. He was surprised to see her, and even more surprised to hear that she had stayed with Meghan and the girls while he was under, leaving only for a short while to handle various issues that had required her immediate attention. When she entered the room, Violet and Katie ran to give her a hug and, surprisingly, she and Meghan also embraced before she finally made her way to Charlie's bedside.

"Looking good, detective," she joked, gesturing toward his vast collection of bandages and the complex network of wires leading to various machines that blinked and beeped incessantly.

"Hey, thanks!" he shot back, a cheesy smile on his face and his words positively *oozing* sarcasm. After a moment, he continued in a more serious tone. "How are things out there, Vee?"

"Depends on how badly you want to be famous."

"Um…not at all," he replied.

"Then things are very bad," she said, leaning back in her chair and stealing an unopened can of Sprite from his bedside table. Cracking open the can, she put her feet up on his bed and took a sip before continuing. "You're really freaking famous."

"Son of a bitch," Charlie groaned.

"You've been there before, babe. It's not *that* big of a deal," Meghan reminded him as she sat down next to Victoria. At that point, the rest of X-ray Team showed up and, noticing that Charlie was occupied, sat down with Violet and Katie and listened to the two girls enthusiastically describe the pictures they'd been drawing. Charlie couldn't help but notice that Meghan and the girls had really bonded with Victoria and her team during the short time they'd known each other. It made him happy that—

"Charles!" Victoria called, snapping her fingers a couple of times to pull him out of his daze. "You still with us, old man?"

"Yeah," he laughed. "Sorry, zoned out for second, there. What were you saying?"

"I was saying that this isn't *anything* like the time when you took out James."

"No?"

"Nope—much bigger. You single-handedly stopped over a dozen of America's most wanted terrorists—didn't you hear?" Victoria winked.

"You *didn't!*" Charlie breathed, already knowing that Victoria had gotten to the news outlets before they could find out what had really happened.

"I might have!" she said, taking another drink. "Public can't know I was here—so maybe I put a wee little spin on the press. You had to be the hero, buddy."

Charlie tried not to laugh. In the eyes of the media, Victoria had just transformed him from one of many people involved, to a one-man army that stopped a highly trained team of mercenaries by himself. It was absurd—he couldn't help but laugh.

He instantly regretted his lack of control as his broken ribs and fresh stitches protested the action.

Victoria giggled and told him to calm down.

"How bad is it?" Charlie asked after he'd relaxed, resigned to the fact that there was nothing he could do about it.

"I'll try to put it in perspective for you. You remember a few years back there was a guy on the news in Los Angeles—FBI agent or something—that found all those nuclear warheads in that unopened theme park? It was on the news for like a month straight after that," she reminded him.

"Yeah, Jack something—right? That was huge."

"Yep," she stated, gazing at him expectantly and nodding her head slowly. She took another sip from her pilfered can and waited for the groggy detective to catch on.

"No!" he protested.

"Bigger."

Whether from the shock of the news or from the lingering anesthetic—Charlie promptly passed out.

§

Finally back on Disney property, Charlie felt exponentially better—his mood soared. Even after all the terrible things that had happened, it was still his favorite place on Earth and he was with the people he loved most. All were safe and everyone was happy. Meghan's cut hadn't needed stitches and her bruises had almost faded away entirely. Her right wrist, however, was adorned with a bright purple cast, which she didn't seem to mind. Charlie found it curious that both he and his wife had injured their right hands striking the same man.

The girls were overjoyed to be back in their beloved pirate suite. They jumped from bed to bed, screaming and giggling with delight. Avoiding his airborne children, Charlie sat down to enjoy the familiar smells of the room and the pleasant coolness of the air conditioning.

Holloway's taunts about his vanity lingering in his mind, Charlie declined to speak to any reporters, instead allowing Victoria to take the reins. He was finally able to read the story that she had fed to the media outlets—and it was absolutely *ridiculous*. He almost couldn't believe that they'd bought it. Apparently, a terrorist cell planned on targeting the parks for unknown reasons. Somehow, Charlie had discovered their plot before they could act and risked life and limb to prevent them, resulting in the deaths of fourteen mercenaries and only few injuries to himself. A lone Detroit detective foiled a grand terrorist scheme—it was absurd.

At the hospital, the detective in him forced him to ask Victoria how she planned to deal with the very real fact that a CIA agent had been killed in action and that rounds from six different firearms—instead of one—were being extracted from dead mercenaries by investigators. She'd simply told him: "The Company already handled the locals—and what the media doesn't know won't hurt 'em."

Deciding that it was far above his pay grade to understand the strange ways in which the Central Intelligence Agency worked, Charlie let the issue die. He had concerned himself with too many strange things in the past few days to care about something so trivial—especially since he had recently started looking for new ways to simplify his life. Relaxation seemed like a good place to begin.

As he'd suspected, representatives from Disney had spoken with Victoria and offered to extend the Walkers' vacation package for as long as they'd like, free of charge, and to reimburse him for the time he'd already spent on property. They were eager to reward the man who had saved their park—but Charlie had only accepted a handful of extra days after a quick call to okay it with Pete. He still declined their offer for reimbursement, feeling it would be taking advantage of his situation.

Even so, Disney was Disney, and they were determined not to let his actions be forgotten. Victoria had shown him a picture on her phone, just hours after he'd humbly declined reimbursement. He had to squint to see the screen and at first he didn't understand what he was seeing. Eventually, he recognized the familiar sight. He looked upon the Christmas scene of the Carousel of Progress. At first glance, nothing seemed out of the ordinary.

"See anything different?" Victoria asked, a knowing tone coloring her words.

"No, not yet. I don't—wait. There," he pointed to a spot next to the grandmother, just behind the presents on the floor. "Is that—?"

"A *walker*," Victoria had finished his sentence for him, unable to hold back the smile on her face. "Clever bastards, aren't they?"

Sure enough, peeking out from around the presents stood a toy AT-AT from *Star Wars*. Victoria was right—it was devilishly clever and it didn't fail to put a smile on his face. The company truly was full of geniuses of the highest caliber, and this little nod to the man who had saved their park was absolutely incredible. He almost couldn't contain his excitement that he had been immortalized—however anonymously—in one of his all-time favorite attractions. No amount of money could have meant as much as this gesture.

§

The last day of their stay had finally come, and they'd boarded the Magical Express for their return trip to Orlando International Airport. X-ray Team had also come along on the massive bus since their flight home departed an hour after the Walkers'.

Charlie hooked an arm around Meghan, who had fallen asleep with her head on his shoulder almost as soon as they'd sat down. Victoria sat in front of them with Violet and Katie, and the three chatted excitedly while watching the video that played on the screen above their heads; the girls telling Victoria about everything they'd done over the past few days. Victoria listened intently, laughed and smiled genuinely—even though she'd heard the stories several times.

Sitting across the aisle from Charlie, next to McCoy and behind Jen-Jen, Kalani casually leaned over and spoke softly to Charlie, so as not to wake Meghan.

"You can have her," Kalani joked, motioning toward Victoria. "Looks like you could use a good babysitter, eh, braddah?"

Charlie laughed lightly. "Then who would keep you from falling out of helicopters?" he shot back.

"She told you about that?" Kalani winced.

"She did," he admitted with a grin. "What's next for X-ray?"

Kalani shrugged nonchalantly.

"We've been called in for debriefing at HQ. Probably going to catch hell for bombing those cars."

"Was it all worth it—everything that you went through?" Charlie asked.

Kalani thought about the loss of Mason and it hurt him deeply—Mason had been one of his closest friends. He weighed this terrible loss against everything wonderful that had been gained. Kalani thoughtfully looked at Victoria, animatedly chatting and giggling with Charlie's two adorable little girls. Then he gazed for a few moments at Meghan. The beautiful woman was still fast asleep with her head on Charlie's shoulder; both husband and wife bathed in the golden glow of the late afternoon sunlight filtering in through the tinted windows. This loving, talented family of amazing individuals was safe, alive and happy—Mason had not given his life in vain.

"Yeah, braddah," he said, settling back into his seat with a smile. He thought he might just rest his eyes for a while, as well.

"It was all worth it."

ACKNOWLEDGEMENTS

And now, the moment you've all been waiting for: the credits! (Stick around afterward for a scene featuring Samuel L. Jackson asking Charlie and Victoria to join S.H.I.E.L.D.) Seriously though, I would like to take some time to express my appreciation and gratitude to all who had a hand—big or small—in making this vulgar, vicious and violent monstrosity a reality. In no particular order, I would like to thank:

Mom, Dad, Jake and Savanah for dealing with my never-ending insanity. My fearsome German shepherd, Sam, for being world's greatest protector as well as the inspiration behind the Walkers' dog, Zeus. Leonard and Pentakis for completely disregarding the aforementioned insanity and welcoming me to the family nonetheless. Hugh Allison for having the eyes of a hawk and making sure I didn't make a complete ass of myself. Payton Craft for the killer artwork. Jeff Heimbuch for some serious support and encouragement. George Taylor for his dislike of Charlie Boats. Michael Dickerson for his knowledge of bus radios. Nomeus Gronovii for lending his knowledge of places most have never been. Adam The Woo for stealing the show in chapter twenty-four. Hoot Gibson for fully supporting this crazy idea. Norm, Jayna and Dallas Stachulski for being my second family and (usually) never complaining about it! Kris and Sarah Roe for forcing me to leave the house during a rough time when all I wanted to do was hide inside. Sean Cecil for being crazy enough to still hang around me after twelve years. Nick and Colette Prainito for being the best metaphorical brother and niece on the entire planet. Chelsea Mee for being an amazing person and a great friend even after all these years. Laura Golden for always being ready with a positive word when I had nothing but negative things to say. Zach Bridges for never saying no to a Qdoba run and always pushing me forward when I try to turn back.

Last but not least, I'd like to thank you. No, not the guy creepily reading this over your shoulder (gotcha!): You.

You bought the book. Or you downloaded it. Or you borrowed it from a friend—maybe even stole it! Regardless, you read it, and I hope you had as good a time reading it as I did writing it.

Thank you!

ABOUT THE AUTHOR

Nick Pobursky is a child trapped in a man's body and lives just a handful of miles south of Detroit, The Most Depressing Place on Earth™. It's no small wonder that he spends most of his money on trips to Walt Disney World.

While spending time as a touring guitarist, he realized that life on the road just wasn't for him. During that period, he wrote his first novel, *Deadline*, and decided that writing was a hell of a lot more fun than sleeping on the floor of a dirty van.

Hollow World and its prequels are his first releases with Bamboo Forest Publishing, but they will not be the last.

And he's always wanted to say something like this:

Charlie Walker will return....

Made in the USA
Lexington, KY
12 December 2013